ALSO BY KATHLEEN CAMBOR
The Book of Mercy

In Sunlight,

in a

Beautiful Garden

In Sunlight,

in a

Beautiful Garden

Kathleen Cambor

Farrar, Straus and Giroux

New York

Farrar, Straus and Giroux
19 Union Square West, New York 10003

Copyright © 2001 by Kathleen Cambor
All rights reserved
Distributed in Canada by Douglas & McIntyre Ltd.
Printed in the United States of America
Designed by Jonathan D. Lippincott
First edition, 2001

Library of Congress Cataloging-in-Publication Data
Cambor, Kathleen.
    In sunlight, in a beautiful garden / by Kathleen Cambor. — 1st ed.
        p.   cm.
    ISBN 0-374-16537-8 (alk. paper)
    1. Johnstown (Pa.) — Fiction. 2. Capitalists and financiers — Fiction.
3. City and town life — Fiction. 4. Dam failures — Fiction. 5. Disasters —
Fiction. 6. Floods — Fiction. I. Title.

PS3553.A4277 I5 2000
813'.54 — dc21   00-034772

Excerpts from *Meditations of Marcus Aurelius* © 1993 by Shambhala Publications, Inc. Reprinted by arrangement with Shambhala Publications, Inc.,
Boston, www.shambhala.com

For Kate and Peter
And in memory of those who died in 1889 in Johnstown

AUTHOR'S NOTE

This is a work of fiction, but characters appear in it who actually lived through and participated in the historical events described in these pages. I have made every effort to represent the outward particulars of their lives with accuracy, but I have also taken a novelist's liberties in attributing thoughts and feelings to them, and in elaborating on incidents that are only touched upon in the biographical and historical works which are available.

I made use of a number of sources in the writing of this book. Chief among them was David McCullough's *The Johnstown Flood*. Other works which were essential include *History of the Johnstown Flood* by Willis Fletcher Johnson, *Through the Johnstown Flood* by the Reverend David J. Beale, *Johnstown the Day the Dam Broke* by Richard O'Connor, *The Life of Andrew Carnegie* by Burton J. Hendrick, *Andrew Carnegie* by Joseph Frazier Wall, *Mellon's Millions* by Harvey O'Connor, *Henry Clay Frick, The Man* by George Harvey, *Dickens* by Peter Ackroyd, *A Gift Imprisoned: The Poetic Life of Matthew Arnold* by Ian Hamilton, *The Mind of the South* by W. J. Cash, *The Insect World of J. Henri Fabre*, translated by Alexander Teixeira de Mattos, and *Tableaux vivants, Fantaisies photographiques victoriennes* (1840–1880), Reunion des Musees Nationaux. The remarkable documentary about the Johnstown flood by Charles Guggenheim gave me a haunting sense of life both in Johnstown and at the South Fork Fishing and Hunting Club.

I'm very grateful for help received from the staffs of the New York Public Library, the Johnstown Public Library, and the library at the University of Texas, and I'm indebted as well to staff members of the Johnstown Flood Museum and the museum and park which are located at the site of the dam.

"I have been watching you; you were there, unconcerned perhaps, but with the strange distraught air of someone forever expecting a great misfortune, in sunlight, in a beautiful garden."

—Arkel to Mélisande,

MAURICE MAETERLINCK, *Pelléas and Mélisande*

In Sunlight,

in a

Beautiful Garden

PROLOGUE

To understand the geography was to understand the place. Three points on a Pennsylvania map connected to create a scalene triangle, an intricate and unequal geometry. From Pittsburgh it was ninety miles east to Johnstown, from Johnstown, fifteen miles northeast into the Allegheny Mountain Range to the little town of South Fork; then another few miles to the earth dam, the enormous lake contained by it, and the South Fork Fishing and Hunting Club, whose buildings flanked the lake's far shore. The South Fork depot was on the main line of the Pennsylvania Railroad, making access to it from Pittsburgh simple and direct, a manageable two-hour train ride through the scenic countryside. The speed and ease of the trip and the comfort of the Pullman cars allowed the wealthy members of the South Fork Fishing and Hunting Club to take little notice of life in the varied mountain towns and cities through which they traveled on their summer sojourns. The club's need for chambermaids and stable boys and wait staff brought some of the locals into the range of the club members' vision, so it was understood that townspeople existed, and understood as well that strict rules about access to club property would have to be established, precautions taken. For the sake of privacy, fences were constructed, NO TRESPASSING signs were posted, and fish screens were built across the dam's spillway to ensure that none of the club fish found their way over the top and down into mountain streams, and onto the fishing hooks and into the mouths of strangers. Shots were fired more than once at poachers, fishermen, or hunters who chose to ignore the signs, creating from the outset anger and tension in the minds of the valley citizenry.

Mythologies developed in Johnstown and its neighboring boroughs about life at the club. It was said that the members dressed in evening wear at dinner; that some of the young girls, daughters of members, were engaged to European noblemen; that the lake was so well stocked the fish leaped out of it, into the waiting nets of clubmen; that repairs to the old dam which the club had made were woefully inadequate, that it could fail at any time. Parents warned their children about the dam, and newspapers ran speculating editorials, especially in the springtime, when rain and mountain runoff caused valley streams to swell and overflow into the Johnstown streets and, it was supposed, also caused the level of water in the lake to rise to a dangerously high level.

Daniel J. Morrell, Johnstown patriarch, Quaker, head of the Cambria Iron Company, had been concerned enough to send his chief engineer as consultant to the contractor in charge of the dam's initial, hasty repairs. The details of that consultation were not made public, but the very idea of it, of Mr. Morrell intervening, reassured the populace enough that their anxiety about the soundness of the dam was somewhat assuaged, and the very real and present worries about families, work, untimely deaths, and plaguing illnesses elbowed aside the vague and unspecific fear about the dam and lake. An engineer had been sent, Mr. Morrell had spoken for them. Except in springtime, the club and lake were rarely thought about, and when they were, the thinking took the shape of fairy tale and legend. They have sailboats, someone said, and as unbelievable as that seemed high in the Allegheny Mountains, no one doubted it.

As to mythologies among the club members about their mountain neighbors, there were none. Mythologies require curiosity and interest, and the members felt neither. Their train trip to South Fork from Pittsburgh was direct, the landscape beautiful. The presence of the other did not impinge on them. At the lake they led an unencumbered, peaceful life. A summer idyll. The life they felt they'd earned.

The streets of Johnstown proper were laid on a grid, as if its founding fathers had a sense that order was essential, that the gods smiled on any enterprise that had precision at its core. Main, Washington, Lincoln, Vine ran east to west. The north-to-south streets included Walnut, Union, Franklin, Park. So touchingly American, those names, so infused with a sense of home. Only Stony Creek Street had a curve and sway to it as it coursed around the southern edge of town, shadowing the river whose name it bore, street and stream both winding toward the point where the Little Conemaugh River, which bordered Johnstown on the north, joined the Stony Creek and a newer, faster, deeper river, the Conemaugh, formed. Just downstream from this juncture was a great stone railroad bridge, its six arches yawing like stone jaws, strung from shore to shore across the Conemaugh, looking to travelers on approaching trains like a kind of monument to all the things that had made the city prosper—commerce, locomotion, the willingness of men to quarry stone, carry it, and shape it.

By 1889, the city and its surrounding boroughs, East Conemaugh, Woodvale, Morrellville among them, had quivered into bright life and filled that level floodplain at the bottom of the valley, a valley that deepened steadily and quickly from the higher points along the Allegheny Mountains, from the reservoir and the South Fork Dam. It was fifteen miles from the earth dam to the stone railroad bridge. The elevation dropped by about 450 feet. Thus the hills that surrounded the city—Laurel Hill, Prospect Hill—were exceptionally high and rose with the suddenness of walls, so steep that to look at them was enough to make one breathless. To climb them required strong legs, sturdy shoes, and a willingness to rest, panting on a rock or leaning on a tree. So deeply sheltered and surrounded was the site that it was as if nature's true intent had been to hide the place, to keep men from it, to let the mountains block the light and the trees grow as thick and gnarled as the thorn-dense vines that inundated Sleeping Beauty's castle. Perhaps, some would say, years later, that was central to all that happened. That it was a city that was never meant to be.

MEMORIAL DAY, 1889

"Nature's law is that all things change and turn, and pass away . . ."
—Marcus Aurelius, *Meditations*, Book XII, Number 21

Frank Fallon lay awake after a night of dozing, waking, dozing again. A night of restlessness. A night of decisions.

Each of the two bedroom windows of his house on Vine Street was opened a crack, just enough to let in the first spring air. May nights in the mountains. Air with a freshness to it. As if, finally, it really was going to bring a change of seasons. As if it might bring rain.

Frank's hands were clasped behind his head, his eyes long grown accustomed to the silver-blue darkness. Eight years in this house, he knew it well: the way the floorboard creaked on the third stair, the nighttime sound of brick-and-plaster sighing and settling into itself. There was a porch and parlor, three good-sized bedrooms, a bay window in the dining room. A sycamore tree stood grandly in the back yard, bringing welcome shade in the summer. Wayward branches touched the house possessively. Downstairs, Frank knew, the pies Julia made at midnight sat on the kitchen table, and fat lemons filled a glass bowl, waiting to be squeezed. The iron skillet had already been placed on the stovetop, and on its seasoned surface chicken would be fried as soon as dawn broke, so it had time to cool before the parade and picnic. It seemed an odd thing to him, the idea of picnicking at the cemetery, an old rough blanket spread across the graves.

"But that's exactly the point," Julia always reminded him. Memorial Day, she said. A day for being with them, for remembering the dead.

As if anything about Frank's life allowed him to forget.

From downstairs he heard the sound of the piano. Julia, restless too, trying to ease herself, to pass the night by playing. It was one of the first things he had given her, four years after they were married. He knew that she had had one as a girl in Illinois, a rosewood Chickering, a stylish square piano with intricately carved legs and scrolled lyres. So for four years he'd saved money in a sock. Three days a week he gave up his stop at California Tom's on Market Street, gave up the shot of whiskey that cut so cleanly through the phlegm and grit that always clogged his throat at the end of his shift. For four years, three days a week, he gave up the quick camaraderie with friends, the talk that was impossible on the mill floor, where your very life depended on concentration, focus, where the screech of the Bessemer blow, the wild vibration of machinery drowned out every other sound. Finally, $137 accumulated in the sock. In 1869 it had felt like a small fortune.

The piano was a Fischer upright, used, old already when he bought it. The ivory of the keys had aged to a lineny yellow, and spidery cracks marred most of them, as if a small, light-footed bird had left its footprints as it practiced avian scales. But what they found was that the instrument's age, its years of use, had given it an organic, mellow tone. John Schrader, who sold furniture on Clinton Street, came once a year with his pitch pipe and his small felt sack of tools to keep it tuned. The sound of it, and the image that came to Frank's mind as he lay abed and listened—of Julia sitting on the round stool, leaning earnestly into the keys, eyes closed to better feel the melody—still had a power over him. After all this time. After everything that had happened.

Frank Fallon was fifty-one years old. And he planned to march, as he did every year, with the Grand Army Veterans. His uniform from the war was folded on a chair beside the bed. The 113th Pennsylvania. He'd retrieved it from the attic trunk the night before, and when he'd taken the jacket by its shoulders and let the careful folds fall from it, he'd thought he could smell Virginia mud on it. Still. Twenty-six years later. There was a tear in the threadbare right pant leg where a Rebel shell had grazed him.

They would begin gathering for the parade at noon. Stores would be closed today, school canceled. Even the iron works was shut down. It cost a lot to let those furnaces sit idle, a rarely heard-of thing.

He did not think much about the war, except on mornings like this when some ritual holiday required it. It had been foggy at Fredericksburg the night before the battle. The picket lines of the Union troops and the Confederates were so close to one another that conversations could be held between sentinels standing guard. It had snowed throughout December, and Frank remembered how cold his ears were, how he kept rubbing at them with his worn wool gloves as he tried to ward off numbness; how he feared the cold, the dimming of cognition and sensation that came with it. At first he thought that the freezing temperature and exhaustion were going to his head, that he was hearing things, when someone with a harmonica started playing "Dixie."

They'd been camped for days, waiting for pontoon bridges to arrive, so they could be placed across the Rappahannock. Around the campfires loose talk flowed easily, full of bravado. Talk about how quickly Fredericksburg would be taken, bets placed on how many weeks would pass before the war ended. Youth and the rightness of their cause had stirred in Frank and in all his Pennsylvania regiment some ennobled sense that God was on their side, a belief that sound planning and foresight had been part of the strategy that had brought them to this place.

As the Union troops moved toward Fredericksburg in mid-December, the townspeople moved out; several thousand Virginians trudged, with the few belongings they had rushed to gather—plucked chickens, bags of flour, Bibles—past the enemy marching to displace them. A child had broken rank that day and run from his mother's side to hurl himself at Frank. Yankee filth, his mother screamed.

Behind his closed eyes, in his dark bedroom, Frank imagined flags flying from every house and shop in Johnstown in the late morning. The swoop and drape of buntings hung, the flowers spilling from second-story windows all along the parade route. The columbines and buttercups and piney buds shaped into wreaths by the Women's Relief Corps to be placed on Union soldiers' graves. The Odd Fellows would march this year, as they always did, along with the Hornerstown Drum Corps and the Hussar Band in gold and scarlet. Train after train would bring visitors from Altoona and Somerset with baskets full of flowers. Bonnets would protect pale faces from the sun. He imagined Grace McIntyre among the celebrants, without a hat's protection because she tended not to like the fussiness of hats, or any of the strict and arbitrary demands of women's fashion. He imagined how she'd look—her thin hand arched across her forehead, deflecting the sun's rays. He would have to check himself to keep from going to her.

The parade would begin on Main Street, as it did every year, then continue past Mr. Morrell's house, the Presbyterian church, and Central Park, its cinder paths and benches packed with people. The arched necks of the four stone swans that formed the center fountain of the park would be encircled with apple-blossom garlands. Then the parade would turn south at Bedford and press on toward the Sandy Vale Cemetery to pay tribute to the dead. Heads would be bent and prayers said. Guns would be fired by Union veterans. The shots would echo eerily from hill to hill, as if a distant war were still being waged.

At Fredericksburg, Frank had plugged his fingers in his ears when the Union cannons fired. Two hundred of them, aimed at that unlikely small Virginia town. When he raised his head that day, after the firing ended, all he could see was smoke, as if the world he knew had vanished and smoke had arrived to take its place. His eyes teared and he pressed his kerchief in the wet snow, then held it to his mouth to ease the singe and cut the ashy taste.

A squat stone wall where Lee had massed his artillery to cover all approaches stood at Marye's Heights, at the bottom of a sloped plain. When orders were issued, line after line of Union soldiers advanced across the field, falling in waves, until the snow mixed with grass and mud and became a bloody porridge, black with bodies. Waiting for his turn to go, Frank felt the muck suck at his boots. "Lead with your shoulder," Bill Jones had warned. "It makes for a narrower target. You'll take it in the shoulder instead of the chest." Frank had nodded thanks, the chill of the day drained out of him by then, replaced by a sick, hot fear. The smoke had cleared enough for him to see bayonets flash in the distance, behind the wall, what looked like thousands of them, the wall itself appearing to rise out of the smoke as if produced by the artifice of some magician. We're going to die like dogs charging that wall with all those men and muskets massed behind it, he thought. He bit his lip so hard it bled.

There was a time when Frank would have gotten out of bed, gone down the stairs, Julia's music growing more distinct the closer he got to it.

He would have moved behind her, gathered her loose hair from around her shoulders, arranged it neatly, with his big hands, down her back.

Frank heard the squeak of the bedroom door just next to his, the sound of footsteps. "Daniel?" he called out.

The footsteps halted, then changed direction. The door to the bedroom opened. Music, hall light entered as his son did.

"Yes. It's me."

"It's early yet. A day off like this. You should be sleeping."

Daniel shrugged. "And you, too."

Frank swung his legs out from beneath the covers. Sat on the edge of the bed, watching Daniel, lit by the lamp he held, his long shadow wavering at the door frame. Shirtless. Pants riding loosely on his hips. Frank noticed how broad those shoulders had become, the mass and sinew of the muscles in his upper arms.

"Will you march with me today?" Frank asked. "With the Sons of the Grand Army Veterans?"

"Sure I will. I always do. But I don't think I'll go on to the picnic."

"Have you plans, then?"

Daniel hesitated. "Yes, you could say that. I have plans."

Hands on his knees, Frank brought himself to his feet. The moon shone a patch of light on the cool plank floor.

"I was going to miss the picnic, too, but then thought better of it," he said.

Daniel, who'd seemed about to turn and descend the stairs, took a step into the room.

"I'm glad you did. She'd be disappointed," he said.

"She'll be disappointed either way," Frank countered. "I . . ." He wanted to tell Daniel something. "I just thought that this year I might want to do things differently." He wished he could say something that would make Daniel understand.

"What is it, Da?" Daniel took another step into the room. He had Frank's curly hair, a sound of worry in his voice. "If it's about the marching, you know I won't miss that. I'll march with you."

He was close enough then for Frank to move toward him, to reach his arm around his shoulder. Frank admired that about himself. The easy way he had of loving. The boy was twenty-three years old, and Frank never tired of touching him.

His only son. He wondered what the day was going to bring. Sorrow, he supposed. Betrayal. He hoped that when it was done, Daniel would find some way to forgive him.

"Yes," he said. "I know you'll march with me."

At Fredericksburg, Frank had heard a hiss and then a fleshy rip before he knew that he had been hit, before the pain seared through his brain, threatening to blind him. Which would have been a better thing, he thought later as he lay through the long night in a field of dead men, taking what warmth their stiffening bodies had to offer, hearing the moans of the wounded as they cried out for their mothers or their wives or water. He remembered how quickly all that blood had spread its color through the mud. The smell of it.

His knee was shattered. But he lived to go on fighting. At Chancellorsville he lost part of an ear and was finally sent home, to the Pennsylvania mountains, to make steel again.

Some would say that it was awful work. That the pay was poor and every day was a danger, but it was, God help him, the world of making, and because of what Frank did, buildings were built, rail was laid, and a son of his could go to a university in Philadelphia. Working night and day, four thousand men had turned a little mountain town into a small metropolis. He defied anyone to tell him he should not be proud of it. He was fifty-one years old, a foreman, and still, after twenty-nine years at it, he and his men dressed for payday. They wore their Sunday clothes on Saturday. Clean shirts, buttoned jackets, starched collars. They'd grown used to 120-degree temperatures on the steel mill floor, used to sweat, but they never grew used to the way those collars grooved their necks. They wore them anyway. And bowler hats, their hair slicked back and clean. As a sign of respect for who they were and what they did. When Daniel goaded him as he sometimes did, about the money and the hours and what he called the exploitation, Frank stopped him, raised his hand against all criticism. Daniel meant well, Frank knew. He'd been radicalized by his time away and only wanted change. But this was his work and Frank would not let his son speak against it. He would not be made ashamed.

Sometimes Frank hated what he did. But the truth was, it was more than he ever thought he'd be. And there was a strange seductive power to it. Those giant furnaces. That liquid iron flowing into molds, which held a white light like no other on earth, as if the heat and power of the sun itself were coursing past his feet, controlled by him, shaped into whatever form he so desired. When he was young, before the war, he imagined being a sailor, he imagined foreign ports, mysterious tongue-twisting languages, and a voyage back to Ireland to see the place where his parents had been born. But war intervened, and instead of going to sea, he went to Antietam, where he shot men at point-blank range, pierced his bayonet into the throats of teenaged boys, of children. They killed each other as if they were killing animals. They walked across fields so thickly strewn with corpses that the ground could not be seen, as if the dead men were stepping-stones. He never entered a church again. He imagined, after all he'd done, that he had no place there. He knew too much. He knew what, in their blindness, men could do to one another.

It was May of 1889, the thirtieth. A Thursday.

Frank took the jacket of his uniform from the back of the chair, slipped his arms into it. The blue had hardly faded.

At the Johnstown library, Grace McIntyre awakened with a start from her fitful sleep at her long desk. From the corner of the large room there had come a sudden clap, and her head snapped up at the sound. For a moment she could not place herself—the darkness disoriented her. Her neck ached, and the arm on which her head had rested tingled and was numb. She pressed fingertips to forehead, focusing, until recognition dawned. She had stayed late the night before to tidy up (or so she told herself), and then stayed on. Unwilling to go home. Hiding out, she said to herself. Trying to clear her head.

Her face bore the crease mark of the blouse sleeve on which her cheek had rested. The seep of nighttime saliva had left a circle of dampness on the blotter on her desk. Her throat felt raw; the fire in the woodstove was down to a few brave embers. The shawl with which she'd draped herself was poor protection from the chill, but she was glad to be there nonetheless, and as she rose to tend the fire, she thought how much of a home this building had become to her. The patrons were like a large surprising family. She could hardly remember her life before she came eight years ago. She could not imagine leaving, starting again. Weeks earlier, she had let herself begin to sleep at the library, either at the desk or curled in one of the reading chairs, as a way of saying a long goodbye, in anticipation of the possibility of leaving. Her bags were packed, just in case, her affairs in order. Notes of apology and farewell written. She had shelved the most recently returned books yesterday with a tender and exquisite care, had replenished the wood box by the stove, polished the frame of the portrait of Daniel J. Morrell, who had gazed on her so steadily and gravely throughout her tenure. And now, she realized, the last thing had been accomplished. The sound that had awakened her had been the mousetrap she had set the night before. The cheese had proven irresistible, the page-nibbling predator had been caught. The books were safe now. She could leave knowing she had done her best and everything was safe.

Just past dawn, and the streets were empty on her brief walk home. Families taking advantage of the holiday were sleeping late, or cooking hearty breakfasts, or freshening up in preparation for the parade. Grace thought she would weave flowers into her hair. Foolish perhaps, the vanity of girlhood in a forty-five-year-old woman, but she would do it anyway. Frank's eyes would find her in the crowd. She wanted to be beautiful for Frank.

In Pittsburgh, in the earliest hours of morning, parades were being organized in several neighborhoods, church services had been scheduled. But for Henry Clay Frick, thirty-nine years old, buntings, picnics, memories of a war fought and friends lost in it were not part of the day's commemorative plans. For him the Civil War was an episode of history, nothing more. He rose early that day, as Frank Fallon had in Johnstown, but not to dress in uniform for marching. Instead, he would make tea, work at his library desk, prepare himself for church, enjoy the holiday luncheon Adelaide had planned, to which Andrew Mellon was invited and Andrew Carnegie was not. Even though Carnegie had just made Frick the chairman of Carnegie Brothers and Co., chief of the largest steel enterprise on earth, things between them were not easy. Frick knew he had been chosen not for his business acumen alone but for his reputation as someone who was unyielding with labor. The perfect business partner for the affable Carnegie. Carnegie, the generous, expansive; Frick, the cold, the dour. A dichotomy, Frick thought, easily enough admired by outsiders who were not on the receiving end of it.

Careful not to awaken Adelaide, he was silent as a thief in his dark house, a house they called Clayton, without the slightest sense of irony. Named for him. Twenty-three rooms of Victorian splendor, three young children, and the modest beginnings of a collection of art and objects. His dressing gown was a lightweight wool, maroon, tailor-made for him. He was vain about such things. Adelaide often teased him about this sartorial indulgence. Who sees you in your dressing gown? she had asked just yesterday, standing next to him at the long mirror in his room. They had watched themselves and the furniture and carpeting behind them in reflection. A tailor had stood just to his right, shown in by one of the several servants. He had come to drape and fit; a sallow-skinned man, mustached, obsequious, a tape measure looped around his neck. Perspiration left a wet ring on his well-starched collar. He clasped his hands together, nodded, and bowed repeatedly, addressing questions of taste, offering expert judgment. Tweed of course, but the imported wool (he shook his head slowly, appreciatively, to show how fine it was, how words failed him as to its quality), there's nothing like it. Frick saw in the tailor's face what he always saw when such men addressed him—a certain fear, an eagerness to please. A wish to be consulted, valued, heard. The tailor had draped a length of the recommended fabric across Frick's shoulder. Does Mr. Frick approve? Husband's and wife's eyes met in the mirror. Did Mr. Frick approve?

He wrapped the robe around himself, tied the braided cord.

The clock struck as he descended the stairs, moved through the vestibule, the south hall, the living room.

Such well-proportioned rooms, such lovely objets d'art. He ran his hand lightly over his possessions as he passed them. Proprietary, a little careless. There was a risk in handling a small Ch'ing Dynasty porcelain, a Limoges enamel; if harmed they could not be replaced. His was the pride of ownership; he felt entitled to touch, to be a little casual about them. He loved them, they were like children to him. And like children he thought they should be touched when passed, stroked a little, smiled upon, enjoyed. The few paintings he'd recently acquired were for viewing, for the eyes' delight, and the soul's, of course. They were for solace. He was developing specific tastes, making those tastes known to dealers. He planned, in his collecting, to use discerning judgment. Would each new acquisition fit among the others? Were they representative of a given artist's finest efforts, did they please the eye? He wanted nothing violent, nothing harsh. Sometimes a dealer came to him, insisting that a work was "important," that, for all its frankness in depicting some dark subject, it was an eloquent depiction of a time. Such persuasion never moved him. This was his house. Grim reality was for his other life, his business. He wanted beauty in his home.

Steam rose from the hot tea, morning light filled the Clayton kitchen. Memorial Day, the end of spring, the start of the summer season. In another week there could be sailing at the South Fork lake. Odd, how five or six years earlier he had looked forward to those times—the lavish dinners in the clubhouse dining room, the horseback rides, the fishing. He felt finished with it now. Bored and beyond its simple pleasures.

A pity, he thought. It was a time when he was still capable of pity.

At every stop along the train route from Philadelphia, flags flew from flagpoles or were draped from depot windows. Each time the locomotive braked, Nora Talbot paused, looked up from the reading she had brought, as if in mute acknowledgment of those who'd died in war. She had lost no one in her life. Such sorrow she could only imagine.

"Meet me," her father had written in a letter, and she had said she would. She had rushed to catch the noon train from Philadelphia—twenty years old, pretty enough, but striking only in the long black braid that arrowed down her back, the mail-pouch satchel slung over her shoulder, worn the way a boy might wear it, worn the way that she imagined Daniel Fallon probably had when he was a young, ardent scholar. Now she was the ardent one: student, scientist, worried daughter, eager lover.

On the train Nora reached into her satchel, drew out papers, pen, her diary. For years now she had taken a journal everywhere with her. The pages were ragged, thumb-worn, the index and third fingers of her right hand stained with ink. Nora, the recordkeeper, the gatherer of facts, of history.

There were times when I thought he loved South Fork more than he loved me.

So she had written once in another diary. The memory came to her sharply, suddenly. She would have been fourteen that summer of 1883. She remembered the day she first told him that his love was a worry to her.

"Not at all," her father, James, had tried to reassure her. "I don't love it more." He and Nora had just gotten off another train, were watching while their things were loaded onto the spring wagon. They'd left Pittsburgh early in the morning, ridden, as they always did, in a Pullman parlor car. She'd sunk happily into the velvet cushion of her seat, crossed her ankles, pressed her gloved hands together in her lap. Her father knew how much she cared and so always saw to it that she sat beside the window. At the insistence of her mother, she had obediently brought handiwork to do, crewel, as well as a little swatch of white-on-white embroidery, but she planned to keep that folded in her needlepointed bag. She had thought perhaps she'd read, so she'd brought *Bleak House* with her. But she knew it was more likely that she'd just watch the river from the window, press cheek to glass while the downtown buildings, the steel mills, and the tenements they'd spawned all disappeared from view. She'd sit quietly, let her mind roam. Imagine life stories for the men and women who lingered on the platforms of the little towns they lumbered through. A man with just one leg, swinging himself with crutches toward a slowing train. A woman whose face was buried in an unwieldy extravagant bouquet of fuchsia flowers, surrounded by anxious well-wishers, saddened, Nora guessed, by a heart-wrenching adieu.

People believed in the Pennsylvania Railroad, James always said, the way they believed in God. The railroad was the future, it would take men and women across the continent, to Western territories. Nora didn't know much about that, about its power or reputation. She just knew she loved the train. She loved the rainbow-making crystal chandeliers and pressed-tin ceiling, the high, etched transom windows, the porters with their smart brimmed caps and pocket watches that always kept such perfect, honest railroad time. She loved the way the porters offered her a hand when she stepped into her car or stepped down from it, as if she were someone of consequence as, indeed, she planned to be. She loved the little sandwiches they served, but really, there was no end to her list of loving. And primarily she loved being alone with her father. Her mother, Evelyn, would come later, after they'd claimed their clubhouse rooms and gotten settled. Then things would change. Evelyn would bring her Saratoga trunk and evening dresses. She'd bring a list of the other families that would be with them at the club for the first two weeks in August, with a complicated set of checks and dots and numbers ranking them in order of importance. But for the first few days it would be just Nora and her father. They'd take walks together. More than anything, she wanted him to teach her how to sail.

As soon as she had gotten off the train that summer, Nora had rushed to the end of the station platform to look down toward the little town of South Fork. It mattered to her that nothing had changed, every detail was just as she remembered it. Stineman's General Store and Pringle's drug-store stood importantly on Railroad Street. The weather-worn frame houses where the 1,500 townspeople lived still stippled the hillside, rectangles of enduring, subdued color in the smothering forest, a rising sea of green. She wondered what creatures watched her from the underbrush. What deer families had had fawns, what had happened to last summer's vixen and her cubs, the rambling family of raccoons. Nora had been told that a panther had been sighted once, not far from here. One more reason, her mother always said, to stay close to the lake and clubhouse, to stop wandering.

"Careful there." At the platform's edge her father had supervised the transfer of luggage, the loading of the wagon. Trunks, valises, his casting rod and tackle box. His creels and reels. His gun. Everything they'd need for their two-week summer stay.

"Good to see you, Tom," James said, allowing his hand to be pumped eagerly. A greeting for the bucktoothed farm boy who always came to drive them to the lake.

As Nora wandered farther, train and depot noise receded. Coal falling from coal tipple to train car, the hiss of steam gave way to the sounds of country life—moving water, the raucous cries of birds, the silken shimmy as the wind brushed the serrated leaves of a towering white ash tree. Just down from the depot, with wires threading from it, stood the telegraph tower, a two-story wooden sentry. Nora knew that a Western Union operator was on duty on the second floor, receiving messages, relaying them with the tap of a practiced finger. By that agent's authority, news was spread up and down the railway line. News of delays or trouble on the tracks; news of late-spring flooding. Nora's father had told her that here, in South Fork, the operator was a woman. Nora wished she could meet her. She wanted to find out how it had happened; how, in a world where men did everything, a woman had been allowed to ascend the tower, to learn the secret, wordless code.

"Nora." James's voice again. He waved her toward him. The length of his fly rod, extending from the wagon's bed, looked like a sword flashing in sunlight, the overburdened wagon like the last of a supply train of some ragtag retreating army.

"Come," her father called. "It's time to go."

She was small and pale that July, her wayward, wavy hair tamed into a thick rope-like braid. It was the club's third season, the Talbots' third summer at the lake. She shook her head, brushed her father's hand aside when he reached to help her climb into the wagon.

"I can manage," she had said. She hiked her skirt up, hooked her foot on the toe-shaped ring, and, with a push, was up and in. She called the horses by their names. The black horse, Jenny, whinnied; Jock, the bay, swished black flies off his wide rump with his tail. Tom shot her a timid sidelong glance, tipped his straw hat in greeting. Then he clucked at Jock; the wagon jerked, they pulled away.

The clip-clop of the horses' hooves was like a metronome, it made her think of Madame Corsca and Chopin études. Of E minor scales. Of her lesson-dense life at home. The summer had been dry, and dirt stirred by the horses' feet dusted her dark stockings, the hem of her voile dress. South Fork Creek showed itself through the trees, in sudden argent glints, and she could hear the spit and gurgle of it as it smacked the rocks and the fallen limbs that were strewn across it. When she saw Lamb's farm and Lamb's Bridge ahead, she held on to the wagon seat, steadying herself in preparation for the climb. They'd be going up now, through the valley, toward the bottom of the great earth dam.

Her first sight of it each summer stunned her, the way it rose up steeply, suddenly, seemed to grow out of the valley floor. Seventy-two feet high, nine hundred wide, her father said, and she believed him. It was like a pyramid, or the wall of a lost city, something an archaeologist might find. Dirt and rock, tree stumps and rubble. Crevices so deep, so shaded, that even in the summer chunks of winter ice still glinted from within. Manure had been used to reinforce the dam as well, and the rich, organic smell of it mingled with the scent of pine needles, columbine, and mountain laurel, and the grasses that silted the dam's steep, earthen side. The dark faces of spiderwort pocked the surface. Honeysuckle blossomed. Life sprouted from the dam. Nora had closed her eyes and imagined she could hear it breathe.

"Of course you're right in one thing," James had said suddenly. "I do love it." They had been silent since they'd left the station, and she had to think a minute. What was he saying? What was it that he loved?

"I love it hugely," he'd admitted.

She looked up at him. Dark hair, muttonchop whiskers, russet, just beginning to gray; veined cheeks prominent above them; his voice a little louder than it needed to be. "I love it, child, because it's ours, and because it's beautiful. *Our* land." He squeezed her hand for emphasis. "Our safe retreat." Another squeeze.

The wagon angled as they rose. The horses strained. Sweat sheeted Jock's hindquarters, his muscles flexed and pulled. At the top, the road forked. The horses veered right across the dam's broad crest and paused midway, as was their habit, because they'd learned that everybody wanted to stop there, have a look. To the right, the steep drop down into the tree-filled narrow valley. To the left, the lake.

"Our lake," James had continued, gesturing broadly. A blue jewel, her father called it. Its trembling edges lapped at the fragrant, pine-dense shore. Spruce and black birch also grew in the forest around it, as well as hemlock and hickory, sugar maples so well fed by silt-rich earth that they oozed syrup in the fall when there was no one there to claim, collect it. Except for hunting season, in autumn most of the cottages were closed, the members gone. For them the beauty of the club was the summer, just after spring rains combined with the runoff from the snowy mountains, when wildflowers sprang up through the loamy forest floor. Spiderwort and periwinkles inched toward what little sunlight filtered through the trees and webbed the path that wound round the lake in smoky blue and dusky amethyst, darkly mottled, the color of a bruise. When she was young and dreamed of flying, Nora used to think of how it would have looked from above, the sun-reflecting lake, the purple ring around it—as if it had been chosen, marked as a sacred place by Druids or by unknowable, approving gods.

Purple-ringed. Protected. Man-made. And not by ordinary men, she knew, but by men who understood the work of making, shaping, insisting that the world conform to their particular, exacting standards. Andrew Carnegie, Henry Clay Frick, Andrew Mellon. Henry Phipps. But in Nora's mind, the lake, the dam, the club were all just South Fork, and for two weeks every summer it was her home. It was no Tuxedo Park, was modest, she'd been told, by Newport's standards, but important men were members: a wealthy man's retreat. Her father, a lawyer, was the least of them, but good enough, it had been decided; discreet, trustworthy. Someone who would do.

From the beginning, she had known that she and her family were peripheral, that they existed on the shadowy edges of the other clubmen's favor. They owned no cottage, no private carriage met them at the train to drive them to the club. She had been fourteen years old that summer of her diary-keeping. She spoke French, read Shakespeare and the poems of John Donne. On Pittsburgh's East End, she was schooled with rich men's children. Perfectly, properly schooled. She had a place among them. But she was not rich, nor was she foolish. Each summer from her coach car on the train she saw other trains, coke-carrying, steel-carrying trains; she heard the distant echo of plant whistles from the valley below. She knew as surely they all did that there was other life besides theirs in the mountains, but she kept that knowledge vague and shrouded in some closed-off, unused portion of her mind. Even so, and in spite of her willed ignorance, she sometimes saw hints of what was out there, what might come. Because, as sweet as the wild strawberries tasted, as crystalline the lake, sometimes an acrid, bitter stench invaded paradise, crept up the mountains, fingered its way through the shielding trees. Once when she wandered too far on the solitary walks she favored, dusk overtook her, and with the lights of the clubhouse and the lakeside cottages far behind her, she could see from the dam's high crest that a fierce red glow lit the valley. When the next day she roamed farther down, much farther than she knew she ought to, she saw that the very trees that flourished with such exuberance around her lake were leafless, black, ash-encrusted in the smoke-filled valley. With a fatidic clarity that comes only occasionally and only to the young, she understood that, like the mythic marking of her purple-banded lake, this too was a sign, an omen. A warning that things are not always as they seem, that everything she thought was predictable and certain was ephemeral, passing, and one day the life she knew would change unutterably.

And so it had, but not as completely as Nora had once imagined. The lake remained the light, bright center of her world, and in 1889 it was her Memorial Day destination. There had been trouble in her life the last two years, but she had managed to retain a singular, insistent, optimistic stance. She tried not to think about the changing world as her train rushed toward the South Fork depot. Her focus was tomorrow and the next day—that brief, happy future.

————

James Talbot thought of Gettysburg as he did each year on this day of remembrance. He closed his eyes and leaned back into his seat as his train rasped, chugged, and lulled him from Pittsburgh to South Fork. He imagined Abraham Lincoln rising slowly to deliver his address. That creased, pocked face which James's father had so hated. Twenty-five years, James thought as the train rocked around a curve. Was that possible? Had it been so long since the consecration of that graveyard? James wondered if there were names on the hundreds of markers in the cemetery. He could find that out; the information was available, but he liked to speculate instead. Would there be names? Could he find the one he was looking for?

He thought of how empty the clubhouse at the South Fork Fishing and Hunting Club would be. The summer season not yet begun, the Launching of the Fleet in early June was still in the planning stages. He and Nora would have it almost to themselves. They could sit together on the wide porch that overlooked the lake.

Love was the thing that brought him there, as it had brought him there each of the last eight summers. Love—of cool nights, mountain breezes, of loons and larks and butterflies. But for James, a sense of burden mingled with that love now. His was the guilt of duty neglected.

He wore a small paper American flag pinned to his lapel, the mark of a mourner, of a man who'd lost loved ones to a war.

He had read once that besides the eight thousand men who had been killed at Gettysburg, five thousand horses and mules had died as well. So many dead. And there had been precious little time to bury them. The suffocating July heat, the swarming bluebottle flies, the stench of rotting flesh had made haste imperative. The initial graves were makeshift, shallow. Householders returning to their homes after the fighting had to plant around the half-buried bodies in their fields and gardens.

Gettysburg was so near South Fork, a half day's journey. He wondered why he had never made the trip, for what he had been waiting.

Through the train's smudged window James could see that the sun had already reached its peak and begun its steady slide toward afternoon. Darkening clouds were forming, graying the sky in the far distance. Snapped twigs swirled in the wind raised by the charging locomotive. He guessed it was close to two o'clock; in less than an hour he would be at the South Fork depot. He imagined the little cupola perched jauntily mid-roof; the brougham, with the horses harnessed to it shooing at the ground, made restless by the electric tinge of rain in the spring air. He envisioned Nora arriving just before he did, standing on the platform, patient as she always was. Waiting for him.

There were things that he should tell her. Not now, not this weekend, but when they returned to the lake in August. In August he would make his long-overdue pilgrimage, and he'd take Nora with him. He'd confide everything.

Yes, this would be the year, he thought. No, promised. Swore. This would be the summer he would make the trip to Gettysburg.

In his room in his parents' house, in the late afternoon, Daniel Fallon placed an extra shirt, two apples, a slicker, and a blanket into a roll that could be tied behind a saddle. Tense with anticipation, he had arranged to let a horse from Snavely's livery in the early morning and had mapped in his mind his fifteen-mile route through the hills and underbrush, over one of the many paths that veined the wooded countryside and led to the lake. He would leave early, allow plenty of time. Today there had been a parade and he and his father had marched in it. Tomorrow he'd see Nora, tomorrow they would meet. Briefly, intensely, as they always did. Hours snatched, confidences exchanged, futures planned and spoken of, without any suggestion, any hint, that their futures might be spent together. Theirs was a relationship lived solely in the fleeting present.

Because they were able to see each other so infrequently, letters, small gifts, tokens had become the touchstones that attached them to each other. His gifts to her included books, flowers, the feather of a bird. For tomorrow's meeting he had purchased a pair of tweezers for her. An instrument of science, an honoring on his part of what she wished to be— a naturalist, an entomologist, an explorer of the plant and insect universe. He was the first one to know that secret wish of hers, the first one to witness, to understand, to be ambitious for her. Prior to him, she had been alone, so set apart by her interests and curiosity that she had almost lost sight of who she was and what she wanted. He had reminded her. His notice of her, she told him later, had been unlike any other she had ever known.

He was seventeen when he first saw her, twenty-two when they first spoke. He had hesitated, waited, because he had been afraid that contact would somehow spoil what he felt for her. He who planned to make agitation his life's work, the labor movement his vocation, had been shy when it came to one rare girl. For five years he had watched her rather than risk approaching.

Once he did approach, once he went to her, he found that she would listen, that she could be trusted. Her gifts to him? A pen with which to record his theories about the rights of man; a scarf to wear to union meetings, red wrap of defiance, reminder that she was with him, on his side; a knife with which he might protect himself if he was threatened with violence. She had read in the newspapers about the measures employed to thwart disruptive unions. The knife had surprised him. It made him think that he ought not to underestimate her frankness, her ability to be unflinching. It made him regret that he had not approached her sooner.

What would become of the two of them? He did not know. He knew only that tomorrow he would go to her, that they would be together at the South Fork lake.

Beginnings:
The Portage Railroad

"How many in whose company I came into the world are gone away . . ."
— Marcus Aurelius, *Meditations*, Book VI, Number 56

How did they choose? Frank Fallon often wondered when he thought about his parents. He had a vague, disjointed memory of his early childhood before they immigrated to America, and in it he saw a rock-strewn Irish hillside, the stone walls of the cottage they had lived in, ever damp, his tall father having to bend before he entered in order to clear the low-hanging pitch-and-straw roof. Frank remembered straggly, undernourished sheep, two pigs, their haunches slapping wetly as they rolled themselves in cooling mud. He wondered if, when they decided to leave Ireland, his mother and father had made a map, if his father had taken it to the pub and thrown darts with a wanton carelessness at the stars he'd formed to mark the biggest cities in America, trusting luck and fate, as was his inclination, willing to bet everything on his arm, his aim, the torque of a flying feather-festooned pin. Or, Frank mused, had his mother pressed for small-town life? A place where there were trees, and grocers who might give credit in lean times, and neighbors whom you'd get to know, friends you could call upon, who'd help you? Frank never thought to ask when they were there for asking. The past seemed unimportant to him then. It was a time when looking forward was the thing, when what had been left behind was best forgotten.

But he, their baby, must have felt *something* about the leaving, longed for something that was lost to him. Isn't it a thing like need that starts the sucking of the thumb? Because there he was, vivid in his own memory, three years old in 1841, red hair tucked into a trim little cap, tattered rag-that-used-to-be-a-blanket dragged behind him everywhere, the hemmed and patched and rehemmed edges of it caked with mud. Right thumb in his mouth, digits fisted at the tip of his nose. You're too old for the thumb, his mother had said just after they'd arrived in Pennsylvania, and she had gone to war to wean him from it. She had made pastes of benign but bitter herbs and smeared them energetically into the skin, and when that failed, she had soaked it in whiskey, then gloved his hand and pinned it to his pillow when he slept. But his attachment to his thumb had been a powerful thing, and even then, when he was just a toddler, there was a wiliness about him. So he had learned to restrain himself in her presence, in the revealing light of day and in the circle of her scrutiny. He'd kept his hand out of his mouth. He'd tried to occupy himself—playing with a dour, forced diligence, as if play were work—with a tin of mismatched buttons, a sack of fabric scraps; he had prodded little crawling bugs with sticks. And for hours at a time, forgot his thumb. But he had sucked it at night, facing the slatted wooden wall, in the strange new wood-and-windowed house, in the corner of his parents' room in an unfamiliar little bed. Secretly he had sucked by day as well, when he gathered eggs from the three-member chicken family they kept penned in what they called their yard. When, inevitably, his thumbnail grew mushy and the skin surrounding it became inflamed and puckered, he had learned to hide it from her—by stuffing the offending hand into his pocket or tucking the thumb, with a practiced casualness, into his palm with his other fingers closed loosely around it. But his mother had been every bit as shrewd as he, and when the nail disintegrated, her attack on his habit, on this residual of babyhood, had intensified. "This just won't do," she had said officiously. The sound of her voice had made his throat ache with worry. He loved her, and he wanted to be good, to be pleasing, but the comfort of the thumb felt necessary to him. Had he had language enough, he might have tried to shape his complex feelings into words, but at three, all he could articulate was need. When she chastised him about the thumb, he had only stared, hands clasped behind him, the fingers of his left hand stroking the injured, injuring thumb as if it were a felled bird, a tiny dying animal.

Finally, after a year of struggle, his mother had wrapped the thumb mummy-style, with clean thin strips of rag to make a gross unwieldy bandage, too big to fit into a boy-sized mouth, too cumbersome for hiding. The Battle of the Thumb, he called it later, when he was a man, when he'd learned in that Irish way to make a joke of everything. But at the time, the wrapped thumb seemed like a mean indictment, an advertisement of his flaws, and it became a stinging source of shame to him.

They were six months into it, the Battle of the Thumb, on the day that Charles Dickens arrived.

"Charles who?" his father had asked, home from work at the canal basin, where he manned one of the locks. Barrel-chested, a voice that had been bred in a world of earth floors, stone walls, spongy absorption; in the wooden house, it had bounded from the walls like a ball thrown hard against them. Throughout his life, whenever Frank thought of him, he thought of the red stripe of sunburned neck as he bent over the washbasin, the spray of water flying from his cupped hands toward his boyish face, the way he shook his head and let the water centrifuge into a baptismal rain around him. Frank had liked standing next to him, squinting his eyes in preparation for the shower, feeling cool and clean beside his father. He was a man who loved to hear the twee and sigh of floodgates opening, to watch the big boats rise in rising water. The kind of man who liked to feel things happening. Not the kind who reads.

"Charles Dickens," his mother had said, impatient with him, as if any fool would know, as if Dickens were a king or a president. "The English writer."

His dad had gone off then in an Irish tirade against Britain, and young Frank could see his mother steel herself against it. Sometimes he imagined he could see her ears close when his father got that way. She had waved a shushing hand at him. Be still now, Jack, the waving hand said. She wanted assimilation, knowledge. Her attraction was to all things modern. Old grudges were old news to her. She didn't want to hear or think about them.

It was the canal that had brought them to the Allegheny Mountains, and as far as she was concerned, it had lived up to its promise. The canal and portage railroad had been the project of the Pennsylvania Railroad. The Western Division linked Johnstown and Pittsburgh; to the east it continued on to Philadelphia. There were canals and five inclined planes on each side of the mountain, to which a narrow-gauge railroad delivered cars so that they could be hauled with hemp rope over the mountaintops. It was called the Portage Railroad, and because of it Philadelphia had access to the Ohio River. For the visionaries in charge of this project in the 1840s, making sure that the Western Division had enough water through the long, dry summers appeared to be the only problem. For that, the original South Fork Dam had been built.

The railroad's decision to locate the canal basin in Johnstown had turned the borough into a small city. Lime had to be produced for making the cement out of which the canals themselves were constructed. Carpenters came to build canal boats, oars, and the locks that raised and lowered the level of the water. Travelers appeared out of curiosity. Hotels were constructed to house the travelers, butchers were needed to cut the meat for the new hotels. The population of the city quickly multiplied.

"It's a wonder," his mother had said to Frank. She took any and every opportunity to supply him with statistics. "The Pennsylvania Main Line Canal," she said, while hooking buttons through the stitched holes of his boots, "covers 394 miles, with 16 aqueducts, 64 locks, more than 150 bridges. A towpath and basin right through Johnstown." Her tone when she was lecturing was unlike what Frank thought of as her motherly tone. There was nothing soft about this woman—so businesslike, so full of information, insistent and didactic.

"And the Allegheny Portage Railroad," she added while she licked her thumb to wipe a dirt mark from his cheek. She bent to give a smart, efficient pull to his small waistcoat, to check to see that his knees were clean, his hair in place, his thumb-wrapping intact. "It's very modern, Frank." She was a short, squat woman, but as she prepared him to stand beside her and watch and worship at the shrine of progress, she did not seem small. It was as if she gained stature when she spoke about the growing stature of her town, as if watching the canal boats made her a partner in this engineering wonder. And as partner in so grand a thing, she became grand, too.

She had worn black for mourning when the funeral cortege of William Henry Harrison, the one-month President, passed through. Frank had just turned three then, but he thought he remembered the sweet brackish smell of camphor emanating from the deep folds of the wool dress she wore that day. It was spring, but cold; too soon in the mountains for so much as a hint of spring. In the early morning a thin gray mist rose from the channeled water. Fog sifting down the hillside seemed eerily infused with color—a dim blue-green, as if, when it had formed itself among the pines and birches, it had leached some of the color from them. Frank could hardly see the other citizens who'd gathered on the sides of the towpath, waiting.

"Like bogland at home," his mother bent and whispered to him—the only time he ever heard her speak of Ireland. She'd tied a woolen scarf around his head and neck against the cold, but thin wool couldn't save him from it. His baby teeth chittered against each other so uncontrollably that his jaw ached from the effort of trying to stop them. He pressed his hands against his cheeks, then nudged his face into his mother's skirt.

A small brass band played something slow and sorrowful, so unlike the oompah music he'd heard them play on Sundays in the summer that he imagined one of the players or one of the instruments was crying. The respectful and the curious crowded against him and his mother, and Frank, at knee level, was swept along when the crowd drew back, like a pulled bow about to launch an arrow, to make way in the towpath so the horses could pull the canal boat through. A taller boy beside him rose on his toes in a hopeless effort to get a better view. Afraid he'd miss the moment, Frank's mother lifted him into her arms, shifted her weight so she could hold him high enough to see: an honor guard of soldiers spread in rigid flank on either side of the simple casket, a spray of baby roses, a pink intrusion cast on board by a teenaged girl at the prompting of her mother. "Look," Frank's mother said, and he saw how slowly the canal boat that carried the black-draped coffin moved, floating, floating, parting the mist the way the prow of a sailing ship might cleave a heavy sea. "Tippecanoe and Tyler, too," a lone voice called, in tribute to the dead President, a last shout of his campaign cry.

Months passed and hundreds of other living travelers arrived as well, to fill hotels and walk through the not-yet-paved streets in city clothes, eager to indulge themselves in mountain wonders. Locks ground closed, creaked open, and swaybacked horses strained at their work on the towpaths, pulling one boat after another. But even in a town grown used to wonder, this English writer, Dickens, brought a sense of celebrity with him when he visited in 1842. It was said that he was showy, unabashed, without the reticence one thought of when one thought of writers. Newspaper reports about his visit to America had found their way into local papers, the *Freie Presse* and the *Tribune*. Boston reporters, it was claimed, had swarmed the *Britannia* when it arrived in Boston Harbor. There had been a great celebration, the "Boz Ball," in New York, Frank's mother read aloud at the kitchen table, and three thousand guests danced quadrilles around him. Danced the night away. His mother's plump little face warmed as she read, as she thought of it. A dancing man. A writer.

"He wore a Prince Albert frock coat, a red vest, a scarf adorned with larks," she continued. Young Frank liked to watch his mother's mouth when she was reading, the way she shaped the words, the quick press of her lips together, the tiny thrusts of tongue. He'd begun to make a connection between the ripple of marks across the printed page and the sound of his mother's voice, and the mystery of that link held him in its thrall. Often, when she'd finished with the newspaper, he'd take it to his bed and open it, and wait for the black-on-white marks to take shape in his mouth the way they had in hers. On the day she read to him of Dickens, he thought he could see in her eyes the plans that she was forming. "Imagine it, Frank," she said. "On his way West he's coming here."

On the morning of the scheduled visit, Frank and his parents were among the first to arrive at the canal basin. It had rained the night before, and the downpour seemed to have rinsed the cloud-strewn sky, cleared the air, made everything tremulous with color. Later Frank would remember the day with a riveting precision—a curl of orange peel on the path, a morning glory's dew-dazzled brilliance, little knobs of sunlight reflecting from his own freshly boot-blacked shoes. He remembered his amazement when his father had relented and agreed to join them on his one day off. In his flushed anticipation Frank thought that the only thing that could make the moment more perfect would be his thumb in his mouth, tucked into his palate. But one parent claimed each of his two hands, and he found that to be a surprisingly pleasing substitute. With his hands at ear level holding theirs, he found his parents were unexpectedly willing to lift their arms and let him take a little running step, then swing him between them.

No one dared believe that Dickens would disembark when his boat arrived, would actually walk among them. And when he did, when he tossed his extravagant long hair and reached out to shake the hands that the pressing crowd extended to him, the very air thrummed. There were cries of pleasure, autographs were sought and received. There he was—the scarlet vest they'd read about, the disarmingly young face, the showman's ready laugh. This time his father lifted Frank up and pointed—See—and in that moment Dickens made a movement toward them. Noticing, perhaps, young Frank's red hair, or his sun-flushed cheeks, the bandaged thumb on the hand that the child waved in imitation of the others. Dickens reached through the crowd for that small hand, and then, perhaps because he missed his own children, whom he'd left behind in England, he stepped forward and took Frank from his father and jostled him about, with a father's rough, generous affection—stroking his back, holding up for closer inspection the grayed and sweat-soaked bandaged thumb.

"So," he said to Frank. "I see what you've been up to."

Throughout his life, what happened next was obscured and blanketed in the chamber of childhood memory. But Frank recalled the burn of shame he felt, the way his muscles tensed in panic, the way he tried to pull his hand away, to hide it. Then, surprisingly, he heard a gentle voice, a soothing sound when he'd been expecting ridicule and mockery. "It's a comfort to you now, I know," whispered Dickens about the thumb, and he said the words as if he'd lived Frank's life, as if he remembered being four and saw it as something deeply complicated, as if he'd felt that raw, unnamed need that Frank felt—for the home they'd left, the thumb he loved, his mother. Such sympathy. Such knowledge. Frank had let himself lean toward that sympathy; his little body sank against the writer's. Frank's forehead touched the cool flesh of Dickens's exquisitely formed chin. "But the need will pass," Dickens whispered to the boy. "I promise."

Years later, when Frank was twenty-three and preparing to go to war, to join the Army of the Potomac, he found in a mail-order catalogue an advertisement for several of the works of Charles Dickens. *Oliver Twist, Nicholas Nickleby, American Notes*, each costing a two-cent piece. His mother was dead by then, the canal-and-portage railroad system over the mountains had been replaced by rail, and his father, who'd never really taken to life in America, had returned to Ireland as soon as his wife was gone. Frank had been told, of course, throughout his growing up, that he had met the writer Charles Dickens, that when he was a child Dickens had held him in his arms. So from the catalogue he ordered the books, compelled by some unidentifiable but nagging need, some sense that there might be something valuable in them that would be useful now that he was alone. Frank had been working six years in the iron works, and already had his own small house, a little clapboard nothing, but he cared for it. He'd made a home for himself, and he spent the last of his civilian days sorting through letters and clothes and the few small things his mother had left—a ring, her mother's Bible, which she rarely read but had put to good use pressing mountain flowers. His wish was to leave as little as possible behind for friends to have to dispose of should he not survive the war. Once that was done, he was free to spend the last nights reading Charles Dickens. For three evenings he sat until late into the night, elbow on table, fingertips pressed to forehead, his thumb stroking idly at his own unshaven cheek, the kerosene that fueled the lamp the amber color of his mother's hair. He saved *American Notes* for last, and it was only the day before he left that he came to the section in which Dickens's travels through the Allegheny Mountains on the portage railroad were described.

"It was very pretty traveling thus," Dickens had written, ". . . along the heights of the mountain in a keen wind, to look down into a valley full of light and softness . . . [at] children running to the doors; dogs bursting out to bark . . . men in shirtsleeves . . . planning out tomorrow's work; and we riding onward, high above them, like a whirlwind."

Throughout his preparations for going to war, Frank had been surprisingly without emotion. He'd paid a farewell visit to his mother's grave in Sandy Vale Cemetery, had walked past the house his family had rented for so many years just across the Stony Creek on Morris Street, the house for which his father, in the end, appeared to have no feeling, no attachment. He'd attended to these departure rituals like a monk who'd forsworn love, possessions, all worldly things. But when he read those words of Dickens, saw the valley as Dickens saw it, the sense of all he loved and all that he was leaving appeared with a wounding clarity before him. Dickens understood, Frank thought. Twice now, in his life, at crucial times he'd taught him things that he needed to know. First, that the pain of growing up does finally pass. And now, before war, there was this reminder—that his life in a small town in the mountains was a worthy thing. That even if you've sailed on the *Britannia*, even if you've danced the quadrille in Manhattan in a room ablaze with light, you can still see how lovely a mountain valley is, how valuable an ordinary life.

And so while other men took photographs of parents and locks of a lover's hair to war, Frank Fallon took Charles Dickens in his haversack. For luck. For cushioning his head. A comfort.

He first saw her in the early winter of 1865. Julia showed Frank how to shuck oysters with a knife. Julia Strayer, twenty-one at the war's end, a lover of apples and dogs and small sweet things. Figs. Hot-cinnamon candies. Oysters when they first arrived in Johnstown. Sweet as the sea that bred them, freighted in on dry ice all the way from Philadelphia by M. D. Jones, the grocer on Railroad Street. "The-best-goods-for-the-least money" M. D. Jones, Grocer, as he advertised himself in the *Tribune*. M. D. Jones, who, at a time and in a place when oysters were unheard of except as something served in coastal cities, in restaurants that could only be imagined, believed his good neighbors deserved exotica, deserved the freshness of the sea.

Julia's hands were deft and strong in ways their small size and fine-boned shapeliness belied. Frank had come to the grocer's for tobacco, and as he stood at the counter waiting to be served, hands in his pants pockets, he looked at the floor-to-ceiling, carefully shelved merchandise—all the things that Jones provided. Queensware, glassware, a display board of buttons; a thousand chips of color, which, seen from the entrance, made the far wall appear to be a dark mosaic, something stolen from a mountain castle in Bohemia, from the bedchamber of a love-starved, bitter, brooding prince. Frank had been back from the war just six months. He was working at Cambria Iron again, living alone, glad to have the chance to shop, glad to see his neighbors. Frank stood off to one side of the counter near the bean and flour bins, when the back door opened and a gust of cold air sent a shiver through the woman standing next to him. Who she was he did not know. In her simple, dark alpaca dress, gray pelisse, and narrow velvet-ribboned bonnet, she looked like someone whom the train had brought, a passenger who'd decided to take a turn through town while the engine took on coal. Jones struggled with the wet, warped barrel, rolling and pivoting it in from the back alley. Frank stepped forward to offer help, as did several other men, but Jones would have none of it.

"Thanks, Frank, but I can manage," he'd said, using his apron to wipe sweat from his bald head. And then, once he had the barrel righted, he'd strained with a crowbar to wrench the salt-streaked lid off. Proud of his strength, magnanimous in offering his neighbors briny wonders from the sea.

There was a wooden groan, a moan, a splintering. And then the sudden smell of sand and salt, of ocean air. Bracing, pungent. Frank inhaled deeply, as did the girl beside him, and the small circle of shoppers that had gathered round to watch, to take part in the theater of it. In that brief moment, in that first inhalation, they let themselves imagine sand and sea grass, let themselves imagine that the gray, moist mounds of oysters were wave-struck rocks.

"May I?" The young girl's light voice broke the communal reverie. And as Jones nodded yes, Frank saw her reach into the barrel and then turn to him, who stood beside her, an oyster in her hand, the gnarled, pocked shell caught in the cup of her palm. He watched her take the knife Jones offered her and urge the flat blade into the shell's slim crack. Then came the pry, the turn, the sudden springing open, the shining bivalve exposed to the glare of light and air, its surface shimmering and glinting.

She cocked her head—another "May I?" in her eyes—this one, to Frank's surprise, addressed to him. And as if she expected yes, as if she was a girl who'd grown up expecting it, she turned toward him and took his hand and showed him how to hold the hard shell to his lips and let the slickness slide into his mouth.

"Oh no, don't chew," she'd cautioned, when she saw his jaw shift, his teeth about to bite into it. "You let it linger on your tongue, just to get the taste and feel of it before you swallow." She swallowed, too, then, her own mouth empty, but as if to help him in his effort, the way mothers sometimes nod and mouth words for their tongue-tied children. "It's a part of the experience," she offered, smiling.

And although Frank's mouth filled with a fishy aftertaste, and his stomach soured at the thought of having that raw, gray, uncooked globule descend into it, he returned her smile and even nodded yes when her raised eyebrows and reaching hand wondered if he wouldn't like another. Because, already, pleasing her had begun to matter to him. This stranger. Her smile, the obvious pleasure she found in feeding him, made him reluctant to move from his place beside her. Her hair was a shade of rich sweet butternut, a small mole dotted the peak of one cheek, surprisingly full eyebrows crowned her wide inquiring eyes. Later, long after they were married, sometimes when he watched her forcing a window open after spring rain, or diapering a baby, or moving her warm wet lips across his chest, defining with her mouth his ribs, his hips, his abdomen, he'd think back to that day, to how love begins. Not with lustful dreams or vague inchoate longings. Those came, of course, and like a fury, but those came later. At the start of it he'd felt only a sudden overpowering wish to make her happy. To see her smile again.

She was the daughter of a doctor who had killed a man in Chicago in a botched surgery. There had been an inquest, a vengeance-seeking widow, searing public questions from the coroner and an older, more traditional physician. The doctor's supporters, who believed in him and his experiments with the newest surgical techniques, wrote to newspapers, made placards, staged rallies on street corners, held public meetings in church basements on his behalf. But even after the proceedings ended and it was concluded that he was *not* to blame, that the tumor sinewed around the dead man's vena cava would have killed him even if the surgery had not, it became clear to Dr. Strayer that he could not stay. His life in Chicago, his house just blocks from the lake, his practice would have to be abandoned. Julia, nineteen at the time, old enough, most certainly, to remember the awful details—the dead cat thrown at their front door, its stomach slit; the jeering shouts of "butcher" that greeted their arrival at the courthouse steps—in fact remembered little. The image that remained in her mind throughout her life was her father's empty office—the spokes of the hat rack, the empty chairs in the room where her father's patients had coughed, and cried, and waited.

Her father wrote to physician friends, made inquiries. If a move was necessary, the farther away the better, Dr. Strayer had concluded, where word would not have traveled. In his letters he told his story truthfully. He'd never be dishonest with his colleagues, but he hoped that discretion could be employed in his new situation, wherever that might be, that patients would not have to know of his recent troubles. Without patients, income, economies had to be employed by Julia. She was housekeeper in the most literal sense since her mother had died. Pike instead of lamb. She learned what seemed like a hundred different ways to make potatoes. At his desk in what had been his consulting room, her father wrote letter after letter.

As the war drew to a close, scores of wounded returned home. It further pained Dr. Strayer to know to what good use his skills might have been put, the surgeries he might have done. The war slowed the mails. The cold Midwestern winter was excruciating. Julia had almost abandoned hope—who wants a disgraced doctor after all?—when a letter came from Johnstown, Pennsylvania, from Dr. Lemon Bean, with whom her father had trained in Philadelphia. Bean's letter made it clear that, because of all that had happened, his surgeon friend would have to join him as assistant, that there would be no surgery, no inventive experimental treatment in a practice whose focus was the treatment of "lingering and obscure diseases." But it was a busy practice, there was much to do. The city was growing, and Bean needed help. Strayer would be welcome.

"A much smaller city. Mountains. Just what I'd hoped for," Dr. Strayer had said in a rush of heartiness, of forced good cheer, when the letter came. Focusing on the kindness of the offer, the opportunity to start afresh. The pleasure of being in a place where no one would have heard of him, where no one knew his name. Julia, so supportive, so like her mother, joined in his optimism, in his show of eagerness, bravado. They sold the house with its first-floor doctor's office, and all its equipment, for which, in his new circumstance, he'd have no need: chairs for waiting patients, the examination table, the cherry-wood desk from the private anteroom where he did consultations. He and his only child packed their clothing to take with them, sold a good bit of the furniture, and arranged for other items to be stored temporarily and shipped later. They were to take the train east, see if Johnstown was to their liking. They would live for the time being in an establishment Bean described enthusiastically in his letter to them. The Merchant Hotel. "Four stories," Bean wrote, November 14, 1865. "An elaborate crystal chandelier in the main dining room. Quite grand." Lest they think that they were coming to a second-rate place, lest they think this was a lowering of themselves, a lessening. And while Dr. Strayer checked in at the Merchant Hotel, while he signed the ledger, approved the third-floor rooms, Julia took a turn through town, saying to herself with each step, "Home, home, home," as if to convince herself; memorizing street names, trying by sheer force of will to persuade herself that this was where she lived now, this was the place to which fate had brought her. Ever practical and with an eye toward what she might need in a life there, she took note of the names of merchants—Fockler and Levergood, Dry Goods, Notions, Hats and Shoes; Lorenz Nothhelfer, Tobacco and Cigars; John Meyer, Shaving and Hair Dressing Salon, "Cupping and Leaching done in a Skillful Manner." A dress shop where she might find employment clerking or sewing if things didn't work out as they'd planned with Dr. Bean; C. Keim Marble and Granite Works—Monuments and Tombstones. A lump formed in her throat. In case they died there. In case they stayed. Julia Strayer, small hands tucked in a muff against the surprising mountain cold, little silk purse in her fist, hat pinned to her tightly tucked hair, trying to ward off the utter strangeness she felt. Then unexpectedly came a wish from out of nowhere, a wish for water, for Lake Michigan. She felt suddenly, acutely claustrophobic, sickened by the mountains, by the overpowering encroachment of the sky-obscuring hills, the dark conspiring pines.

It was by sheer chance that she wandered onto Railroad Street, saw, through M. D. Jones's tall glass front windows the grand display of buttons, a reminder of her need for thread and needle, the hem she'd torn on the train's high step. Who knew when she stepped inside that she would wander into the arrival of the oyster barrel, the celebration of exotica, the goodwill attached to welcoming in a still-small town—oysters, pretty strangers, the pleasure taken in the everyday surprises that the railroad brings? She had always thought herself shy, but suddenly she was at the center of a kind of tableau, demonstrating oyster shucking, sliding oysters into the mouth of a young man she did not know. A veteran, she realized, when she noticed his mangled ear. The train that had brought her and her father here had been full of soldiers coming home or, in the case of Southerners who'd lost everything, running from it, shirtsleeves pinned to hide rude stumps, crutches placed beneath seats; a man who'd been blinded, whose lids were puckered by the burns' scarring, being led to his seat by a patient porter. It made her glad in a way she'd never been before that she was an only child, that she hadn't had a brother. From her father, an ideologue, as inflexible about patriotism as he'd once been about his right to practice medicine the way he saw fit, she knew that men with money, in both the North and the South, had paid others to fight in their stead; $350.00 dollars and you could find some hungry, foolishly patriotic boy. A believer. You could stay behind. Such a bargain. And on the train, as she settled herself and looked around her, trying to keep her eyes from wounds, trying not to stare or, worse yet, show signs of feminine concern, unwanted pity, she found herself assuming that to be a young man without a scar, a wound, an absence was a sure sign, not of luck, but of prosperity, cowardice, dishonor. In a country already so divided, how much would that widen the breach between men? The triumphant North and the defeated South. The haves. The have-nots. How could any of it be spoken of, ever? she wondered. She'd noticed since the war's end how quiet young men seemed to have become. How the rowdy, random foolishness, the exuberant goodwill she'd always thought of when she thought of boys seemed to have been replaced by a bitterness, a blankness. On the train she could not meet their eyes.

She told Frank this, on their wedding night, eight months later, after a brief, impassioned courtship. Theirs was a very short engagement, but every kind of postponement, every kind of waiting seemed a foolish waste at the war's end. Blood on the sheets that night, their wedding night, but not virgin blood. That she'd shed weeks earlier, in his house, his bed, in the bed that had been his mother's. A house, he told her proudly, that he'd bought with money he had earned. She wasn't sure why, but she was surprised by that. Surprised by such domesticity in a man. She had thought that someone so young, so unencumbered, would take rooms with a family or in a rooming house. When he'd brought her there the first time, she'd admired the way he'd made a home of it, the books he owned, the embroidered tablecloth which offered kindly cover to a piece of furniture whose legs revealed how rough, how less-than-fine it was. There was a little watercolor on the wall, the kind of thing that might have been bought from a street fair, from a troupe of artisans who moved from town to town. A mountain scene, a waterfall, the red leaves on a lone maple tree made three-dimensional by the use of thick, raised daubs of painted color.

"It's not so much," he said to her as he showed her in. But she could see that his modesty was false. That he was fiercely proud. In the last few weeks she had discovered that she liked having pride in her life again, she, the daughter of a defeated surgeon. Frank had been quick to find her after that first meeting at the oyster barrel. Scrubbed and soap-scented when he appeared in the hotel lobby to call on her, to meet her father. Resourceful in finding her despite the fact that they had not exchanged names at Jones's store that day. No questions asked. With her father's approval, she agreed to take a walk with Frank when he came calling. She wore a pelisse and an ornate little hat, overdressed for a Sunday stroll. Reminded once again that she was not in Chicago. He surprised her by asking, boldly, she thought, if she would like to see his house. And she surprised herself by liking the boldness, by agreeing to go with him. Once inside, once he'd closed the door, he stepped toward her and eased the hat pin from her bonnet crown.

"I'm alone in the world," he said softly as he placed the hat on the table. He took her hand, glad when she didn't withdraw it or scold him. He wanted to show her everything. The kitchen, the wide-planked floors, the steeply rising stairs. In one of the two small bedrooms, she ran her hand along the windowsill, the bureau, the simply carved headboard of the bed. It was as if she had to touch a place to know it.

"I've never been alone in a room with any man except my father," she said. "Do you think that's odd? I'm afraid I've lost my bearings recently, so I don't know what is odd and what isn't. My father and I have had a difficult two years." She drew the curtain back from the window, looking out toward Prospect Hill, the spring green of willows bending toward a far-off stream. It was as if every other color were gone from the world. The green of the hillside, the green pattern of his mother's quilt. "In Chicago I could see the lake from my bedroom window. I could open any window in our house and smell the water." She let the curtain fall back, turned to him. "Do you think I'll ever grow accustomed to it here? What do you suppose will become of me?" There was a look of quiet desperation on her face, just weeks into this new life, one she hadn't wanted. Frank didn't know what to say.

She looked down at the floor. When she raised her head, it was with the look of someone determined, someone game, prepared to try to make the best of things. Needing help, but willing to try. And he found himself wanting very much to help her.

"Why don't you tell me the good things about living here." She smiled, but without enthusiasm. "There must be scores of good things. Tell me about them. Make a list for me."

"Fish," he said, without really thinking, saying the first thing that came to him. Then, as if to justify himself for reminding her of the water she so missed: "Different fish than you're accustomed to, I imagine. Catfish. Mullet. Walleyed pike." She laughed at that unlikely name, and he thought, There! I can make her smile.

"What else?" she asked, shyly able to engage a little in the enterprise. She was on one side of the bed, he the other. She stretched her arms out toward the mattress, leaned on her hands, toward him. "What else?"

"Ice skating on Von Lunen Pond. With white arc streetlamps glazing the surface with a spectral light."

"Spectral light?" She cocked her head to one side, impressed. He thanked God for Dickens.

"And a horse-drawn streetcar that travels down Maple Avenue to Moxham, the prettiest street in the valley. The streetcar itself is yellow."

Her lovely pink lips had spread into a grin. "Yellow?" She laughed, as if reluctant to be engaged, interested in the way she was. "Can we take a ride on it?"

"Only after we have been to see *Uncle Tom's Cabin* at the nine hundred–seat opera house."

Her grin grew wider. "So players come? There's theater? You're not just teasing me?"

He shook his head. "And fortune-tellers," he mouthed, as if sharing a secret, something no one knew but them. "And roller-skating. And sleigh rides at Christmas time."

"Thank you," she said, serious again, reaching out a hand as if to touch his cheek and then withdrawing it, embarrassed. She almost volunteered to stay then. She could imagine living in that house, with him. A home instead of a hotel, a place of her own, a family. She thought of turning the quilt back, turning to kiss him. Instead, she glanced again at the window, noticed darkness settling in.

"My father will be waiting," she said simply. "But I'd like to come again. May I?"

He said yes. And so she came again. And again. And then she married him and came to stay.

ATTACHMENTS

"Man must endure whatever wind doth blow
From God, and labour still without lament."
                    —Marcus Aurelius, *Meditations*, Book VII, Number 51

From the very beginning Julia wanted babies. Four. Frank, in love with her, wanted several, but thought four might be too many, might require too much of them.

No, she'd said to Frank, four was not too many. What's too many when so much can happen, when such things go wrong, but even when she said that, as if four were a kind of insurance against losing one, she never thought she would.

The first baby was Daniel, a boy, a son. Wee bit of a red-haired thing. A little miniature of his father. Frank was stupid with the joy of it. When the child was only days old, Frank held and rocked him, Daniel's small hand looped over Frank's index finger. Frank prayed he'd never suck his thumb.

And then, just after Daniel took his first steps, came Caroline. Three years later Louis, followed by the baby, Claire. For Julia it was easy to be pregnant, easy to deliver each child in Frank's mother's bed. For her and Frank, two only children, it seemed like an entrée into another world, an unlikely adventure. Babies everywhere. The sweetish smell of breast milk, diapers nipped with wooden pins to the back-yard line like white flags of surrender—to parenthood, to sleeplessness, to the lust that kept the babies coming, even when good sense told them they should plan a little, slow down, wait.

The proliferation of Fallons mirrored the proliferation of every kind that marked the decade after war. Cities, businesses flourished. Rockefeller started Standard Oil, Charles Darwin shocked the world with his evolutionary theories. Henry Clay Frick began his coke-mining operations. Andrew Carnegie "got the flash," as he liked to characterize his flights of inspiration, and began his manufacturing of steel. When Jay Cooke's railroad ventures failed in '73 and brought "The Panic," expansion paused. But not in Johnstown, where hotels were being built, saloons sprang up. Gautier moved its wire works there, and Mr. Morrell had plans drawn for a new library.

After Caroline was born, Frank used money he had saved and bought Julia a piano. She had taken lessons as a child while in Chicago, and he wanted to have music, for her and for his children. Sometimes when he'd worked the long turn, when he'd come home bone-tired, wanting nothing more than Julia and sleep, he'd sit briefly on the small piano stool and run his fingers silently, almost lovingly across the keys. This instrument, this almost sacred object, seemed emblematic of the life he'd made, and just sitting next to it, his dark hands shadowing the ivory, brought a tightness to his chest.

With four children Julia became used to colds and fevers, to the way fierce short bursts of illness passed from one child to the next. Each of them sick in quick succession. Mountain winters were the worst, of course. Who could keep any house warm enough against the dank, blanketing snow, the tree-bending, penetrating winds? And spring was bad, too, when snowy runoff left water standing in the streets, a breeding ground, her father said, for germs and biting insects. When she was old enough, Julia had helped him in his office in Chicago, taking her mother's place after she had died. Nothing truly medical, just small things—changing the sheets on the examining table, boiling instruments, feeling a flushed forehead for signs of fever. She'd come to know some basic, simple terminology. But she felt inept and stupid at the beginning, when she was new to mothering, when she had only Daniel. All knowledge, all judgment seemed to vanish. With the slightest heat rash, the slightest sign of restlessness or irritability, she summoned her doctor/father, bombarding him with questions. "What about that rash—is it scarlet fever? Smallpox?" Or: "His coughing is a fearful thing." Her ear pressed to the pink arc of Daniel's baby chest, listening for danger signs, for roiling phlegm, for strident breaths, for wheezing. "Pneumonia?" she asked. "Whooping cough?" Fearing in a way that her father thought was unnatural to her. But as the children thrived, Daniel's beaming, red-haired presence setting the tone for the family, she grew easier. Not quite complacent, but easier. About Frank she worried more. She knew that steel making was rough and risky. But by the time Claire had lost the first of her milk teeth, Julia had come to feel secure in a way she couldn't quite explain about the children. She thought love sheltered them.

Louis in his rimless glasses was nearsighted and small. Claire, the princess, was five in the summer of 1879, fussed over by Caroline, twelve, earnest, and determined to be mother's helper, mother's sidekick, mother's sweetest pal. And Daniel, the reader, was thirteen, a charmer and full of purpose—everybody said so—a boy who would make something of himself, already working two days after school at Central Drugstore and on Saturdays for David Snavely at the livery. Now, there was a boy. No one worried about Daniel. So when he first fell ill, when he first *complained* so uncharacteristically, Julia thought little of it. She even flattered herself by thinking that it was his way of taking a day from school, of being babied, fussed over by his mother. A little sore throat. That was all. Something easily looked after. Something simple and routine. Hot tea with lemon, poultices to keep the thing from going to his chest. Her father would come later in the day to check, he always did when the children took ill, but by then, she thought, Daniel would probably already be feeling better, wanting to play chess with Louis, who was too young, really, not much good at it. Wanting to read Dickens late, a book checked out from the library, long after he ought to have been sleeping. But he stayed in bed all day, curled into himself to keep the chills from coming, and then, when she took him broth at suppertime, she saw the fever had risen, that he'd stopped making sense, and he frightened Julia when he said he couldn't swallow.

Her father spent much longer than he usually did examining, percussing Daniel's chest, pressing the stethoscope too long to his heart, and then, oddly, Julia thought, to his throat. As if he expected to hear something there. There seemed to be much more of a production made of checking eyes and ears, even when Daniel, in his fevered thrashing, knocked the otoscope out of the doctor's hand and sent it flying. "Bring the light closer," her father said to Julia, again paying a special kind of attention to the throat, barking, "Hold him still now," to Frank, whom he'd always treated with the deference he felt was due a son-in-law. He was short with him now. Terse with all of them. He avoided Julia's eyes when he finished the exam, sat instead beside Daniel on the bed, took his pulse again, once more counted the quick rasping rise and fall of his irregular and noisy breathing. Until Julia wanted to scream at him, What's all this fussing, hurry now and say what you always say, cold compresses for the fever, see that he rests, he'll be like new by morning. Say it, she thought. Just say it.

Instead, he took Frank by the arm, motioned to the other children, who'd gathered themselves in an anxious little circle on Caroline's bed in the farthest corner of the room. Even Claire, the baby, sensing something bad, a wrongness here, was sucking her thumb while Caroline held and rocked her. Come, the doctor's gesture said. Out of this room now. Follow me. And it was only after Caroline had herded Claire and Louis down the stairs that he put his arm around Julia's shoulder. I can't be sure, of course, he said, his usual confidence in no way evident. Then he said, *I've been wrong before.* The first and only time he'd ever made reference to the lapse of judgment, to the fatal error that had brought them there.

"Just tell me," Julia whispered. "What point is there in going on this way? What is it?"

"Diphtheria," he said, leaving Julia feeling suddenly off balance, as if the earth had tilted on its axis. Suspended between knowing and the refusal of knowledge, between the father who understood what diphtheria meant and the husband standing helplessly beside her, his arm around her as her father's was, as if asserting his rights as protector, as the one who keeps tragedy at bay.

Julia remembered against her will what she knew from her days as her father's nurse substitute. She remembered the awful, choking, murderous trajectory of the disease. Because she'd helped her father in his office, she knew better than Frank did about the virulence and contagion. The tough, sinewy membrane of dead cells that webbed and blocked the throat, that stopped breathing, invaded kidneys, livers, lungs. That finally and fatally inflamed the heart.

Her mind rushed beyond Daniel, beyond the room and the moment. To the other children. To saving them. It was then that she heard her father speaking to Frank, that she heard him say *Quarantine*. A sign would have to be posted. Her home declared a death house. If they were quarantined, the other children would have to stay here. She'd lose the others, too.

"Take Caroline and Claire and Louis," she said to her father. Crazed with the thought of how quickly, how easily they'd be infected. She began rifling through the cupboard where their clothes were kept. A drawer for each child, their modest accumulations of underthings and small necessities. Striped socks and dark suspenders, Caroline's favorite blue woolen dress, and Claire's cape, which Julia had trimmed by hand with scarlet piping. Toothbrushes, hair ribbons, a wide-toothed comb. All thrown with mad haste into the pouch she was making of her apron. Gathering the things they'd need for their escape. "We've got to hurry," she said to herself as much as to anyone. "We've got to get them out of here."

"You know I can't do that." The doctor reached for her arm and tried to turn her toward him, imagining, perhaps, that eye contact would restore reason. As if reasoning hadn't already given way to near-hysteria, to panic. "To my rooms, Julia? To a public place? It would be unconscionable. They may be fine. There's every chance that if we're careful now, they won't be stricken, but if one of them is infected and they leave here, it could start an epidemic. You know I can't do that."

But of course, she didn't know, she refused to know; what does any mother know when it comes to saving her children? She was wild-eyed when she turned on him, the father to whom she was so thoroughly attached, with whom she'd survived disgrace and banishment. She'd try anything, any threat, any cruelty to force him to help her. If you ever loved me, she cried frantically, not caring if the children heard, not caring how she made him suffer. I'll keep them from you if you deny me this . . . If you ever want to see your grandchildren again . . . If you want to make up to me for all that's happened. Accusing him. Finding any words she could to wound him.

Bedlam ensued, bedlam reigned. A word that came out of nowhere to

Frank. Claire, downstairs, began crying when she heard her mother shouting. Louis was racing up the stairs, calling his mother's name. And then suddenly Daniel sat up, eyes wide and bloodshot, as he retched, coughing and choking, and vomited in bed. Frank ran to him, used his shirttail to clear the blood-tinged mucus from his mouth. He wished that he could reach down into his throat, or place his mouth over his son's. He would have sucked disease right out of him.

It was Daniel who brought an end to hysteria and mayhem, Daniel's bluish face that restored clear-thinking, usefulness, some semblance of sanity. "Get me alcohol, Julia! Hear me, child. Be quick," Strayer cried, and he used the rye whiskey Julia brought when nothing else could be found in a hasty attempt to sanitize the scalpel that he ripped from its cloth enclosure in his bag. Wiping vomitus aside, rinsing the throat with a bedside table glass of drinking water, finding, as only a surgeon could, the precise spot, inserting the scalpel just so in the trachea, hearing the soft pop as the cartilage snapped, hearing the rush of air. Seeing immediately the return of color to the sick boy's face.

Frank pulled Julia to him. Said irrelevant and private shushing things to her, to stop her weeping. Julia's father's face was the color of ash; his hands, so steady when they had to be, when the cut was made, were trembling. Again he reached into his bag and withdrew from it a flanged metal insert of his own design which he worked into the tracheal opening to assure it would not close and choke the boy. He kept two such implements in his doctor's bag, and other small pieces of equipment he'd designed himself, the secret inventions of a man who'd once lived for the advances he thought he could bring to medicine.

Strips of bandages ribboned from the flanges that lay in a flat square on Daniel's throat. Strayer pulled these around the boy's neck and tied them, making all secure. Only then did he allow himself a grandfather's feelings. He bent to stroke the wet hair from the boy's hot forehead and sat heavily on the soiled sheets so he could kiss the child, unmindful of the vomitus, wanting only to watch his grandson sink dully back into his pillows, wanting only to watch him breathe.

"Let him rest a bit. Then this mess can be cleared." He was gathering his instruments, burying things in the dark depth of his bag.

There were instructions on airing the house, placing pallets in the kitchen to make a separate sleeping place for the other children. Treating the fever, using lye to disinfect the bedclothes. He kept his eyes averted from his daughter's, the threats and fury not referred to, the hurt relinquished. He had to go to his office, he said. There might be others. Yes, yes, of course he'd come back soon. Of course. Just see to yourselves, and keep a close eye on the others, he said at the front door. Pulling Caroline and Claire and Louis to him one more time, holding each an extra moment, letting his hands linger in their hair.

Frank slept with Daniel that first night. Don't get too close, his father-in-law had warned, and for a time he sat in the chair beside the bed, watching the miracle of the tracheotomy, the miracle of breathing. But how long could that last, with the child so ill? How at such a time does a father keep his distance? Frank slid his arms under Daniel, disturbed by his lightness, troubled by the sense that illness had already drained some essence from him. He was tall for thirteen. Work at home and at Snavely's had given a muscled heft to his arms and shoulders. But Frank found that it was easy to slide him on the soft sheet to one side of the bed. Frank removed his own boots, his coarse work pants, and lay down beside him. How hot he was, how flaccid his long arms and legs! He pressed the whole length of himself against the boy, as if contact could bring cure, as if he thought he could force escaping life back into him.

Daniel, fever-ridden, deranged, dreamed that night that he had left his body, that he was sitting in the chair beside himself, watching the limp thin boy in the bed as he worked, *worked* at breathing. He thought about that boy, the sick one. You should get up, Snavely will be waiting for you. In his dream he smelled horse, smelled something acrid, burning, the scent of horse hair and flesh right after it was branded. He felt the warmth of animal skin against his hand, as he did when he brushed Pearl or Cricket or one of Snavely's other horses after school. Get up, he said to his sick self. You promised you'd take Louis fishing on his birthday. Snavely, who never let horses to anyone so young, had promised to break his rule for Daniel. Just this once. As a reward for hard work, an acknowledgment of how steady a helper he'd been. Reins, bit, harness . . . In his dream Daniel got it all wrong, outfitting the horse improperly, and there would be no brooking that, all bets would be off if Daniel couldn't get the gear on the horse correctly. Snavely said so. Whether I've got a soft spot for you or not, there'll be no horse for a careless boy, for a boy who can't remember. Daniel had been figuring the logistics of the fishing trip—a rod and reel for Louis, the horse letting, the extra food for a picnic—for months. He'd been scouting spots on Bottle Run and the Rorabaugh Creek. He had over and over again imagined Louis standing in the rocky creek bed, fiddling with his rod and reel, fiddling with his glasses. Get up now, Daniel said in his dream to his sleeping self. And be mindful of Louis, hold tight to him when Pearl starts trotting, as you've seen her do. See that he doesn't fall and cut himself on a sharp rock. See that he doesn't hit his head. Mother never would get past it if you let her favorite hurt himself. *Louis, Louis.* In his dream Daniel tried to call his name, but something . . . what? . . . the bandaged place on his neck . . . made it impossible to speak. He struggled, tried everything he could to make a sound, but nothing came. So he could not call Louis, who, he saw, was wading far too far into the water, gesturing with wide arcs of his arms. Come on, Daniel. Follow me. Daniel strained against the hands that pressed him back into the bed. He pulled wildly at the coarse fabric knotted around his feet and ankles, the restraints that had been deemed necessary to protect him from his delirium and thrashing, that tied him to the bed. Get up, he urged himself in his dream. Louis has gone too far, the water is rising to his hips, the current eddying around him, making him uncertain and wobbly. Hurry. The word buzzed in Daniel's brain. Come back, he called, but soundlessly. No voice, no strength. His warning unheard and so unheeded. Louis drifting off away from him. Louis lost. Nothing, nothing but the sound of moving water. Waving over the tops of rocks, carrying surface detritus away.

No one blamed him, of course. For bringing death into the house. For bringing the disease that infected Caroline and Claire and Louis, and then, miraculously, recovering, while the other children lay in phlegm-bound stupor. Julia's father had been right to fear. It was an epidemic, after all. Disease was rampant, mostly among children. Such easy marks, their immune systems so undeveloped, so tentative and struggling. It wasn't Daniel's fault that he was among the first to get it. It wasn't his fault that he got well, while it killed so many others.

The diphtheria epidemic of '79. More than 130 children were dead in the space of three months. Epidemic. Did it help to give an official title to it, create some referential phrase that could, over time, make the memory of the dying more abstract, and in its abstractions, somehow more bearable? When a stranger asked, two, three, four years later, "How many children have you?" one could say, Julia could say, four until '79. Two now, and no further explanation would be required. You could count on being left alone about it. Not pressed with questions or fumbling, well-intentioned sympathy. The pain could be sealed off and contained that way.

Or so hoped the parents of the 130 dead.

That thinking might have helped some, but it did not help Julia. She'd grown up in the harsh and often disappointing world of medicine at a time when medicine was palliative, when recovery and cures were more often hoped for than expected. People died young, she knew. Children died. Cholera had killed her mother. Childbirth killed, and then there were wars and accidents. She was just thirty-three and a half dozen of her girlhood friends were dead already. She understood that people had large families to ensure against such dying. Death was excruciating, painful, but it was not supposed to be surprising. One was not allowed to be surprised. Or stricken. One was not supposed to wallow in it.

It meant something to Julia to be the one to wash the bodies before the undertaker came. To leave Caroline's sickbed long enough to tend to her two youngest children. To fill the basin with water warmed by the woodstove, to smooth the hair, to touch and trace their flesh one last time, memorizing them again, as she had right after she had birthed them. Touching toes, chin, the curled cusp of ear, the rounded mound of cheek, the dips and promontories of their supple spines. Frank couldn't bring himself to watch. He wanted to remember them as they'd looked living. And in any case, he'd been preparing himself, letting go, applying himself to the business of mourning as soon as he saw how much sicker the two babies were, how much more virulent the disease had gotten, as it moved from child to child, as if it had gained force and strength as it sapped strength from one and then the other of them. He could feel himself detaching from them, shocked by what seemed an ugly, self-protective instinct in himself. The instinct to prepare, to find strength where none existed, to struggle toward some power that he might use to shield the others in his dwindling, diminished family. Julia. Daniel. Caroline. As he watched Claire and Louis dying, he struggled mightily for some artificial, temporary courage. And when the end came, he felt weakly, stupidly grateful; that they had not died in some brief moment when he and Julia weren't in the room, and that it was late at night, so Caroline and Daniel hadn't had to watch, because they were sleeping. Frank had already begun the strategy that would make continuing to live possible for him. The strategy of clinging to what had not been lost, the impossibly small blessings.

He stayed with Caroline and Daniel in the kitchen in the morning while their mother washed the babies. Knowing that *they* knew what was happening upstairs. Knowing why they were forbidden access. An eerie quiet filled the house. Frank had expected something uncontrolled from Julia. Some keening, wrenching sounds. But the only sound he heard coming from the second floor was the sound of water trickling back into the basin as Julia wrung the washcloth over it. Dipping, soaping, wiping, wringing. Her footsteps on the floorboards as she carried the basin from one bed to the other.

She left the calling of the priest to Frank, the choosing of the stones. She let her father buy her mourning dress.

They laid them next to Frank's mother. Louis 1871–79, Claire 1874–79. The Epidemic. Loved. Missed.

And tried to begin to live this altered life they had been handed. The life of two beds in the children's room instead of four. The truncated, stunned existence on the other side of the impossible abyss of child loss. Children snatched, their vast unfolding futures left to the day and night-time dreams of shattered parents.

Frank wanted to be kind to Julia. He wanted love to reassert itself and save them. He wanted her to want that, too. He tried to find a way to think of himself as lucky. Lucky that two of them had lived. Lucky that he and Julia were still young enough to have another child if that's what they decided. Surely, he told himself, they'd satisfied the gods now. They'd lost enough that they'd be spared all further grief. They'd grow old together. They'd live to see their grandchildren get married. If they lived long enough, he tried to convince himself, they might find something resembling happiness again. He could not know that all such avenues had closed for her. That unlike him she was strangely, surprisingly, without resources. That the charm, the tenderness, the wit she'd always counted on, that her mother always said were part of her good character, had disappeared like so much smoke. She was left hollowed, fractured, parched.

The Charter

"Your principles are living principles. How else can they become life-
less, except the images which tally with them be extinguished?"
—Marcus Aurelius, *Meditations*, Book VII, Number 2

In the month that the Fallon children died, James Talbot was given a routine matter to handle at his Pittsburgh law firm. It had to do with a charter
for a club—a mountain resort in the Alleghenies near the little town of
South Fork—a two-hour train ride east. According to the documents
there would be privately owned cottages, a clubhouse where members
would take their meals, and, most incredibly, a 450-acre lake. When James
took a first, cursory look at the documents, that fact had caught his eye.
He knew the Allegheny Mountains; he'd stayed once, before he'd married,
in the Mountain House Hotel in Cresson, where Andrew Carnegie spent
time, and James remembered well that the only waters there were rock-
strewn mountain streams and rivers. He wondered if there might have
been some error. He couldn't imagine how there had come to be a lake.

"We want you to give this special attention," one of the senior partners
had written in a note attached to the thick envelope. James was thirty-
three then, married eleven years, father of a daughter who was ten. He had
worked at the firm three years. "Special attention." The names of Andrew
Carnegie, Henry Clay Frick, and Andrew Mellon made him pause as he

read. Important well-placed men—clients or associates of theirs. He dared to hope that this was the assignment he'd been waiting for.

The day the documents arrived, he'd looked up from his reading, gazed absently at the artifacts he'd placed with so much care on bookcase and desktop, things meant to give his office an identity as his. A horn box shaped like a small sarcophagus. A curved tusk from some sort of small-tusked animal. Indications of trips taken, souvenirs acquired, of a life lived with propriety. His favorite bibelot was a little pearl-encrusted pillbox that he'd seen in the window of a shop and bought. "My mother's," he said with a soft reverence whenever someone admired or asked about it. All around him he had placed these mementos of his created, carefully constructed past. He ran his finger over the raised surface of the pillbox lid. So often had he mouthed the words "my mother's" that there were moments, when he was tired and working late, when darkness seeped through the windows and the smudgy flame of his kerosene lamp filled the room with wavering shadows, that he almost believed the little jeweled box *had* been hers, that it was, in truth, something of herself she had left to him. A trick of the imagination, fantasy. A flaw, he thought, in someone who so valued clearheadedness, practicality. He gathered the pages he'd been reading through, tapped them smartly on his desk to even out the edges. He pulled at the starched cuff that had ridden up beneath his dark suit sleeve. He had never imagined he would be a lawyer. He had thought that, like his father, he would be a gentleman, a planter, that he would never leave Virginia.

The clock gonged with a hollow precision in the reception area just down the corridor from his small office. He imagined the day he would be asked to become a partner. He imagined the other partners gathering to greet him, a circle of dark suits and bent heads opening to him. On that day, he thought, even though it would be afternoon, there would be a brandy bottle and glasses on the table. Handshakes would be long, congratulations fulsome. Throats would be cleared before words of praise were spoken. Glasses would be filled and raised.

He imagined telling Evelyn, how pleased she would be. She had been patient with him during their marriage, during his seeming incapacity to find a career that suited; silent while he moved from one job to another—bank clerk, seller of farm equipment, shipping broker—until he finally decided on the law. But James knew that patience had its limits, that she was ready for the success that had eluded them.

The clock continued striking. Eight, nine, ten. A hunting-and-fishing club, a lake. A simple thing, and yet, perhaps, the key to a bright future. If he stayed late again, he thought, as he did so industriously and often, he could complete the work that night and file the papers in the morning.

It seemed to James that the last years of his childhood had been years of losing, of tabulating loss.

"They are just things," his father had said. James knew that it was a point of honor to his father that he could divest himself so easily. That he could stand up, be counted, make sacrifices for a cause that he believed in. Southern independence, the rights of states, the right of a man to his own property. That for the sake of principle he could sell a sideboard brought by ship from France, rugs woven by nomadic tribes, porcelain painted by rice-eating Chinese peasants. Furnishings that James's parents had bought on yearly trips abroad, explorations of the continent—Vienna, Paris, Rome. Even, once, just after they were married, Constantinople. A name to roll on the tongue, to savor. Cities, James thought when his father spoke about them, that were named with the same care as plantations across the South had been. The Hurricane. The Pines. The Glimmer Glass Plantation.

Just after the war began, his father insisted that the furnishings of greatest value be carted off in wagons, with the understanding that everything would be taken directly to the president in Richmond. He was certain that Davis or some close associate would see to the selling of the things himself. A symbolic gesture, a show of solidarity. If sacrifices had to be made, he would be among those making them. James, fifteen at the time, watched from the deep veranda as his father supervised the loading, placing discarded quilts or torn feed bags with a hesitant, self-conscious tenderness around the delicate whorled feet and slender cabriole legs of a rosewood table in order to protect them on their journey. James saw his father stand in the driveway, hands clasped behind his back, watching as the wagons departed. James went to stand beside him.

It takes money, his father told the boy, to raise an army.

Up until the war, James's father had been thought of as an aristocrat, a gentleman, born to a life of ease, of education, with the kind of rich, meandering mind that was so unsuitable for a life of planting. He lacked the edginess that planters needed, the gambler's flare, an ability to accommodate to the absolutes of land and weather. It was a good thing, admiring friends said, that he knew to hire a savvy overseer. A good thing he had slaves.

He studied plant rotation and variety, what he called the science of cotton and tobacco farming. In his mind's eye James could still see his father standing in one of the far fields, feet apart and planted as if rooted to the earth, hands in his pockets, head bent, listening and nodding. A dark-faced figure standing beside him, sweat-stained palmetto hat in hand, being encouraged to tell the master what *he* thinks about the drought, the soil, those cotton-eating weevils. What *he* thinks the master ought to do.

There were those who said it was less a plantation than an agricultural experiment. James's father tried crops that had never been planted in Virginia before. He kept goats and sheep, peacocks and milking cows, and let his four sons name farm animals as if they were house pets. He himself had been raised on myths and Bible stories, and from them he'd plucked the names of gods, holy men, or characters from literature for the baby James and his three brothers to choose from. A little group of cows kept in a grassy pasture near the house were named for the Muses, daughters of Mnemosyne: Calliope, Euterpe, Erato, Melpomene, Thalia, Terpsichore, Polyhymnia, Clio, Urania. The bull was Zeus. Pigs and horses were named for characters in Shakespeare's plays. Will, the oldest son, raised lambs by hand. Charles built a many-chambered hutch where he housed rabbits. Martin, the shy one with a stutter that kept him largely silent, trained bird dogs so well, so patiently, that men came from all over Virginia each time his bitch threw a litter. At the bottom of the green sweep of lawn behind the house, an antique rosebush called Jaune Desprez cascaded over and camouflaged the fence that surrounded the menagerie. James's nursemaid, Lacy, called it Noah's Ark. "This is a plantation," she said flatly to James one day in the kitchen, her quick hand and short knife sending carrot scrapings flying. "No place for playing." What would become of such a master? she seemed to wonder. What would become of such a master's sons?

At his desk at his law firm, James dipped his pen in his inkwell, preparing to take notes. On page 2 of the papers to be filed, he saw that there was an earthen dam involved, designed for the state by a young engineer. Begun in 1836, it was part of a plan to provide water year round for the canals that had been built to facilitate an over-mountain portage railroad.

He placed an asterisk beside that fact. There must be some reference, some book, about how such dams should be constructed. For the sake of thoroughness, in order to do the most impressive job, he made a note to learn more, to go to the library in the morning.

Lacy had been wet nurse to James when he was a baby. He'd attached himself to her, clung to her much longer than he should have. As a small boy he'd learned girl things from Lacy—how to churn butter and roll biscuits, how to sew a running stitch—and boy things, too. She smoked a little hand-carved pipe sometimes, and she showed him how she put tobacco into it, how she tamped it down, what kind of short, puffed breaths worked best to keep the little hump of hot tobacco burning. Once, after his mother had read him a tale of Roman soldiers, James had drawn Lacy a picture of a gladiator's helmet, of his long, sharp sword. And that night she and her husband, Moses, had fashioned rough replicas for her young gladiator and his gladiator brothers—headpieces of bent hammered metal; in place of feathered plumes, a length of sanded wood. The muted thud and click of wooden swords beneath the live oaks surprised the named, penned animals. Erto looked up from the grass she chewed to watch them, flicked a cow ear, trying to cast aside the clatter.

James and Lacy. So bound to one another, his mother noticed, relieved that he, her baby, was so well cared for, perhaps a little jealous of the love between them. James slept with his hand curled, as if Lacy were holding it in hers, as if they were setting off across the grass to feed Malvolio and the other rabbits. And because James loved her so, and knew how she loved him, he began to think that she was his. Her voice, her muscled little body, the fulcrum of her elbow as it worked her veined brown arm. So one night when he was six, he didn't think she'd mind when he reached out to her plate while she was eating supper in the kitchen, helping himself to her steam-clouded biscuit. Family dinner would not be served until much later, candlelit and in the dining room. He was hungry; he thought she'd want him to have it. It was the only time she ever struck him. Her hand was swift and sharp as a strap across his wrist. Too stunned to cry, he yanked his welt-streaked arm against his chest and looked up, wide-eyed, at her.

"Do you *see* me, child?" she said hotly. "*Me?* What I have here on my plate is not yours just because you want it. Everything does *not* belong to you."

He'd fled from her, soaked a corner of his pillow with his tears, hugged his chastised hand to himself until he fell into a hurt, self-righteous sleep. Years later, long after he was grown and she was gone, he'd wished he had found a way that night to go find her, to say that he was sorry. They'd made up, of course. He'd picked a small bouquet of the antique yellow roses and left them on the kitchen table for her. Days later she'd used a tiny, needle-sharp awl to etch what she hoped was a Romanesque design across the face of his small gladiator helmet. His blindness, his presumption, was never mentioned again. She let it go because of love, but perhaps she shouldn't have. Because blindness to the other is an awful flaw, a deadly sin. It would have been better had he purged himself of it that night. He'd missed the chance to speak to her, to be forgiven.

His father did not give up everything at first. There seemed no need. Southern pride and Southern confidence were bolstered by early victories. Manassas and Bull Run were routs, everyone believed that the Federals would lose heart quickly. So the family kept the large carved beds, the Hepplewhite chairs with the shield-shaped backs, the ornate mahogany table in the dining room. But after Shiloh, after all that bloodshed in the peach grove, Southern need began to seem much greater. Armoires and chiffoniers and piecrust tables were given up, a dainty writing desk that had been a gift to his young mother. By May '62, when the Seven Days of battle raged in an effort to repel the Yankee advance on Richmond, a good part of the furniture was gone. Then the call went out for horses for the cavalry. They gave up eggs in Lent that year, to honor the suffering of Jesus, his mother said, but the boys all understood that it was more complex than that, that she hoped that God would take note of their sacrifice and look with favor on their cause. Late that same summer the family gave up eggs again, then never ate another, because the chickens were all killed to feed the army.

How habit-forming, how seductive loss and sacrifice become. When the draft began, all men with more than twenty slaves could count themselves excused. James's father, with thirty, fell under that protection and could have extended that protection to his sons, but he chose not to. Will and Charles were eighteen and twenty, and he knew they'd make fine soldiers. He imagined uniforms and glory for them, he envisioned them riding next to Lee. He still believed that the war would be a brief one—everyone had sworn it would be brief. He thought when the family had gathered in the entry hall to say farewell to the boys in the cloying heat of August, that they'd be back to help carve pumpkins later in the fall. He shook their hands. *Forgo all show of sentiment*, he had advised his wife and two remaining sons about the farewell ritual. *Show them how confident you are.*

Treasures collected on his parents' wedding trip to Europe were hard to part with, but once the slaves began to leave, once deserting, sick Confederate soldiers began to appear at night to beg for bread, that, too, seemed necessary. The winged gold cherub balanced lightly on one foot, his plump arms encircling a small clock face, tiny chips of sapphire embedded in the spots where numbers ought to have been. The salt cellar made of a fragile, iridescent, pink-hued shell, a remnant of their one trip, as a family, to the sea. On that journey to Savannah, the big boys had carried James and Martin on their shoulders, out beyond the froth of breaking waves. They'd taught them how to press shells to their ears so that once they'd returned to landlocked rural Virginia they might still hear the throbbing of the sea.

The remaining few cows went last, because they were needed for milking. Then one by one James and Martin said goodbye to them as well. Erato the desirable; the singer Polyhymnia, known by all of them for her oboe-lovely moo; Clio, the glory giver. Hamlet, the pig James had raised by hand, was sacrificed for ham and ribs and bacon. James watched his beautiful mother—her high forehead, her heart-shaped face, her exquisitely dimpled chin—become transparent, guileless, a shrine to willingness. Ladders were brought in, and flounced drapes were taken from the windows in the dining room and parlor. The silk, his mother reasoned, could be used to make dresses for war widows and children. That afternoon, as James and Martin were dismantling the back-yard pens, they could hear the snag and rip of fabric—the long air-shredding tears. The endless repetition of it, a symphony of tearing, as his mother made strips of the drapery lining, rolled yards of sun-faded jaconet for bandages.

When the gladiator Will died at Fredericksburg in December 1862, Martin, seventeen, self-fashioned patriot, left by night without asking his father, right after the news of the death was brought to them, vowing in his farewell letter to take his brother's place. At night James, the only child at home, grew restless. Dreams disrupted the current of his sleep. Vague scenes from the Bible. An angry God, the curtain in the temple rent. He spent the long nights listening to the jump and buck and roar of cannons being fired.

Charles died in what came to be called the Valley Forge of the war that winter. Cold gripped the Virginia countryside, winds brought blizzards, and pneumonia spread among the depleted Southern ranks as if it were a plague, another awful weapon. When the news of Charles's death came, James waited for the world to stop, for the sun to fall in a hot, annihilating streak out of the sky. He wanted his parents to rail against this loss, to curse God for it, but for them, the stoics, the heroes of sacrifice, it became another opportunity for bravery. They buried a second son with military honors, with gunfire salutes and sacred songs. James and his father had dug both graves themselves, pickaxed their way through frozen earth just beyond the side porch, under the magnolia tree, in a spot where his mother could watch them from the dining room windows. She did not cry, but for endless hours in the weeks and months that followed she stood at that window. Like a sentry standing watch. It was as if they were alive still, towheaded stubborn children who might wander into danger in that aimless way that children will. If she could see, then she could save them. James watched her press her forehead against the frosted window. He feared that she would turn to stone there.

For his parents' sake, James gave no sign of his own suffering. That spring he helped his father with the planting, worked in the wan sun with Moses and Lacy and the few other slaves who had not yet gone away. But at night, while cicadas washed the spring air with their song, he crept out to his brothers, wrapped a light wool blanket around himself, and sat on the damp earth, cross-legged between them. Smoothed their mounds of fresh dirt with his hand and gave up, with deep shame, the things he'd hidden, squandered, kept back when all else was so heroically being given away. A rabbit's foot for Will, who'd always been the lucky one, and for Charles, the winner, who'd never lost a thing before he lost his life, his cat's-eye marbles. With his thumb James made a row of holes in the packed dirt for each of them. Dropped the marbles one by one, as if he were hoping for a harvest, as if he were planting seeds.

He felt that he was old enough to fight. In preparation, he wrote long letters to his remaining brother, Martin. "I am not afraid," he wrote, as fear rose in his throat.

Then on May Day, the day when they had always had a party, when, in his boyhood, the house had been full of guests and tea sandwiches and flowers, he came into the kitchen to find his mother taking family photographs from silver frames and placing the frames carefully into a pillowcase. She removed from her own ears her mother's tiny gold-and-emerald earrings and added them; she gently wrapped and included in the bundle a mauve glass dinner bell. James watched her lips part with each divestment, as if she was about to speak, to say goodbye to these last cherished objects. When she laid the sack on the kitchen table, when the open edges nodded toward each other like the petals of a flower closing, James thought that all that was left was the tying of it, that she was going to the basket in the corner where she kept the string. But she was simply freeing both hands for the greatest effort. She spread her fingers, raised them to her mouth, and began to moisten her ring finger. She curled her wet pink tongue around it, twisted her reluctant wedding band, then licked again. Eased it toward the knuckle, licked once more. Looking at her made James wonder if stoicism had no limits, and if it did, how one reached them, what those limits might finally be.

Then he found out. One of the soldiers who had been briefly bivouacked in the house that winter took James's silver baby cup. Dented, tooth-marked, its handle bent. His mother had kept sugar cubes in it after he stopped using it for milk, filled it with hard candy and placed it at his elbow to entice him to greater effort when he studied. She'd found it to be especially good for mixing whiskey, tea, and honey when the boys were young and their throats were raw, before she rubbed their chests with liniment and wrapped them. This little cup. Her tongue grew thick, her hands trembled as she tore through drawers and cabinets. Where could it be? she asked James and his father. Please, James. She gripped his shoulders. Her fingers dug into his flesh. Tell me that it's here somewhere, tell me you've seen it.

She wept for days. For the first time James saw her cry, and feared that this would be the beginning of some great cataclysm, that now that she'd started she'd lose herself in weeping. Spring rains began and dripped from the oleander trees, sleeted the white fragrant petals of the magnolia, fell in sheets from the pitched roof, leaked through it and made stains on the ceiling in the dining room. To James it looked as if all God's world was weeping with her. She sat in the kitchen in a straight-backed chair. His father knelt beside her, took her hand in his, and placed his smooth face in her palm, then kissed it—the raised dark veins, the fingertips. Begging kisses. "Don't," he whispered. James left the room.

So it was decided that after so much letting go, she would be allowed to keep him. James. One small thing.

James begged to go to war, threatened to run away in spite of them, feared that cowardice would color his life if he was kept from it. Instead, he was told that his mother had a girlhood friend who lived in France. They would send him there to save him.

He would have been at Gettysburg if he had stayed. Perhaps he would have been at Seminary Ridge with Pickett. In the Luxembourg Gardens he read his mother's letter and wondered how differently things might have gone if he had been there. Poor gut-shot Martin, the soft lead bullet exploding in his belly. Maybe he could have pushed the ribbons of intestines back into Martin's abdomen, maybe he could have led the charge and fallen in his stead.

The fighting should have stopped at Gettysburg, James thought. Seven thousand sons of the Confederacy fell the first day of the battle. There was no reason to go on with it another day and then another. How do men live, he wondered, with being the cause of so much suffering? On the third day, Pickct and Pettigrew had advanced sixteen hundred yards toward the Union line from Seminary Ridge. They still had fourteen hundred yards of open ground to cover. Pickett ordered fourteen thousand Rebels to leave the protection of the woods to form an assaulting column. Fourteen thousand men marched across open land into aimed artillery—shot and shell and canister. The first gray wave fell, and then the second, and then the next was brought down with a firestorm of musketry. All it would have taken to have stopped it was a white scrap of a mother's drapery lining tied to a stick. A simple no. James imagined his brother curled on the ground, trying to use his knees to seal, to close, his blasted belly. He thought about how frightened he must have been. He knew he should have been there, too. He should have gone to join his brother instead of going to Paris. One year apart, they'd shared a bed when they were young. From their window they had counted stars together. They'd planned to get hats, boots, and lariats and drive the muse-named cows to Mexico. They'd had pillow fights until they'd stumbled, defeated, into a tangled heap across the bed. They'd fallen asleep in each other's arms.

James was the first to arrive at his law firm's offices. He was waiting when the partner arrived.

"Early, aren't you?" The partner seemed surprised to see James. He shifted his briefcase from his right hand to his left, slipped his watch out of its pocket, used his thumb to click the gold case open.

"Yes, I suppose I am, sir. I just wanted to be sure to find you first thing. I'd like to speak with you if I might."

"Certainly." A frown. "But if it could wait . . ."

"I'm sorry, sir. I think it shouldn't. I believe we have something of a problem."

"Problem?"

"Yes. With those papers you sent me yesterday. About the club."

"Aha," the partner said slowly. "A problem about the club." He looked at James appraisingly. "Yes." He nodded. "I think you had better come in."

Once inside the office the partner gestured toward a chair. Positioned himself behind his sprawling desk, his back to the window. Even there, a good distance from the Edgar Thomas and the Lucy furnaces and the other steel mills, the air was blighted, the skies seemed overcast, the glass through which James looked were filmed with soot.

An onyx desk set, a maroon leather blotter, a beveled walnut humidor. The partner rested his elbows on his padded leather chair arms, wove the fingers of his hands together, brought them to his chin.

"So?"

"I'm afraid we cannot file the charter here, sir. In the city. In Allegheny County."

"Can't?"

"No. The charter must be filed in the county in which . . . well, to quote exactly from the statute, 'in which the chief operations are to be carried on.' "

"I see." The chair tipped back. The partner's forehead creased with a worried frown.

"Naturally, I stand ready to go to Cambria County and file it there. It should be quite simple, really. Two hours up, two back." James smiled to show his willingness. "I can do it in a day."

A nod. "A day."

"Yes. I've done all the preliminary work. Now it's just a matter of the filing, of making it part of the public record."

"With the names of the founding members, of course."

"Yes. Of course. That would naturally be part of it."

"I see." The partner swiveled in his chair. Right, then left, then right again. It was honey oak, massive but flexible, capable of tilts and turns and odd maneuverings. When he stopped, he leaned forward, eased the lid of the cigar box open. Gestured for James to take one.

"No thank you, sir. A bit too early for me."

The partner nodded again, and resumed his swivel.

"So." James had a great deal of other work to do, and he didn't want to waste the partner's time. "When would you like me to attend to this?"

"Immediately, James."

James was surprised to find himself addressed by his first name.

"Very well, then. Shall I make plans to go tomorrow?"

"No. I think you can take care of it today."

James checked his watch. "All right. I'll just check about the train and . . ."

"No, no, no," the partner said, smiling indulgently. "It won't be necessary for you to go to South Fork. I'm sure we can take care of everything here."

James cleared his throat patiently. "It is certainly not my wish to contradict you, sir, but I don't see how we can. The law on this is clear."

The partner waved his hand. "Yes, I know, I know. But tell me, James, did you notice who some of the founding members of this club are going to be?"

"Yes," said James. "Yes, indeed."

"Good. Good. And you know, of course, that these are important men, men of substance."

"Yes and . . ."

"Men who prefer that some of their business dealings be handled privately. This is simply a club, after all. It's not as if they are trying to begin a business or some major enterprise. It is just going to be a few fine families gathering together to hunt and fish, to indulge themselves in much needed mountain recreation."

James had an agile mind; he was a very careful lawyer. And because that was the case, he understood that the time had come for him to listen. He sat back in his chair; he meant to look relaxed, receptive, open, but, in fact, he was completely focused, attuned to nuance, curious to ascertain where this twisting road might lead.

"Yes." He nodded. "A club."

"Yes. And frankly, James, since so many of their business dealings take place here in Pittsburgh, and since we, their lawyers, are here, too, it seems much wiser to just go ahead and file the charter here."

"I see." James thought a moment. "Well then, sir, I think that just leaves two problems to be solved."

The partner raised his eyebrows quizzically. "And what might those be?"

"The first is, since the law is so explicit about this, that we'll have to find a judge willing to . . ."

The partner waved his hand lightly, sweeping problem one away. "There are so many who would sympathize, who wouldn't wish to inconvenience us or our clients."

James nodded understanding.

"And the second problem?"

"What will they think about this in Cambria County? Once they get word. I mean to say, sir, that with a dam involved, a dam, I might add, that is old and in ill repair, which will hold back an enormous weight of water, don't you think, once they get word, objections will be raised?"

"Objections? I can't imagine what they'd be. The dam and the surrounding property have been purchased. It is no longer a problem for the county or the state. It is now a question of private property. Besides, discretion will be used. And once progress on the club begins, assurances will be given."

James was silent.

The partner swiveled in a half circle to look out the window. Paused. Swiveled back again. "So, James. Does this sound like something you feel capable of handling for us? Or should I assign this project elsewhere?"

It was James's turn to weave his hands together. He knew that what was being proposed was wrong. There was no threat in the partner's voice, his tone throughout the conversation had been businesslike and even. He could simply say no and let the matter be handled by another. His father had given up everything for his sense of what was right, and James understood that he, his only living son, should possess that kind of courage, too. But his parents and brothers were all dead, the Virginia house and property were gone. His whole future was here. His East End house, Evelyn and Nora. He had no place else to go. He thought of the price his father had paid for principle, and in a flash he smelled whiskey in a baby cup, saw his mother's ringless hand. He thought that if he was made partner, Evelyn would stay with him. That they'd have the son he so wanted, that he'd name the son for his brother, Martin.

James rose, smiled reassuringly, reached out his hand. "I'll take care of everything," he promised. He meant the charter, of course. But in his heart, the honorable heart that he so cherished, he was making other promises as well; he was making bargains that he could not keep. That he would find a way to join that club, that he'd make himself personally responsible. He knew that people lived below that dam. And he swore to himself that no harm would come to them on his watch, that not one life would be lost because of him.

THE CLUBMEN

"Men look for retreats for themselves, the country, the seashore, the hills . . ."
—Marcus Aurelius, *Meditations*, Book IV, Number 3

H. Clay Frick. Frick, Henry C. H. C. Frick. It was H. C. Frick that he finally decided on, after years of boyish struggle about what his official signature might be, and it was as H. C. Frick that he affixed his name to assorted documents on the sunlit desk. His father had always thought his pride in his handwriting was overdone and had told him so repeatedly. But a certain vanity, a certain foppishness having to do with appearance, had made him preoccupied with such things from an early age—his ophidian penmanship, his obsessively polished black boots, the careful arrangement of his thick, dark hair. He had begun his working life when he was just fifteen, as a store clerk; a few years later he became a book-keeper. In his role as the latter he believed that, when the books he kept were scrutinized for accuracy, so would his script be subject to evaluation by others. For this reason he could not bear it to be anything other than a study in perfection—elaborate, arresting, worthy of notice and admiring comment. So it had been in his young manhood, and so it remained.

In May 1880, H. C. Frick was thirty years old, keen on the idea of travel. If he'd been asked, he might have said that he had been waiting his whole life for it, and he was lost in busy preparation—signing documents, arranging for his mail to be held or forwarded as necessary, writing lists in his beautiful hand, of hotels where he'd be staying, the name of the ship that would take him to the Continent, the things that would have to be attended to in his coal mines during his absence. On his birthday he had gone to his company store on his way home from a chess game with one of his cousins to take "a look at the books preliminary to the annual accounting." The double checking was a bit of self-indulgence which he had allowed himself when he turned thirty. There was no need to check—he knew his cash-flow situation precisely from one day to the next—but it had pleased him to examine the books that night, to run his finger slowly down each column of figures, to calculate once again and to feel the impact of it. He was a millionaire. On that night he'd entered his store, savoring its nighttime emptiness, the lack of customers and clerks. He had walked through the aisles of Christmas wares—paper ornaments and rag Santa Clauses—and unlocked his office door. His grandparents were both dead. There was no one with whom he could celebrate, so he celebrated alone, congratulated himself in his grandparents' stead. "Happy birthday to you," he said aloud. Then he rose and went out into the store proper, to the shelf on which tobacco products were kept, reached into the box where the best cigars were secreted and ran a five-cent Havana beneath his nose so he could savor the scent before he smoked it. "Happy birthday to you," he had said again.

He decided to add Venice to his itinerary, and penned the word carefully, admiring the perfectly curved tail on the end of his *e*.

He knew the reputation he was building, the way other men regarded him. The barbs, the slurs, the damning adjectives. Cold. Ruthless? He did not mind being thought of as ruthless. He wanted success, not admiration. Being disliked and feared, he thought, could only work to his advantage.

His business was the manufacture of coke, a by-product of coal. When he had been just twenty-one he'd been consulted by a much older cousin, Abraham Tinstman, over a game of chess—the arena in which all serious discussions took place in their extended family. That night Tinstman had solicited his opinion because he feared he'd made a bad investment—the acquisition of five hundred acres of coal-rich land in Connellsville, near the family sinecure. With the acreage came a partner who believed money could be made from mining coal and manufacturing coke from it. Clay Frick moved knight and rook, gave up his queen that night, and gave every appearance of paying close attention to the game. But it was this other "game" that was of interest to him. Coal land in Westmoreland

County, Pennsylvania, was relatively inexpensive; coal was needed to make coke, coke was a useful, perhaps even necessary fuel for firing the Pittsburgh furnaces that were producing steel. When coal was baked in beehive ovens (built of brick, with a circular vent in the roof through which the coal was fed), sulfur and other impurities were burned out of it and released into the air as flaming gases. That process caused the coal to form into a cake of almost pure carbon—a much more efficient, longer-burning form of fuel than the coal or charcoal that had been used in blast furnaces earlier. And 1,700 pounds of it were needed to smelt a ton of pig iron. It was true that the work of tending to the beehive ovens was hot, horrible, and killing to the lungs, but labor could be had for next to nothing. While he and his cousin set up the chess pieces for another game, Frick began calculating how cheaply more coal acreage could be bought, the cost of constructing additional beehive ovens. He wanted to buy in.

Once the partnership was established, Frick, the youngest and the least experienced by far, urged expansion. The others weren't as convinced as he, but his was a will not easily resisted. Twenty-three more acres of coal-rich land were acquired. Frick's contribution to the enterprise was his total absorption, and every bit of cash he could spare from the money earned at his day job—bookkeeper in his grandfather's distillery. In a gesture that he thought munificent, he also offered the use of his name: H. C. Frick and Co.

The company barely survived the financial crash of 1873. Frick spearheaded all efforts to keep the ovens up and running, borrowed money, and, when he inherited $10,000 from his Overholt grandparents, plowed it all back into the business. He even allowed his father to mortgage his small farm to help him. He didn't admire his father, but he had no qualms about taking money from him. Such was his determination, and his certainty that he was in possession of a kind of prescience that enabled him to understand what others had not yet—that steel was the metal of the future and that coke was the most efficient fuel for making it.

When cash was scarce, he opened a store for his employees and issued store certificates called scrip in place of U.S. currency. With scrip he paid their wages, giving them no choice but to trade with him. Complaints of miners and coal heavers were met with swift and unequivocal retribution. He was young but imperious. His rules were simple and he posted them at the pay window. Work the way Frick wished you to or don't work at all.

His partners finally gave it up. The precarious finances of the venture would have been enough to make them think of getting out, but then an explosion caused by faulty excavation buried thirty coal miners alive. Tintsman became an old man overnight, haunted by dreams of how it must have been for the men who died: the first creak of beams giving way, the quake and heave of the earth collapsing, the futile, terrified attempts to run. He and the other partners couldn't imagine facing all those families. Frick saw opportunity and seized it. He secured a loan from Judge Thomas Mellon in Pittsburgh and bought his partners out.

H. C. Frick. Small in stature, slight of frame. Delicate features, a prominent proud jaw. He had been weakened as a child by illness and would always be thought of as physically "frail," but in every other way, in mind and will, he was unassailable, someone who used power easily. When the countryside around his coking operation became unlivable, when local workers left, he sent agents of his company to southeastern Europe to hire Hungarians and Slavs, whom he believed were ignorant and thus more easily managed. His focus formed him, fixed his character. In a matter of a few years, his capacity for sympathy and sentiment diminished. He became implacable and unrepentant, capable of cruelty.

Now, at thirty, he was known, his reputation was secure—"the king of coke"—and he was about to go on a European tour with the somewhat younger but equally aspiring Andrew Mellon. The time had come to indulge himself a little, after a decade of privation, of focus on balance sheets and ledgers. It was just days before his June departure. He had seen a blue jay earlier that morning, honeysuckle struggling to flower. In the early months of the new year he'd grown a beard, and he had noticed in the hallstand mirror just that day that his hair had begun to recede. To his mind both things—beard and hairline—contributed to making him seem older and established. It was a look that pleased him.

For the trip he'd bought new clothing, an extravagance that he could finally afford and one that mattered to him. He moved from his desk and his list-making to his trunk and the last of packing. He'd found a cutaway jacket for more formal, evening wear, several short sack coats that had newly come into style for daytime, an assortment of stiff, standing collars, six soft silk ties. He had also acquired an array of guidebooks, both to the cities they planned to visit and to the art collections he hoped to see. Paintings were his weakness. He had always thought himself closed to sentiment, so it surprised him when he discovered, while still a boy, that he loved the painted image, that the mix of texture, color, light was so appealing to him. He and Mellon would see the Wallace Collection in London, the Louvre in Paris. But above all, he longed for Venice. He had imagined every step they would take there, every work of art they'd see. The mosaics of Saint Mark's, the Bellini altarpieces in the Accademia. He adored Bellini, adored him. The word felt alien to him, and he flushed when it rose unbidden to his lips, but he could think of no other. The idea of standing in the presence of those altarpieces made his mouth dry, caused moisture to gather in the creases of his palms.

A European tour, the frank approval of Judge Mellon implied by his willingness to let young Andrew accompany him—he was taking his place in the world. Then, most recently, he had been approached about a club that was to be formed in the Allegheny Mountains. It was to be exclusive, private (membership never to exceed one hundred), with a magnificent 450-acre lake. Shares were being offered. Frick, after examining the proposal, had insisted on buying three. He had been told by Benjamin Ruff, the contractor who'd bought the site and developed it, that everyone of influence in the city would be part of it. Members would spend two weeks there every summer, escaping the filth that had become so much a part of city life, the stench of the foul and fetid air.

A lovely spot, he had no doubt of it. And the idea of the venture, of participating in the creation of a resort to rival Newport or Saratoga, pleased him inordinately. He foresaw a future in which his name was as known as the names Cooke, Vanderbilt, and Morgan. He imagined inhabiting their world, and he thought that a fishing and hunting club, secluded, private, was a step in that direction. A lake in the mountains— unlikely and extravagant. Something to be noticed, admired, envied.

But first, Venice. He closed his eyes, pictured cathedrals and the Palazzo Ducale, a hotel on the Grand Canal with shuttered windows. Hard rolls and savory meat on his breakfast tray. Or eggs, or fragrant, overripe Italian cheese. Or anything he wanted.

He placed his silk ties in a drawer in his large trunk.

He could have anything at all.

In late afternoon of that same day, Andrew Carnegie slipped into the suite of rooms at the Windsor Hotel where he lived with his mother, Margaret, on Forty-fifth Street and Fifth Avenue. He was forty-five, hair and bush-of-a-beard already becoming gray, but he had the round cheeks and eager energy of an expectant, charming child. There was high color in his face, his bright presence charged the air. He'd just come from horseback riding in Central Park.

The key turned easily; the click-clank of the lock was emphatic, weighty, emblematic of the solidity and importance of the Windsor. He quietly closed the door behind him, trying not to draw attention to his arrival, feeling not quite ready to see his mother. Her rooms were across the drawing room at the far end of the suite, his were off a short hallway just inside the door. He could easily go undetected.

He had made his home in New York hotels for almost thirteen years, first at the St. Nicholas, then at the Windsor. The original move had come when he'd grown tired of Pittsburgh, tired of the constant petty pressures of his corporate life. His brother, Tom, was his capable, if somewhat uninspired (to his way of thinking) first lieutenant and could be trusted to manage the day-to-day operation of Carnegie Enterprises—the payroll, the ordering of coke and pig iron. And Andrew Carnegie had found that he felt more masterful in New York, at some distance from his Pittsburgh-based business. He believed that he could prod and press more persuasively with frequent inspiring wires and telegrams, without the daily ordinary burdens which ran counter to his sense of himself as visionary leader.

When Andrew Carnegie and Tom were boys, immigrant children of a penniless Scottish weaver, Andrew made promises to his sweet-natured younger brother about the business they would have one day. It would be big, he promised grandly, and called Carnegie Brothers. Initially the Carnegie enterprises included the Keystone Bridge Company and the Union Iron Mills, as well as steel mills—the Edgar Thomas and the Lucy Furnaces. The products of Carnegie steel buttressed many of the engineering wonders of the day—the Brooklyn Bridge, the elevated railroads in New York. It was becoming evident that steel was the great new thing, the metal of the future, and that the technology for producing it was going to grow complex and competitive. Andrew Carnegie claimed as one of his several mottos "Put all your eggs in one basket, and then watch the basket," and he acted on his own wisdom when he combined all the Carnegie holdings into a single entity called Carnegie Brothers and Co., Limited, with steel as its sole product. It marked a change not only in name but in management style as well. Brains and daring replaced old wealth and good connections as qualities necessary for success. Carnegie was beginning to understand that young H. C. Frick had both, as well as the coke he needed to make steel. It was on a walk near his Cresson home in the Allegheny Mountains that Carnegie first said to a friend, "We must attach this young man Frick to our concern." Already inquiries were being made. What did Frick want? How could he be seduced to join them?

Carnegie liked New York. He liked the lack of heavy industry, the fact that mills and plants and factories did not clutter the landscape but had been consigned to locations elsewhere. And the possibilities of intellectual pursuits intrigued him. He had aspirations in that regard. Ideas spewed from him, and a natural loquaciousness impelled him to give voice to them. He'd become a regular at Madame Botta's Murray Hill "salon," an unlikely participant among the likes of Henry Ward Beecher and Charles Dudley Warner, but he was representative of the type of nouveau riche American that aroused so much curiosity among the thinkers who gathered there. The question when he'd first come to the city was a question still asked, all these years later. Who was this busy little millionaire? What place did he hope to occupy among them?

He could discourse at length about Herbert Spencer's *First Principles* and the works of Auguste Comte. He was invited to become a member of the Nineteenth Century Club. Thus far, New York suited him, and it more than suited his mother.

He and Margaret had left Pittsburgh when Tom Carnegie married. Up until the arrival of Lucy Coleman in their lives, the three Carnegies had lived happily together in a tawny-colored house, with Norway spruce trees shading the wide windows and enough land for his mother to have a flower garden. Carnegie had thought that the three of them had achieved a perfect harmony. Only when Tom brought Lucy Coleman home did he realize how much Tom had chafed at the pressures of so much "family," where so much submission was required of him. An autocratic, clinging mother, a brother whose ebullience overpowered him. When Tom married, he split the family, gave his allegiance to his wife and then to a growing brood of children. It was at Margaret's insistence that the family home was given to Tom and Lucy. It had surprised Carnegie that the negotiation of so large a gift was so simple. On the day he and his mother left for New York, Margaret handed Tom their two sets of keys. A carriage had been hired to transport them, their packed clothing and small mementos to the train station. They left almost everything behind: the overly elaborate furniture that had been purchased for Margaret: the cretonne-covered divan, the Louis XIV dining chairs, the mantel and floor clocks, the kitchen tools, the china. All abandoned. In New York they would not require household goods. Their hotel suite would provide them with pristine European towels and linens, even-more-gracious furnishings, meals prepared and served by a meticulously trained staff, which could be taken in the hotel dining room or in their private quarters, whichever was their pleasure. Ever since they had left Scotland and first lived in two crowded rooms in Slabtown, that had been Margaret's wish. To be unencumbered by details of domesticity, to be waited on, deferred to. And Andrew always acceded to her wishes.

The only house, the only real "home" he had now, was in Cresson, where he and Margaret spent four months every summer. He had named it Braemar Cottage, and it had pride of place in Cresson Springs, with a view of all the blue-gray mountain peaks and ridges in the distance. Often in the early morning, when he arose before his mother did, he could stand on the long porch and watch as low-lying clouds severed the distant hilltops from their bases. He loved Cresson; it reminded him of the Scotland of his boyhood. He and Margaret took large parties of friends to Cresson every summer and housed them in the Mountain House Hotel. Other millionaires collected art. He preferred collecting people. Even now, he was trying to make the acquaintance of the poet Matthew Arnold. He wanted to bring him from England for a speaking tour.

Just a week ago, he had signed on for a piece of another mountain paradise. This one with a lake. Although he doubted that he'd go there much, he thought it wise to become a member of the South Fork Fishing and Hunting Club. Young Frick and Mellon, Pitcairn of the Pennsylvania Railroad, all were joining. An eye ought to be kept on such a group. Tom might take his many children there, or perhaps some other trusted counselors of the company could go. He only cared that Carnegie Enterprises not be excluded from it.

In his rooms he placed his riding crop, his silk hat on the bed. A sitting area was attached to each bedroom in their suite. There was a long salon in which they entertained. The lamps had flounced silk shades, some walls were covered in Lincrusta below the dado rail, others were wallpapered in tartan plaid, a somewhat overdone tribute to their Scottish heritage. The carpeting was thick and scarlet. It muffled footsteps, absorbed all human sound.

Only recently had Carnegie begun to resist having his name linked so automatically with Margaret's, especially when he knew the one she really loved was Tom. This was never spoken of directly, and if it had been suggested to her, Margaret would have denied it. But it would have been a denial without the power to persuade. She was subtle in this, all her cruelties were subtle, but Andrew knew. He understood that she was proud of his incredible success. She was vain as well, and eager for the adoration he showered upon her. But Tom was her baby, her adored sweet boy, and everyone who knew the family realized it.

So Carnegie had taken her from Tom. He hadn't framed it in his mind that way, but that was, in fact, what had happened. Tom got Lucy Coleman. Andrew claimed his mother. He moved her to Manhattan, to the luxury for which she'd longed. Carrara stairways, frescoed painted ceilings, the walls of the hotel lobby decorated heavily with tapestries and mirrors. Now she was his. But in his eagerness to punish Tom, what he had not considered was that the counter of that, the flip side of the coin of his possession of her, was hers of him.

Now he had met a woman. At forty-five he was as flushed as a boy, throwing his riding coat carelessly across a slipper chair. He wondered what had taken hold of him. For all his worldly manners and intellectual pretensions, when it came to women he had always preferred the company of flighty girls, girls who posed no threat to what he thought of as his freedom. But today he had taken Louise Whitfield riding. The daughter of a man he had considered a friend. Carnegie had issued the riding invitation as a courtesy—she was young and unduly burdened by responsibility—her father recently dead; two younger siblings, still in school; a high-strung, dependent mother. He'd asked her to spend the afternoon with him as a favor to Alex King, a Scottish thread merchant.

"She is a bit taciturn," King had said, always undervaluing any suggestion he offered Carnegie, fearful of misstepping or disappointing and then being held accountable. "Thin as a blade. But an excellent horsewoman."

Which was enough, really—a good horsewoman. That was enough for an afternoon of riding, an investment of a few hours on an exhilarating, fresh spring day.

In his room, Carnegie sat in his Boston rocker. He knew he should change clothes, work his way toward evening, but he felt restless, at odds with himself. He had even forgotten to have his carriage take him to his office after the ride. He ought to have sent telegrams, checked those that were waiting for him. He wondered at this unaccountable lapse. He, the astute and tireless steward of his empire.

At the stable, as they prepared for riding, he had noticed the confidence with which Louise Whitfield stroked and reassured her mount, noticed that he didn't mind the fact that she was a little taller than he, that he had to look up a bit in order to admire her.

Her mother was a semi-invalid, she said. She spoke of how much she missed her father, about the fact that, since his death and her mother's illness, it had been necessary for her to assume responsibility for the running of the house. (How well her riding habit suited her.)

On long, open stretches of the bridle paths they had let the horses have their heads a bit. An easy trot broke the monotony of a high-headed canter, and Miss Whitfield had laughed and agreed readily when he suggested it. (No, not taciturn. Not taciturn at all, he realized.)

He often took young ladies riding in the park. He liked to flirt, to play, without intention or design, and part of the play involved a testing of his theory (he had many theories, strong opinions on all subjects) that one could tell a great deal about a woman from the way she sat astride a horse. So as he rode with the quiet Louise Whitfield, he evaluated, judged her. The vaporizing breath from the horses' nostrils clouded the clear air; the tentative green of new leaves on high tree branches, the hot yellow of the first brave daffodils surprised the eye. She spoke softly, made no effort to impress, and he had thought, There is some substance to her. It was certain she would need that if she were to involve herself with him. He could not, then, know the details of the future, but he was aware that he understood nothing of the requirements of an intimate attachment to a woman. He suspected he'd be bad at it at his age, that he would be difficult, deceitful, that he would make her suffer, make her wait; that he would be ambivalent and thoughtless, offer love, then, frightened by the offer, take it back again. He wondered as he rose to pace his sitting room if she'd have the stamina for him, a bachelor twice her age, an aging, selfish suitor.

From the far end of his suite he heard his mother call his name. The last soft syllable of "Andrew" lost to the burr of her Scottish accent. She liked to be kissed when he returned after an afternoon of riding. She liked him to read a Robert Burns poem to her while they sipped their sherry, before they went to the hotel dining room for dinner.

In the summers, when he trudged alone along the mountain trails in Cresson, he recited favorite literary tracts to the trees, the startled birds, the drooping clusters of wisteria. He liked exercising his oratorical powers. The poems of Robert Burns were among his favorites, as well as Othello's speech to the assembled senators—"Most potent, grave, and reverend signiors." He admired Burns, but his poems were poems of nature, and as Carnegie dressed for dinner, as he fixed his tie and plucked a wisp of lint from his dark sleeve, he realized he needed something more than nature poetry this night. His volume of Burns's poems lay on the tallboy chest, beside his silver-backed hairbrush, the gilt-framed looking glass. He reached for it, thumbed its pages, in search of something that might match his mood. A verse about the Scottish Highlands would not suffice. And certainly no elegy. "Delia: An Ode"? "To a Kiss"? And then it came to him. He would find the poems Burns had penned in honor of a Glasgow surgeon's daughter. He would read one of the Clarinda poems tonight.

> *She, the fair sun of all her sex,*
> *Has blest my glorious day;*
> *And shall a glimmering planet fix*
> *My worship to its ray?*

Spring floods that May filled Johnstown streets and sent water creeping into the first floors of buildings and houses. The city was built on a level floodplain at the bottom of a valley at a point where two rivers converged. The rivers ran high every spring. The residents had come to expect the floods. They'd learned to live with the nuisance of them, and to value the beauty that spring rains brought in the weeks that followed. The wildflowers that bloomed so brightly through the summer. The way the sourgum trees in the mountains flamed into shameless, scarlet splendor every fall before they fell into a faded carpet on the forest floor.

November brought hard frosts to western Pennsylvania, and brought Frick and young Mellon home from their European tour. Thanksgiving dinners in both families were celebrations of their safe returns. The conversations over turkeys were replete with long descriptions of the churches, parks, the palaces where monarchs reigned, the flags they'd waved on July Fourth, the day they'd kissed the Blarney Stone. Dublin, Belfast, Glasgow, London, Paris. Andrew Mellon, at his family's Thanksgiving table, was circumspect and understated in his telling, careful not to let his father know that fun had been a part of it, that there had been some foolishness and laughing, self-indulgence and pleasure. Such things would be disapproved of, Andrew knew. At the Mellon house, Judge Thomas Mellon and his wife, Sarah, sat formally at each end of the table and asked questions of their young traveler as if reading from a list. Was the crossing calm, seasickness avoided, had the strange French food been to his liking? "I myself have never been tempted to travel," his father said. Andrew did not doubt him.

Judge Thomas Mellon had made his considerable fortune first in real estate, then in banking. He had grown up on a farm in a place near Pittsburgh with the unhappy name of Poverty Point, and his son always suspected it was that that had produced in him a single-mindedness about all things financial, a flinty lack of sympathy for anyone who had not prospered as he had, for anyone whom he considered "weak."

When Thomas had been a young man, he realized that in order to finance the education he would need, he would have to find ways of making money. To this end he taught Latin, sold books (Hallam's *History of the Middle Ages*), organized a kind of summer camp for scuffed, frayed children. To finance his study for his law degree, Thomas Mellon worked as a clerk in the prothonotary's office, handling mortgages, deeds, liens, and notes owed. Even then he stood firmly against pleasure. His life as a young man was a ceremonial of self-denial. He ate sparingly, slept only when exhaustion felled him, eschewed the company of women, kept two books, his bedding, three dented pots for cooking, a change of clothes, and nothing more in his spartan rented rooms. It would have been impossible for a small kernel of self-righteousness not to grow in such a fertile field.

When he was thirty years old, he chose a wife. Neither love nor lust propelled him. He was looking for a helpmate. He calculated time invested in wooing against desired outcome and made lists of essential wifely qualities. His bride would need to be someone of good family, without traits that might prove irksome. (Among these were independence and a love of music, two things he mistrusted in women.) Elaborate background checks on would-be candidates were undertaken. Hereditary consumption was among the potential blights that had to be ruled out. Thomas was a blunt, impatient lover.

Sarah Jane Negley was plain, but not without a muted, understated beauty. Her manner was unaffected, matter-of-fact, and she was an heiress of the sort that particularly appealed to Thomas, with a fortune in land—a substantial parcel of it in a place that seemed a likely site for urban sprawl. Romance seemed not to have played a role in their brief courtship. She wanted conversation, soft pleadings, cut flowers wrapped in grosgrain ribbon. He hoped to quickly close the deal. To his way of thinking, at thirty he was no longer young, and a longing had come over him. For children, for some easing. It unnerved him to be struck by longing and he wished to satiate it quickly.

In the years after his marriage he became a judge and a banker, all the while keeping close track of the properties he was eagerly accumulating. He and Sarah had eight children—six boys, two girls—and from the outset he determined that his sons would go into business. He built a schoolhouse on his property so he could educate them at home, thereby offering protection from public-school boys, who were likely to be "coarse and low by nature." (So he wrote in his self-published memoirs.) A tutor was employed, but the curriculum was designed by Thomas. "For businessmen it is unnecessary to waste much time on the classics and special sciences," he decided. And although he himself liked reading—Gibbon, Herbert Spencer—he didn't encourage such diversions in his boys. As to the girls—forget the girls. They, and one boy, died in childhood. The judge saw to it that the mourning period was brief. "Daughters who die young," he wrote, "need not be greatly lamented."

Thomas Mellon had chosen Sarah Negley because he thought she would "wear well roughing it through life." What she thought of him was not recorded.

Andrew was twenty-five years old when he returned to Pittsburgh from Europe in November; and when he went back to work after Thanksgiving, to T. Mellon and Sons' Bank on Smithfield Street, it was with a new eye, an eye accustomed to the streets of Paris, short cobbled alleys where soap, antique pens, and large ruffed bouquets of flowers could be bought. He had seen how sunlight could make rooftops shimmer. The bank building, which his father had designed and built himself, which had once seemed so magnificent to him, with its four imposing stories, the arched windows crowned with cornices and keystones, the dark, stained hardwood paneling that made the lobby so inexplicably imposing, now seemed like the product of too much effort. He thought it imitative, an expression of a failed attempt at beauty. It would be only a few months until his "real life" reasserted its power over him. But in the days after his return, the words "chiaroscuro," "palazzo," and "oeuvre" crept into his vocabulary. He was unable to resist them.

His office was adjacent to his father's, and there was catching up to do. Well into December he worked late every night in an effort to learn all that had transpired in his absence. On December 20, his father stayed late with him, to review files and papers that required his scrutiny. The judge's mind was still alert, but at sixty-eight his eyesight had begun to fail. Together, he reasoned, he and Andrew could accomplish much.

Andrew read the first paragraphs of the assembled documents aloud to his father, the chronicle of business from the last six months, and the judge then provided a narrative of the strategy behind each contract or agreement. Gaslights hung suspended from hinged brackets on Judge Mellon's office wall. A kerosene lamp sputtering on the desk illuminated their faces and their figurings. Andrew turned each document facedown when they'd finished with it. They were almost to the bottom of the pile.

"The South Fork Fishing and Hunting Club," he read.

"Ah, yes. A necessary business venture."

Andrew read further. "So we are members, then?" He could not hide his surprise. It seemed a most unlikely venture for his father.

"Everyone important has become a member. Read further, find the list." Judge Mellon gestured impatiently with a bent, arthritic hand.

Andrew riffled through the paper pile, then began reading: "Robert Pitcairn, James A. Chambers, Frank Laughlin, Henry Phipps. Carnegie?"

"And you and Frick, and all those others. I believe the term is 'founders.' I know, I know, it must seem foolish to you. It did to me as well when I was first approached—some lodge in the Allegheny Mountains. But then I saw what others were to be invited to participate and I decided it was imperative to join them." He squinted as he took the list from Andrew. "It will be a summer place; some structure, some sort of clubhouse is to be built. There will be hunting and fishing, as I understand it. An old dam is to be reconstructed, a lake for recreation, sailing, and such will accumulate behind it."

"Fishing?" Andrew asked. He was quite sure that he had never seen his father fish.

"Fishing, hunting, boating—it's all written there. And horses. Stables. A summer place." The judge seemed somewhat embarrassed by this, eager to move on to the next transaction.

"You'll go there, then? You'll actually spend time?"

"Good God, no. But you might. There might be business to be done there. It could do for you."

Andrew read more carefully. There had been a charter filed, the work had started. The clubhouse would be ready for summer occupancy. Seventeen thousand dollars had been spent on repairs to a large earth dam. Not much, he noticed. But if not much was done, little must have been needed. The Pennsylvania Railroad ran a line from Pittsburgh to the South Fork station.

Andrew had heard much about the beauty of the Allegheny Mountains, but he had not seen them. He tried to imagine what the club might look like—a tree-fringed lake, the blue firs darkening the hillsides. It brought to mind Corot landscapes he had seen in Europe. *Paysage au clair de lune. Ville d'Avray.* How alarmingly original they had seemed to him. How redolent of tender feeling toward the land, the lake that was being rendered on the canvas. Corot had painted tree branches thin as spiderwebs, he'd used sheer washes of paint to create the sense of a magical and muted world. Thin, light colors, almost transparent greens and browns. Andrew had read that Corot's wish in painting landscapes was to render the impression, the *effet*, rather than the realistic details, and so he had. Standing for long hours before those paintings, Andrew came to feel as if he knew the places, as if he had walked along that lake. How he had admired Corot's landscapes. Before he saw them, he had not thought of the obvious benefits of making money, of the possibility of spending it. But in Paris, in the presence of those paintings, he'd had dreams of acquisition, of owning one one day.

The Allegheny Mountains. Not the French countryside, to be sure, but in his office at his father's bank that night Andrew Mellon wondered if the moon would hang as hauntingly in the sky at South Fork as it did when Corot painted it streaked by clouds in Ville d'Avray.

Snow had begun to fall heavily outside. Fat wet flakes clung briefly to the windowpane, then melted. A good thing, this. There would be snow for Christmas.

A retreat. A summer place. Andrew imagined a lake, a breeze, a sailboat slipping through clear water. He thought perhaps he'd go there. He thought perhaps he'd find an overgrown, secluded lakeside spot and take up painting.

THE DAM

"Remember how long you have been putting off these things, and how many times the gods have given you days of grace, and yet you do not use them."

—Marcus Aurelius, *Meditations*, Book II, Number 4

Perhaps Nora had been right about the dam when she was young, right to imagine that it could breathe, that it was in its own way a living thing. It was, after all, rock shards and earth, tree stumps, a mulch of disintegrating leaves and splintered branches and manure. A great organic giant. And it was fed by mountain springs and streams that coursed through layers of the earth like arteries through limbs, their currents so quick, so urgent that even after those waters combined and spread over the lakebed and grew calm, some memory of movement still stirred within them. The gathered waters pressed at the dam's earthen side, pulsed heavily against it. Seeping water oozed from its face, where twigs and budding flowers trembled, brushing softly at each other with crackles and little whispered purrs. When standing close to it, more than once Nora had thought, Yes, it might be breathing. More creature than artifact. A giant with its own long history dating back to 1836, the year that Emerson published an essay in praise of nature. In that same year Jean-Baptiste-Camille Corot, of whose work Andrew Mellon was so enamored, had painted *Diana Surprised by Actaeon* in Paris. Davy Crockett, not yet a legend, died bravely defending a Texas fort and mission called the Alamo. And in the Pennsylvania legisla-

ture a vote was taken, a course decided on. A dam would be built on the
Alleghenies' western slope, so that water could be had for a canal system
linking Johnstown to Pittsburgh. Canals? the skeptics wondered. In the
mountains? It would be like a transportation system from a fairy tale,
a mad inventor's fantasy. The triumph of optimism over practicality.
It would be called the Portage Railroad, and because of it, Philadelphia
would have access to the Ohio River. The Allegheny Mountain Range
would cease to be an obstacle to commerce. Train cars on barges would be
floated, hoisted, railroaded up and down, across and over. For the visionaries in charge of this project, seeing to it that there was enough water
through the long, dry summers to supply the canals appeared to be the
greatest challenge. For this a dam would be required.

The site was chosen fifteen miles north of Johnstown. Hundreds of
acres of trees were felled and cleared. A bright-eyed young engineer
named Morris was given responsibility for its design. Earth dams were of
the most common sort. He had studied earth dam construction, he knew
what was required.

1. The core will be made of stone and will extend twenty feet above
the normal water line. The stone core must be filled with earth and
clay, and its outer surface riprapped, reinforced with rock. Some of
the rocks ought to be gravel-sized and packed down tightly. Others
should be so huge that harsh hemp rope would need to be tied
around them, teams of horses used to haul them to the site. The
base of the dam will be 270 feet thick, planted, anchored to the valley floor. The width will gradually narrow as it rises. The thickness
at the top should be approximately 20 feet. The outside wall ought
to be steep and strong, the inside gently sloping.
2. Good engineering practice dictates that the spillway be cut into
the rock of the hillside to which the base is anchored, not through
the dam itself. Wide enough to handle any overflow, kept clear of
all debris.
3. Five cast-iron discharge pipes, each two feet wide, will be placed
in a stone culvert in the center of the base. If the water rises dangerously, the discharge pipes can be opened, and the water released. A
wooden tower will be built on site and manned by a well-trained
watchman, who can thus be made aware if the lake level begins to

rise. So warned, he can crank open the valves and control the release of the excess water.

4. Because the water can be released, the final rule of earth-dam construction and maintenance will be adhered to. The water must never flow over the top. The top cannot be breached.

The proposed dam would be 900 feet across and 72 feet high. Mountain streams and melted snows could be counted on to supply the 20 million tons of water that would be called Lake Conemaugh. Nothing to it, one young engineer said to another over dinner in a saloon in Philadelphia. A 1,400-ton steamer had just sailed from England to New York in fifteen days. A simple earth dam? The young men clinked glasses in a toast to progress. They predicted that the dam would be completed in a year.

But the job went slowly, and in 1842 the state ran short of funds and stopped work on the half-completed project. For four years nothing was done. But while the dam sat idle, cholera came to the valley and outwitting death became the business of the day. No one thought about the dam, and more years passed. In West Overton, not far from Johnstown, Henry Clay Frick was born. Readers wept over the newly published *David Copperfield*.

Finally, in 1850, work on the dam was resumed, and in June 1852 the sluice pipes were finally closed and the lake began to fill. But it had been twenty years since the inception of the plan, and for the Pennsylvania Railroad, the romance of canals had lost its luster. An all-rail route across the mountains from Pittsburgh to Philadelphia had just been completed, so a few months after the dam was finished, the water that it held was no longer needed. The whole enterprise was obsolete. Three years later the Pennsylvania Railroad bought it all—canals and dam and inclined planes—from the state, just to get the rights-of-way. Then allowed it to sit.

1857, 1858, 1859. The dam, a sleeping giant. A beast in hibernation. In winter, snow dusted, then crusted its surface, ice glazed the riprapping rocks, forming crystals, white gems, jeweled growths extruding from its side.

In Virginia, James Talbot was fourteen years old in 1860. The snow was light in Virginia. A traveling theater company was coming to Richmond. They would perform *Twelfth Night* with sets and props and elaborate Elizabethan costumes, and his father had promised that he would take his sons. It would be the first time James had seen a play, and long after the other boys had gone to sleep, excitement kept him fidgeting in bed. Finally, his mother came into his room to sit beside him, to close the draperies against the lunar light.

In Russia Czar Alexander II initiated the emancipation of the serfs, James heard his father tell his mother when he should have been asleep. He heard his father say it raised questions in his mind. But no questions were raised in James's. His mind was full of the play he would see, of twins, mistaken identities, and shipwrecks. He wasn't familiar yet with Shakespeare's tragedies. So he knew nothing of the world of which his father spoke, of kings and slaves and free men, sleeping giants. Russia could have been in another universe as far as he was concerned. He'd never even heard of Johnstown.

Each spring, rising temperatures melted winter snow that ran into the dammed reservoir; spring rains swelled the mountain creeks and streams that fed the lake. Little hemlock saplings, volunteers, took root in the dam's damp face, spurred petals of columbines nodded pinkly from their stems; the dark earth blushed. Nesting birds left semipalmate tracks as they pecked and rooted for building fodder. Dense clouds formed shifting continents above the trees.

1861. Now a war was being fought and the abandoned dam was long-forgotten, weedy, wild, and feral. Someone should have been assiduous, careful. Someone should have been watching. But no one was, and what ought to have been impossible began to happen. As the captive water lapped and smacked and heaved against the earth containing it, slowly little rivulets began to burrow through the face of the dam. Small rocks on the outer surface, made smooth by driving rain, had no rough adhering edges and lost their grip in the sloped earth.

In 1862 the Union Army struggled for a foothold in Virginia. Heavy spring rains in the Alleghenies caused mountain tributaries to roar over their banks. Water wasn't oozing through the earth dam anymore; it was sieving through the face of it. What had been small holes were becoming large pressure cuttings, and finally, yielding to the strain, the dam gave way. A flaw in the foundation, the stone culvert was the cause, the locals said. Thank God, the level of the lake was low, good thing the sentry in the wooden tower acted quickly to open the discharge valves. Weren't they lucky there was so little damage. Nothing more serious than what they'd come to expect from the occasional spring flooding. The first floors of some houses in the valley had water in them, and at the point in Johnstown where the Little Conemaugh meets the Stonycreek, the streets were like small rivers. Catastrophe had been averted. Thus drained, the lake became a small and docile thing. A duck-filled pond.

A dry summer gave rise to brushfires. One of them licked and spit its way through dead wood and undergrowth to climb the sides of the watchtower. The clapboard structure, the levers that controlled the discharge system burned. Since there was so little water in the lake at that point, the Pennsylvania Railroad saw no need to build another. Naturally, since there was no post to man, when the old sentry died, a new one wasn't hired. Grass sprouted in the dried patches of the lakebed. A South Fork farmer found it a good place for grazing sheep.

Then, in 1875, a Pennsylvania congressman named Reilly bought the dam and surrounding property from the Pennsylvania Railroad, for next to nothing. The railroad was happy to be rid of it. The dam was by then just a creased and riven earthen heap. It would have been hard to call it a dam at all. Morris, the young engineer who first designed it, was a grandfather now. On holidays he bored his children with stories of how humbling it was to stand beneath it after work on the dam was finished. How noble an achievement it had seemed.

In 1879, Benjamin Ruff, a contractor, bought the dam, the lake, and the property. He had heard from business associates that a lake was wanted, a mountain retreat for the newly rich. And Reilly, trying to salvage something from his bad investment, removed the discharge pipes before the sale was final.

Eager to get on with the business of the club, Ruff spent $17,000 hauling rocks, mud, hemlock boughs, and hay in a flimsy, unscientific effort to "repair" the dam. A meager sum, but money, it was reasoned, would be better spent on the clubhouse and stables, things the members could enjoy. So insubstantial were these efforts that on Christmas Day of 1879, right after they were completed, a downpour carried the repairs away. Ruff might have stopped then, consulted experts, gauged the cost of real repair. But instead, no thought was given to replacing the discharge pipes. No one worried that the elaborate network of logs and screens built at the top of the spillway to keep fish from being washed out of the lake might block the spillway, compromise the dam's integrity.

By March 1881, the new lake had become deep enough for the owners to begin to stock it; work on the clubhouse was being hurried along in order for it to be completed in time for the club's grand opening. Architects used rocks to anchor their meticulous and detailed drawings, to keep March winds from sending them, like paper seagulls, over the lawn and across the water. With the foreman they consulted the plans, reminding him that the finials still had to be placed on tower tops, that a shed roof was the one they'd decided on to shade the porch. Ruff himself saw to the installation of the billiard table. The grounds were being groomed and mulched, fruit trees were brought by wagon, orchards planted. But in relation to the dam, no one sought the advice of an engineer. Men who were to become cabinet members and congressmen, ambassadors and statesmen, who oversaw the smallest details of their business lives, the railroads they ran, the mills they built, the daily tonnage of the steel produced, the mines they dug and the ovens they built for the coke that they were making, the precise schedules of the trains that carried steel and coke to markets—these men who kept obsessive track of all their holdings, their vast properties, had no interest in the safety or the structure of the dam. It was as if no people lived below it, no world existed in the mountains but the one they were creating.

Someone should have been assiduous, careful. Someone should have been watching.

TO THE LAKE

"Love only what falls to your lot and is destined for you; what is more suited to you than that?"
        —Marcus Aurelius, *Meditations*, Book VII, Number 57

Thinking back to the time just after the epidemic and the deaths was difficult for Daniel. The way the house changed, the way cheer of any kind departed as if banished from the place. He had been thirteen and was slow to regain the weight he lost during those days when fever racked him, his throat was cut, and he could barely swallow. He was still "not himself," as his father said, when they came to take the coffins from the house, wasn't even strong enough to help with the carrying of the caskets. And they were little things, those caskets. Small and neat and as finely made as the children who were carried in them. Later, he felt ashamed that he hadn't insisted, ashamed that he hadn't carried his brother that last time. Horace Rose helped. He was a lawyer and had been a school friend of Frank's; as boys they had played round ball and quoits together, until Rose had to go to work at the tannery after both his parents died the summer of his thirteenth birthday. Lemon Bean helped, because he'd come to admire Daniel's grandfather. Tom Davis helped, closing his saloon—California Tom's—that day, putting a black wreath on the door, which was a more effective way of spreading the news of the deaths of the Fallon children than an announcement in the *Tribune* would have been. Captain Bill Jones came all the way from Pittsburgh to help, because he and Frank had fought and lived through Fredericksburg together, because he'd made a place for Frank at the iron works after the war and taught him all he knew about steel making before Carnegie hired him to run the Edgar Thomson Works in Pittsburgh. John Fenn helped, as a way of appeasing what he feared were jealous gods, gods who had spared his own three children in an act of arbitrary mercy. And the Reverend Chapman helped because Christian fervor made him overlook the fact that the parents never came to church, and instead of responding angrily, he thought it would be a spiteful thing if no one said a proper prayer for those two babies, parishioners or not.

Daniel remembered a day of much standing about and whispering. The two downstairs rooms of the little house were too full of people, the air was close, and men he barely knew kept shaking his hand and reminding him to be strong now, saying how they were "sorry for his troubles." Standing by the kitchen stove, watching women move pots from front burner to back, he thought it odd that anyone could eat, that ordinary life was going on, uninterrupted.

His mother had not moved once from her chair in the corner of the kitchen, gripping the same cold cup of coffee since coming back from the cemetery. His sister, Caroline, eleven and ashen from her own long days of fever, hovered near Julia like a stunned, uncertain bird. Her black dress had been borrowed hastily and was too large for her. The long sleeves hanging limply, and her wrists and hands disappearing in them, made her look even more frail and insubstantial. Throughout the afternoon Daniel stepped outside frequently so he could be alone. Prospect Hill began its rise just beyond their back yard, and its dark immensity felt like protection, the one remaining constant.

Late in the afternoon Horace Rose also stepped outside, thinking to smoke his pipe, stretch his legs, get some air. When he saw Daniel a few steps distant from the back door, a forlorn-looking figure, he hesitated before approaching him. He thought it might be best if he pretended not to see the tears, not to interrupt them. But concern got the better of him and he walked toward the boy, warning of his approach with an exaggerated throat-clearing. Rose did not speak at first but stood briefly beside Daniel, looking off into the distance, drawing on the stem of his pipe, letting the sweet smoke drift lazily between them.

"Your father says you like to read," he ventured after a moment, stroking his hand across his full red beard.

A non sequitur. What does reading have to do with anything? thought Daniel. He wondered if this was the way it was going to be for him now, if all conversation was going to seem foolish and irrelevant. He wondered if he would turn into a cynic.

"Yes," he had finally said.

Rose nodded, puffed on his pipe again. "You might know, then, that I'm the founder of the Johnstown Literary Society. Did you know that?"

Daniel had wanted to run. He felt as if he knew nothing about how to go forward with this, how to speak. Only the good manners learned at his mother's knee kept him from doing what occurred to him, from screaming, "Don't you understand? I am not capable of this." He had a sudden wish to make this clear to everyone, the fact that these deaths were not like any others, that these deaths were particular and cruel and not to be borne. Too much, too much, and the family that was left behind could not be asked to bear it.

"I ask, because I thought you might want to borrow books from me. Things I have that the library does not." Rose hesitated, and his voice, always soft, never to anyone's knowledge raised in anger, dropped further, as he fumbled to explain himself, to give the crying boy something, anything. "It is just that I have found literature to be of great consolation . . . myself . . . When I was a boy, that is, and lost my parents." His voice broke on the last word, as if even at that moment, so many years later, he felt it freshly, lived with the pain of that loss still. He thrust his free hand into his trouser pocket. "The Russians especially. Works that are newly translated. You might like them. They seem to have a great understanding of life, the Russians. Reading them makes me want to see that part of the world. I would like you to borrow them. Whenever you feel ready."

Daniel had not known what to say. And he had not, for even a moment, believed that there was any consolation in the world for him. But Rose's struggle to comfort him, to grasp so eagerly at anything that might give solace, moved something inside Daniel. The weight of his grieving did not lighten, but it shifted. Briefly. Barely detectable, that shift. But it made him think for just one moment that he might not feel this way forever, so sick at heart, so wounded, so responsible, and without the slightest notion of what to do.

"The Russians," Daniel said, wiping his wet face with his shirtsleeve, not looking at Rose, instead looking off with him toward the far hills, the pink-edged clouds, the fading light.

"Yes," Rose offered, eager now, pressing forward with his plan. "Pushkin, Turgenev, Dostoevsky."

There was the sound of music in the names.

"When you're ready, then," said Rose, still not looking at Daniel, knowing not to be a witness to the crying. The boy would be ashamed. And he didn't want that. But as he turned to go back into the house, he felt the need to briefly lay a hand on Daniel's shoulder.

A few months after the babies were buried, Daniel had gone to Rose's house. It had been difficult for him to imagine a room in a home given over to books, although he had certainly read and heard about such things. But these private libraries, these lavish extravagances which he'd pictured in his mind so often, were in other places, European cities primarily, London or Madrid. Not in a place the size of Johnstown. Although it was true that Mr. Morrell had a greenhouse, a conservatory. And now Mr. Rose had a library. A wonder. It had made Daniel curious about what other wonders waited behind the closed doors in this town, or on the outskirts. What other mysteries were hidden in the mountains.

Rose's library was small. There was room in it only for the book-filled shelves that lined three of the four walls, one faded green velvet-covered chair, and a small table on which an oil lamp was placed. For reading, Daniel guessed. He imagined a book opened on it, a chair drawn to it. It was a room in keeping with the rest of the house, well tended, with no apparent clutter. It was a larger house than Daniel's, to be sure, with a mansard roof and a gabled window. Imposing, Daniel noticed in his quick pass through, on his way to the little library in the rear. Rose had opened the door to his book-filled room with a kind of reverence and spoke in the same hushed tones one used in the public library in town. He explained in some detail the ingenious cataloging system he'd devised, the pleasure he took in his position as the head of the Literary Society, although it was certainly not the greatest of his accomplishments. (He had also been district attorney of Cambria County, had served in the cavalry and in the state legislature.) The books, Rose explained to Daniel, had been acquired in much the same way that the Fallon family's piano had been—with careful planning, diligent saving, the only sure way to betterment.

"There are no shortcuts," Rose had said, hands clasped behind his back, nodding his head as if agreeing with himself.

It sounded so much like something Frank might say that Daniel understood immediately why Mr. Rose and his father had remained friends in spite of the different turns their lives had taken. And as to the books and how Rose chose them—that, too, Daniel learned, was the result of eschewing shortcuts. "I began with the Greeks," he said. Sophocles. Aeschylus. One or two books purchased when business dealings took him to Philadelphia. Gifts from his wife, who was always kept abreast of what volume he was hoping to acquire next. Patiently he watched his shelves fill, reveled in the gradual accretion.

Daniel was thin and inordinately quiet, as if the very idea of speech exhausted him. Rose watched him scan the shelves, his head tilted so he could read the titles. Amazingly patient in the way he touched the spine of each one, as if they had all day, a lifetime. Rose had made a kind of tally sheet for him that would remain on the table, so if Daniel wanted to come borrow something, and Rose or his wife or his children weren't there (the door was never locked), Daniel could help himself, sign the book out on this makeshift chart. It was all very well-thought-out, very much appreciated by Daniel. What he couldn't admit was that he had heretofore been, at best, a desultory reader, a seeker of pleasure more than of culture or information. Or consolation of the kind Rose had suggested the Russians might provide. Never avid. Not passionate about it. But who can account for avidity, the development of it, what takes root in a life and becomes a source of passion? He took the first book just to please Mr. Rose, who seemed to want so much for him to read it: the *Odyssey*. "An adventure story," Rose said as he pressed the volume into Daniel's hand. Detailed plans were made for their next meeting. Rose confessed to hoping that Daniel would become the Literary Society's youngest member.

Two children, Julia had said to herself again and again in the year after Claire and Louis died. Two children. And Daniel with a scar thick as a finger on his neck to mark him. Every time she saw that scar, she thought of

Claire and Louis. And it made looking at him a searing, painful thing. Impossible to get beyond. Impossible to conquer.

She did everything she could. She made the house a home for four instead of six. Smaller meals, less laundry.

For Frank it became a matter of loving the two remaining children more, of focusing four-child-love on two. Like the potent coffee he and his friends drank before each shift, his love was thick, intense, dark as the shadow he cast over them on nights when he sat beside them, watching them sleeping. He honed his powers of concentration, precision, exactitude, and it made him sharp and volatile and quick. How bittersweet it was when he made foreman in early January of 1881, a promotion that was the product of a focus and single-mindedness that was unavailable to him when his heart, his head were so intent on keeping up with the children. For the first time in his life he felt the weight of irony.

Frank's promotion enabled them to move into a bigger house. Two stories, red-brick, and on a street lined with birch trees, with a sycamore and two cherry trees in the small fenced yard. There were three bedrooms instead of two on the second floor; on the first, besides the kitchen and a smallish dining room, was a front room with two arched windows, a room that could be called a parlor. It was a proud thing for a workingman, a man who'd gotten ahead by his own labors. A proper place for their piano. Forget that it was dusty. Forget that Julia hardly touched it now.

They moved in June 1881. And while the wood floors were being polished to a soft, buffed luster at the South Fork clubhouse, Julia Fallon, unaware of the glittering world about to spring into being fifteen miles away, was on a ladder hanging curtains in her new house, from a rod above her tall parlor windows.

Yes, there were sailboats. Nora would always remember the first time she saw them, the first time she came up the hill to the lake during the club's inaugural season. It was 1881, and she was twelve, in so many ways a little girl, excited, caught up, her face candid and transparent. The horses' hooves slapped the packed dirt road. Her lips were caked with coarse, stinging dust. She heard the prodding click of the wagon driver's tongue; squinted when they emerged from shadow-dappled woods into the open air and the wagon in which they rode turned onto the dam's broad breast. On her left she saw it suddenly, the azure lake, dazzling in the hot sun, absorbing the sword-shaped shadows of tall pines.

When she first looked out across the water, she was not sure what they were. She'd seen pictures, of course, watercolor renderings of sailing ships in books. Here, on an ordinary day in summer, they seemed out of context, out of time. In Pittsburgh the rivers were umber-colored, foul. You looked upon them from a distance, and then saw only tugboats, barges, smoke from mills and factories ribboning toward the water, puffing through the sepia-stained air. Barges were boats, thought Nora. But these were apparitions, bright white crescents sprouting from the narrow polished hulls. Three of them glided over the water in formation, precisely angled toward the wind. Tiny doll-like figures rested in them, distant, impossibly delicate, their dresses making a ruffled band of blending pastel colors separating skiff from sail. In one of the vessels, a girl's hand was pressed to the crown of a broad sunbonnet; her other arm, bare, extended, drifted dreamily through passing water while a boy in a boater steered.

From the second boat an arm was raised as someone waved. Excitement, pleasure made her forget herself, and Nora, imagining the wave was meant for her, leaned forward, to see past her father, to wave her arm in exuberant reply. She heard giggles from the parasol-protected lovelies in the wagon just behind them, where another family rode, and realized, blushing, that the wave was one of recognition, meant for them. She straightened her back, raised her shoulders, touched her flushed cheek with her hand. She'd learned early how to do this—to pull back, withdraw, reclaim the territory of decorum, and affect an air of indifference. She straightened her skirt, turned from the lake to look the other way, and told herself that it was the sight of the sudden drop away from the dam's steep rock-studded face into the valley that made her dizzy, that took her breath away.

"Slings and arrows. Sticks and stones. Remember who you are." Her mother's speech was riddled with these sayings. Nora thought of it as a kind of Morse code, and early in her childhood she'd learned to fill in the missing words, complete the thought. Perhaps that's why her diary entries were so dense and overdone, her ideas so hectic and cluttered. She wanted to probe, to understand; in the world that she created for herself, where she was in charge, she wanted everything explained. From the corner of her eye she checked her mother, who flanked her father on his right, to see if she'd observed her faux pas, her unbecoming overeagerness. If she had, there would be a lecture later. Nora knew this, wait and see. But perhaps her mother had looked away at just that moment. There was no hint of approbation, no stiffening of spine, no sigh. Nora's father took one of hers, then one of her mother's hands in his.

"Almost there," he said heartily. The wind cutting across the lake had shifted. The sailboats in the distance came about, then skimmed away.

Eventually there were sixteen cottages. But that first summer there were just the boathouse, the stables, and the clubhouse, all arranged just back from the water. A boardwalk made it possible to stroll between them. Flags and buntings were draped for the occasion. There was a German brass band playing celebratory music. The air smelled of just-cut wood. A light wind troubled the newly planted trees and shrubbery.

Their rooms were on the third floor of the clubhouse at the far end of the hall, adjoining. Each had wide windows overlooking the lake, the better to see the moon, her father said approvingly. Nora had watched him press a bill into the porter's hand, explaining that they'd prefer to be a little distant from the others, his wife slept lightly, privacy was needed. Nora, in her room, let their voices recede from her. Her bed was brass. Sunlight sifting through lace window panels webbed the dark wood floor. The washbasin was fringed with a painted border of forsythia and ivy. She was startled when her father approached her from behind to show her how a penny dropped against the china surface made a ping. How clearly she remembered that first day of that first summer.

Nora's room was in a corner, and her bed was so much grander than her bed at home, the mattress so deep, the frame so high, there was a little stepstool next to it. She walked respectfully around it, admiring the pale blue coverlet and matching pillow shams, the goose-down pillows fluffed and full. She thought of how smooth, how comforting the sheets would be. Perhaps, she thought, it was a feather bed. She was a child much given to imagining, and so she imagined herself a member of a royal family, the daughter of a king. She wondered—was she as sensitive as the heroines of fairy tales?—she wondered if she'd feel a wrinkle in her sheets that night. The Princess and the Pea.

They ate, as all the members were required to, in the dining room among the other guests downstairs, later that evening. There was a certain magic to it all that first "season." Miter-folded linen napkins, crystal glasses shaped like tulips, candles flickering in breezes drifting in from open windows. Rhododendrons that bloomed in hot profusion rose bright-faced from small silver vases, their placement among splendor a nod to simplicity, to native growth, the common touch. Flannel shirts and crush hats, the garb of country life, were put aside at dinner. Nora's mother was resplendent in black silk, the sleeves of her dress edged in beaded scallops, the neckline scooped, the wasp waist cinched and small.

Young women from nearby towns stood in a line, backs pressed to the far wall, waiting to serve them. They wore black dresses, with pressed white fichu collars and white aprons to offset them. Dark-haired, red-haired. Nora saw that some had Irish freckles. She'd heard her mother say that people here were Scottish, Welsh, and German, that there was a hint of Gypsy blood among them. Nora scanned the wall until she found a Gypsy, or so she thought. At least she had the well-formed cheekbones, the dark eyes and honey-skinned beauty that Nora thought of when she thought of Gypsies. Nora watched as her mother leaned to whisper to her father. She heard her call them "girls." Not so, she thought, looking at the smocked and ribboned bodice of her own dinner dress, flat as a pan. She touched the ends of her wiry hair, made civil only by the binding force of her thick braid. Too old to play, according to her mother, too young for other pleasures, certainly. *I* am the girl, she thought, as the servers, competent, contained, stepped forward from their posts with foot-soldier precision, each with a small white service towel draped over one bent arm. Silently they moved through swinging doors into the kitchen.

When they emerged, Nora saw that the waitress assigned to them was the dark beauty, the Gypsy. She served sir and madam first, and as she passed behind her, Nora smelled wood and wash soap, lilac-scented cologne. Her hand was graceful, shapely, the color of a nut. The nails were rounded, the half moon at the cuticle was perfect and pearl-toned. So beautiful, thought Nora. She wanted to reach out, touch that hand. Nora looked up eagerly into her face and smiled. The hand stopped as it placed a bowl of hot pea soup before her. The server paused, as if deciding. And for a moment Nora thought she was going to return the smile, or smooth Nora's collar, anoint her with some unexpected kindness.

Nora's mother, watching, said her name sharply, shook her head, and frowned. Nora straightened her spine, turned her eyes down toward her lap. Then looked up, sighing, thinking, Time to eat, but when she reached to retrieve the soup spoon from the array of silver spread like wings from the circle of her plate, she stopped suddenly, confused. Too many spoons. Which for the cream soup, which for dessert, which for consommé? She had been trained in this, it was something she should know. She dared not ask her mother. She tried to catch her father's eye, willed him to pick up his spoon first, to start to eat, but he'd had several bourbons and three glasses of the garnet-toned Cabernet. He'd already slipped into his dinner-table vagueness and did not see her predicament. Her mother blew a kiss to an acquaintance at a distant table, then leaned and whispered something coy, some bit of insider's knowledge, into her father's ear. He laughed a bit too heartily, kissed her hand. This was part of their performance. Everyone should look now, see how gay they were, how lovely. Nora twisted her folded hands, picked at a jagged cuticle until it bled. She imagined that everyone was watching her and judging, that perfection was her responsibility. And as if in a dream the table lengthened and her parents began to slip away. It seemed as if they had been set adrift, were disappearing from her, gliding toward the far end of the room; that even if she called to them they wouldn't hear. She gripped the handle of one of the spoons so tightly that the escutcheon carved into it made an imprint in her palm. And through some intricate and anxious reasoning, she came to understand that they would come back only to the child they *wished* they had, the faultless child; that their return to her depended on not giving her stupidity away. Too many spoons. She had to get rid of one. Without knowing why, she slipped the rounded one into her pocket.

Nora swallowed, blinked; her parents had taken their place again across from her. Her mother's eyebrows rose when she saw Nora dip into her cream soup with the dessert spoon. Nora held the hot pea soup in her mouth, not daring to swallow. Her father in his munificence gestured to her mother that the proper spoon was not there. And when Evelyn realized that the table had been set improperly, that a lapse in serving etiquette had occurred, she beckoned coolly to their server and, in a voice thick with asperity, began a haughty reprimand. Nora saw her mother's lips move, heard the key words. Click, click, double click. The Morse code. "Careless . . . inept . . . foolish." The dark-headed, dark-frocked server nodded, apologized, and said, "Yes, ma'am," repeatedly. Respectful, Nora saw, but at the same time there was a hint of insolence about her; she'd do what she must do, but she was unimpressed by Nora's mother, anyone could tell she'd seen haughtiness before and was impervious to it. Nora, relieved, thought, It's going to be all right now, this is over. She could eat her soup, get through this meal, go up to bed. It was only when the Gypsy maiden turned toward Nora, when she glanced at Nora's pocket on her way back to the kitchen for the proper spoon, that Nora realized that she'd seen, she knew, and had chosen, for reasons of her own, not to betray her.

That night Nora lay in darkness and heard her parents talking angrily in the adjoining room. She heard her mother call her father spineless, foolish. She thought about how wise her father was to want these corner rooms—a bit apart from all the others. Nora slipped the spoon out of her pillowcase, where she had hidden it, slipped out of bed, knelt on the floor by the opened window. The moon was full. Nora held the spoon up to the light. Her hair, unbraided, was a great cascading wave of blue-black curls, a gift, she'd heard her mother say, a token, a dark taint from her father's ancestry. She looked at her reflection in the spoon's round dome, her features broadened by its concavity, thickened, made plain even in the moon's kind light. Out of the nighttime silence she heard shoes ticking softly on the boardwalk, saw the wood planks, new and yellow-brown, a pale ribbon stretching along the shore into the water. Nora peered into the night. Laughter. A boy, a young man, hoved into view, no club member clearly. His shirt was collarless, a work shirt; his suspenders hiked over his shoulders and hooked his waistband; the uncuffed edges of his pants legs slapped at his shoes. A toss of his head and his wavy hair flew back out of his eyes. His hand was stretched out behind him, pulling, and her server from the dining room came out of the doorway, out of the kitchen's demanding livid glow into the creamy, moonstruck night. She wore no apron now, no collar, no towel over her arm, no signs of obeisance. When the screen door slammed behind her, he pulled her to him, into the shadows, took her face in his hands and began to kiss her. Nose, cheek, chin, mouth. Nora was glad her room was dark, that there was no silhouetting light behind her. The girl let her hands fall to her sides, tilted her face up to him. She seemed to know that he wouldn't harm her. Surrender, Nora thought. She would use that word later when she wrote about it in her diary. It would be new for her to think of love this way, as a willing thing. Below, the girl leaned heavily into the boy's broad chest. Her hand toyed with one of his suspenders. He stepped back from her, arm extended once more, pulling toward the boardwalk's end, the trees. He jumped from wood to earth, turned to lift her into the air, to bring her down to the soft earth with him. Nora remembered that her father used to lift her in the air that way when she was small. She closed her eyes, wished he would do that now. She wished he were still strong enough to lift her.

She lingered at the window after the lovers were gone. Stretched herself, lay down on the floor, her white gown, like a dropped handkerchief, pleated and spread around her, the spoon held to her chest the way another child might hold a doll. Her eyes slid shut, momentarily she dozed. And when she awakened from her dream-laced sleep, her arms and chest and shoulders ached, as did her determined spine. She smiled. Aha, she thought dreamily. Just like in the story. I *am* a princess. In spite of all the cushioning, I feel the irritant, the flaw, the wrinkle. She moved from her spot at the window, climbed into the feathered bed. The Princess and the Pea.

Nora hardly knew just when her life at South Fork began to seem like her real life, her only life, when two summer weeks in the mountains were the time she lived for. But she thought it began that very first summer, the night she saw the lovers on the boardwalk. At her window watching them, she felt some difference in herself, a separateness. Some sense that the window, the clubhouse room, that moonlit lake—that this was the magic place, the kingdom where she could be happy. When she awoke the next day, when she drew her curtains back to see the lake, she felt an eagerness that seemed wholly unfamiliar to her. She dressed as quickly as she ever had, pulled on her pantaloons and cotton combinations. She stood at the window, spread her arms, let the lake breeze cool her pale, bare skin. Glad for once to be twelve, young enough to still wear the slightly shorter skirt of adolescence, one that just touched her boot tops. Young enough to not yet be required to wear a crinoline cage, young enough to go without a bustle. From her trunk she chose a dark plaid dress that wouldn't show the dirt, pulled it over her head, fumbled with the buttons. In defiance of all standards set for grooming by her mother, she braided her own thick hair, not caring when she missed a strand, not caring how it frizzed and fought with her, not pausing at the mirror long enough to see how haphazard the end result was, how wild she looked, how untended, how unlike the city child she was. It was dawn, the clubhouse still. She cracked her door to see the long hall empty; she tiptoed on the stairs. The dining room was quiet, the tables set with flower-patterned china, but the kitchen purred with sound. The air was thick with the smells of baking. Fly rods for early-rising fishermen were propped against the hallstand in the entry, thin sentinels casting blades of shadow in the gathering light. Fresh fruit filled a bowl on the sideboard in the dining room, and Nora helped herself. A peach for her breakfast, an apricot and two dark plums for lunch, for later. Her first experience with thieving. She thought of the Gypsy princess, who'd not betrayed her the night before, who'd been her silent ally. She told herself that the Gypsy girl would have wanted her to have this fruit. The pieces all fit snugly in her pockets. The front door creaked when she drew it open, as if awakening; the hinges squealed. A bird cried shrilly. Her boots tapped time across the porch, then she was in the grass, dewed heavily, the air misted by what must have been a late light rain. So many paths led off behind the clubhouse that it was hard for her to choose, hard for someone who was given so few choices. A chipmunk appeared, and Nora let herself pretend it was a prince cursed by a toothy witch, herself a lost and wayward princess. So she imagined, and so she spoke, in a voice that was new for her, imperious, commanding. "Lead on," she charged. And when he ducked into the underbrush, she pulled a branch of a pine tree back and followed.

In Johnstown that same morning, Daniel J. Morrell rose moments after Nora did, dropped to his knees beside his bed, began the day, as was his custom, with a prayer. He asked God to bless his enterprises, Cambria Iron, his company store, and especially the new library which would be dedicated that day, 7,000 volumes, an imposing new building—thoughtfully situated at the corner of Washington and Walnut, between the lower works and downtown Johnstown, equally accessible to businessmen and steel workers coming to or returning home after their shifts. Over his breakfast Mr. Morrell read his "Guide to Quaker Practice," then prayed again, for humility, for wisdom, for grace and good faith in his business dealings.

His large house and the grounds surrounding it occupied an entire block on Main Street. Chimneys for the eight fireplaces rose above the mansard roof. Bay windows extended grandly from either side. A glassed-in conservatory with wicker chairs and a table overlooked a small garden devoted exclusively to flowers that bloomed white. The house was palatial to be sure, more grand by far than any other, but not too ostentatious for a man who had done so much for the city. Besides, he believed that passersby enjoyed his landscaped lawn, the flower-filled beds, the mani-cured boxwoods as much as he did. One of his greatest pleasures was to share his cuttings, to talk flowers with friends. He grew everything from seed, coaxed and tucked and tended every would-be plant himself in the three-room greenhouse he had built, the only one in Johnstown. It was to the greenhouse that he headed, eager to open the door into it, eager for the fecund smell of earth and moisture, bright light and face-flushing humidity. While watering his orchids, he reminded himself to keep his breakfast reading in his heart throughout the day, to let Quaker practice guide him. He had left specific instructions for the dedication ceremony with his secretary, with the librarian. He wanted no speeches that offered praise and thanks to him. "Praise God instead," he rehearsed his planned speech to his just-sprouting tomato plants, "and your own hard work, for making the profits that enable Cambria Iron Company to do this."

The new library (and here he'd stop to mention his plan to hire a sec-ond librarian, a helper for Mrs. Hirst) will mean more lectures, more classes there and at the Morrell Institute. Metallurgy. Accounting. More chances for his workers to improve themselves. Praise God for that, he planned to say. And as he mouthed the words, the need to pray came over him, a need to which he promptly responded. Daniel Morrell, of the broad chest, large heart, of the neat, trimmed whiskers. The good, pater-nalistic, well-intentioned lord of all he sees. In his greenhouse, in his nightshirt. On his knees.

Seven thousand books. Waiting in boxes and crates, stacked in shad-ows, the varnish on the shelves that will house them so newly applied, so fresh, it was sticky, barely dry. Some of the volumes had been packed and moved from the library's old location; others were new acquisitions, care-fully selected by the librarian, who happily accepted suggestions from the Literary Society members, the butcher or the blacksmith, anyone who wished to offer it. Morrell was especially pleased by the new books, smelling still like paste and glue and printer's ink, spines the colors of river rocks, washed shades of softest leather. He'd gone the night before to walk through the place, to sit alone at the checkout desk, to savor what he'd wrought. Books that would serve the populace, be lent for free to any citizen. His gift to his people. But even as he envisioned the crowd that would come to the dedication, the way they'd chant his name, another image vied for prominence in his imagination. Because he had heard that this was also the day when twelve railroad cars, tank cars, were unloading 1,000 black bass into South Fork Lake. Black gold, Morrell thought. He'd heard they'd been purchased for the great price of $1 each.

When he'd first learned that the dried-up reservoir and crumbling dam had been bought by Benjamin Ruff (entrepreneur, skewed visionary), with an eye toward selling shares for the creation of a sporting club, Morrell had contacted him to offer engineering help. There was a science to earth-dam construction, for safety's sake it ought to be done properly. Morrell had heard that Ruff was selling shares to Pittsburgh businessmen at $800 each. The plan—a clubhouse, "seaside cottages," boating, fishing, and hunting, except on Sunday, when no killing was to be allowed. In November of the year before, Morrell had sent John Fulton, geologist, trusted colleague, chief engineer at the iron works, up to take a look, to meet with E. J. Unger and C. A. Carpenter, two members of the club. Fulton had spoken with their contractors, stressed to them the necessity of retaining engineers to supervise the project. He worried at the slipshod nature of the rebuilding and repair. "The discharge pipes have been removed by the previous owner," Fulton wrote in his report about the dam. "Poor repairs have left a large leak in the face, which continues to cut the new embankment. Should the dam break with a full head of water behind it, in a flooding season . . ." Morrell, alarmed, immediately wrote to the clubmen. "We do not wish to put any obstruction in the way of your accomplishing your object in the reconstruction of this dam; but we must protest against the erection of a dam at that place, that will be a perpetual menace to the lives and property of those residing in this upper valley of the Conemaugh, from its insecure construction." He reiterated Fulton's recommendation of new discharge pipes; he wrote that the iron works would be happy to share the cost of real repairs. On December 2, 1880, a letter arrived at Mr. Morrell's office, dismissing all his claims and interest. "You and your people," Ruff concluded bluntly, "are in no danger from our enterprise."

"You and your people." Eight months later the condescension in those words still stung. As if "his people" were a subspecies, not quite human. He had swallowed his pride (his Quaker faith required that) and joined the club for the sole purpose of keeping himself apprised as to how things were going there. He wanted to stay informed, to have a vote, but he vowed that he would never partake of the club's idle pleasures, and he never did. Bitterness remained. When he saw the club roster, he noticed that Andrew Carnegie was among the members, and the bitterness turned to bile. Carnegie, who'd been so ruthless a competitor, who'd stolen Captain Bill Jones, one of Morrell's best men, from him.

"Don't think of it," he chided himself as, back in his bedroom, he dressed that June, chose a fresh, crisp collar. His head ached, and a brief uncertainty descended on him. For a moment he forgot why he was taking so much care with his appearance, for what he was preparing. He felt a kind of panic setting in at this confusion, a confusion that seemed to afflict him more and more. What day was it, whose house was this, where was it he was going, and when was he supposed to be there?

"Ah, yes," he said, and the confusion, like a curtain, lifted. Books. The library. He took a deep breath, reassured that his memory had returned to him so quickly. If he weren't abstinent, he'd bring champagne and break the bottle on the building's fresh façade, christening the brick prow as they'd christened the new boats at the Fishing and Hunting Club three weeks earlier, at the Launching of the Fleet. He smiled at his reflection in the mirror. "Faith, Daniel," he said to himself wryly. "Trust in the Lord. Forget strong spirits. A prayer will have to do."

In Boston, Grace McIntyre returned earlier than usual from her morning walk. She'd left her house at five—no point in lingering in bed when sleep so thoroughly eluded her, when every thought that came to her mind made her feel like weeping. Better to be up, she'd decided, to be dressed, alone, outside, better to step quickly through the still dark and empty streets, to hear the waking birds coo to one another in the trees in Boston Common. Her husband had not returned home as he had promised to when he'd left the previous evening. Another night spent at his club, she thought. Another night spent elsewhere.

By seven she had returned home, removed her pelerine. She stood at the mirror that hung over the little marble table in the entry hall in order to remove her hat and gloves. The morning sun shone through the narrow sash windows and dusted the encaustic tile floor with light. As she placed her bonnet on the table, she saw that yesterday's newspaper had been carelessly left there. Someone had folded it open to a page of brief advertisements. Homes were for sale, housemaids needed, job opportunities available. "Wanted. Librarian. Johnstown, Pennsylvania." She touched the newsprint with her finger.

Lucille, the maid, had placed Grace's calendar on the tray with the tea and toast that was routinely left in the library for her each morning. Grace glanced at the opened leather volume, the almost blank page—lunch with her father, volunteering at the local hospital. She shook her head when she saw so much empty time. The unaccounted-for hours felt like an accusation. Perhaps this would be a good day to tend to the task she'd set for herself just a few days earlier. She would contact her physician friend, hope that he could help with her problem.

She was thirty-six years old, eight years married. If she had been a boy, she knew, marriage might have been avoided. But she was not a boy, and although she was as intelligent as one, and had, since young adulthood, spoken publicly and well at all her father's rallies, had won footraces and Latin prizes as a child, had made herself into a small girl wonder, he had not forgiven her, would never, for not being a boy. It didn't matter that she'd gone to Radcliffe, trained as a librarian, been hired by the Harvard library right out of college. It didn't matter that she loved her father with a helpless, hopeless craving. What *he* knew, what he was certain of, was that when twins were born to him, the wrong one, the boy, emerged blue and dead. His ambition was to be governor one day. Either that or stand for Congress. Her father reminded her repeatedly that his fate was linked to hers, that it would matter that she marry well. Frederick's father was a judge, politically active, with many influential friends. When the marriage was proposed, Grace could have said no to Frederick, could have asserted her formidable will. She realized that now. But resistance had seemed beyond her. She'd already been required to reject the Harvard job; she knew that while she remained in her father's house, meaningful work would be denied her. Acquiescence had become her habit. Frederick was unknown, a risk, but perhaps a risk worth taking.

Eight hundred people had attended the wedding. Calla lilies filled the vases on the altar. The scent of incense made Grace fear she'd faint, the sight of so unfamiliar a lover standing next to her before the dean of the cathedral made her feel unaccountably frightened and alone. In the receiving line complete strangers, friends of the parents of the couple, kissed her cheek. What great good fortune for them, the guests effused when they were introduced to her. How handsome a couple, what a brilliant political alliance.

Johnstown. Grace wiped toast crumbs from her lip with her damask napkin. Not the great unknown that most runaways would dream of. She would not have to cut off her hair, disguise herself as a boy, stow away on a tall-masted ship, be washed ashore on a deserted island where there were only wild berries and tree bark to eat. As escapes went, this would no doubt be a simple one—a matter of consulting train schedules, packing a bag. She'd leave no letter of apology behind, invent no explanation. It would be cruel, she knew, to leave—father, husband, friends—that way. She'd never been purposely cruel before, but the impulse didn't surprise her. Her life thus far had trained her well for it, she thought—for simple, thoughtless cruelty. She'd leave her hospital volunteer work early, come home in the afternoon, open the atlas on the table where she sat now, sipping tea. She would write to the man, Morrell, who'd placed the ad. It would be a simple inquiry. "Seven thousand books, a large new building," the copy stated. She read pride and a kind of touching boastfulness between the lines. She read freedom.

Daniel Fallon, fifteen years old, waited for his parents in the parlor of their house on Vine Street, in the room set aside for visitors. One lady's chair, the taller, grander one meant for a gentleman, the antimacassars embroidered, starched, placed to protect the fabric chairback from the gentleman's hair pomade. Gentlemen rarely came now. House-proud, Daniel's father had once said about his mother, long ago, pleased by it, by the pleasure she took in the home they made, so pleased that he was happy to give up one entire room of it so Julia could turn it into a parlor. "Striving," Frank had said when Daniel asked him once why he worked so hard. "We are striving," he'd said then, in what now seemed like another century, another lifetime, "to make a better life for ourselves, and you and Caroline." The shoes he wore then, before he became foreman, when he worked on the hot mill floor, were thick, wooden, shoe-shaped platforms, attached to his feet by coarse rope laces that wound up his calves and around his thighs, that left welts in his skin beneath his wool pants, in spite of all their padding. Daniel sometimes watched him dress and undress, took instruction from the watching, preparing himself for the day that he'd work with him.

Now, as he waited for them to come downstairs, Daniel could hear his parents argue. He stepped out onto the small front porch, trying to put some distance between himself and the sound. Daniel hated the way it had become between his parents. Fifteen years old and he'd started to hate his life.

His sister, Caroline, had gone ahead with friends and a picnic lunch. Library Dedication Day, any excuse in Johnstown for a picnic. For a walk in Central Park, with its picket fence and clipped grass and neat trimmed paths designed for strolling. Daniel imagined a brass band playing at the dedication.

"This is your life, Julia. You must take it up again." He heard his father, his voice both cold and at the same time pleading. This is your life, Daniel thought, alone in the unused parlor, wishing he could be anywhere but there.

He went to the kitchen, found a pencil, wrote a note. "Gone ahead," he wrote. Then he slammed the door behind him.

From her hideout in the tangled underbrush, Nora watched as the wagons brought the fish tanks up the steep embankment toward the dam. She'd heard about them from her father but had not realized that today was the day. That explained the fly rods in the clubhouse entry, the tackle boxes ranged along the far end of the long veranda. Her heart went out to the burdened horses, pulling the heavy, heavy load of fish and water up the steep hill. She stood well out of sight of Mr. Unger and his laborers, hidden by the trees. Brambles in her hair, dress sleeves rolled up above the elbow, matted wet grass smearing the edge of her starched petticoat. In one pocket of her dress she had placed two bird's eggs and several feathers; in the other (peach-stained from the fruit's lush ripeness) twelve rocks of startling shapes and hues. In her left fist she held a bunch of wildflowers, names unknown, species she had never seen before, collected to be pressed, catalogued, and identified much later. She had tried to convince herself that her mother, the self-proclaimed flower lover, would be pleased with this small offering, but she knew that she was lying to herself, and for the first time she faced the truth of her mother's disappointment in her. Of her repeated failure to please. She thought that such a certainty about her mother's feelings for her should make her cry, but no tears came. She was twelve years old and was a princess, after all. And she had read somewhere and knew with certainty that a princess never cries.

Commands were shouted: "Stand back, now." Metal rods with hooks on the end of them reached to undo the metal latches on the side of the first tank car. "One, two, three!" The rod wielders worked in synchrony. With a sudden crash, the door swung open, and the water rushed from the tanks into the lake, as fish flew from it, as if mad to escape. From where Nora stood, as they leaped and plummeted toward the lake's smooth surface, they looked as if they were trying to save themselves. They looked as if they were drowning.

They did not drown, of course. They swam and spawned and grew fat through the summer. More than a few were caught and eaten. The club cooks became expert in black bass preparation—cooked over an open fire for woodland authenticity, or sautéed in brown butter in a manner the clubmen considered French. And then, at the end of August, the fish were left to their lake, left to grow sluggish in cooler water, the first season of the South Fork Fishing and Hunting Club having come to an end. The clubhouse emptied, and the fall brought only a few weekend hunters for deer, grouse, and pheasant. Throughout October the sound of gunfire ricocheted from hill to hill. A skeleton staff remained at the club—three cooks, six servers, two men to mind the stables. The boathouse was filled with the sculls and skiffs of summer, locked and secured against the coming snow. A time for men only, for deal-making, cigars, the camaraderie of huntsmen. The giant fireplace in the main room of the clubhouse, with its great carved corbels, dried logs tepeed on the dog grate, the fire itself crackling and blazing, warmed the vast room, and the cold hands and wind-chapped faces gathered around it.

An icy wind brought a storm with it on the first day of winter. By early evening the snow had drifted into mounds that looked like whipped cream. In Philadelphia, New York, and Pittsburgh, a new season had begun in earnest, and each week brought another round of dances, teas, skating parties, concerts. Already Andrew Mellon was having trouble differentiating one party from another. He'd begun to think that all those East End Pittsburgh mansions looked the same. The elaborate plaster ceilings of Italianate design, the paneled wainscoting, the slate fireplaces, the overmantel mirrors. He had changed in Europe; he'd come home looking fit and older.

He arrived a little late to the dance that night; the weather made it difficult for his carriage to get through. He placed his thick vellum invitation on the silver tray extended to him at the door when he arrived, allowed his overcoat to be taken from him, the snow brushed from it. At the threshold of the ballroom he quickly scanned the crowd for Frick and his fiancée, Adelaide Childs. Familiar faces. Since his time in Europe he was less tense than usual at this sort of affair, where so much talk, so much interaction, was required, but still, it was never easy for him to be social.

The center of the room was filled with dancers, while small, tight circles of young people bent on conversation fanned out around candlelit buffet tables on the room's periphery. He knew everyone, but no one well, so he moved quickly in and out of conversations that were already under way, that would require no input, no cleverness from him. In this way he hoped he might go unnoticed. His curse, the thing that made his wish for invisibility so impossible, was that he was startlingly good-looking, mustached, erect, his blue eyes bringing light to his narrow face. He turned from a group to move toward the food when suddenly she was there before him, breasts blossoming from the neckline of her off-the-shoulder gown, hair pulled back from a clear expansive brow. Pretty, dressed in tulle and satin, but in no way extraordinary or arresting. A girl like any other girl.

"Are you vain?" she asked.

Or, he thought at that moment, perhaps not like any other girl. He was unaccustomed to such forthrightness.

"I beg your pardon?" He stood very tall when he was offended. He liked to think that tallness intimidated.

"I asked if you are vain," she repeated, taking no notice of the offense he'd taken. "I ask because I would think you must be tempted to it. Because you are so handsome. Are you tempted?" A waiter passed them with a silver tray of filled champagne glasses. She stopped his progress with a white-gloved hand and took two of the flutes from him.

"Do . . . do I know you?" He was aware of a slight stammer in his voice.

"Laura," she said. "I am Laura. And I can see that I've embarrassed you." And then it was her turn to be embarrassed. "Oh," she said softly. "Oh dear. I was too bold. Please, you must forgive me. My brothers tell me that I am wanting when it comes to charm. They say I have no social graces. Do you think they're right?"

Until she asked that question, she had seemed to Andrew to be utterly oblivious to the rules of etiquette, of social discourse, the need to be oblique, discreet, and shy. But she looked absolutely vulnerable when she asked him about her social graces. He wondered if he had the same stricken look on evenings such as this one, when he felt so out of place and awkward. He imagined that he did.

"Am I graceless?" she asked again.

"No," he said slowly. "No. I wouldn't say graceless."

"What would you say, then? If you were required to, how would you describe me?"

Andrew wished to escape, but he could see that there would be no release from this. No one was coming toward them, no vague acquaintance was moving from the dance floor, no one was waving an invitation to him to join in any of the chatter. To fortify himself, he raised his glass to his lips and drank eagerly from his champagne.

She looked self-conscious when he did not answer her.

"I've asked too much," she offered, the sparkle, the banter in her voice gone. "And I'm keeping you from this lovely party. You must have many friends here. Let me allow you to join your friends."

What made him hold on to the hand she offered in farewell? How did he know that he should keep her?

"No. Don't leave," he said. "As to your question—how would I describe you—I think you are . . . fearless." He smiled, pleased by the unlikely adjective.

"Fearless?" She seemed to be considering: was this a compliment, a tease? Could he be trusted?

"Fearless." She said it again as if measuring the word, translating from a foreign language. Then she smiled. "I would love to be thought of in that way. It is a thing I dream of." She looked up at him. It was only then, her face tilted with the full glow of light on it, that he noticed how pale she was. Hair the color of winter wheat, cheeks unblushing.

"You've dreamed of being fearless?" he said, an ease coming over him. "Something we have in common, then. It is a dream of mine as well." He could have asked her to dance then. He could have gotten them two more flutes of champagne. But he thought that movement, speech, might shatter the accord that had sprung up between them. So he did not speak. But he did gesture to her, turning so that they were more side-by-side than face-to-face, indicating, suggesting, that they might stand together and admire the dancers.

Once he found that she was not put off by silence, that she could bear it, he did, finally, ask her to dance. He offered his arm to her, his elbow bent and ready for the placement of her hand. He had learned to dance in Europe. The acquisition of that skill was one of the things that had given him heart enough to launch into the social season. He was lean, moved easily. He showed her how it was done on the Continent.

SECRET KEEPING

"Withdraw into yourself; the reasonable governing self is by its nature content . . ."

—Marcus Aurelius, *Meditations*, Book VII, Number 28

Daniel didn't know quite what to make of Grace when he first met her. He had always dealt with old Mrs. Hirst in the past when he went to the library and only sought out Grace at Mr. Rose's insistence.

He was sixteen, she'd been in Johnstown less than a year. He'd seen her, of course, someone new to town was always noticed, but familiarity made him go to Mrs. Hirst when he needed help finding something particular. He went to the public library often: he had long since read his way through Rose's books (where he *did*, in fact, find some consolation in the Russians). Now, said Rose, it was time that he go on to further feats of learning with Grace McIntyre as tutor. In conversations with Daniel, Rose referred to the new librarian as learned.

"I have approached her on your behalf," said Rose, who was keen on the boy learning Greek. "Now you must advocate for yourself."

So he had gone to see her, and he was surprised by what seemed like a dismissive response.

"Greek?" she said, with no sign of enthusiasm. "For what do you need Greek?"

He had become used to Rose's encouragement in relation to everything he did. When Grace McIntyre was short with him, he was angry. He deemed her ugly, condescending, not worth his time. She was standing beside a cart of books that she had filled, and she was preparing to wheel it down the length of the room to shelve them. He was taller than she, this "learned" newcomer, and he had a moment of wanting to return in kind what felt like her contempt for him. To walk away from this rejecting woman, from the "who do you think you are?" tone of her voice. But suddenly, inexplicably, she frowned. She brushed her hand quickly across her eyes before she reached out in apology to touch his arm. "Forgive me," she said, looking vulnerable, embarrassed, engulfed by some unnameable tide, he thought. Perhaps the very tide that had brought her here—single, alone, a stranger. Everyone in town knew that about her. Everyone was curious to find out more. "I am too quick to speak sometimes," she ventured.

He felt some urge to reassure her. The same urge that he felt sometimes toward his mother.

"I have books that we can use for this project," she said, "but I haven't yet unpacked them. When I do, we'll try it, shall we?"

Mr. Rose had said that there was much to be learned from Thucydides and Herodotus, Greek chroniclers of war. He said that the stated intention of Herodotus was to preserve from decay the remembrance of what men have done. Looking at Grace McIntyre, Daniel realized she had all that at her disposal. He was still stung and a little angry, not inclined to trust her. But she had books, knowledge he wanted. He could read a poor translation from the Greek or be given access to the original.

"We will become historians together," she said.

The Russians with Rose, the Greeks with Miss McIntyre. Soon she was insisting that he call her Grace.

On his own he read works of more contemporary writers, Henry James and Stendahl's *The Charterhouse of Parma*. Grace told him that memorization was good exercise and made for an agile mind, and so he allowed her to lead him to poetry. Keats and Tennyson, and the more current Matthew Arnold.

> *But often, in the world's most crowded street,*
> *But often, in the din of strife,*
> *There rises an unspeakable desire*
> *After the knowledge of our buried life;*

A thirst to spend our fire and restless force
In tracking out our true, original course;
A longing to inquire
Into the mystery of this heart which beats
So wild, so deep in us—to know
Whence our lives come, and where they go.

Nora had always wished to have a grandmother. It had begun when she was a small child as a kind of vague, impressionistic fantasy—graying hair, skin so delicate that the briefest touch of cold wind rouged and chafed it. Small suede-slippered feet. Two mother-of-pearl bracelets. A trembling, glinting laugh. Over time, on Nora's walks to school and back, she shaped this grandmama, she dressed and groomed her, she blessed her with a life. She saw her in a snow-flecked gray Toulouse cloak, she gave her brooches shaped like small exotic animals; she dreamed of a jungle bird for her, a parrot, tame enough to leave his ornate cage and to sit astride the arm that she curved toward him. A husband? Yes, but one long gone, lost in war, perhaps, or disappeared at sea while on a voyage of exploration. Grandmother had admirers, of course, many of them, who joined her on Wednesday evenings at the salon she held at her house. She was beautiful, beloved; she refused marriage proposals as frequently as her friends rejected dinner invitations. She loved her independence, enjoyed the variety that such independence brought her.

The children of this grandmother, Nora's father among them, loved but did not completely understand her. But her grandchildren—many of them, cousins for Nora, children who looked and thought and saw the world as she did, who shared ancestors and Sunday suppers, aunts and uncles, a many-branched and lushly blooming family tree—worshipped Grandmère; they adored her for the eccentricities that were such a puzzle to their parents. And among these cousins, Nora was Grandmother's favorite. In this contrived world, in the world that existed only in the span of time it took Nora to walk to and return from school, Nora was adored.

In her actual life, Nora did not really know who she was, what her place was in the world. In her family no records seemed to be kept, there were no Bibles, no photographs, no smiles with which to compare her own smile. Questions went unanswered. She sensed, she feared, that shame was part of the secrecy, and wondered what cause there was for it.

So much curiosity, so utterly unsatisfied. In school she found a channel for it. In subject after subject, the unknown presented itself, waiting to be studied, to reveal its secrets, if one was only willing to spend time unearthing them. The secrets of the French vernacular, the algebraic equation, the movements of the fluctuating stars. Understanding was possible, available to her finally, within her grasp. She found that she was undisciplined in the beginning, unable to focus with so much to choose from. Her curiosity about the world, the other, her exploration of it became an antidote for her ignorance about her immediate, familial world. Her curiosity became her raison d'être. She fashioned a self from her necessity to *know*. And in her diaries she recorded the observations and knowledge that she accumulated. When the time came one day, when she was asked to share her knowledge with children, or nephews, or a husband, or the entire world, she would reveal herself completely. There would be no mysteries.

"And is it true? Was she so beautiful?"

Spring 1883. Forsythia were budding in yellow profusion, cut and artfully arranged by Evelyn for the round center table in the entry hall, and it was the first thing Nora saw as she descended the stairs of her Pittsburgh home for dinner. And the first thing she heard: her mother's voice, raising the question of beauty. James and Evelyn were already at the dining table waiting for her. Nora paused on the staircase. The runner itself was not Persian, not Chinese, not in any way as fine as the runners on the stairs in other East End houses, but serviceable, Nora had discovered years earlier, thick enough to mute her footsteps, to make her parents unaware of her approach. A furtiveness had developed in her. A sense that the only way to know her parents was by indirection, intuition, fantasy. Snatches of conversation overheard, looks passed between them when they thought she wouldn't notice. She regularly and secretly perused the card holder in the entry hall, the collection of engraved calling cards accumulated there enabling her to ascertain who had come calling and, sometimes, more important as far as the mysteries of life revealed themselves, who had not. Nora, fourteen, stood at the foot of the stairs, head cocked toward the dining room, fingertip tracing the ornate pattern of a turned-oak baluster.

"Yes. Apparently so. Quite beautiful. But tuberculosis . . ." Nora imagined her father shaking his head. "It is so withering. So wasting. By the end she must have been quite . . . altered." His voice was rich with sympathy, with feeling.

"It seems odd for Andrew Mellon to have betrothed himself to a girl who was so ill, to have been so devoted to someone like that. Really, James, it's quite out of character for the Mellon men. The judge lacks sympathy, and has made it clear, I understand, just how little use he has for women. Could Andrew be so very different?" Her mother had a way of taking the measure of a man, pronouncing judgment on his character. She always had an air of certainty about what a man, or woman, was or was not made of.

"Well, love . . ." Nora imagined her father shrugging in a way that suggested how unknowable the world was, how unexpected the power of strong feelings. "It's been known to alter men. I've heard that throughout her illness, during the entire year, he saw her every day. That he read poetry aloud. That he sang to her to soothe her."

"Sang? Somehow I doubt that, James."

Nora, on the staircase, gathered her skirt, careful to shush the crunch of petticoats as they scratched against each other. She sat on the last step, let her head rest against the newel post. She had seen young Andrew Mellon many times at church, and once, last summer, at the fishing and hunting club at dinner. She remembered him as being spindle-thin, with deep-set, hooded eyes. An unlikely little mustache, an affectation, Nora had thought at the time, some effort to look older than he was, to look old enough to be a banker. He had looked too young, certainly in Nora's estimation, to even think of getting married. She wondered if perhaps he'd been robust once and had only grown frail as his fiancée had. Maybe in a kind of exquisite romantic sympathy he'd become as consumed by her as she was by disease. Nora imagined him sitting carefully on the edge of the bed of his beloved, so as not to disturb her, his head bent toward her, his lips close to her ear. His singing voice, reedy and wavering.

In the gloaming, oh, my darling! When the lights are soft and low . . . The tune played in her head. It was the song that everyone had loved so much last summer.

Only recently had she let herself think much of love, only lately had the possibility of it formed clearly in her consciousness. The monthly bleeding, the onslaught of womanhood the year before, had brought strange new feelings with it. Prior to it she had convinced herself that she'd resist the pull of love and marriage, that she'd become a female Charles Darwin, a naturalist, an explorer, a rare woman devoted to her work. Now, imagining young Andrew Mellon, she wondered, fleetingly, if she could ever inspire such passion, such devotion from a lover. Her cheeks flushed. She pressed her palms to them to take the heat away.

Will you think of me and love me As you did once long ago?

"We should go to the funeral," Evelyn said.

"Or allow a private man his private grief. We hardly know him, my dear."

"There are church and South Fork connections. And for you, James, business oncs as well."

"A discreet note?" Nora's father ventured, hoping to deflect her, hoping that they would not have to discuss this far into the night. Discuss and argue, until finally, typically, he gave in, let her have her way.

Nora moved then, with a bit more noise than was required, forewarning them of her arrival, smiling as she entered, sliding the pocket doors closed behind her.

"Nor-a." A shift in tone. Her father always said her name as if he loved it. The consonants and syllables, the *a* rising away at the end of it. As she always did, she hurried to his side to greet him. A kiss for his cheek, the anachronistic curtsey that her mother still required. Her father's teasing, chivalrous kissing of her hand.

"And how was your day, dear one?" he asked as she slid into her chair, obviously happy to be diverted by her, his only child, his charming young distraction. He cared for her elaborately, but carefully, knowing, as he did, how much is risked with too much loving. Because of that he was demonstrative in a hundred superficial ways. She was praised for her decorum at the table, applauded for her forced and amateurish efforts at piano. He took unseemly pride in her when she avoided the colds that were so common in winter, as if good health were an art, a thing perfectible if practiced. She was quick to learn new poems and recite them, to struggle through the intricacies of Bach on the piano, because Bach was James's favorite. He knew that now, at dinner, with just a little prompting, she would launch into a detailed accounting of her complex, internecine social life at school. But he kept himself from the depth of her. To go deeply into her was to invite her curiosity and queries, would require him to obfuscate and alter and dissemble in order to keep who he was hidden from her.

"Where *did* you grow up?" she'd asked two summers earlier, during their first visit to the club. James had said he would accompany her down to the boathouse, so she could see firsthand the sailing boats tied at their moorings. James had made vague promises to Nora about the time they would spend together at the lake. There had been talk of horseback riding, sailing. But he had brought work to do, contracts and several wills, and the days had slid by as summer days have a way of doing, until he realized that the end of their two weeks was upon them and he had disappointed her. Disappointment etched her sober face. So he made plans with her at breakfast on their second-to-last day there. They would meet at ten and walk together down the boardwalk and then the footpath to the boat-house; they'd introduce themselves to the two boating instructors.

"Perhaps they will suggest books or sailing manuals that we could read together over the winter months in preparation for next season," he had said, the pancakes on his plate growing cold as he grew more and more expansive with the thought of a winter's worth of evenings spent in study-ing together, a winter's worth of father-child attachment. "We will get lengths of rope and practice tying knots," he had said.

And she had grown expansive, too, so eager for his company, so will-ing to let hope triumph over experience. She had been like that, ready to forget his past neglect, his absences; ready to take his hand, to trust him. So off they had gone, toward the sparkling lake, toward the lake breeze wrinkling the water. Her hand in his; the easy way he swung it as they walked thrilled her. They would learn to sail next summer. Alone in a sail-ing skiff, she'd come to know him. Innocence and ignorance made her think she could begin the process even then, while they were walking. "Where did you grow up?" she had asked.

"Curiosity killed a cat," he teased, as if amused, patting at her hand, his way of ending conversation. There, there, the pat said. Enough of that.

"Was it here in Pennsylvania?" Who knew what had possessed her that day, what had made her think her questioning would yield answers?

"Did you fight in the war?" she'd persisted.

"What is this, Nora? You know all you need to know—that I'm orphaned, that you and your mother are my family now. The war, those times are far behind us, thank God. I'd rather forget them."

What was it that first summer that made her want to know so much? Made her flush with curiosity?

She had an easy grace, an unconscious generosity that flourished in spite of all Evelyn's efforts to subdue her. She was brown from two weeks of summer sun, her eyes were patient, penetrating, fixed on him. She was eagerness personified. Words rushed from her. She said she had been studying the War between the States at school.

"You were too young, I imagine, but you must have wished you could fight." She gripped his hand more tightly as if to emphasize the urgency she felt. It was as though she'd been waiting to have this talk with him, waiting for the chance to find out everything. He and Evelyn had tried to raise her to be polite and nonintrusive, and they thought they had succeeded, but there she was, full of twelve years of unanswered questions. He felt bombarded by them. "Miss Alfry says that everyone remembers where they were when John Booth shot the President. Where were you, Father? Did you cry when you heard the news?"

"Nora."

There was no lilt to the sound of her name when he said it then. No loving.

"I will not be questioned this way." His voice was a mixture of weariness and anger. "Do not interrogate me. The war is *over*, I was left *alone*, and I prefer not to speak about it. It is forward and unkind of you to bring this up when you know how I feel. I am ashamed of you for your insensitivity."

Ashamed. The word hung in the air between them. Had he been watching her instead of staring ahead, he would have seen her spine stiffen, her skin blotch as the blood rose to her face.

It was a time when children were often treated thus. Silenced swiftly by parental dictate, parental will. A different child might have recovered quickly from it. But for Nora it cemented the way it was between them, it solidified what she thought of as their surface life, it closed off access to the deep elaborate underground where the real child, Nora, lived, making their father-daughter bond one composed almost entirely of ritual. The kissing of the hand, the curtsey. And over the years the handing of his glasses to her, for her to buff and polish, before she gave them back to him. Gestures, tokens, affection barely hinted at. Hurts avoided scrupulously or, if inflicted, carefully ignored.

But that was then, and this was the spring of 1883. In the dining room Nora's mother moved her toe to the buzzer skillfully imbedded in the hardwood floor, summoning Eliza from the kitchen. Evelyn reached for her napkin and nodded to Nora that hers, too, could be unfurled.

"Perhaps, after a proper amount of time has passed, we could have a little dinner," Evelyn said with the youthful eagerness that came to her voice whenever she thought of parties. "Old friends, a few of the younger people, including Andrew Mellon." When she saw James about to object, she quickly added, "He wasn't married to her, after all. There won't really be an official mourning."

And so her parents' talk turned to the pros and cons of having the proposed dinner. And Nora's thoughts turned back to what she'd heard while on the stairs. Again the song that had been so popular last summer played in her head.

Tho' I passed away in silence, Left you lonely, set you free . . .

In the song the lovers are compelled to part. One leaves, hopes to be remembered lovingly. Nora found herself thinking of Andrew Mellon's young fiancée.

It was best to leave you thus, dear, Best for you and best for me.

Nora wished she knew her name. As she took a spoonful of the peas from the bowl that Eliza held at her elbow, as she watched her father rise to begin carving the meat, she tried to picture the young lover. She imagined a profusion of fair hair, thin little bird wrists, freckles perhaps, yes freckles on her nose. Nora imagined the early hope she must have had when she first fell ill, that, with rest, she would recover. How that hope must have been gradually replaced by the relinquishment of every dream—dances, walks in moonlight, the chaste kisses of courtship, marriage to her slender lover. Perhaps she'd tried to release Andrew from the promises he'd made to her, and he'd said never, and kissed her, openmouthed and with surprising ardor, flaunting his love, defying contagion. Nora could almost see her weeping once he had left that night and she was alone, weeping quietly and with relief because he'd refused to be set free. Nora wanted to believe that in the final days her chest cleared slightly, her fever lifted. That she'd gotten, briefly, strong enough to be of some small comfort to him, well enough to return his kisses, to trace with her fingertips the orbits of his dark, troubled eyes. That she'd had a chance to let him know how much she loved him.

Nora. Fourteen years old. Thinking of love's large implications. Crossing her ankles, eating her peas.

———

"Beloved Child." It was what was written on the marker at Laura's grave. And it was that sentiment that had made her who she was, Andrew Mellon discovered in the months after he'd met her. Her energy, her enthusiasms captured him. She took him birding, to a lecture about parasites, to a tree-planting in honor of a dead friend, to tea with her three brothers. She had lived a childhood softened by affection, an adored only daughter whose parents, after a brief early effort at trying to mold her, to make her fit into the requirement of the times, relented to the urgent press of her true nature. She was impulsive, contradictory. Easily caught up in new ideas. She attended a church of a different denomination every Sunday in search of a theory of God that suited her. She distributed pamphlets at street corners denouncing "yellow dog" contracts offered to the steel workers at the Homestead Mill. She had literary aspirations, penned feuilletons and sent them to magazines in full expectation of having them published. Full of high purpose, she could also be frivolous and extravagant, buying a dress with soutache trimming for herself on one day, giving it to a clothing drive the next. She was unlike her brothers, unlike her poised, articulate, calm mother. She was as original as he had imagined her to be when they first met.

She and Andrew went sledding at midnight on New Year's Eve. He gave her two lilac bushes to celebrate the first mild day of spring. That summer, he took her to South Fork for the opening of the club's second season and rowed her to the lake's unfathomable center, her hand trailing in the water, her head resting against his chest, the sound of his heart, the rhythm of the dipping oars lulling her into a brief, light slumber. They had not yet recognized it as a symptom, the way she tired so easily. They had told themselves that summer brings that on sometimes, or perhaps his wooing, the pressing of his suit had fatigued her. She joked, when she accepted him in the fall, that she had agreed to marriage in self-defense. That his daily visits, his attendance, had convinced her they would have to live together; that to rest, she'd have to marry him.

The diagnosis of tuberculosis came on the eve of Halloween. Everyone but Andrew agreed that the wedding would have to be postponed. Proposals were made for healing trips for Laura, who would be accompanied by her mother—to Italy or the French Riviera. Greece was briefly considered. Umbria finally chosen, the climate deemed dry and warm enough to be restorative. Laura's father would go initially in order to get his wife and daughter settled. It was decided that they would leave right after Thanksgiving, and that Andrew would come for a long visit in March. No one imagined how quickly she'd become too unwell for travel.

The world shrank under the heavy press of illness. The short walks she was permitted when the winter thaw came soon proved to be too difficult for her. She was easily made breathless, and it was decided that she should conserve herself by staying in the house. By the end of February 1883, dressing had become a labor, but one she struggled through because she wanted so much to see him, and feared that, even in her forward-thinking family, she would not be permitted to be alone with her fiancé unless she was properly attired and in the parlor. She underestimated them in this, and in mid-March, when almost constant bed rest became necessary, her parents moved a sofa, a chair, a small French writing table into her room, so that Andrew and she would have a place of privacy, where they could be alone together, where they could move together precisely and inevitably through her illness. The short walks by then were from one end of her room to the other; she leaned heavily on Andrew's arm. Weight fell from her in spite of all her mother's culinary efforts. She made Laura the food of childhood—custards, potatoes mashed with butter and heavy cream—then watched her devour it, but no amount of food could fortify her. The bones became prominent beneath her fragile skin; her long limbs, the source of so much pleasure to her, which had once been part of her beauty, seemed grotesque. She felt ape-like, scraped, deformed.

"I feel seared," she said to Andrew. "I feel as if my skin is burning."

The singing began toward the end of her ordeal. Laura had been resting with her eyes closed. The tiny threads of blue veins on her white lids trembled. She was sleeping so much by then, he was spending so much of his time watching her sleep, that he had come to notice the smallest things about her—the mole on her wrist, the slash of a scar on her impeccably smooth forehead, vestige of a childhood fall.

Her cheeks had a remarkable flush to them that day, caused, he knew, by fever, but it made her look almost robust to Andrew, like someone who loved the out-of-doors, who'd just come in from an afternoon of too much sun.

"Will you do something for me?" Her voice came from deep within her, resonant, hoarse, from a throat made raw by months of coughing.

"Anything." It had become his answer to all she asked of him.

Laura opened her eyes and smiled. "I woke up in the night thinking of all the things we've done together. I dreamed I heard your voice, the voice you use while reading to me. And it occurred to me—don't laugh, promise that you won't think it's foolish—but it occurred to me that I've never heard you sing. Would you do that? Would you sing for me?"

He smoothed the covers over her legs. Of all the things he would miss about her he knew he would miss this most—her ability to surprise him. To call forth from him capacities he never knew he had.

But sing? What did he know? A hymn? He rarely went to church. In his parents' home there had been no lullabies, none of the singsong games of childhood.

She saw him hesitate, and she shook her head forcefully. "Don't be cautious now. Remember, we have banished caution. It doesn't matter what you sing. Just sing to me."

He'd been to the Paris Opéra on his European tour and read in the program that the diaphragm must somehow be engaged, that breathing mattered, that any halfheartedness would work against him. So he concentrated with a seriousness that was complete. Breathe in, breathe out, then in again. He felt the tremor in his throat, the push of exhaled air before he actually heard the sound of his voice. It was rich and full-throated, a dark deep baritone. And the song he sang: "Silent night, holy night." Even he knew Christmas carols.

He had not been aware until he'd met her how small and mean his life had been, without adornment or refinement. He had been raised by aphorism and admonishment.

"Make no friends until you know their private moral character."

Never serve your country in the army. "Those who are able to pay for substitutes do so," Judge Mellon wrote. "There are plenty of other lives less valuable."

Eat meat, be diligent and shrewd. Avoid the company of woman, avoid light literature. The former "unfits a man for business," and the latter "unhinges the mind."

With Laura he had forgotten all those warnings. With her he had become, briefly, a slate swept clean.

"Sle-ep in heavenly peace," he sang. "Sle-ep in heavenly peace."

———

Soon singing was all she wanted.

"Beautiful Dreamer," "I'll Take You Home Again, Kathleen," "In the Gloaming." He learned song after song. Then lost them. They left him when she did, so swiftly, so utterly, that it was as if they had been excised.

He was twenty-eight when she died, wealthy in his own right, judged to be the son most like him by his father. He had innate gifts for finance, although not the passion, at least not while Laura was alive. But once she died, he turned himself totally to business—with his father, with his brother Richard, and with Frick, his best, his only friend.

For Andrew Mellon, the South Fork Fishing and Hunting Club was a business arrangement. During the years of the club's existence, when he went there he went alone, and ate alone in the clubhouse dining room, or occasionally shared a table with Frick and Adelaide. He was not interested in the other members, to his mind they were acquaintances, colleagues, nothing more. He felt no need to know them. And the incuriosity that developed during that time marked the beginning of a life that would be invested in not knowing—if a worker he employed was starving, if the iron and coal police he hired were armed with machine guns, if an earth dam of which he was part owner was sound or flawed. He was grieving in the years that the South Fork Fishing and Hunting Club existed, he was out of his mind with grief. But even had he not been, it is unlikely that his character would have led him to be diligent in affairs that did not concern him. His people were at the clubhouse. He had no interest in imagining who lived below.

In June 1883, at the South Fork Fishing and Hunting Club, workmen finished painting the last of the latticework of the last of the sixteen cottages. The feverish sense of building and expansion that had so colored the first two springs and falls and summers—the smell of new wood, the relentless buzz and rasp of sawing—was coming to an end. What had begun as a single clubhouse had been transformed into a colony, with each cottage some slight variation of the others.

The cottages were private homes, owned by men like Mr. Moorhead, Mr. Knox, financiers, lawyers, industrialists. The Moorhead house was Queen Anne–style, seventeen rooms, a steeply pitched roof, an intricately constructed turret, third-floor windows hidden in deep gables, draped in almost transparent summer sheers. Some cottages were Stick-Style, with a two-tier porch design; for others no expense was spared when it came to decorative elaboration. Novelty siding had been brought from Germany, vertical and horizontal treillage built, textures meant to resemble a shoji screen were handwrought, hand-surfaced, fashioned painstakingly by skilled laborers brought from far away. Clapboard-sided, gable-roofed. The porches overlooked the waterfront, as did the balconies above, the second-story bays. A few of the cottages even had widow's walks at the crest of the roofs' steep peaks, as if the cottages themselves were about to pull away from their stone foundations, break the boardwalk, slip down the narrow strip of grass, and set sail across the water. So beautiful. The boathouse fit snugly at the shore's edge. The stables were cloistered in the woods. Each house was built on a cut-stone foundation, for permanence, a legacy for children, maybe even grandchildren, one day. Romances were meant to blossom in this effulgent setting. The boys could wear flannel shirts and crush hats for hunting and hiking, the girls wore riding costumes, simple sun hats, dresses made of lawn. Here the children of the best families rode and sailed together. On rowboats, at night, songs were sung and banjos played.

That summer, gardeners knelt in the flower beds that skirted the clubhouse's wide veranda, that trailed along the boardwalk's edge, so many kneeling men in their dark shirts and dark wool trousers that they looked, from a distance, like mendicants, like monks. With hands and hoes they turned the soil, cleared weeds and the debris of winter, to make way for the flats of pansies arrayed in rings around them. An edge of crisscrossed wood was added just beneath the rafters on the clubhouse porch, a place from which, at the height of the summer season, magic lanterns could be strung. The wide doors of the boathouse were opened, the stables filled with spring-fresh hay.

Daniel Fallon, seventeen, stood on a wooded rise just beyond the cottage that lay farthest from the dam, bit into the apple that he'd brought, spent a long time watching.

He had originally started coming here because he liked the fishing, or so he'd told himself. But there was fishing in dozens of streams that were a great deal closer, that didn't require a horse and whole day's expedition just for the sake of some fish to fry for supper. No, it was not the fishing that drew him. He'd come repeatedly these last three summers because it was a place where he was not allowed. Somewhere, in an office or a conference room, or perhaps in the very clubhouse that sprawled so grandly below him, rules were composed, inscribed, and agreed to by a group of men, designed to keep him out. And he denied their right to do it. Every time he crossed the invisible border onto club property, each time he defaced with his knife, or a stick, or a jagged edge of rock a NO TRESPASSING sign, he was resisting the forces that would hold him back, that would tell him what he could not have.

But in another sense he came to the lake for the same reason that the clubmen came—in order to get away. He took another bite of his apple, and the spray of juice across his chin felt sweet and good.

He had thought that there would be only workmen on the grounds just after Memorial Day, just prior to the gala season opening, so the appearance of a young girl standing on the clubhouse steps surprised him. He tended to stay hidden in the woods once the members had arrived; he liked the sense of secrecy, evasion. He felt an odd lack of curiosity about the members of the club. He didn't wonder what they wore, he didn't want to see them. But there one was, or the child of one, a girl just shy of womanhood. Hair plaited in a thick braid down her back, her hand at rest on the railing. He was struck by how stiffly she stood, as if her spine were a stick, without flexibility. He had imagined that money made for easiness. Perhaps not, he thought, watching her, she who for all the world looked like a figure from a painting in a dank New England attic, the mute mad wife of a sailor lost at sea. Standing, looking out over the water. Shouldn't someone so young have been running on the boardwalk, up the wooden steps that terraced the hilly lakeside, that joined one flat stretch of boardwalk to another? Why wasn't she sitting on the dock's edge, shivering as she dipped her bare feet into the icy water?

Daniel heard the sound of a man's voice, deep, but the words were indecipherable from where Daniel stood, nothing more than a wash of sound. Then the main door to the clubhouse opened, the man appeared and walked the several steps across the porch to stand on the veranda steps beside her. There was enough of a resemblance to suggest father and daughter, and Daniel imagined a quick trip to the lake, inspired by the father's need to tend to some club business. The father's lips moved, but whatever he was saying was meant for her and her alone. He leaned toward her with a warm familiarity and laughed, let his forehead touch hers. Then, as he continued speaking, he removed his glasses and held them at arm's length, out beyond the porch shade toward the light, as if to check for smudge or a fleck of dirt, or some flaw in the lens that might distort his vision. She moved too, then, and raised her arm so that it extended beside his, as if in imitation of him, and to Daniel it looked as though they were actors in a staged performance, following directions, gesturing together and on cue. But then he saw that she had reached to take her father's glasses from him, to wipe them with a section of her skirt. She made small buffing circles, held the lens to the light to check it, buffed again. This had the feel of ritual to it, and there was something achingly precise in the performance of it. The father smiled when the glasses were returned to him. Touched the ribbon that had come untied at the bottom of her braid.

A caterpillar fuzzed its way along the trunk of the tree that Daniel stood beneath. Leaves above him rustled as a nesting bird slipped through them. He saw her speak. The father's head turned—no, he seemed to be saying. But in their conversation all the affect, all the feeling seemed to come from him. He gestured to one of the gardeners to a spot he'd left bereft of flowers, stroked his trim beard, sat on the top step, leaned against a porch-supporting column. Something about him seemed to require movement, talk; he seemed unable to be still. It was as if he were the child and she the calm unruffled parent.

The sun was veering high into the sky. Daniel knew he'd lost the best part of the day for fishing. Still, something made it hard for him to leave, to throw his apple core into the underbrush, to retrieve the horse he'd left tied to a tree on the hill behind him. Somehow he'd thought that the summer people would look different, would be of another species. That they of the private club, the sailing boats, the miter-folded napkin dinners would wear their pride like a breastplate, their wealth like a cape. But the girl with the braid, except for her stiff dignity, could have been any one of the girls he knew, although the girls he knew seemed much more of-their-time, their hair beribboned and bedecked, intended to look womanly and chic, coiled into a bun, with just a fringe of curls left free to frame the face. This girl seemed strangely unmarked, unaware of fad or fashion, someone caught outside time, adrift in an unfamiliar universe. Daniel, who had begun to think of college at the urging of his father, wondered if this is what the girls in Philadelphia would be like, if they would seem so illusory and still.

Only time would tell.

A workman emerged from the boathouse, a cloth parcel tucked beneath his arm. And at the dock's edge, where a tall pole stood, imbedded in a lake-edge mix of earth and muddy water, he raised the flag, and the wind unfurled it. On the clubhouse porch steps the father rose to his feet and angled a stiff hand toward his forehead. It was a gesture Daniel had seen his father make a thousand times, a soldier's salute, the mark of a man who'd been in battle. Red, white, and blue. Catching the wind. Beautiful, really, as it curled on itself, then spread its colors as if to cast them on the canvas of the high blue sky. It made Daniel think of the buntings hanging from the windows on the Memorial Day parade route through Johnstown every year. The colors of equality and freedom, flying in the air above a closely guarded, private lake.

At the South Fork Fishing and Hunting Club that August the Talbots' stay passed quickly, and after two weeks Nora's summer in paradise was coming to a close. Nora and her family were to depart the following day, and she spent the early morning saying goodbye to the lake. She walked through the woods. Fallen twigs cracked beneath her hard-soled boots, her bark-brown skirt swished over the forest floor, the sturdy fabric resisting the snagging efforts of bramble and thorny underbrush. Besides, the fabric of the skirt was already nipped and pulled and patched; it was her hiking gear. It was a skirt meant to be of service in the country, and when she took it home each year at the end of the summer season (to wash it by hand, herself, she wouldn't let Eliza or her mother touch it), when in her room she took a needle and thread to make post-season repairs to it, she had the pleasure of finding in the drooping threadbare hem an accumulation of organic remnants of the summer—pine needles and torn blades of grass, clay-colored dirt, and tiny pebbles. In her Pittsburgh room, as she sat on the edge of her bed, head bent toward her mending, she could gather the remains of summer in her hand, crush the grass against her palm, smell it, and be lakeside in the hot sun, sitting on the shore at Sheep's Head Point again.

Later, as she stood in her South Fork room at her washbasin, the one into which her father had dropped a penny two years earlier, she used a small hand brush to work the dirt loose from beneath her ragged nails. Her mother would be checking. She would treat her daughter as she always did, as if she were twelve years old, not fourteen. As if her hair, her nails, her shoes required constant monitoring. More than once she had checked Nora's teeth. "As if I were a horse," Nora had complained one evening to her father. Allowing herself a small burst of anger, some brief rising up of youthful independence that had in the past expressed itself in bouts of heaved unhappy sighs, and moodiness, pursed lips, pouting. But in the last year all such self-indulgence on her part had come to seem unduly burden-some, more than her already burdened father could be asked to manage. No more of this complaining, Nora, his eyes seemed to say as he folded his paper, trying to be attentive, trying to act as if he was listening to her.

"Like a horse," she'd said just a week ago about the inspection of her teeth. James was on the clubhouse porch, creaking back and forth in a wicker rocker. A stack of legal papers sat on a table just beside him, his glasses smudged because he handled them so much, took them off and on, chewed absentmindedly on the c-shaped earpiece whenever a problem vexed him, whenever he was thinking. On the porch that day she'd extended her hand to him, the way she always did, took the glasses from him. She looked right and left to be sure one of her mother's friends was nowhere near, then used her skirt to clean them.

"She does these things because she wants you to look beautiful," he said as he nodded thanks and took the glasses from her. "She fears that you're a little careless about such things sometimes." He drummed his fin-gers on his stack of papers. "She checks the way you look, Nora, because she loves you." And to himself he said, I've told you this a hundred times. Why, I wonder, do I always have to tell you?

There was a time when he did not bring work with him when they came to the mountains for the summer. A time he'd spent more than just a fraction of their two-week vacation fishing, picnicking, and hunting. But he heard a rumor that his name was going to be raised again, that he was going to be made partner, and he wanted to impress the other partners with his diligence and industry. He wanted, as he told Evelyn when she complained about it, to "put his best foot forward." He began to bring briefs and files, lead pencils worn to nubs by note-taking and writing. Only after drinks and dinner did the working stop, when the sun had set and the sunlit day had ended. Then he would join the other guests in the lounge, or on the porch, where families gathered, where one of the young men sat on the steps and played harmonica. On those nights, along the whole long clubhouse porch, the wicker rockers stopped. Sometimes there was even a furtive handholding among the married couples. Courtships in other places were recalled. *Drink to me only with thine eyes* . . . Sometimes there was singing. From her place, sitting on the steps among the men and women, although she could not see him, Nora imagined her father's face relaxed and smiling. She thought she heard his tenor voice blend with the others.

For the first two years that they were members of the club, Nora had wanted her father to sail with her. She wanted to feel the hull tip up out of the water, to keep the sail full; she wanted a callus on her hand from managing the tiller. The first summer they'd come to South Fork he'd promised her. With an uncharacteristic defiance in the face of Evelyn's purse-lipped disapproval, he'd told his wife that she shouldn't worry so about decorum. That it didn't matter. Decorum, he'd told Evelyn, could wait a year or two. Then suddenly and without apparent reason or explanation, he could see the wisdom of it. Of having Nora sit back. Of encouraging her to wait until some good-looking boy would want to take her. Just as he could make a case for teeth inspection. But what Nora gleaned from conversations with him, what she saw in the fingers drumming, drumming, drumming on his papers as he spoke, was an eagerness to get back to work, eagerness for peace between "his girls," for Evelyn to be content, for Nora to be less obstinate, more pliant.

When he saw her on the edges of what club members called "the young crowd," instead of in the center of it, when he saw her coming toward the clubhouse from a wooded path alone, instead of walking on the boardwalk toward the boathouse with the Scaife or Clarke boy, or one of the others, he wished she understood how hard he'd worked to see to it that she "belonged." He had shed his Southern ways and Southern accent, found a woman of ambition who would require ambition from him, studied law although he hated it, learned to keep opinions to himself if such opinions were not shared by those around him, how to negotiate and deal, and smoke cigars and drink with men who would lie to him without thinking twice about it. He had done everything he knew to assure stability. And on the porch that day he wished she could see that. He wished she knew how many sacrifices he had made. And even though he felt petty and unworthy when the thought occurred to him, he wished she could be grateful.

Back in her room, Nora's ring, the one her father had given her on her tenth birthday, which she now wore on her little finger, pinged against the flowered basin. She shook the soapy water from her hands. Knuckles and cuticles scrubbed pink, but spotless.

"No-o-ra." Evelyn knocked at her door, but only for formality. She didn't wait to be invited in to enter.

"Yes, Mother?" Nora folded her hand towel carefully, used dampness from her wrist to smooth a wandering hair back from her forehead. She had failed thus far in her efforts at pliancy, but she had learned how to pass inspection.

Evelyn opened a watch that hung from a chain around her neck. Tapped it lightly with one smooth-tipped nail. Tilted her head to look out the window toward the water. "Five minutes, Nora. Hurry on, now. Really." She took Nora's straw sun hat from the bedstead where she'd hung it. "Go along," she said, frowning impatiently. "Or the boat will leave without you."

The kitchen help had packed hampers with chicken and deviled eggs, and Mason jars of lemonade, each lid tied decoratively with grosgrain ribbon. Canoes had been hoisted off wooden racks and placed in the water, but several of the party would take sailing skiffs and use the summer wind to navigate the lake. Lewis Clarke had designed and built a steamboat that chugged and coughed and split the air with its shrill whistle, but that was out of commission. At the dock Nora hesitated. Couples were forming, negotiations were under way for who would get to share whose blanket. She would rather stay behind; she'd found a clearing with rare flowers in the woods and she would have liked to spend the time exploring. But she knew her mother, only half hidden by blowing curtains, was standing in her upstairs window watching. She could feel her eyes on her, they pressed like palms on her back, requiring her to move forward. Elizabeth, who didn't like the boy she had been left to sit with, rushed forth to take her hand, to insist that Nora join them in their boat and on their blanket. Nora gathered her dress up, let her hand be taken, let herself be guided as she stepped from boardwalk to canoe. All around her on the sun-glazed water there was high, bright laughter. By summer's end, matches would have been made. In the fall her parents would go to betrothal dinners, there would be a dance at Christmas at the home of Mr. Frick or Mr. Knox. The members of the club would enjoy these off-season reunions.

You see, they'd say to one another, watching the lovers dance together, how wise we were to find a place where we could summer.

Evelyn Talbot, née Morgan, had been an adolescent during the war. Affairs of state were of little interest to her. Hers was a family of the merchant class, or so her father called it, people who had worked for, not inherited, their money, which suited him. He was a clothier who owned a store, and because he served his clientele so well (he was the premier clothier in the city), it was assumed he had some larger connection to his important patrons. In the modest city of Wilmington, he and his wife and young daughter were invited to Christmas parties and summer picnics, and other inclusive functions in the best and largest homes. Their own house was small but "charming," the furniture was tasteful and expensive, and what her father referred to as modern, which meant a little avant-garde. Chaise longues where there should have been divans, heavy velvet curtains when flowered silk would have been more fitting, less theatrical. Evelyn had inherited her father's eye for line and form and understatement, and because of that, even as a young child she realized with wise relief that it was fortunate that her mother preferred going to other houses rather than having people in theirs.

When Evelyn was fourteen, long after the three of them assumed that their family was complete, her mother revealed that she was pregnant, late in her marriage and, as these things went, relatively late in her life. She was forty. What became clear immediately, although it was never spoken of, was that the pregnancy was viewed as something shameful, a sign of lust and indiscretion, evidence of a wanton sexuality. One ought to have given up sex completely by her age or, at least, have learned to be discreet about it. Now here was evidence that sexuality had not been put aside. Her mother rarely left the house for the whole of her pregnancy, giving a new meaning to the term "confinement."

The issue of this pregnancy was another daughter, one who nursed poorly and whose tiny newborn features gave way in the first few anxious weeks to wide-set eyes and a broad flat nose, and whose inability to sit alone, or crawl or feed herself, led the doctors to declare her to be defective in a way that they could not explicitly define. What they could speak to with some authority, and did, was the clear necessity, for the sake of the child, of keeping little Adele sheltered, out of sight, and under lock and key at home.

Evelyn's mother, who had always had a buoyant, easy air about her, and who had charmingly regarded herself as something of a bohemian, turned suddenly pinched and worried and domestic in the presence of this second child, whose care required so much of her. Help was hired, but help, to her mother's way of thinking, could not replace the ministrations of a doting (and, it could be said, guilty) mother. So not only Adele but her mother as well took up a housebound life, in which a particular love and duty linked them. Adele's speech never progressed beyond that of a young toddler, and soon no one but her mother could understand what she wanted and required, the nuance of her needs. Evelyn's father made great shows of patience and indulgence, but when it became clear that his exclusion from that mother-baby bond was total, he turned to Evelyn to take his wife's place as the woman in the family. The housekeeper who was employed (just for cooking and cleaning; she was not to minister in any way to Adele's needs), who came with fifteen years' experience and a highly evolved sense of who she was and what her duties ought to be, soon came to understand that she was *not* in charge. That Evelyn was the mistress of this house. And so, at the time of Adele's first Christmas it was young Evelyn (in a velvet fur-trimmed cape and matching muff) who appeared at the round of Christmas parties on her father's arm. She who commented politely on the lavish decorations, on the petits fours; she who wrote the notes of praise and gratitude. That first Christmas she had feared there would be questions, inquiries. "How *is* your mother, Evelyn? And the baby?" But it was a time when good manners dictated that shame could stay a hidden thing. Evelyn found that fellow party guests asked after "the other Morgan women" as if they were on a holiday in Switzerland, rather than sequestered in a house in which the velvet curtains were most often, even in the heat of summer, drawn.

When the time came for the girls of Wilmington to be introduced to society, it became clear that Evelyn would not be one of them. The daughter of a clothier would not quite do. Out of courtesy (and pity, she thought, when she let herself think of it at all) she would be included as a guest at many of the functions, her father told her one night at dinner. Just the two of them—Mother took all her meals in the third-floor playroom in which Adele lived and slept. Evelyn would have preferred not to go at all, not to participate if she could not be fully included, but she knew such a stance on her part would be viewed as ungrateful and petty. She had simple dresses made, ordered matching satin slippers, consoled herself with the fact that the "season" was going to be abbreviated and subdued that year, in any case, in keeping with a generally felt end-of-the-war sobriety.

It was on the night of the first of the festivities that spring, 1865, that Adele ran away. A certain wildness had developed in her—as it might in any spirit so confined. Evelyn, who visited her mother and her sister every morning just before she left for school, from which she was soon to graduate, might have seen it coming. Adele, dressed in crinoline, hair tied back in a bow, the little queen. More than once in the mornings of the weeks preceding her escape, she tried to follow Evelyn when it came time for her to go to school.

"No," Evelyn said the first time it happened, and the second, and the third. She knelt beside Adele, cupped her sister's little flat face in her hands when she addressed her. She had learned that these were the things that helped her understand. Touch. Simple words and sentences. She stroked her cheek as she might have stroked a cat, to quiet her, to soothe her. "You must stay here." Eager to leave, disguising all that eagerness with the low purr of her lying voice.

That May, Evelyn had chosen a dress of coral-pink grosgrain with an overskirt of point lace in preparation for the late-spring party—white was reserved for the lovely inductees. She curled her hair and pinned it up, wound pink roses and leaves and dainty ribbons through it.

Did her mother fall asleep that afternoon? Did exhaustion and unhappiness undermine her vigilance? Evelyn never knew. All she knew was that as she was at her mirror, in her room, pinching color into her cheeks, preparing for departure, her mother was rushing down the hallway crying. The moment Evelyn saw her face and listened to her sputtered, disjointed sentences, she knew: Adele had run away.

That morning her father had gone on a buying trip; there was no one to summon. No one to take authoritative charge. In the entry hall she and her mother developed a hurried plan—one of them would go into the wooded area that trailed off behind the house, the other would take the street that led, through a labyrinth of turns and angles, toward the center of the city. Evelyn took the town route, hoping that the proximity and silence of the woods had beckoned her sister, hoping that the carriages and street activity would have scared her away from the route toward town. She wanted very much not to be the one who found her.

Evelyn called her name. "Adele. A-dele." Discreetly. Lightly. Imagining that the little queen would emerge from between two houses, take her hand, and they could return home quietly. That Adele, the secret, would go undiscovered. But as darkness gathered like a garment, different scenarios began to occur to her. There were people on the streets, carriages and hurrying pedestrians. If Adele had come this way, someone was sure to have seen her. Evelyn called her name with greater urgency. Her voice a little shrill by then, a little shaky. In a rush of feeling she hoped that Adele had not been injured, that she'd found her way home. That she could laugh about this later when Adele was behind closed doors again.

Just as Evelyn had convinced herself that her sister had gone the other way, and was about to give up and go home, she saw a small crowd gathered at a street corner. She paused. Then made herself move forward. One foot, then the other, until she could press her way past them, until she could see what had drawn them there.

Adele was sitting on the sidewalk, Indian-fashion, among the gathered strangers. Using her own poor language, she must have tried to tell them who she was. One young boy whom Evelyn did not know was engaged in a mocking imitation of Adele's idiosyncratic speech to the man beside him, but everyone else was silent, watching. Adele's crinoline was torn, her hair loose and disheveled. She rocked back and forth in solitary agony. The odor emanating from her told Evelyn that she had soiled herself. Lucy Kyle, a doctor's daughter, a familiar face, not quite a friend, stood in the circle opposite Evelyn and looked across the space at her. She was dressed in white, obviously a debutante, one of the honorees that night, waiting for her carriage in front of her father's house, about to take her place in good society. This was her street, Evelyn realized suddenly. She must have just stepped outside and seen the little gathered crowd. Lucy locked eyes with Evelyn, then blushed, as if uncertain what to say or do.

Evelyn stepped into the circle toward Adele, who threw herself in crazed relief against her sister. Poor babe, she thought, but even as Evelyn's throat closed in some mute sympathy, she could not find a way to translate feeling into action. She knew she should have bent to her, she should have wiped her nose, cupped her flat face in her hands. Instead, she stiffly pried her sister's arms from around her waist.

"Come," she said, brushing dirt from her own dress, reaching stiffly down to grasp at Adele's wrist. She led her home that way, without word or sympathy or sentiment. Delivered her into her room, into their mother's waiting arms.

Pride moved her to change her dress, to dust the dirt from the long walk from her pale satin shoes. To summon her father's carriage. She knew that word of Adele's misadventure would have spread quickly, that other partygoers would have seen the sisters, would tell the tale to all the others. There would be talk that night. Everyone would know about the failure in her family, about the blight that marked them.

The fan she carried was arrayed with painted butterflies. At the party she fluttered it beneath her chin. It was on that night that she developed a kind of stiffness of the spine that years later her daughter would inherit. She kept her head extremely high. But at the same time she wanted very much for someone to speak to her, to bring her punch, someone who would save her. It was at the moment when her longing reached its peak, when she thought she might die of longing, that a young man approached her, bowing slightly, gesturing toward the place beside her on the divan. She smiled wanly, nodded, hardly able to look at him. His gracious manners saved her, his slightly Southern accent, his verbal ease. He was a distant cousin of someone whose name was unfamiliar to her. A visitor. Oh, sweet relief. Someone she'd never have to see again. Someone to whom rumors would mean nothing. He suggested a stroll among the partygoers, guided her with a subtle, confident pressure on her back.

James Talbot was about to relocate to Pennsylvania, to take up work in banking. He didn't say from where he was moving, and she felt no need to ask. But as she listened to him talk, she imagined going with him. Love did not enter into it, of course. After twenty minutes of conversation she certainly could not say she even knew him. She could not imagine love. But she could imagine leaving her home, her not-quite-acceptable family behind. Living in another city, becoming someone else. As the evening ended, as the tapered candles arranged so artfully around the room burned low, as the flowers began to nod, smothered by the room's close atmosphere, James leaned toward her with a look of so much trust, so much presumption as to her sympathy, her capacity for understanding, that she felt frightened, aware that he was going to tell her everything about himself. Secrets. Confessions that she didn't want to hear. "I was in Paris," he began when she had asked about his occupation during the war. Paris. He licked his lips, overcoming hesitation.

"Don't," she said. "It makes no difference. The war is over." Looking up at him, into his naked, hopeful face. It was as if she was vowing to herself and him that what they'd been before would never matter. "It's a new world. You should forget the past. You can become anything, anyone you want to be."

For their wedding she wore a dress of Swiss muslin, a blond tulle veil. No mention was made by Evelyn or either of her parents of James's lack of family, his vagueness about where he had grown up, what his father did, how he'd lost his brothers. She and James revealed their secrets to one another only gradually, only over the course of years, always politely. They struggled to become people to be reckoned with, a couple who belonged. They pretended that disappointment wasn't a large part of what they felt for each other, and were surprised as the years passed to find that the truth about each of them, once revealed, revealed itself to matter after all.

Evelyn, at the clubhouse window, watched Nora move forward into the crowded press of the young, the entitled. She watched her daughter gain what she had always wanted and never had. A place on the boat.

A mix of pride and jealousy swept over her.

AMBITIONS

"All things are in change, and you yourself are in continuous alteration . . ."

—Marcus Aurelius, *Meditations*, Book IX, Number 19

"It is accomplished," Carnegie wrote to Louise Whitfield in the fall of 1883, as he wrote all news to her, his secret fiancée. "Matthew Arnold has agreed to come."

The letter writing was essential because Andrew Carnegie had taken to traveling so much. His wanderlust had been ignited on a coaching trip to the British Lake District and Scotland in 1881, in the company, as always, of his mother. The culmination of that trip was a triumphant visit to Dunfermline in Scotland, the town they'd left years earlier, ashamed, escaping grinding poverty. WELCOME, CARNEGIE, GENEROUS SON, the banners had read on his return. His plans for donating a library to his birthplace had been well publicized. His arrival was treated with the pomp and ceremony reserved for a member of the royal family.

Carnegie had invited Louise to go with him and his party on that trip—with the obvious understanding of the need for chaperones, for the requirements of decorousness. She had said yes without hesitation. He had kissed her hand in recognition of a promise made. Shopping, the seamstress's visits had thrown the normally quiet Whitfield house into a whirl of enthused activity. Anticipation, happiness had marked the preparations.

Feelings that seemed to have died when her father did were resurrected. Her mother's uncertain health was, at least temporarily, restored. It was Margaret Carnegie who had interfered, who had paid a visit for the ostensible purpose of formalizing Andrew's invitation and instead convinced Louise's mother to deny permission, to question the invitation's propriety.

Recently Andrew Carnegie had acquired a newspaper syndicate in Britain, and more trips abroad became pleasing necessities. He loved travel, the freedom of it, the sense of going to the farthest reach of the tether that attached him to his mother. Louise knew that, between his mother and his businesses, responsibilities weighed heavily upon him. She respected his many burdens, did her best to understand him. But there were times when his letters seemed to her to have the character of taunts—full of hints of affectionate attachment that stopped shy of fervid feeling. He gave her no sign that he felt a passion that could not be stilled. Even their engagement, kept secret as it was, had a false, inconstant feel to it. When he was in New York, the rides in Central Park continued. They went occasionally to the opera and to concerts together. But, inevitably, their brief times together were followed by long silences which she was left to interpret as she might. She scrutinized his letters, read them repeatedly, in an endless search for clues to his true, unarticulated feelings.

Even her own feelings, of which she'd felt so certain, had become muddied and unclear. "I am so unhappy and miserable," she wrote in her diary at about that time. "I feel so old and strange. Nothing is certain, nothing is sure." But each time a letter came, her feelings for him rallied. Even as she thought of how much time this Arnold visit would devour— one more thing to keep her beloved from her—she was glad for Carnegie. She knew how much it would mean to him to have acquired such an articulate, important friend. "The most charming man I ever knew," he wrote of Arnold, and this American lecture tour was taking place at Carnegie's initiative.

"I want him to be treated splendidly, so he'll visit often. I'll prepare a suite for him and his wife and daughter at the Windsor with floral pieces over the doors, each inscribed with the title of one of his books. Pansies for *Literature and Dogma*, pink tea roses for *Culture and Anarchy*." Louise could not help but smile at the idea of these floral tributes. Such was the extravagance, the attention he showered on his friends. Andrew Carnegie, affable little white-haired Santa of a man. Voluble in friendship, taciturn in love.

Louise imagined herself becoming an aged, shriveled virgin, growing bitter while she waited for him. More than once, and against the grain of her good nature, there were times when she regretted having met Mr. Carnegie. (So circumspect was she, so given to propriety, that even after their secret betrothal she continued to refer to him as "Mister" in her diary.)

More than once she had had to ask God's forgiveness because she wished his mother dead.

It was Julia's father who spurred her to it, who summoned Julia to his consultation room and required her to occupy the chair reserved for patients. "You must find something to distract yourself, child," he had said. "Some useful occupation. Watching how you pine is killing your family. It's killing me." It was four years after the funerals, four years during which the smallest effort at engaging herself in the living world felt impossible to her. She had been dutiful, of course, always dutiful. She fulfilled responsibilities, but her connection to them, as threads in the fabric of her life, had been severed. Her mind was elsewhere; she was not engaged.

How vividly Dr. Strayer saw himself in her as she sat across from him. Her hands folded in her lap, her head tilted slightly to one side in a failed effort to indicate polite interest in what he was saying. He suspected he had looked quite like her in the early days of his banishment. Waiting to be told how to behave, what would be expected, how much grieving and self-pity the world would tolerate. The difference was that he had been the architect of his own trouble—a visionary surgeon who'd taken a chance on the new, the experimental, someone who had gambled and lost. In this, he supposed, he was unlike his hushed, dear daughter. Although, he thought as he looked at her, weren't they essentially the same? Hadn't she, too, risked everything? Marrying, having children, betting on love that way. He ought to have warned her.

He had turned his failed life into an outward success. As Bean's assistant for more than fifteen years, he had been cautious and methodical, unimpeachably correct in all his medical endeavors. Fifteen years of conservative, time-honored treatment—he had earned back the respect that he had lost in Chicago. But at what price, he sometimes wondered. He felt thwarted, held back; his growth and imagination stunted. The small pieces of surgical equipment he designed (in private, in his rooms) could not be used, the experimental procedures he imagined, procedures he believed could save lives, could only be written about in notebooks, kept for his own perusal. His knowledge was useless to him in his practice. Perhaps one day he'd find some young doctor to whom he could leave his notebooks. Someone more courageous, someone undefeated. Julia, Julia, he wanted to say to his child, sitting across from him. Don't let yourself be defeated.

He took her hand. He reminded her of how skillful she had been as a girl with thread and needle, the eye she'd always had for what might be called "fashion," the subtle, discriminating taste she'd acquired from her mother which had always set her apart. "Enhanced her beauty" was what Dr. Strayer said. Beauty. The day her father had lectured her, the day he had used that word in reference to the brittle person she'd become, their conversation had brought tears to her eyes. Unlikely tears. She wished she could explain to him that it was not just the loss of the children but what that loss had revealed to her about herself. She was a woman who could stop loving her son, who could blame her own child, when blame should not have been a part of it.

A freezing rain scratched at the window glass. She wondered if the ice would cling to the sycamore's bare branches.

Years earlier, in Chicago, in the face of her father's disgrace, she had stood unwaveringly beside him. She had held her head high during the inquest into his alleged malpractice. She had not cringed when he was called "butcher"; she had scooped up and buried the eviscerated cat found on their doorstep as if it were something well-bred young women such as she did every day. She had left the home she loved and moved to a city buried in the mountains, determined to be dutiful, resilient, vowing to make the best of it. Circumstance, not choice, had brought her to this place. Circumstance had brought Frank into Jones's grocery that first day. She had allowed herself to believe that the unexpected, startling love she felt for him, the children they would have and the life they'd make, would be her reward, finally, for having been stalwart. Now she saw that all her efforts had been false ones, that she was not resilient. She had no idea, really, what she was. She was thirty-nine years old and wanted to run away, return to Chicago, take up the life that had been ripped from her.

Impossible, ridiculous wishes almost two decades later, the wishes of a girl, but they did not feel ridiculous. Looking at her father sitting across his desk from her, she thought what a stunning confession it would be, this confession of her wish to abandon her whole family, to go back to Chicago and pretend she'd never left. She could not act on it, but every part of her being wished to.

"Try the sewing," Dr. Strayer insisted.

And finally, to please, to placate, she said she would.

She was tentative at first as she began to think about a life, *her life*. Who was she, after all, to trust any impulse toward action, any possibility of hope in something new? When shopping for staples she allowed herself to finger bolts of fabric, at Baer's and Jones's and Charles Leventry's on Cherry Street. Cambric, cotton, flannel, and, for women of means, women who indeed might wish for the services of her deft hands, there were small swatches of fabrics that could be custom-ordered. Pink surah, gauze-thin grenadine, etamine. Lovely, she said to herself, touching the fabric samples; the feel of ribbed silk against skin. While clerks boxed Julia's supply of flour, cornmeal, salt, she paged furtively through the ladies' magazines that were on display: *Godey's*, *Peterson's*, and *Demorest's*. She realized she had grown out of touch. It would require work to familiarize herself with the new trends in style and fashion. The cuirass bodice, the gored polonaise, the elongated slimming lines were not what she had sewn before. At her house in the evenings, after Caroline and Daniel had finished their schoolwork at the kitchen table, she herself sat there, doodling in a lined notebook she had bought, calculating fabric yardage, the cost of trims, making sketches of gigot sleeves, basques, pointed shoulder capes, and wide-brimmed hats with plumes. In her notebook she wrote *Julia Fallon: Dressmaker*, imagining cards that she might have made by C. T. Schubert, who did job printing. She revealed nothing of this nascent fantasy to Frank, or even to her father, imagining that it was best to deny hope to those she loved until she could live with that hope a little, see where it led her, test it to be sure it wasn't an illusion.

It was in this spirit of testing that she had first gone to the library. She had heard about the new librarian, a helper for Mrs. Hirst. There were rumors about a dark past, lost love, sordid longings; that she'd arrived in Johnstown fresh from being spurned. She came from Boston, lived alone in the rooms above the pharmacy, but for the most part seemed to live at the library, unpacking books, making little cards, one for the book, its partner in a drawer. Daniel, the reader in the family, always eager to engage his mother, searching relentlessly for *some* way to engage her, had talked of the library at length with Julia. The Dewey decimal system, the narrow oak drawers of the card catalogue. Julia, ironing, steam and the scent of hot cotton rising to her face, had stood listening to him as he spread his books out on the kitchen table. She had always loved the way he used language. Even when he was a little boy she'd kept a bound book filled with Daniel Words, Daniel Phrases. Lost now. Momentarily, while ironing, she had wondered where it was. She had put it away, as she had all the things which were part of the before of her before-and-after life.

The librarian. A professional lady, a Boston spinster. A novelty in a city where Julia knew almost everyone. Just the sort of woman who might want dresses designed and made for her. Julia could test herself on this new woman, test her own ability to implement a plan. No one else would have to know, no one who cared for her would be disappointed if she failed. Julia imagined a Medici suit and hooded cape for this Boston woman, a polonaise round skirt. The latest thing.

Julia liked the musty smell of the library, the spread of shelves along the far wall, the dull colors of the book spines filling them. Seven thousand volumes, Daniel had said. Not like the libraries Andrew Carnegie had begun to build in bigger cities, but Julia knew how fortunate they were to have one at all. She took a book from a basket piled full near the door, turned it in her hand. The tag on the basket handle said "Book Return." She let the book fall open in her hands. *Huckleberry Finn*. It gave her momentary pleasure to think about someone by a fireside reading it. She tried to imagine, of all her neighbors, whose eyes, whose guiding finger had recently run down that page. Behind the desk, off to the left, Julia saw an open door, a glimpse of a lectern, rows of chairs. Last week Daniel had been to a lecture here. Julia closed *Huckleberry Finn*, dropped it carefully back into the basket.

She looked down each row of bookcases as she passed it. She thought of calling out, but it seemed wrong to disturb so deep a quiet. A wall clock chimed. She was about to give up, go, when she heard the sound of wood on wood, something being dragged across the floor not far from her.

In the next aisle of books Grace was standing on a little ladder, stretched on tiptoe, reaching toward a high shelf, slipping a book into the shadows. Tall, Julia thought. For a woman. Also prettier than Julia expected her to be, and younger. In the gauzy light of afternoon Julia could see that her hair, so neatly tucked and pinned, was graying, but just a bit. Too thin, Julia thought. Forget sewing. Someone should cook her meals. Someone ought to feed her. Grace had caught her tongue between her lips as if it helped her with the long reach or with her balance. Louis used to do that with his tongue when he first learned to fasten buttons.

She cleared her throat. "Excuse me."

Grace cried out. Her hand raced to her chest.

"I'm sorry." Julia spoke quickly. "I didn't mean to frighten you."

"Oh." Grace laughed then, at herself. Her lips were full, her mouth and smile were generous and wide. She shook her head, patted her chest with her hand, making light of fear, of how startled she'd been. "No, no. It's just *so* quiet here." Her eyes grew wide in emphasis. She laughed again. "Really. Have you ever been in any place so quiet?" She looked to Julia like someone who had a way of finding something a little odd, a little funny, in everything. Her voice had that kind of undertone in it.

Grace had gathered her skirt in one hand and was backing down the ladder. Then she held her hands beneath her chin, blew a little cloud of book dust from them before she reached out to introduce herself, to shake Julia's hand. Yes, Julia thought, there was something of the city about her, but she thought that the rest of what she'd heard was wrong. The part about the spurning. Not likely. Whatever brought her here, it wasn't that.

They walked back toward the desk together. A picture of Daniel Morrell hung just inside the entry, above the woodstove.

"Do you know him?" Grace asked, when she saw Julia looking at it.

"Everyone knows Mr. Morrell."

"Yes." Grace folded her arms over her chest and gazed up at him. "He seems to have had his hand in everything. The Savings Bank, First National Bank, the water and gas companies. Two terms in Congress. President of American Iron and Steel." She glanced at Julia, sensed her surprise at all that she knew. "Among the books here is the Cambria Iron history, and I thought I ought to read it." At that moment, in the western sky, some shifting cloud banks moved away to make room for a beaming sun. Shafts of light slanted through the window on the far wall and fell across Morrell's dark eyes. Grace laughed. "Look," she said. "God has shone his light on Daniel J. Morrell." Julia laughed, too, surprised at how easily Grace used God's name. But even as she laughed, she found her courage flagging. The idea of offering her services as seamstress seemed embarrassing, as well as presumptuous and foolish.

"I should go." Julia turned to leave, knowing that Daniel and Caroline would be coming home from school soon.

"But you haven't told me why you came. You've borrowed no book, you haven't asked about the lecture series."

"No," said Julia. "No, I haven't." Then, searching: "I simply came to welcome you." She smiled apologetically. "I know you've been here quite a while, and I'm a little late as these things go, but I wanted to tell you how glad we are to have you. *I* am to have you." She was thinking then about Daniel, about how kind this stranger had been to him at a time when she, his own mother, had so little to offer. "I think you know my son. Daniel."

"Daniel?" Grace nodded. Tilted her head to one side, appraising. "Yes, I should have known. He looks a little like you."

Julia blushed.

"No, really. He does. And what a reader." She moved behind her desk, eased into her chair, leaned her elbows on the blotter, and cupped her chin in her upturned hands.

"Yes." Julia felt shy then, out of words. "Well . . ."

"You know, you should come with Daniel sometime. There are books here you might enjoy."

A little flurry of negatives rushed from Julia's lips. No time, not interested.

Grace had taken up her pen again and seemed not to hear her. "Or don't come with Daniel. Come alone. And really, you'd be doing me a favor." She smiled up at Julia. "I'll lose my job if no one reads."

Julia looked back over her shoulder at the rows of shelves lined up like dominoes down the length of the room behind her. It was as quiet there as any place she'd ever been. She had loved to read as a girl. And Daniel talked so often about how it was possible to lose yourself in books.

"So next week, then?" Grace brushed a strand of hair back from her cheek. "There is a kettle here, and cups and saucers. I'll make tea?"

"Tea?" Such a strange word to find its way into this valley, into this world of hard work, long days, dark sludgy coffee. Tea. To Julia it sounded mysterious and foreign. It made her think of kings and courtiers. It carried her away.

Next time she'd mention sewing. Next time, she told herself, she'd implement her plan.

Grace undressed later that night by lamplight. Stockings, shoes, muslin dress, petticoat—too many clothes, she thought. Why do women wear so many clothes? In her rooms, with their spare insubstantial furnishings, she felt as if she were at a cabin or a summerhouse. A beach. Her dressing table was a grouping of crates, disguised by faded fringed shawls draped, skirtlike, over them. The little framed aquarelles on the far wall were of sand dunes, sun-glazed seascapes, gulls. Seabirds in the Allegheny Mountains. Columbines, pansies, and buttercups, which she picked on days when she was not working, were arranged in an old tin pitcher. The mirror was chipped, its warped edges brown, wavy. Everything looked temporary, expendable, as if it had been collected with an eye toward the day when a storm would blow in without warning and take it all away. It made her think of the beach at Marblehead that long-ago summer. It made her think of Matthew.

Barefoot now, freed of everything except her light slip and ruffled camisole, she pulled a chair up to her dressing table. Angled her chin to look at herself in the little strip of mirror that was as yet undamaged. Her arms were shapely, thin. Lifting, boxing, shelving books had worked the muscles, given a surprising definition to them. In the glow of gaslight, her shoulders seemed peach-tinted, and again she thought of Marblehead, the rise of color in her sunburned skin that summer, the cream she had rubbed into it to take the sting away. She touched the graceful bow of her clavicle, the blue-gray slice of shadow lying in its hollow like a little shallow pool. A gust of wind rippled the window curtain. A pin fell from her hair.

She wondered about Daniel's mother. How young she still seemed after—what had Daniel told her? Four? Was it four children? There was a roundness to her—hips, cheeks, bound and buttoned breasts—that made her look girlish, modest, sweet. Daniel must be seventeen. How old would she be? Grace remembered friends from grammar school who'd married, how young they'd been. Nineteen, twenty when they had their first babies. If she hadn't gone to Radcliffe, she might have done that, too.

Almost forty, then? Could Julia be the same age as she? Four children. Absently Grace ran her hand over her flat, taut, unstretched stomach.

A train whistle sounded. A locomotive rumbled its way to the Conemaugh yard. Her library, she thought, was the only quiet spot in town. She had expected a peaceful little place tucked in the mountains. Industry, commerce, rough bustle never crossed her mind. She'd read about this job in the paper. "Wanted. Librarian." How they came to advertise as far away as Boston she never knew. But for her, those two words contained every truth about her. The latter was a thing she was, the former something she wanted desperately to be. At her dressing table she reached for a jar of cream, dabbed into it, and worked the emulsion into her palm, then into her slender hands. The finger where rings had been was narrowed below the knuckle.

It's so simple, really, she remembered thinking when she saw the ad. The way things just come to you sometimes.

"I'd really rather not talk about this," her husband, Frederick, had said just two nights earlier. He'd sat across from her. Since it was to be just the two of them, she'd had a small table set by the fire. She'd arranged the napkins in their silver rings herself. Candles were lodged on silver prickets. She'd placed her mother's china carefully—the pattern with the painted Chinese dragon on the rims. As she prepared for the evening, she sipped wine for courage. To curb her nervousness she tried to smooth things. The tablecloth and draperies. She smoothed her skirt and smoothed her hair.

Mushroom soup. Turbot in champagne sauce. Frederick sat elegantly across from her. For the third time that evening the napkin slid from her silk-skirted lap onto the floor. Gracefully, she dipped to fetch it.

"Yes, I know. But . . ." She hesitated, using the napkin as opportunity to pause, collect herself. "We can't decide about this if we don't talk."

"Decide, Grace? Talk?"

They were going to join his mother at the symphony right after supper. The white tie of Frederick's evening attire moved ever so slightly when he swallowed, as his Adam's apple rose and fell.

He had told her that he was planning to go on an expedition. He'd spoken without anger, with great authority. He'd thought of East Africa; he'd been hearing of the rare beauty there, trees bowed by plain-driven winds, the crystallizing mountain rains, the possibility of buying land and growing coffee. But recently he'd been told of a group headed for the upper edges of the world: Scandinavia, Finland, the northern lights. That night he'd used the butter dish and salt and pepper shakers to give her a sense of the size of the expedition, the way the flotilla might form itself, the number of boats they'd need. In this pantomime of travel the linen tablecloth became the sea. She knew without asking that his mistress would be taken along as secretary to the group, as executive assistant. That this woman who for ten years had been like a second wife to him would be going, too. At Marblehead that summer Grace herself had been indiscreet. Matthew was a surgeon. They'd met at a small party. "Did you know," he said to her after they'd talked awhile, "that wedding rings are worn on the third finger of the left hand because of an ancient belief that a vein runs from that finger directly to the heart?" He asked this as he offered her his arm to escort her to the dining room for dinner, touching her wedding band as he spoke the words, turning it as if to admire its antique setting. The touch both clinical and startlingly intimate. And where had Frederick gone in that moment? Only later did she remember how eager he'd been to introduce her to her would-be lover. Only later did it occur to her that he might even have planned it. Her indiscretion would allow him to go off with his mistress.

At dinner in her Boston townhouse, Grace's napkin had slipped again. But that time, as she bent down to retrieve it, a wave of nausea swept over her, almost brought her out of her chair onto the floor, onto her knees. She had dared to hope for something different. She'd planned to tell Frederick about the baby. Her own liaison was long over. Although Frederick came to her infrequently, there could be no doubt. The child was his. She'd placed her hand on her stomach; she'd touched her stomach that night, too. This baby was something that she wanted badly. She had been prepared to beg. But as the tablecloth grazed her cheek, as she took in little gulps of air to try to fight the nausea, as she used every particle of strength to keep herself from falling, she understood that begging was impossible, out of the question. That everything about her life had been a begging, and that begging would no longer do.

She had straightened herself in her chair. Wiped her mouth with her retrieved napkin, dabbed at the ribbon of perspiration that had gathered there. She decided she would have to go to Matthew one more time. He was a doctor, she would ask for his help, the last time she would seek help from anyone.

Daniel was convinced that it was Horace Rose who enjoined his father to let him go to university. Rose had never had the opportunity for formal education, he'd "read law" in John Linton's office, then opened an office of his own. An education like the one he might have imagined for Daniel, his protégé, was like a dream to him. Daniel, at eighteen, had never thought of it; he'd always assumed that he would join Frank at Cambria Iron, apprentice himself to the muscled work of making steel.

Throughout the period he'd worked with Grace, Daniel would have said that his only goal was self-improvement; he had not really connected the reading he was doing to a future plan. Workingmen were often learned, autodidacts. Captain Bill Jones, once Morrell's man and now Carnegie's, was known for his love of Plutarch. Daniel's own father had read his small volumes of Dickens so often that he had to tie each one together with a length of string because the bindings had become loose and worn from use. Mr. Rose said that everyone was reading *The Meditations of Marcus Aurelius.* "Wipe out imagination; check impulse; quench desire; keep the governing self in its own accord" (*Meditations*, Book IX, Number 6).

Whose idea was it, then, when it was finally mentioned? The University of Pennsylvania? How had so far-fetched a notion ever found its way into the Fallon dinner-table conversation?

Quiet had replaced the typical clamor and happy disarray that had swirled around the table when there were younger children. The sound of a voice speaking had become an oddity in recent years, seemed loud and intrusive in the muted atmosphere in what they persisted in calling the "new house," in the dining room.

Frank used his bread to skim the gravy from his plate. Tilted his chin toward the plate to prevent dripping. "Horace Rose has been telling me about a well-known university in Philadelphia. He has a friend from the legislature who could help work things out so that you could go there."

Caroline, sixteen, who'd somehow missed all hints of this that might have surfaced in other family conversations, looked up, blinked. "Philadelphia?" Of all of them, she was the one with a real wanderlust. "Might I go, too? If Daniel goes, could I go with him?"

Julia intervened. "A young man doesn't take his sister with him to university. That's not the way it's done." As if she were some kind of expert.

"You've mentioned this before," Daniel said, trying to sound respectful to his father and at the same time to make his feelings known. "I'm not certain that I want to do it."

Daniel stared at his mashed potatoes as a way of avoiding looking at his mother. Everyone expected some objection to this plan from her, an expression of a wish to keep her only son at home.

Julia put her fork down, touched her napkin to the corner of her mouth, a linen napkin that had been her mother's, much used by now, overwashed and over-ironed, less crisp than it had been when she first was married, but it was a nicety that she'd always insisted upon at dinner. She even had a book on napkin folding. That night, when they seated themselves at the table, they had found their napkins tweaked into the shapes of swans.

She glanced briefly at Daniel, then focused her gaze on Frank. "And what is it that he would study? What would be the point of this?" she asked.

Daniel opened his mouth, but Frank placed his hand on his arm, spoke for him. "The classics. Science. Mathematics. If he chooses to, he could be a doctor. You can train to be a doctor there." Like her father. He hoped that connection would add to the appeal of the plan.

Frank had injected a particular kind of excitement into his voice, an enthusiasm that he did not feel. He knew that Daniel and Horace Rose, and now, no doubt, Caroline as well, thought that letting the boy go off to school would break Julia's heart, that she'd be the one to yearn for him to stay, to think of reasons to keep him close to her. Only Frank knew the truth of it, a truth he kept from everyone. Julia had confessed to him the first night they'd made love after the funeral, four months later, after the first frost had crusted the markers on the children's graves. Lovemaking was perhaps not quite the term for it that night. It was more a frantic, violent coupling, an act of openness and penetration that they both hoped would somehow link them again. She held Daniel responsible, she said. She didn't want to, she'd tried everything she could to rid herself of the feeling, but every time she looked at him she saw the scar on his neck and was reminded again, excruciatingly reminded, that he was the one who had brought the fever to the house. She wanted it to be different, but every time she saw that scar, she said, her voice so faint that he could barely hear her, she thought of Claire and Louis.

She had expected Frank to pull away from her.

"You hate me, don't you?" she had asked tonelessly. "Say it. Go ahead, say it. I hate myself, I know that what I feel is unnatural, but I can't make the feeling go away."

He hadn't turned from her. He had been still, and he had held her hand while light snow fell, until she slept. He realized then that everything about her had begun to seem unfamiliar to him, that she fit less perfectly than she had once into the long angle of his arm. Her breasts, her neck, the curve of which his mouth had memorized from chin to sternum. She seemed to have grown smaller. He pulled her sleeping figure tightly to him.

Snow accumulating on the window ledge formed a brittle crystalline crust on the panes, closing them in their bedroom, off from the world. He had wished, momentarily, that all of them—Caroline, Daniel, he, and Julia—would die that night. That the woodstove would fail, the temperature drop, that they'd all be found by the neighbors frozen in their beds. He was married to a woman who couldn't love his son. And he didn't know what he could do about that. Love had vanished. Oh, who can account for love, he thought. Who can explain the things that kill it?

So he had added to his protective plans relating to his family a plan to keep the truth from Daniel. Coming between the boy and his mother, intervening, joking in a way he rarely did, talking too much in their presence, keeping the conversation light, buying high-necked shirts for Daniel, to keep the scar from showing. He developed a prizefighter's bob and weave, thrusting at the truth, keeping the truth off balance or on the mat, blocking the punch of it, the pain his son would feel if the truth touched him. It was why he'd attached himself so eagerly to the idea of Daniel going away to school, even when Daniel said he didn't want to. When Daniel said, *I want to stay with you. We should stay together now. It would be too hard for Mother.* Frank could see it that night at the dinner table in Caroline's face as well. Poor Mother. He knew all the while what relief Julia would feel, he knew that his was the heart that was breaking.

Julia spoke into the protracted silence at the dinner table. Daniel had expected her to side with him, to speak on behalf of the impossibility of him leaving. "It sounds like an opportunity," she said instead. Quietly. Looking into his eyes, fixing her gaze on his eyes. "Something you should try." Then she reached for his hand, surprising everyone by touching him, leaving Caroline shocked by the surprise she felt, unsettled by some dawning recognition. "What harm can trying do?" Julia went on. "Besides, the library there must be much more complete than what we have here. Think of that, Daniel. That alone is a reason to try it." For a moment, only a moment, there was that old sweetness between them, a moment that made Frank think that if Daniel did go away, if letters full of love were exchanged between them, if time was allowed to pass, then perhaps it would bring a change in the way she felt. He'd fall on his knees and pray for that if he thought it would help. But he knew the best he could do was to make this separation happen, to give the boy and Julia this chance.

He could let a room from Horace Rose's friend on Locust Street, close to the university. He would buy a new valise for traveling. The boy had wanted to use the satchels that his grandparents used when they came from Ireland, but Frank said no. He wanted a proper traveling bag for his traveling son. They would order new boots from the shoemaker, Lewis Weinzierl, a few new clothes—a guess, really, about what a college man might wear. They went to George Heiser's store on Washington, where George produced a catalogue, and they all got into the spirit of it. George said his son Victor would be the next to go; Daniel could mark the path for Victor to follow two years later. The boots were ordered for Daniel, as well as a shorter sack jacket, a vest, a wide tie to wear under the turned-down collar of his shirt. It was the first such excursion for son and father; ordinarily clothing was purchased one piece at a time, out of immediate necessity, and this outfitting was awkward initially. Daniel was unaccustomed to having his body scrutinized and measured. George Heiser squared the jacket on Daniel's shoulders, checked the length, pinned the trouser legs so that Julia could hem them. They looked alike, Frank thought. He and the boy. Daniel was already big like he was, long in the torso, with beefy, muscular arms. A head of red-brown hair, Daniel's being darker. Square, brutish Irish jaws, hands like paws, good hands for puddling. Louis had had the small features and exquisite fine bones inherited from Julia's mother. Lovely hands. Julia had hoped to buy a violin for him. She had imagined that he'd spend his life making music.

On the September day of Daniel's departure, Frank walked him to the station, insisting on carrying his bag. It was a beautiful autumn day—hesitant and muted morning light, mountain mist. Elm, laurel, and sugar maple trees posed like elaborately costumed actors in the wings, waiting for the sun to crest the hill and light them. The leaves were always most vibrant when there had been heavy April and May rains, the predictable spring flooding. A day like this made them agree that it was worth the ankle-deep water in May on Main Street, if that was the price you paid for such a fall. Daniel and Frank mounted the steps of the B&O depot, right across the street from Heiser's, an old converted schoolhouse. Frank could never quite take it seriously as a train station, given that he'd gone to grammar school and learned his sums there. The place where the teacher's desk had been was now a ticket window, and Frank paid Daniel's one-way fare. Once they were seated on a bench on the platform, Frank took his hat off, fingered the felt brim. Daniel blew warm breath into his cold, cupped hands.

"So Christmas, then?" said Frank.

"Yes, Christmas," Daniel answered. "Unless things don't go well, unless I change my mind."

"Let's have none of that now," Frank said. He pulled a pamphlet that the school had sent out of the inside pocket of his coat. He and Daniel had looked at it a hundred times, but Frank opened it again, holding it a little distance from his face, joking with Daniel, making an exaggerated show of how old he was getting (even though he was only forty-six), how hard it was for an old man like him to see. " 'Begun by Benjamin Franklin,' " he read about the university. " 'Home to the Continental Congress.' And here, Daniel. You didn't show me this." Frank pointed to the place in the text that had been underlined in red. " 'The student body publicly performs the plays of Aristophanes together.' One of those Greeks. You've been reading them, haven't you?"

Daniel reached to take the pamphlet from him. "The master of Old Comedy," he said. He leaned back on the bench, stretched his legs out in front of him. "You'll save a place for me at the iron works, won't you? I've always thought we'd work together there. That I'd go to night classes at the institute. That I'd learn what you know. Would you mind that, really? If I stayed with you?"

Because Daniel had become such a man in his size and bearing in the last year, Frank realized that he had begun thinking of him as a man. In his enthusiasm for this project, this going away, he had forgotten just how young he was. He dared not look at him. He looked at the rim of his hat instead.

"Take this chance, boy," he said. "See about some other place. It's a thing a young man ought to do. I did it; not like this, of course, but when I went to the war. I traveled, I saw some things. I came back by choice then. That's the thing, Dan-o. The thing is to make a choice." Frank looked up at him, forced a smile, gave him a fond nudge on the arm with his bent elbow. Trying to get them through this talk, this bittersweet farewell. "Come back a doctor. Or better still, come back and run the iron works." He let a laugh out, and even got a reluctant smile from Daniel. "Now that would be something, wouldn't it? Mr. Morrell is wearing down a bit, he'll need help, I'm told. Wouldn't it make you proud to come home to do that?"

Frank saw the train, the distant flat face of it, before he heard its whistle; it seemed suddenly to arrive in front of them, stopping with the heave and sigh of halted locomotion, hissing steam. And then the handshake, the boy's back as he turned to board the train. Frank handed his bag up to him, needing to touch his fingers one more time, just a touch. Best to forget the way his stomach lurched as the train began to struggle forward, as the engine forced the wheels to turn. He waved his hat, made a great to-do of waving, for a foolishly long time, until the train was out of sight, until it was safe to drop his arm, to drop the pretense. Safe to slump back on the bench and cover his face with his hands, and gather himself, force himself, to face the day ahead, and the days that were to follow. All the days until the winter came, then, finally, Christmas.

The girls in Philadelphia were not like the girl at the lake. Or perhaps they were and it simply didn't register with Daniel. Because his studies busied him extraordinarily? Because city life held more attractions for him than he would have guessed? No. Rather, it was the case that something about the girl at the lake had remained with him. He thought of her costume, a loose white tea dress. Dishabille, he would later discover it was called, this brief new look in women's fashion, uncorseted, unbustled, an early-in-the-decade flirtation with comfort, ease of movement. He didn't know a whit about such trends. He simply registered the difference in how she looked. The dress, the simple hair cast her in an aura of lightness, gave him the sense that beneath her apparent gravity there was something unrestrained.

And at the university, a certain sense of being unrestrained infected him as well. It was as if a kind of fever—of new buildings, new ideas—had struck in Philadelphia. That's how Daniel would describe it later.

Laboratories were being constructed on the campus, which had recently been relocated to the Almshouse farm west of the Schuylkill River. American universities had begun to embrace the notion that their mission was not just transmitting knowledge but creating it as well. New discoveries were treated with the same respect as established wisdom; the possibilities of science, what could be revealed and learned by experimentation and study, were attracting excited attention. The world had begun to seem "knowable." Chromosomes and mitosis, cell division, had been described. Ventures into astronomy had made it possible to list the spectra of 4,051 stars. Robert Koch explained that tuberculosis was caused by a bacterium, that a causal link could be made between a germ and a disease. The streets of Philadelphia were cobblestone, the air electric. Everyone was a visionary. Even Daniel. Especially Daniel. He who had imagined that his fairly standard education and idiosyncratic reading life would lead him toward philosophy or history found himself drawn instead to the social sciences, to August Comte and Herbert Spencer, and inevitably to the laboratories, to the microscopes invented only five years earlier, the Periodic Table, the possibilities that vaccines might be found that could prevent disease. Even the stench of the laboratory chemicals seemed bracing. Everything he knew about working life he had learned in a city whose very existence depended on making steel. He knew the legends of Henry Bessemer like he knew his nighttime prayers, his parents' one nod to religion. In the library at the university Daniel saw charcoal renderings of Bessemer's London stronghold and laboratory called Baxter House—his windowless studio, the skylight barred against spies and intruders. Daniel took a class in metallurgy and an introduction to engineering. Time spent in the chemistry laboratories produced in him a sharp olfactory longing, a wish for home. He felt less a stranger to his life when he was there.

Impossible to miss in any city at that time was the talk of social change. The rights of workers. The need for labor unions. Daniel read early papers that Herbert Spencer had published in *The Zoist*, written when he was still in youthful thrall of mesmerism and phrenology, and later the more elaborate social theories Spencer developed while subeditor at *The Economist*. Spencer preached the doctrine of social evolution, survival of the fittest, and was admired by industrialists such as Carnegie and Frick and Mellon for his clear articulation of a theory they had long believed—that they had succeeded because they'd adapted when adaptation was required. They had become wealthy because, as "the fittest," they deserved it. They were blessed by God and good fortune, deemed worthy. The corollary of this thinking was that other less successful men had not been so blessed, had not adapted, and so did not deserve reward.

In Philadelphia that first year Daniel attended a Knights of Labor meeting and grew interested in the trade union agenda and, in this way, fell in with a group of new friends: urgent, radical, impatient for change, for some new egalitarian era. Young men for whom he felt a natural affinity. What would he be now, he wondered, as he walked to class, as he warmed his hands by the fire in his furnished room? Night after night he struggled to bring these two sides of himself together—the activist, the scholar. What now? It became a kind of echo. And at the same time, even as he went about his studies, and wrote letters home, and did research for a professor of astronomy, and washed dishes at a local tavern as a way of making extra money, the idea of the girl at the lake was never far from him. The more he tried to resist her, the more frequently she appeared. Even when he met and shared meals with and fell vaguely, briefly, in love with other girls, she was with him. Never at the center of his mind—his was a mind too full for that. But off somewhere in the ether, just beyond full reckoning. A shadow. A figure from a dream.

When she began to go regularly to the Johnstown library, Julia did not think of herself as taking Daniel's place. Before he left for Philadelphia, she had gone occasionally, as Grace had invited her to, for tea, for talk. Then, once he was gone, she discovered that she felt close to Daniel there. Sometimes when she visited in the late afternoon, before school was out, when the library was almost empty, she wondered if the chair she occupied was the one that Daniel had sat in when Grace taught him Greek. In this small, barely perceptible way, she began to miss him.

"Was he a good student?" she asked Grace, struck by curiosity about three months after he was gone.

"Wonderful." Grace smiled, remembering.

The teas which were offered varied from week to week. Oolong, Darjeeling, plump leaves from Ceylon. The teapot was a distressed glazed green; the kettle steaming on the woodstove had the gleam of burnished copper. When Julia asked where Grace had grown up, she spoke of Maine, then Boston, the cold Atlantic, the pleasures of living by the sea. Julia nodded. Their talk turned to water, to Lake Michigan. "You should see it," Julia said, smiling. "Chicago is a splendid city."

"So, we're city girls." Grace nodded. "And fate brought us both here."

"Fate," said Julia.

They sipped tea slowly, as if they were women of leisure, without work to occupy them. As if they had all day. It had been a long time since Julia had stopped moving, stopped filling her time with pressured, mind-numbing activity, as a way of keeping feeling, thought, at bay.

"Your father?"

"A judge. And yours?"

"A doctor. He lives here. Dr. Strayer. Have you met him?"

Grace smiled again. "Oh yes. I've met him here. He asked that we sub-scribe to a particular journal for him. He's a very . . . gracious man."

"Gracious? Yes. That's a good word for him. He's worked hard. Patients of Dr. Bean's ask for him by name. He is a fully included partner in his practice now." Julia thought of how he had been during the epidemic. How he had redeemed himself, had rescued the somewhat suspect reputation he'd brought with him when they arrived in Johnstown. Someday she would tell Grace the whole story. Already she could imagine confiding such a thing. She could imagine how quickly she would learn to trust her.

Then she surprised herself by saying, "I am a very fine seamstress. I'd like to sew for you." It was not the circumspect approach that she had planned.

"You sew? What else do you do? What are your other talents?"

Julia blushed at the word. How without talent she seemed to herself. "I also play the piano. Although it's been a while. I seem to have given it up."

"You must never give up such a thing. Such gifts are precious. There is piano music in the library that can be checked out. Did you know that?"

"Someday. Maybe I'll do it. But I'm more interested in sewing now. If you need some things"—she was reluctant to impose on this new friend-ship—"I would be pleased to sew for you."

"I left . . ." Grace began, and then she checked herself. She had been about to say, "I left hurriedly, with almost nothing." A confession that would not quite do. "I could actually use a few simple things. Day dresses. Would that be too ordinary for you?"

"Oh no. I'm trying to gather clientele, hoping word will spread. I'm quite new at this, in fact." Then she was quick to reassure. "But also skilled. You shouldn't worry about hiring me."

"I won't, then. So how do you wish to go about this?"

"At Geis's there are catalogues, fabrics to choose from. If those don't suit, we can order finer things."

"They'll suit. My needs are simple. And fittings?"

"In your home would be best, I'd think. I would come to your home."

Grace nodded. And that simple nod pleased Julia. It felt like a promise, a commitment to a future plan. She could not remember the last time she had felt anything approaching anticipation.

"So, shall we go to Geis's one day next week?" Julia said with the authority of one in charge.

"Next week."

Julia sipped her tea again. Darjeeling. A name as foreign as the life she seemed about to embark upon. A new life. Her tentative, small secret.

By the time six months had passed, Julia's sewing enterprise and her new friendship were both flourishing. In her parlor, Julia sat near the open window, her head bent to her stitching, her small hands as deft as the day she had so capably demonstrated oyster shucking on her arrival in Johnstown. Her skin was not quite so silken as it was then; the veins were more prominent. But they would do, she thought about her hands. They'd do. She had spent her whole life fussing over them extraordinarily, her single vanity. The cream she bought and stored in a bureau drawer and worked so patiently into the skin at night, in the dark, her one extravagance.

Now the beautiful hands did beautiful work. Her needle nipped the gray Sicilienne, her thimble glimmered like a jewel in the lamplight. She was completing a reception dress for Rosina Quinn, who had access to so many lavish fabrics because her husband owned Johnstown's finest store, Geis, Foster and Quinn. If the sewing Julia did was a kind of art, then Rosina could be thought of as her patron. She wore some ready-mades, but she made it known to all her friends that she much preferred Julia's hand-made things. Julia kept baskets full of ornaments and notions—beaded passementerie, butterfly bows, yards of pongee and plissé. But Julia's next project would be something simple—a striped wool dress with a linen collar for Anna Fenn, who was going to sit for a photograph with her husband, John, and their five children. Three more than they had had when Claire and Louis died.

Julia's needle nipped again. She had made many things for Grace, too, in the months that she had known her. A pointed basque of ottoman silk with Byron cuffs and collar; a bonnet of straw strewn with lace and feathers and velvet flowers as a lark, an experiment they'd tried when ridiculous and highly ornamented hats came into vogue; a striking but simple "house" dress, made of Sicilienne of the pale salmon shade called *aurore du Bengale*. When Julia sewed for Grace, they were like girls playing dress-up. It was fun; they laughed together. The measuring and fitting all took place in Grace's rooms, her small apartment. Nothing there reminded Julia of anything. In her own house everything seemed heavy, weighted, so saturated with the past. After she'd seen Grace's rooms for the first time, she was so taken by their lightness that she almost suggested to Frank that they move away, sell everything, buy train tickets, disappear, leaving all behind. She had the sentences, the whole speech formed in her mind, but at dinner that night, she could not broach the subject. How had it happened that she could not find a way to talk to him? Work and friends, Daniel and Caroline had become everything to Frank. How could she ask him to follow her when for so long she had had so little to offer?

She had confided this to Grace. As she confided everything. And Grace shared things with her—at least some things. Julia was sure that Grace kept many secrets. She was hurt by that at first, and then she envied it. Julia envied the mystery, the sense of entitlement to privacy that it implied.

For her part, Grace admired Julia because there *were* no mysteries. Julia revealed herself with a frankness that Grace found astonishing. "We rarely make love," Julia had said early on. And then more recently she had spoken of the loss of her children, the loss of feeling, the loss of something essential between wife and husband. A truth Grace could never have admitted. Grace had been bred for silence and stoicism the way racehorses were bred for speed—with an eye toward what was required to win, to show oneself to the best advantage. She wished she were some other way;

she often felt that because of her reticence, she brought too little to the friendship. But amazingly, whatever it was Grace provided seemed to be enough: tea, books, the potent silence of the library at noon, the freedom of her temporary life, her mementoless rooms. And what Grace got in this bargain was a view into another life. A crumb, a taste, a sense of the possibilities. However lost they seemed to be to Julia now, these things had all been hers: children, sex fueled by desire, marriage to a man who was capable of love, who wanted to be married. She could have listened to Julia talk all day.

They were like favorite cousins, best friends, twins separated at birth by a cruel fate, then magically reunited. Like lovers.

DISCOVERIES

"Remember that to change your course and to follow someone . . . is not to be less free."
        —Marcus Aurelius, *Meditations*, Book VIII, Number 16

Finally, it was the water that drew Nora to them. The other "young people." She had kept herself apart from them the first four summers because she wished to. She preferred being alone. She was the kind of girl who believed that she could live without the things they offered—the thin and temporary friendships, the gossip-ridden conversations, the picnics filled with laughter. She cared not in the least for the fishing or hunting that the boys especially favored. She felt no need to bag a bird, or land one of the black bass who'd gone forth and multiplied since the day she'd watched from the woods as the tank cars spewed them into the lake. She could have lived forever without sun-induced camaraderie, and might have continued in her solitariness had she not so longed to be out on the water. Under sail, or in a scull, where she would be under the power of her own strong arms. Somehow it was only there, on the lake, that all was equalized, that boundaries blurred. There, on the water, the categories that ruled so much of club life grew indistinct and hazy. Which families were assigned the tables by the windows in the dining room, who had private cottages, who occupied the smallest clubhouse rooms, who had fortunes, who did not.

The differentiations disappeared. On the water, even sex was without import or meaning. Girls as well as boys could check sculls out of the boathouse. Could row the length of the lake, explore the farthest reaches of the South Fork property. One only had to be an able swimmer and to learn the mechanics that the different types of boats required. The paid boating instructors, brought from boarding schools in Massachusetts and New Hampshire, had designed a simple test that had to be passed before you could take a boat out alone. You would be taken to a deep part of the lake, dumped into the water, have the boat upended over you. A simulation of capsizing. If you could swim from under it, then right the bulky wooden hull, you could take a boat out on the lake alone. This was done with the sculls and one-man sailing skiffs. Nora had watched the test administered from one of the many vantage points she had discovered in her survey of the paths around the lake. A paid instructor and a member of the boathouse staff, servants of a sort, obliged to call these children Miss and Mister. Required to be respectful, even when no respect was felt. Nora saw through her spyglass the way their faces changed when the instructee was flailing in the water. The perverseness, the satisfaction. The unnecessary roughness of the gesture when they finally lent a hand to pull the weary, if triumphant, swimmer from the water. "Want help, do you?" she imagined the staff members thinking to themselves. "Struggling, are you? Cold?" Every helpful movement had the feel of reluctance and contempt to it. And whose part could she take, sitting there watching? Nora, neither fish nor fowl herself. Not quite equal to the other guests, but not the hired help. She did not dwell on it. All she cared about was the fact that once she'd passed the test, the entire lake would be hers.

Her father was always promising that he'd teach her how to sail. Finally, after four years, she knew it was time to look elsewhere. She began the kind of study that came so easily to her. Watching. Looking up with a practiced casualness from her late-afternoon reading on the clubhouse porch to see, at that time of day when the wind was lightest, whose boat moved most swiftly on the water. Sails in that changing light seemed an even starker white with the orange-turning sun as backdrop. She liked listening to the challenges tossed back and forth across the water, the breathless, mostly male bravado. Most often Louis Clarke in his noisy, rowdy little steamboat would serve as the starter for these late-in-the-day impromptu races, and then as judge. He had a tailored sailor suit with middy collar, cord piping on the pants and sleeves. It made him look nautical, to be sure, but also, Nora thought, a little foolish. Or at least she *had* thought that. But when the slips were launched for racing, when they hovered at the shore, at the arbitrarily chosen starting line, Louis, dressed for sailing, seemed to lend just the right touch. She could hear the toot-toot—the steamboat whistle—as Louis chugged and maneuvered into place. Most times he used another whistle, one he wore on a cord around his neck, for the start. But as he got older, as he became more trusted by his father, he often used a gun. It was a thrilling thing. That single, articulate, sharp sound. Not muffled like the shots of the hunters in the woods were. There was a spirit and incisiveness about it. It made her want to rush to the pier to join the others, to shout calls of encouragement to the oddball little fleet. It made her want to forget her contrived indifference. "Hurry," she'd say, just beneath her breath, her book forgotten, its closed cover pressed to her chest. Whispering encouragement to no one in particular. She had no special friend to cheer.

Putting her book aside, she watched as the boats tacked back and forth, cut the water into curls of froth, caught what wind there was, moving farther and farther from her. Until they became small wavering triangles of white, then lines, then mere points on the far horizon. Each time she watched them disappear, the fates she imagined for them grew more elaborate. They became explorers or mercenaries; they were met by gods at the exact point where the sun slipped into the earth's thin rim. Wings were attached to their slim crafts. The ties of earth and family had dissolved and freed them.

Finally, she decided that she would choose one of the older boys to be her sailing instructor. She would work a little with her hair, think twice instead of not at all about the dress she wore to dinner. Leave her parents' table early to join "the youngsters" gathering for songs on the clubhouse lawn. Sixteen years old. She'd been four years a close observer of the subtleties of club life, it was just a matter of acquiescing to them. To possess the water, she would do what was required.

Batten, tack, mainsheet, boom. Jib sheet, portside, halyard, head. Edward took his role of teacher seriously, drew diagrams for her, made lists of terms.

"But when may I try it, Edward? When may I try?"

He cautioned patience. He was twenty, older, and saw in this a chance to be as doctrinaire as so many of the teachers in his preparatory school had been to him. Once he began Nora's sailing lessons, once he claimed a teacher's power, he began to understand what drove them. For the first time he, too, felt the pleasures of authority, the satisfaction power brings. He didn't wish to torture her, this, the funniest of girls from his point of view. "The pretty pigtailed one," as the boys generally referred to her. He was surprised when she approached him, surprised to hear her voice at all. She'd kept herself so apart from all of them. Then all of a sudden she was there one evening, just standing in front of him and, he found to his surprise, not without her own mysterious charms.

"I've been watching, and you're quite skilled at sailing," she said. Pale moths hovered around the lanterns that had been strung under the eaves of the porch roof. Her lush braid was slung forward over her shoulder, but even so, the frizz of her hair, the exuberance of it backlit by the lantern light, created the effect of a nimbus or a gold dusting of stars around her head. The style for girls her age included artfully arranged curls and short, crimped bangs, complex and tortured hairdos. No one wore her hair as Nora did. What made her think she could do it? Or, as Edward had heard his mother say, "Who does she think she is?" *Who do they think they are?* Without regard for style or custom. Wearing her hair like some wanton thing, some servant. Roaming the paths hacked through the woods. Alone. To what end? Where did she think she was going?

But Edward, youngest, least-accomplished son in a highly accomplished family and unaccustomed to flattery, to such unabashed and charming admiration, was as seduced by it as some other boy might have been seduced by averted eyes, shy maneuverings, and indirection. Teach me how to sail. She all but demanded it.

"It isn't easy, you know. It won't be easy for you. Fair warning, that's all," he said roughly that first night. Dinner had been served at seven, by eight-thirty everyone but parents began assembling on the lawn. The gloaming. Darkness just beginning to extend itself from the velvet blackness of the trees out onto the open spaces. The porch lanterns were hung in such a way that the whole narrow expanse of grass that sloped from clubhouse to water could be illuminated once the last light faded. Someone was stringing a badminton net. Edward had been sitting on the bottom clubhouse step. She dropped abruptly to a place beside him, wrapped her arms around her knees. "I've been watching you," she said again.

"Am I so interesting?" He laughed.

"You're the best sailor here, and I want to learn to do it. You needn't worry. I'll work hard, learn quickly, and be grateful. I won't be a bother," she said after outlining her plan. Simple enough.

"I'm not sure I have time," he ventured, uncertain how to handle this request. There were other girls he would have preferred tutoring, but they were satisfied enough to be passengers of his on the lake, to let him read the wind, handle the sails and rudder. Either of the Lawrence girls, real beauties to his mind, would have been a great pleasure to teach. But neither of the Lawrence girls had asked him.

"Mornings would be best," he said, thinking of her predawn wanderings that he had heard about, thinking that the suggestion of a morning time would dissuade her.

"Fine."

He nodded his head toward her soft hands clasped around the folds of her skirt, around her knees, then reached out, took one of them, and turned it palm up toward the light. "Your hands will become coarse and dirty. The lines make calluses," he said, showing her the thick rough pads on his.

"It'll ready my hands for rowing, then. I plan to row, too." She took her hand back.

"We're only here two weeks. It's not much time." He hated the idea of binding himself to this, to her. He feared how it would eat into his day.

"Look here," she said abruptly. "Will you or won't you? You're pussy-footing. I'd rather have an answer. What do you say?"

Annie Semple had flung herself across the hammock tied between two willows at the porch's edge. She used her toe to set herself to rocking, synchronized the rocking to keep time with some new tune Hart McKee played on the banjo. He was always playing something no one had ever heard of. Ida Irwin was calling to her group, the younger girls, to join her in catching fireflies.

There is something about a summer night. It makes yes so much easier than no. The comma of the moon hung in an oak's high branches. Her shoulder touched his; the swish of the petticoats of the firefly catchers, the intimate hum of moths as they pressed foolishly toward lantern light, the sigh of the elm leaves as they brushed one against the other. What was there for him but to acquiesce? To rise from his seat and bow to her. To promise.

Batten, tack, mainsheet, boom, jib sheet, portside, halyard, head. She'd learn the intricate mechanics. She'd learn to read the wind and water.

Tuyeres, nozzles, stoppers, sleeves. Trunnions and brick converter bottoms. In Johnstown, there were also lists. Memorization was essential there as well. Daniel, home after his first year in Philadelphia, signed on for summer work. It was not uncommon for men to fall victim to heat stroke; extra hands were always needed. He worked one day, sometimes two, a week. He was hell-bent on trying this thing, and Frank had walked him through it, prepared him for what he'd see.

The Bessemer converter, shaped like a pear. A 12-foot-tall pear with a steel exterior, a firebrick stomach, capable of holding the molten pig iron that was poured into it as if it were thick hot soup. Pourable metal, sizzling, roiling, giving off an explosive, sun-brilliant light. So hot. Each man watching, waiting at his station attentively. A glance away, a moment's hesitation could be deadly. Wind of sorts was a factor in this world, too. Levers set the big pear to swinging slowly on its trunnions, waiting for cold air to be pumped into it through tuyeres extruding from its bottom. At the outset of the process, Frank explained to Daniel, expect eerie silence. A few red sparks shoot from the top, the pig iron quietly but steadily grows hotter. Then there is a sound like a whirlwind. The upward suck of cold, converting air.

Two thousand, three, four thousand degrees. Impure silicon breaking its iron bond. The cold air's oxygen binding carbon to it. The molten mass, reluctant convert, begins its heaving side to side. The pear-shaped vessel trembles, shudders, rocks. The pig-iron mass pounds as it tosses, "a tortured god" resisting, with a moan, the alterations it endures. For iron as much as for any live, organic thing, change brings with it a kind of agony. Some men turn their gazes from it briefly; it sounds so much like suffering that it's hard to watch, difficult to be steady in the face of so much pain. And then the moan becomes a roar, a shrieking, and then an arced white light fans a flame of victory high into the air above the converter. Men step back and shade their hurt eyes from it. Frank Fallon, lapsed Catholic, nonbeliever, hail-fellow and cynic, knows he's not alone in imagining that this is the way God will return to earth one day. That He'll bring with Him this shattering, this sound, this earth-illuminating light.

A signal, and the light subsides a little, everyone moves quickly to man his station. The lever tender raises one gloved hand, and the sluices aimed toward molds are checked, moved a last half inch into position. The gloved hand drops; the converter, as if nodding yes, it's time, tilts forward to release its liquid load; and pure steel, thin as water, quick-moving as a sun-struck stream, pours out into the waiting ladle, then into assorted sluices, and finally into the waiting, shape-making molds. Men stand in thick-soled boots just inches from it, from the hottest thing on earth, with poles and prickers and turning wrenches ready to direct the flow. To make ingots, steel bars, rails. To trap each drop before it cools and hardens.

Sometimes the ladle overflows, sometimes the hot steel eats right through it and hits the floor, or splashes up from the pit beneath it. So many variables, so much room for human error. Things go wrong, and when they do, men suffer. Men burn and die slowly, or are burned alive, too stunned even to raise their arms to shield themselves, too dumbstruck to cower. Men rigid with surprise, their straight backs stiff as the wick in a candle flame, the sudden awful pain etching their faces until their faces melt. Quick is the death that everybody wants. Quick is what praying men pray for.

And after each firing, the pit and the ladle and the firebrick belly of the pear converter have to be cleaned, set steel scraped from them, a judgment made about how many blows a lining could withstand before it crumbled. Three? Sometimes just one or two? The foreman has to say, has to live with his fallibility, and when mistakes are made has to tell the wives and mothers.

That was Frank Fallon's job, and his men counted on him. It was one of the first things the men told the boy just after he started working. "Your dad knows, Daniel. Learn from him."

Daniel Fallon. Nineteen. Sweat soaked him and left a salty residue on his shirt. He was sore after his first day, his skin burnished by the heat of the work, the close proximity to fire. He feared he'd grown soft in Philadelphia, that there had been too much time spent with books and in the city. All summer long he would fight against that image of himself. He'd work harder, faster, more. Soon bets were being placed on him, how quick he'd be, how many rails they'd roll on days when he was working. He drank with the men on Friday nights, a pint or two at California Tom's to slake the thirst that had developed in him. That thirst was a sure sign that this kind of work was in his blood, that he was an ironman, his work crew told him. That unquenchable thirst.

It had been easy for Daniel to learn Nora's name, simple to gather information about the club's summer schedule. Young men he'd grown up with worked at South Fork lake that summer, waiting on tables, mowing grass, tending to the trees. Keeping the grounds and cottages in good repair. He had spies everywhere.

And because she had not left his mind since he had seen her the previous August, because he could not manage no matter how he tried to rid his mind of her, the girl at the lake became his other summer project. A horse let from Snavely's, the ride to the lake. He learned that most days she left the clubhouse at first light, that there was boating in the afternoon. But the mornings she retained as her own. The day after his spies said that she'd arrived, he waited in the woods behind the clubhouse, and when she chose a path, he followed.

In this way he discovered things about her. He watched from a distance and learned things that no one else took the time to know. She had made nests for herself throughout the property. Burrows of a sort, where she stashed notebooks, journals, a glass, a magnifying lens. He watched her watch the world. On hands and knees, small prodding stick in hand, she urged ant columns forward. (Once she'd left a spot, he often went to it, to see what had kept her so long in her kneeling pose, what she had been observing. Bug life more often than not. Beetles and ants. Caterpillars organizing themselves for an assault, for the task of webbing trees.) Once out of the clubhouse she rolled her sleeves up, baring her arms. When climbing or wading a narrow mountain stream was required, she hiked her skirt up shamelessly, sometimes knotting it between her legs to create a kind of pantaloon. On one particularly humid day she removed her blouse to splash cool water from the lake over her neck and shoulders, and he had turned away from the curve of her underarm, the sheer, revealing lace of her chemise. Wanting to watch, but at the same time wanting to protect her. Understanding that he ought to respect her privacy. More than once he felt that he shouldn't be there. That his interest was a violation, that his knowledge of her a theft. He had entered her world uninvited.

He made rules for himself. He would allow himself to read the notebooks that outlined her observation of the natural world but would never read her diaries. He would not gain dishonest access to her inner life, her longings. Instead, he read the journals that she had labeled WORKBOOKS. And from those learned some of the essential things. That she thought of herself as scientist. Discoverer. That she feared idleness, valued industry. Time, she declared, in a workbook wrapped in an oilskin cloth and tucked under a rock on the north side of the lake, was the most valuable commodity. She swore she would never waste it. She had the small pinched script he'd seen so often in the science laboratories at the university, and in that script she filled page after page. She urged herself to greater effort, collected aphorisms that inspired. "Do not wander without a purpose, but in all your impulses render what is just, and in all your imaginations, preserve what you apprehend." Marcus Aurelius.

He would have winced at the term "voyeur." He didn't think of himself that way. He simply believed that he wanted to know her, and he could think of no other way to achieve that. Hers was a world quite different from his, there would be no introductions. Nonetheless, he had come to imagine that they were alike somehow. That they shared something essential, that they'd met in another life, that their souls were bound. (Such uncharacteristically romantic notions. Too much time spent in the library perhaps? Too many hours spent brooding?)

He also imagined himself to be her protector. When he'd first seen her at the lake that day last summer, he'd thought her vulnerable. Not weak, but at risk somehow. An endangered species in an unkind world. The head of some resistance movement. Her hair, the emphatic, simple way she wore it, was like a proclamation, a challenge to some enemy. "I am not like you."

He fingered the scar on his neck.

Two weeks, his spies had told him. That was all. He traveled to the club grounds every day that he was not working. He had told himself when he started that that would be the end of it, that in two weeks he would have satisfied himself. But he found as the time of her departure drew near that he was not satiated, that he could not let go of her so easily.

Toward the end of her stay, he began leaving things for her. Tokens. A textbook from the botany class he had taken in Philadelphia, an unusual wildflower (rue anemone) tucked as bookmark in its pages; a handful of freshly sharpened pencils tied together with string. And as he grew bolder, notes: "Have you considered bird-watching? The junco nests near moving water under tuft of ferns. White-crowned sparrows flourish here; the lake is home to loons." Or: "The butterflies are varied, surprising, worth your time." Warnings: "Don't underestimate these woods. There are snakes. Bears. There are dangers here." He wanted to make himself known, he wanted contact of a sort, but he also wished to lay his own claim to this place, declare his knowledge of it. To let her know that it was not her privilege and hers alone to be here. He never stayed to watch her find what he had left. He never learned what his leavings meant to her. It was enough for him to know that his presence had been felt, that an impress of him had been left on her and on the South Fork property.

At the beginning Nora hardly knew what to make of these gifts, these notes, these leavings, the idea of being watched. She felt as if something was being taken from her—her secret, essential life, spoiled, stolen. She imagined another young club member, Frank Willock or George Shea, spying, plotting a cruel public betrayal of her at dinner one night or on a picnic. But as days passed and the notes and offerings continued, she began to imagine that it was not someone from the club but, rather, someone local, a boy, a young man perhaps. Some secret admirer. She blushed, and found that the idea of being watched sent a small frisson of pleasure through her. It spoke to some vanity that she was unaware of, that she'd kept hidden. She was just sixteen. And for the first time someone was struck by her. Someone was watching.

All his early notes addressed her work (she blushed again, thinking how presumptuous she was to refer to her crude observations and accountings in that way), and she found that thrilling. "You are taken seriously," she said aloud to her reflection in the mirror in her room. "You are interesting."

After the first few days, she began to leave things for him as well. Directions to a spot on the South Fork property where she had spotted blue-winged locusts (in case he cared about such things, in case he shared her insect passions). Three plums wrapped in one of her embroidered handkerchiefs. A blank notebook in the event that he, like she, wanted to keep a record of discoveries.

Over the years, the children of Johnstown had often stopped on their way home from school to gather at the ornamental iron fence that surrounded the Morrell property on Main Street in Johnstown. Hoping for a glimpse of Mr. Morrell himself, with his barrel chest and the bib of whiskers on his chin and neck, always happy to stop and talk, never able to walk down the street without speaking to his neighbors, always remembering the names of the children. It didn't matter to the children waiting at the iron fence that, at the time when they were there, late afternoon, when school ended, he was not at home. There would be no sighting. Mr. Morrell was at the iron works, in his office, or on the mill floor watching the furnaces being fired. But a ritual had developed among the children, and ritual does not bow easily to reality; they stopped anyway, hoping for a glimpse, most often having to be satisfied with watching the gardener, who sometimes offered a single rose to each of them, or a small bouquet of lilacs, to take home to their mothers. Distributing them as a priest might bestow blessings, or a prisoner might pass a message through the iron bars of his cell. Daniel stopped there often throughout his years of growing up, intrigued by the size of the house, wondering what use so many rooms might be put to. Without envy, without longing. Happy enough as a child to live the life he lived, to have in his hand the gift of a rosebud with which to surprise his mother.

No one could say with any certainty when it was that Mr. Morrell began fumbling over names, when he stopped going to the library he loved, when the word "Bessemer" first eluded him, the surest sign by far of slippage, the moment when his colleagues realized how serious the problem was. No one could say specifically when this decline began, but George Swank at the *Tribune* and Horace Rose and Fred Grebs, the manager at the Gautier barbed-wire plant, all believed that it began the year the club was built, after his attempt to see to the safety of the dam had failed. His first known failure. They imagined that his mind had simply begun to slowly, steadily shut down against it, to close itself against the idea of defeat.

It was rumored that he had begun talking to his orchids, and that in the mornings, in his greenhouse, he had begun imagining that the phalaenopsis, especially, were answering. Perhaps the currents of air that stirred the greenhouse's moist atmosphere made the frail white blossoms quiver in such a way that they seemed to be nodding, saying yes. Agreeing with him. Perhaps the tiny inner lips of the blooms had looked as if words were taking shape there.

But then Cyrus Elder, the company's solicitor, let slip one day that things had come to such a pass that Mr. Morrell had to be reminded to dress each morning. Long monologues became his preferred way of addressing friends who came, out of concern, to visit. The history of Henry Bessemer was his favorite topic. He was enchanted by the fact that Bessemer had begun his career engaged in operations that were refined and delicate—making dies for cutting lacy paper valentines and machines for cutting Utrecht velvet, the production of a fine bronze powder. He wanted his guests to imagine with him the move from such artistic pursuits to the work of blowing air through pig iron. He wanted them to share his wonder at Bessemer's genius. Morrell himself had indulged in a lifelong fascination with the idea of it. He'd financed a man named Kelly, given him a place at Cambria to work the kinks out of the Bessemer process. Now, with anyone who came to visit, Mr. Morrell recalled himself as a young ironmaster, reminiscing about his pioneering days. As his arteries grew clogged and brittle, as his heart had to labor to pump his own blood through them, he dreamed of the flash and glare of liquid steel as it sluiced lightning fast into molds or into the rolling machine. "Be quick," he barked at his men in his dreams. "Look alive now, pay attention!" The only sure way to avoid injury, to control the process, rather than being controlled by it. In his dreams he heard the sounds and checked the firebrick bellies of the huge converters; he watched their giant pear shapes swinging on the trunnions, gave the signal for cold air to be pumped through the tuyeres. He managed everything himself.

By night, in his dream life, he was an iron man again. But by day he was losing words, then days of the week, the capacity to leave his house, the ability to form clear sentences. By 1884 he had given up his civic life, retired from business. Then on Thursday, August 20, 1885, Daniel Morrell died.

Citizens queued up beside the ornamental iron fence in the days that followed, waiting to pay their respects. Children who had waited for a glimpse of him on their walks home from school, who had accepted flowers as a thin substitute for his large presence, were young adults now, and they waited in the heat with their parents, walked through the gardens, entered the front door, hesitated there. They crossed themselves, or knelt briefly at the open casket in the parlor. On the Monday of the burial, the iron works closed, and the men who worked for him led the funeral cortege. It was agreed that that was the way Mr. Morrell would have wanted it. The workers first, thousands of them, filling the newly paved streets, filing past the Morrell Institute, the hospital, all the buildings he had built, dressed in their best suits, a somber processional. They had the honor of leading, worried about how this loss would change their lives, but putting worry aside to honor him. The police and the firemen, the city fathers and professional men all followed behind them.

As he did in the Memorial Day parade each year, Daniel walked beside his father that day, too. The sun shone wanly from behind great tufts of opalescent clouds. Hemlocks and hickories shaded the streets. The windows of the shops were uniformly draped in black mourning crepe. The city had a dark dignity about it, as if it had willed itself to be a place of muted, shadowed beauty as a way of giving honor. The bells of the twenty-seven churches tolled for thirty minutes in a final echoing salute as Daniel walked beside his father, as he wondered how he would break the news to him. How to say that he was not going to return to the university, to Philadelphia. Because even as he marched in tribute to Morrell, Daniel was planning the changes that might be made at the iron works now that Morrell was gone. Unionization was on Daniel's mind, it was his idea that he would bring the labor movement home. The Knights of Labor organization in Philadelphia had promised seed money; he'd already talked to L. D. Woodruff, editor of the weekly *Democrat*, who did job printing on the side, who could be trusted to be discreet and secretive in producing the leaflets and flyers needed to forward the cause. Two years away had enlarged Daniel's vision. He meant to change the way the world worked.

The library was not on the route of the Morrell funeral procession. But in honor of the day its windows had also been scrubbed clean, and sunlight beamed through the fanlight transom and onto the freckled-wood floor. Grace McIntyre was alone in the building, alone at her desk, and glad of it. At the library there was always catching up to do.

She had been awash in the lovely silence. Except for Main Street, where citizens waited and watched the funeral procession move slowly toward the cemetery, all the other streets were empty, strangely still. Even the railroads seemed to have halted. Their predictable and, to Grace, reassuring clangs and whistles, which studded the air with such piercing regularity, were notable on this day for their absence. She had been listening to two birds call to each other in the large black birch just beyond the window near her desk when the church bells began to toll their prolonged threnody. How moved this small world seemed to be by this one death. She wondered, briefly, what it would be like to be admired, loved that way.

Of course she *was* admired. It was something she felt she had not earned, but nonetheless it had been mercifully granted her. She advised Horace Rose and the Literary Society about books that ought to be acquired for the library's collection. She led small reading groups and had taken to delivering sacks of books to nearby Woodvale, where she began a lunchtime lending library at the woolen mill, for the hundreds of women who worked there. In this way she came to be known. Men tipped hats to her in the street, she had been asked to teach a course on poetry appreciation at the Morrell Institute; she had gained a following, had come to be included.

Daniel Fallon admired her, she knew. When Mr. Rose had approached her about teaching Greek to Daniel, shortly after she'd arrived, she had been reluctant, uncertain about how long she would be staying, parsimonious with her time. But Horace Rose had waxed eloquently about Daniel's gifts, and once she took him on, she saw firsthand how great his talents actually were. More than once as she had sat at the library table beside him, watching his lips shape themselves around the foreign, Greek pronunciations, watching his brow furrow from effort, she thought, had she had a child, she would have wanted such a one as this. His presence in her life—the twice-weekly tutoring sessions, the flowers he often picked to bring to her, the extra work he did so regularly in an eager effort to impress her—so enhanced her time in Johnstown that she had felt a base and wicked happiness when she learned from him about his mother's suffering, a cold thrill at the thought that loss had caused another woman so much pain that she had relinquished everything to it. Even this boy. For months she had thought proudly of herself as Daniel's other mother. The good one, the one who loved and understood.

How hard it had been, then, when Julia first came to the library. Graceful, tentative, hope flickering in her eyes. Someone making an effort, someone trying to re-enter the life she had abandoned. Grace had not expected Julia's visit, she'd had no chance to gird herself against it, against her. She found herself offering tea, solicitude. And then, somewhat reluctantly, as time passed, friendship. She had thought herself generous, magnanimous in offering such a thing, until she realized how long she'd been without friendship's solace, how hungry she was for it. They exchanged small confidences, Julia made clothing for her, they shared books and a nearly grown child.

Grace fingered the chenille fringe on the basque Julia had recently made for her, glad that the church bells had ceased. Later in the day Daniel would stop by to visit with her here. He was good in that way, careful of her feelings, even now that he was away at school, always eager to show his regard. During the academic year, from Philadelphia he sent letters, newspaper clippings that he thought might interest her, and once, a silk-cord bookmark with a tiny ivory elephant knotted at its end. Small tokens. She had not known when she came from Boston that such small things could come to mean so much, that a life could be stitched from them.

She rose to collect the teacups from the cupboard where she stored them. By now, at the cemetery, the interment must be taking place. Images came to her—the fecund scent of just-turned earth, the thready rasp of the coffin scuffing at the ropes that lowered it. When her death came, she knew it would not be mourned as elaborately as Mr. Morrell's had been, and that knowledge didn't trouble her. She had once had grand plans for her life, plans meant to please her father. Now she felt lucky to have made a life at all, to have come to know the value of small triumphs.

Midmorning tea with Julia, a sweet tart shared with Daniel in the late afternoon. A day of pleasures. Even a death could not dim that.

Four years into their partnership, and already there were tensions between Frick and Carnegie. In spite of the fact that Carnegie spent almost all his time away from Pittsburgh, he maintained autocratic control over his business. He chose his partners for their abilities, and then endlessly second-guessed them. Frick, unaccustomed to acceding to the authority of any man, received Carnegie's daily barrage of telegrams with icy detachment and wrote cryptic, short replies.

In the early 1880s, Carnegie had gained a reputation for negotiating with his workers. He gave rousing public speeches on the rights of labor to organize, on the evils of strikebreaking. He put into place an eight-hour day for workers at his Edgar Thomson plant, replacing the twelve-hour shift that had so long been the standard. He was proud of his progressive thinking, but within months had retreated from it.

Because what he discovered about himself was that his principles were fluctuating, dependent always on the bottom line of profit. Frick, who in the early days of their association hoped for friendship, for some affectionate connection to the older Carnegie, grew to hate him for his equivocations and his bow-taking.

"I am in bed with the devil," Frick said to Mellon in the Clayton library on a September night in 1885. It was almost midnight, and Adelaide and the baby were asleep upstairs. Mellon could be counted on for counsel any hour of the day or night. Since the death of his fiancée, it appeared to Frick that he had given up sleeping altogether. His only occupation besides business seemed to be reading aloud to his ailing, almost-blind father.

"True enough, but he is a wealthy devil. If you must be bedded with one, best him."

Mellon was the only person with whom Frick could confide in this way. Discretion was his hallmark.

"He is always allowing himself to be quoted. He writes for magazines, for the love of God; gives speeches in which he contradicts everything, absolutely everything that we both believe in. Wouldn't you think he would have sense enough not to allow himself to be quoted?"

"And you are his partner," Mellon reminded him, his voice subdued, as it always was. Reason prevailing. "Bide your time. Your day will come. You'll walk away with a vast fortune and your freedom. Patience. Be shrewd and patient."

And so he was. His wealth accumulated while he stayed the course throughout the 1880s, the South Fork years. But Frick's distrust never abated, and by the middle of the decade, contempt for Carnegie was festering in him like a sore.

"Dickens?"

"Dickens." Frank Fallon stood patiently at the library desk, hat in hand, dressed in his work clothes, but he was clean. He'd freshened up in the yard behind the iron works, where there were tin pails and strong soap, running water. He was not a man to go out in public with the stench of work on him.

"Were you looking for a particular book by Dickens? Or shall I recommend one?" As if he hadn't read them all, as if he hadn't all but memorized them.

"One of his later books?" he asked politely. Then admitted, "I've read the early work." Early work. Injecting that edge of knowing into his voice, that hint of expertise. He looked down at Grace, seated at her desk, her hair tucked up into some kind of elaborate S at the back of her head, her round face suddenly tilted up toward him. The fact that she was pretty came as a surprise. He'd imagined her as plain. Julia had said that she had never been married. Julia said that they'd become so close that they had talked of everything, confided everything to one another. Grace had told Julia that she'd given up on love. Stopped looking for it.

She had the appearance of someone younger than forty, forty-one, whatever age she was. Maybe she looked that way *because* she hadn't been married or had children; maybe marriage and children, the burdens of those things, aged one. That such a thought could even occur to him surprised Frank. He never allowed regretful or discouraged thoughts to stray through his brain, anything that smacked even a little of self-pity. He feared that the gods would strike at him or his children again if he was ever anything but optimistic.

"Do you have a library card? Perhaps you've been here before, maybe you've already got one. So many people come, it's hard to keep up."

"A card? Let's see about the book first. Then we can talk about a card."

How strange he must have seemed to her, this big red-haired stranger, hair still wet from his freshening-up, a residue of soap clinging to the angle of his jaw, filming his whiskers. And as *she* took *him* in, evaluated *him*, Frank found himself trying to reconcile a surprising mix of feelings. Perhaps not identifying himself, presenting himself under these false pretenses, as some random curious library user, was wrong. It felt like lying. But he'd thought that he needed to approach her as a stranger; he wanted to get a sense of her before he became identified as Julia's husband, Daniel's father. How else would he be able to take the measure of her? To try to see in her what they saw. Even as she spoke, he felt a foolish, humiliating jealousy. How was it that someone besides himself had had the power to bring Julia back to engagement, interest, life? How had it happened that friendship had wrought what love could not? His real wish, felt keenly even as he feigned politeness, was to ask her outright. To accuse her. I've loved her for more than twenty years. What entitles you to interfere?

She pushed her chair back, rose, and gestured for him to follow her. "Dickens's late work?" She barely suppressed a slight smile, and he could tell from the sound of her voice that she was teasing a little. Teasing the self-proclaimed Dickens expert.

"So, *Great Expectations*? *Our Mutual Friend*?

He nodded. "Either will do."

"Come with me, then. Fiction is at the far end of this room. I'll show you." She pulled her skirt aside with her hand, a little easy flick of her muslin skirt and petticoats, as if dancing were part of the plan. He added that to things of note about her. That there had been dancing in her past. She stepped lightly in front of him.

He followed just behind her, listening to her polite, soft-voiced chatter, about the fine selection of fiction that the library had acquired, how she'd worked in larger cities, bigger libraries, and the collection here measured up quite nicely in comparison. There was an undercurrent of pride in her voice, some proprietary sense of pleasure, as if she'd lived here all her life.

She was larger than Julia, a bit taller, her body shaped more emphatically. She walked as if she owned the room, as if the books, the shelves, the lights, the windows, all belonged to her. Like the reigning monarch striding among her loyal subjects: gracious, charming, certain of her power.

When she mentioned other libraries at which she'd worked, he saw an opening, a chance to discover more. "You've been a librarian for a long time?"

"Years," she said. A kind of tension worked itself across her shoulders.

"And where were you before you were here?"

"New England," she said vaguely.

"Here we are." She ran her fingers along the spines of a shelf of books, pulled *Great Expectations* out with one quick tilt, and, with a flourish, handed it to him. "If you'd like to branch out, beyond Dickens, that is, there are a number of things I could suggest."

Frank rushed to defend. "You don't like Dickens?"

"Well, of course I do," she said. "He's wonderful. Of course. But I *am* a librarian, after all. I'm here to help. I was just offering my services to you." She blushed slightly, wondering how this had become so awkward: she defensive, he abrupt. And he liked her then. The combination of things she seemed to be. Assured but shy, confident but somehow cautious. He felt compelled to be honest with her.

"I'm Frank Fallon," he said, extending his hand. Casting aside the plan to know her before he revealed himself.

"Oh. Oh, Julia's husband? Why didn't you tell me?"

He had no answer, of course. Nothing to say for himself. So he said, "Why don't you recommend something else for me? You're right. What good is a librarian if no one seeks her help?"

And so she thought for a moment, hand poised at her chin, index finger tapping lightly at her cheek. She wanted to recommend just the right thing for this surprising man, so intimately connected to Julia and Daniel, two of the people in the town she had come to admire most. Henry James? Jules Verne? Then she thought of Trollope, and since *Barchester Towers* had been checked out, she pressed *Can You Forgive Her?* into his hand.

After his first visit to the library, something drew Frank back again and again. Most often when he went, he sat reading, availing himself of the newspapers and magazines there, the several comfortable chairs arranged around a table with a dictionary opened on it, just a few feet away from the desks where the librarians labored. And in that way he was able to observe Grace. Not that he could be there so much; he worked ten-, twelve-hour shifts, after all, he was not a man of leisure. But with his children grown and his wife so . . . so unknowable to him, he found that he had a little time to spend. And so he spent it there, at the library, as if time were money and this his gift to himself. Grace and Mrs. Hirst both called the library the village well. Central to everything, where people stopped for books, for a list of the lectures to be offered, for the surprise of discovering a neighbor there whom you'd missed, whom you hadn't seen. Another California Tom's, but without the whiskey, with the surprising scent of just-baked bread (women often visited there after getting groceries). Frank did not really think of the time he spent there as having to do with Grace, although he was aware of her. The determined zest she brought to work with her, the flick of her skirt, the fact that she served tea, arbitrarily, to regulars, to favorites. He tried to imagine her as she must have been with Daniel when he was younger, two chair seats touching as they labored over the Greek alphabet. The idea of enlisting her in his campaign to urge Daniel back to school occurred to him. Law, Frank had decided. He could study law. A better use for himself than rabble-rousing here. He had first come to the library resenting Grace's interference, her presence in his life, Julia's attachment to her. Now he wanted her to help him.

The comfort that his library time afforded him was unexpected, welcome. As the weeks passed, he became aware of how much the place, the press, the steady flow of people, the scent of glue and binding, the scent of books pleased him. At first he could not articulate what he felt about it, and then one day he realized that he felt invited into meaning there, that the world seemed large when viewed from the library's broad windows.

I Have Been Watching You

"It is a property of man to love even those who stumble."
— Marcus Aurelius, *Meditations*, Book VII, Number 22

Once Nora had acquired a new, albeit unknown, companion in her summer life, her winter life, her months in her parents' Pittsburgh home, became more and more unreal to her. She performed activities by rote. Her lack of freedom irked her, but she tried to keep her irritation largely to herself. There were mother-daughter tea parties, meant to be part of the ongoing effort to enhance the social skills that would soon be needed by young women in society. There were dancing classes and piano lessons, Episcopal church service, classes in deportment and elocution. There was needlepoint to learn. Only in school did Nora still find small islands of interest and sweet satisfaction, but even there the pleasures waned as the curriculum for older girls began to be geared more and more toward what were thought of as the very different and much more modest educational requirements of women. College, she hoped, would begin to address that problem. She was already anticipating the objections of her parents, who would certainly oppose her going.

What sustained her through the winter months were her thoughts of South Fork. In her room at night she sharpened the pencils that her admirer had left for her the previous summer, and drew intricate and exact pencil sketches of insects of all varieties. On paper she captured the life cycle of the bright-line, brown-eye moth—caterpillar, pupa, and adult; the tripartite bee's body, the legs of ants, delicate as snippets of silk thread. She placed each drawing, when it was finished, in a portfolio she kept beneath her bed. Perhaps she'd leave one of the sketches in the woods during the coming summer for her new summer friend. It never once occurred to her that he might lose interest during the time that she was absent. Or if it did, she crushed the thought so swiftly that it never had the chance to take the shape of fear or threat or apprehension.

Nora, the naturalist, the enthusiast of plants and birds and bugs, turned seventeen in 1886. She had been seduced by the just-published work of a little-known French naturalist, J. Henri Fabre, and in her South Fork room at night she read his account of his life devoted to acquiring a knowledge of the insect world: *Souvenirs Entomologiques*. She read and memorized and colonized his knowledge, made it hers. The first volume had only recently been translated, the second she read in French, pleased to be able to subvert what she knew to be the intended use of French in well-bred girls—the trip to the Continent sometime in the next few years, the ability to chitchat with the natives over a snail and foie gras dinner. Now, the more she read of Fabre, the more specific and obscure her vocabulary became. She had all but forgotten how to say, "It pleases me so much to meet you" and "What is the name of that lovely flower?" but she knew the French words for "grass tuft," "antennae," "tarsi"; she could describe in a flawless grammar how the demure-looking Prègo-Diéu eviscerates her prey. She stopped worrying about her lack of training, her lack of implements. "Time and patience," Fabre wrote, "are my best instruments." She adopted his motto as her own. *Laboremus*. Nora had made a kit for herself which she carried in a charming little drawstring satchel. Notebook, pen, magnifying glass, and little balsam boxes that she constructed for carrying insect specimens back to what she called her "studio," a little unused room next to one of the cold cellars that had been built to house the perishables from the clubhouse kitchen. In the woods, in one of the many little hideaways she had made for herself, she had hidden a net for catching butterflies, an illustrated text that she used as a source when she was trying to identify the flowers that grew in such surprising florid clusters on the sunny hills and in the underbrush. A diary.

She had created a world for herself in the woods, a parallel universe, a secret life. A place where the real child, Nora, lived. But she was seventeen that summer, and not a child, of course.

The two weeks every summer never felt long enough. She was so curious about lake life, so interested in *looking*. At the dragonflies, beetles, and locusts; at what life emerged if she went to the simple trouble of upending a rock. Were she and an aging Frenchman the only ones who knew of this? Of seething life? She found herself wondering. Sometimes on her expeditions, at the moment of discovery (ants parading in a marching column, bees prodding into the deep interior of flowers), she felt her blood rush, an unsettling hum of feeling overtook her, made her light-headed. All else seemed sterile by comparison to what she witnessed in the woods. She could hardly sit at dinner with her parents, she felt so unnerved, so warm that not even the chill of a mountain night could cool her. She longed to be alone to inventory her discoveries, but at the same time she longed for a confidant. Someone like herself. A summer-lover.

Was it that longing that made her change? She hardly knew. In fact, the changes came so subtly she wouldn't have called them changes at all. Is that how it always was? she wondered. That if one wasn't vigilant one could fall under some spell, capitulate to fantasy? She supposed it had begun the summer before, when she joined the others on the water, joined Edward and his friends in boating and in picnics at the spillway. It altered her identity as "other." Unwittingly, she had become one of them. She had begun to think that she wanted both things, a place on the periphery and a place among the others. A dual life. Because in spite of the strength with which she had resisted, she'd come to love the sense of otherworldliness at the South Fork Club, of time and reality suspended.

Everything conspired to support that sense of wonder, fantasy. They were so isolated, so occupied with one another. Any suggestion for new pleasures was quickly taken up. So when someone said costumes, drama, poetry, everyone agreed. Photographs. *Tableaux vivants*. Enactments of the poems of Tennyson?

It had begun simply enough. The idea of dressing in costume, of being photographed, had already captured imaginations on the Continent. It was only to be expected that interest in it would spread across the ocean.

With an eye toward propriety and high-mindedness, the first tableau at South Fork depicted a religious theme. Three girls posed in white dresses, with Christian symbols (doves, white crosses, lilies) as backdrop—a representation of the noble virtues Faith, Hope, and Charity. Nora, in the late afternoon after her morning wandering, her high-noon sails, dressed for dinner, had stood on the clubhouse porch watching the strange scenario unfold at the bottom of the clubhouse lawn. The camera set upon a tripod, the flourish of Louis Clarke as he bent behind it, ducked beneath the drape. She did not participate, she had only watched that first summer. Other girls overcame their shyness, yielding to the tug of curiosity; they primped and dressed and posed, and held their poses until Louis Clarke and his camera could capture the image, fix it.

It had seemed a little foolish last summer, but this summer everyone wanted to join in. Props and elaborate garments were packed in extra trunks and brought by spring wagon from the South Fork station. For the sake of easy access, for the overloaded wagons bearing guests and all their trappings, the road across the breast of the dam had been widened, lowering the dam's height, bringing it surprisingly close to the level of the lake. Club members traveling across it noticed that, on windy days, small lake waves slapped exuberantly up onto the road, eroding its tightly packed edges. Once, when Nora was returning from a morning in the woods, she came upon her father and the club manager, Elias Unger, in heated conversation. She stopped before they saw her, stepped back off the path which trailed toward the clubhouse, thinking it best to remain hidden. From her vantage point she could hear only fragments of their conversation.

". . . not enough difference in height between the dam's breast and the spillway." Her father sounded strident, insistent.

"I oversee everything. Why you cannot take my word for that . . ." Unger's tone suggested that this was a conversation they had had before.

"There should be discussion. An all-club meeting."

"So that the others will be troubled about what I'm paid to do?" Unger sounded less and less placating the longer their talk continued. After a moment more, the two men parted, Mr. Unger leaving while Talbot was in the middle of a sentence, and leaving a sense of unfinished business behind them.

If any of the other clubmen felt concern, it soon gave way as the advantages of the wider road became evident. More props for more elaborate tableaux could be transported. Great sacks of chain mail arrived (where it came from, no one knew). Some unknown club member brought a sword, another brought a candelabrum; yet another delivered a replica of the shield of Lancelot. A plan developed in which the young people were going to take the roles of characters in the poems of Tennyson. Louis Clarke's group staged a stark representation of a scene from *Idylls of the King*. Because of her hair, because it could be let loose and spread like a fan, because it was so impossibly wild when it was unbound, so fused with some fierce energy that it looked like it might ignite, burst into flames, Nora was chosen to lie still in a rowboat at the lake's edge, portraying the Lady of Shalott. George Shea and Frank Willock painted the white lettering on the stern of the boat. Lillie Rankin gave a sotto voce dramatic reading:

> *Lying, robed in snowy white*
> *That loosely flew to left and right—*
> *The leaves upon her falling light—*
> *Thro' the noises of the night*
> *She floated down to Camelot.*

Nora, prostrate in the little rowboat, crossed her hands over her chest and closed her eyes. The robe that she'd been given to wear had voluminous long sleeves. Late-in-the-day sun bathed her face in lemony light. She felt a release, much like the one she imagined the Lady of Shalott would have felt, free of her mirror, her loom, the web she'd been compelled to weave with it.

> *Willows whiten, aspens quiver . . .*

Nora imagined that the willows were indeed whitening around her. The shroud she wore fell in deep folds over her legs and breasts and shoulders. Water lapped at the rowboat's wooden sides.

The next day the tableaux would include Marianne gazing at the shield of Lancelot. The day after, Mary Queen of Scots, bedecked in velvet, attended by the loyal Rizzio. By summer's end there would be a gallery of photographs, exhibited in the clubhouse parlor, admired, then taken home by Louis, who feared that the dampness of the mountains might damage them. Louis Clarke, inventor, sailor, steamboat captain—his skills were manifold. And now he could add archivist to his list of credits. Without elaborate plan or forethought, a record was being kept, evidence that they had been there, at the lake, even when, years later, they all wished to deny it. A history was being gathered. And in this gathering Louis took the role of photographer, the keeper of images. Nora, the diarist, saw herself as scribe.

What *had* come over them that summer? What forces combined to make everyone fall so in love with fantasy? Nora noticed that even the parents seemed susceptible, touched by the romance of it.

How often she had stood on the clubhouse porch at night, looking out into the darkness, toward the boathouse, the boardwalk, toward the lake. The sky was fuzzed with stars, little tongues of cloud obscured the moon. She imagined the scene unfolding behind her, beyond the parlor, beyond the French doors that marked the entrance to the dining room, those doors closed to keep night breezes from chilling the guests, from extinguishing the wavering, bowing candle flames. She imagined her mother or Mrs. Horne or Mrs. Pitcairn reaching to the backs of their chairs to gather shawls around their shoulders, fringes trembling, silk, watery in their iridescence, changing color in the fickle light. The ring of silver against china marked the last of dinner, the dishes being cleared. Nora imagined chairs pushed back, men crossing their legs, the dark V of a knee breaking the perfect drape of linen tablecloth. The men, the members, eager for cigars and port and after-dinner brandies, running careful fingers around the immaculate starched folds on their cuffs. "I'm sorry, my dear," said Mr. Wells or Mr. Woodwell or Mr. Crawford, "I'm afraid I wasn't listening." A hand was caressed in apology for being so distracted. A hand was kissed. The fine wash of hair along the wife's arm rose to her husband's touch.

Nora imagined that it was on such a night that the planning started. A low murmur at first, a mere suggestion, made actual and thrilling by the flush of enthusiasm that wine with dinner brings. They would have a regatta. A daylong nautical event to mark the end of the summer season. Something for the young people, a day in which the purposeful simplicity of country life was put aside. A day of splendor. Scull and canoe races, the bracing exhilaration that competition brings. A program would be printed. Prizes. Ribbons. Trophies, someone must have said, enthusiasm mounting. Silver bowls. Why not? They could afford them. Silver bowls with the date engraved. The club name etched in a permanent testimony to the sun-washed summer days that had filled the months since May. And a name, of course they'd have to give a name to the event, and that was when someone suggested the Festival of Lanterns. After the races there would be nighttime wonders. Boats would form a line off Locust Point, fifty of them illuminated by five lanterns each, an ethereal procession. As a finale they would form a circle, a brilliant swirl of light on the dark lake. Fireworks, someone offered, and a rush of "yeses" and "of courses" filled the room. Ah, fireworks. And prizes given to the winners.

Nora was caught up in the idea of it as much as any of them were, in that summer of her seduction, her capitulation to the romantic whims and urges of the others. It was only when she retired after the planning for the regatta had begun, only after she had brushed her hair with a hundred strokes, and brushed her teeth, and turned her coverlet down, that she saw the folded paper on her pillow. She stood by her bed while she read the note that was written in what had already become a familiar hand.

"You forget yourself. You are not one of them."

She looked quickly over her shoulder, imagining that he was just behind her, that after he'd slipped into her room to deliver this chastisement he'd decided to stay, make himself known to her. She felt her face flush, some mixture of embarrassment and anger. She felt like someone who had been caught doing a crass, forbidden thing. What had he seen of how she'd behaved that summer? Had he seen her in the boat that day, costumed as Tennyson's cursed lady? Could he see into her window now, could he see into her soul? She felt spied upon, and shamed, fearful that he was right in his assessment, that she had forgotten herself, given herself over too much to summer life, to frivolity, to sailing. She extinguished her lamp, sat at her window, watched the moon's reflection on the lake. An owl called from the distance. Her eyes scanned the lawn, the lake's edge, the nearby trees. She half hoped she would see some sign of him. She half hoped she wouldn't.

She rose from her place at the window, went in the darkness to sit at the little writing table in the corner of her room. It was hard for her to imagine anyone else sitting there or sleeping in the bed. It pained her somehow to think that other girls from other families filled the armoire with their clothing during the other weeks of summer. Sometimes she found traces of them—bits of blackened blotting paper in the writing-table drawer, a lace-edged handkerchief, a tortoiseshell hair comb. And suddenly she could see in her mind's eye the end of it all. The days when she would be older, married perhaps, living in another place, without access to this room, this particular beloved landscape. Children who were mere toddlers now would take her place. She would be banished, because of age or geographic distance. Or perhaps because of flaws in herself and in her character—small things that were nonetheless significant. Foolish inadvertent lapses.

"You forget yourself," he'd written.

She took pen in hand, wrote on her vellum stationery, without a light to guide her: "Who are you? Reveal yourself to me." She wrote it again and again and again. One creased note to be left in each of her lairs. Part command, part pleading.

"Reveal yourself to me."

Just as Nora had her off-season life, her life without him, so Daniel had his without her.

He sat at his parents' kitchen table keeping a chronicle of deaths and injuries. He moved the gas lamp closer, rubbed with his fingers at the bridge of his nose to clear his head, his vision. He had just come off the "long turn," twenty-four straight hours tossing billets to the rougher. It was late August and hot, and throughout the long night he'd kept drinking water, jug after jug of it, but he'd just sweat it out again. His arms ached, and he was as tired as he had ever been. But it was important to do this now, he knew, before he forgot, before he climbed the stairs and fell into a dreamless sleep. He reached for his wire-rimmed glasses and awkwardly pulled the earpieces around each ear. He thought he looked too much like Louis when he wore them. So he tried not to let his mother see him in them. He didn't want to be responsible for reminding her of Louis. The ream of paper he had close at hand was newsprint. This was the paper, the pencil he used when he wrote messages for Nora. He pulled a sheet of paper toward him as he licked his pencil tip.

Six from a hot metal explosion, two from rolling accidents, four from falls into pits, one asphyxiation. Three men lost legs in piling accidents, one lost an arm. Herman Fuller, a 'hot-job' man, was still alive, but most of his skin on the left side of his body was burned when molten metal that was being poured missed the sluice for which it was intended and struck the edge of the mold, and bloomed up and over it. Like a wave, the arc swept over him. Eight more men were hurt on another shift when the fluid metal hit the floor, splashed up from it. In that accident, the new boy, Jacob Banyon, lost an eye.

Fifty life-threatening lacerations, one paralysis.

Daniel paused. Thirteen deaths this year and it was only August.

One of the secretaries at the mill had secretly provided him with these numbers. He'd slept with her to get them. He'd offered money; but she wanted him. She'd met him at night, before his shift began, took bulky iron keys out of her pocket, brought him quietly into the secretaries' office. He was wearing his work clothes: ragged trousers, shirt sleeves cut off, boots he'd replace when his shift started with shoes that tied to his calves, that had thick wooden soles, to keep his feet from burning up beneath him. She was younger than she looked, he knew. She'd been a friend of Caroline's in school. Her name was Marie. Her husband drank too much; Daniel had heard that he beat her. He'd been a puddler, she'd explained, before puddling became obsolete, before he'd become a strong-armed, skilled anachronism. Not her fault, she'd said, the first time she and Daniel had met to talk, the first time Daniel had approached her. But when he became angry, who else was there to blame, who else could her husband make suffer? She and Daniel had met in front of Dr. Lowman's house, then taken a turn together through the park. She'd tried that day to keep her bruises hidden, she'd insisted he be on her left as they strolled in the sepia light of dusk, keeping the unharmed side of her small face to him. The cut on her right lower lip, he saw, had swelled like a dark blossom, but the forgiving light of evening obscured it—that and the slight concealing gesture of her hand.

The night he had met her at the iron works, after the office door was closed and locked behind them, she had run her fingers over the knot of muscles in his arms and smiled. By then her lip was healed. She'd raised her skirt, and when he hesitated, she'd undone the faux-pearl buttons on her very proper secretary's blouse. Paper-strewn desks and straight-backed chairs—it seemed the floor would have to do, but on that floor they felt the building roar and rattle—the pressure works was just below them. Window glass quivered as if the earth itself were quaking, as if the very ground were about to break apart and swallow Johnstown whole. The screech of cold saws ripping through steel made speech impossible. He covered her mouth with his hand, a signal not to try to talk. Better this way, in any case, he thought. Best not to say things that were not meant.

She was wet before he touched her; her triangle of hair was slick and matted by the time he pushed her skirt and layered petticoats aside, by the time his fingers found her. In his mouth her nipple was a tight hard nub, his tongue made long, inviting circles around it. He came when she did, took his hand away, and let her cry out. He felt the sound but could not hear it. Her lips were pressed against his neck. Her smooth back arched and shuddered.

He had been glad it was so dark in there, relieved he didn't have to search her face for meaning. He'd reached to take her hand in his as a way of helping her, and himself, across the great awkward divide that comes with the end of sex—nakedness and intimacy on the one side of it, clothes and banal conversation on the other. He wondered, Should they speak about her husband? About the baby that she said she was going to have? But she'd moved quickly, away from him and from all false sentiment, silent in the darkness, her sleek back gleaming in what little night light found its way through shaded windows. She bent to find her petticoat and light woolen combination. She tossed her loosened hair aside as she slipped her arms into her blouse, then used a small embroidered handker-chief to dab her cheek, her neck, her forehead, to wipe the passion and the heat away.

"I've always liked you, Daniel," she said softly, head bent to the task of fastening pearl buttons. "Even years ago, when we were children."

"I know," he said.

She walked the few steps to the desk, pulled a sheath of paper from beneath a blotter. As Daniel folded it to put it in his pocket, it smelled of lavender and semen where she'd touched it.

"Too bad," she said. "That we're not children anymore."

The figures about who'd been hurt were considered confidential because the Cambria Iron Company feared it would be demoralizing to the workers if released. They wished to shield their employees, be protective. When Daniel tried to think fairly about management, when he forced himself to try to understand their point of view, he could imagine how their rationalizing went. How they told themselves that they did a better job than other steel companies, that they were fairer with, more careful of their men than Carnegie and Frick had ever been. Daniel knew that it was true, they had been better; since his association with the Knights of Labor, he'd talked to men who worked in Pittsburgh, he'd been to Braddock once and seen conditions there. But when he was tired he wasn't inclined toward fairness; fairness, he reasoned, was not his responsibility. He meant to tell the truth.

He heard coughing in his parents' room upstairs. His father rising to begin his workday. The bedsprings creaked. He was a foreman, he wanted Daniel to become a craneman, out of reach of the worst danger. What good is a foreman father, he pressed, if he can't move you forward, help you on? What he wanted even more was for Daniel to leave the steel mill, move back to Philadelphia, finish college. Only two more years to go, then he could be a doctor, a teacher, anything he wanted. Why did you start school, Frank pressed him, if you never meant to finish?

Daniel pushed his chair back from the wooden table, walked to the kitchen window. He'd never quite gotten used to the "new house," never grown accustomed to their rise to the middle class, to his father's elevated status. But much of the furniture was old. The kitchen chair legs were uneven because Champ, a dog who had lived among them briefly, had chewed on them when he was a puppy. The horsehair bristled up through one arm of the sofa in the parlor, bit into Daniel's elbow when he forgot and leaned on it. He'd liked the old house fine. All his memories were there. Bean soup in February; checker games with Louis, each of them on their stomachs, elbows bent; the woodstove in the kitchen exuding heat, making everything about the room seem to be tinged with heat and color. The baby, Claire, being bathed in a tub on the kitchen table. Now they had this other house. Three stories, six rooms, and an attic, a front porch, a sprawling sycamore tree shading the back yard. His own room. They'd moved on his fifteenth birthday, and for the two years prior to that, in the old house, he'd shared "the children's room" with Caroline, his sister. A careful arrangement of beds and bureaus had made it seem like two, had made it possible for them to talk at night. They had shared childhood fears then: the fear that the ghost of Louis roamed the yard at night, that their beloved grandfather would die, that the South Fork Dam would give way as older children, in a teasing singsong banter, often threatened it would.

In the new house, too, they shared secrets. They conspired.

"Philadelphia might be far enough for you, but not for me," Caroline had said the night before he was to leave for school. She was sixteen, he fourteen months older. She had come into his room, sat on the floor beside his bed, where he was propped against two pillows reading. She bent her head and threw her long hair forward over it, and was brushing hard, because she'd heard that a thousand brushstrokes would make her hair grow beautifully and shine.

The wind pressed at the rafters. Through the far window he could see the steep bank of Prospect Hill rise away from the Stony Creek. Daniel looked up from his book, over his glasses. He fingered his place so that he could listen to her. She loved an audience, and he was glad to be one. He liked looking at her. Her mouth was a little thin, her brow a bit too high. Claire had been the beauty among them. Claire the beauty, Louis the saint. But Caroline's voice had a particular and haunting cadence to it—everyone who knew her said so—and when she spoke, she became a beauty. It was as if sound altered light, the senses worked together in her favor. That night she'd said she was going to go to Paris. She showed him a sketch she'd made of the soon-to-be-built Eiffel Tower from descriptions of it that she'd read in the *Tribune*. "And you'll be able to climb up inside and see the whole city," she said. "The Invalides, the Arc de Triomphe, the Tuileries." She knew the names of monuments and gardens in a dozen European cities. She'd studied maps and histories, even taught herself a little French. When her boat sailed, she'd be ready. She tossed her head, inched over closer to him, to sit with her back against his bed frame, to weave a braid into her red-tinged hair. "And perhaps," she said with an affected haughtiness, "just perhaps, I'll take you with me." She tapped his foot with her hairbrush. Smiled up at him.

He had laughed and opened his book again. "You'd best be careful with your invitations. I just might go." He picked her sketch up, held the Eiffel Tower to the light. Such a strange shape. By whose design? Whose sense of modern was this? He tried to imagine the steel girders, the men who welded them together. He wondered who made the steel. Steelmen always want to know. On the train to Philadelphia, he had wondered which mill rolled the track.

In the end, she hadn't gone to Paris. With Daniel off at school, Caroline thought it would have been too hard for Julia if her only other child had gone away, too. Then love struck. Or, Daniel feared when she first wrote to him about it, perhaps proximity and need merged into some simulacrum of it. Perhaps falling in love had replaced adventure in her list of wishes. All Daniel knew with certainty was that by the time he returned home for Christmas during his second year away, Caroline was planning to be married. She was eighteen, a girl. Daniel didn't understand it. Her lover, Ezra Kidd, was ten years older, responsible, diffident, phlegmatic, a stonemason, a skilled craftsman, with a hairline already retreating toward baldness. A shy, unlikely candidate, thought Daniel, for this rush toward marriage. He might have tried to dissuade his sister, but something implacable had gripped her. He could see it in her eyes. Her tendency had always been to please, to negotiate. Now she seemed to be daring anyone to speak against her plan.

Two days before Christmas, Caroline and Ezra posed for a betrothal photograph. Julia, wishing to be on the side of happiness, had made a dress for her of amethyst silk, with a high-standing ruffled collar, narrow sleeves, a close-fitted waist—a dress not for a girl but for a woman, someone old enough to marry. Daniel had noticed a difference in his mother since he'd returned home for this visit. In the service of her daughter, Julia had become the embodiment of industry and purpose. One of the white calsimined bedrooms had been commandeered as a workroom during his absence. Prismatic pleats and folds of yard goods were strewn over chairs that had been called into service from the dining room. A dress form stood at stiff attention, the whir of the sewing machine continued long into the night ("$27.00 used, bought from a traveling vendor," his father said laconically when asked about the new contrivance). It seemed as if remnants of what Daniel remembered of his mother's old beauty, the beauty of his boyhood, were returning to her. Her hair was arranged more softly now, collected into waves and pinned. Daniel watched her as he might a stranger, the change in her arresting. He found himself wanting to be near her.

It had snowed the week before, but an unusually warm weekend had caused most of it to melt, and it was decided that the photograph could be made outdoors in natural light. There had been a great show that day of family goodwill and solidarity, with Frank carrying a small bench out into the yard which they might sit upon and Julia worrying good-naturedly that the dampness of the grass might stain the hem of the lovingly made gown. The photographer, an emphatic and officious little man, had guided them in placing the bench beneath the sycamore tree. Following instructions, Caroline sat down on the bench, and Ezra allowed himself to be arranged in a formal frozen stance beside her. It was a foolishly stilted pose, and Daniel had been about to interfere, to say so, when Ezra suddenly and inexplicably grew tired of obedience, of the posing and arranging. He took one quick step and stood behind Caroline, placed his hands on her slender shoulders, on the silk that shimmered there. One of his blunt fingers grazed her neck just above the ruffled collar, and there was something claiming, possessive, in the gesture. In an instant Ezra's whole demeanor had changed. The eager-to-please look he had used to such good effect to convince her parents of his worthiness was replaced by one of frank sexual desire. Only Daniel, from his vantage point off to the side of the tableau, could see clearly what was happening, could see Ezra's hardening, his obvious erection. What he saw as well was the look of pleasure on his sister's face as Ezra pressed himself secretly, urgently into her back, as she relaxed against him. He saw desire there, too, and understood that it was that, not some fata morgana of romantic love, as he had feared, that drove their union and made the wedding such a necessary, pressing thing.

The chill air impelled the photographer to get on with it—it was winter, after all—and he took advantage of the smiles of his subjects, became willing to cede control over the arrangement of the scene for the sake of a photographic print in which the loving couple looked satisfied and happy. The camera shutter clicked, and clicked again, while Daniel walked across the yard to stand behind the photographer, beside his mother.

"Lovely. Good, good, perfect. Just one more." Daniel had heard the photographer's instructive voice, his father warning his mother against lingering on the lawn, fearful that she'd catch cold. In the stew of words in the air, in his head, only one had stayed in his ear, demanding his attention, more weighted and important than the others.

Desire.

He knew all about desire.

And now Caroline was nineteen, seven months married, pregnant.

Happy, she insisted when Daniel went to see her in "her" house (even now the expression seemed alien to him) throughout the summer, to take her a fish he had caught or birds he'd shot and cleaned. To have the pleasure of her company.

When she talked about her happiness, her hand rubbed absentmindedly over her pregnant belly. "I have everything I need. The problem for you, Daniel, is you don't know what you want." How satisfied she seemed to him, how settled. "Go back to school, Dan," she said as she kissed his cheek in thanks for the offerings he'd tendered. She smelled of the fish, of yeast, of quarried stone, of Ezra. "You're so smart, you know so much, Daniel. What are you doing here?"

He was happy for Caroline. But he had work to do. Besides, he'd never want a child.

So what did he want? A young woman he barely knew?

"Reveal yourself," she'd charged weeks earlier.

"My name is Daniel," he wrote.

"Why did you choose me?"

Why indeed?

A relationship of sorts had begun. They left cryptic messages at agreed-upon places, exchanged works of reference, transcribed poems. Poems? He'd thought he had to put aside such things in his life—his new life of hard work and high purpose. But what he discovered as he came to know her, to know about her, was that in his life, which had been so *other* than hers, he'd read many of the same things. Two years at university, a long life of reading. He easily knew more than she did.

"The Russians," he had written on a slip of paper he tucked into the pages of Turgenev's *First Love*. A gift for her, whom he had begun to address as Nora. Nora. "They seem to have a great understanding of life." He had chosen the book with exquisite, exhaustive care. The nature of the binding mattered to him. The quality of paper. He had left it next to the net with which she captured butterflies.

Now he stood at his parents' kitchen sink, gazed out the window. Outside, the sky was brightening. The night was always red-tinged here, the gaping furnaces gave darkness a depth and substance, hue. But even though daylight had come, the sun wouldn't really rise until ten or so; the surrounding Allegheny Mountains kept it from them. During the two years he was in Philadelphia, at the university, he rose early every day to watch the miracle of morning, the wonders of a rising sun. Of course the drawback there had been that there were no mountain pleasures. No deer to hunt, no grouse. None of the dazzling, fast-moving, fish-filled mountain streams. It was his day off, the one he had every two weeks, after the long turn. He would sleep a little. Then get his rod and reel, his gun. Get a horse from Snavely, ride up into the woods, where he could expand his lungs and stretch his legs. He thought of Thoreau, *Walden*. He'd head toward the reservoir, "the Club." Search for Nora. Stop at the beautiful spillway, dip his kerchief into the cool cascading water, drape it around his neck, feel the heat rise out of him.

He would stand briefly, take in the beauty there, then walk past the posted sign that declared the lake, the 160 acres that surrounded it—PRIVATE PROPERTY. Climb the fence. They'd threatened locals, even shot at one, but he knew he was better in the woods than any of them were. He knew they had brought black bass in palace cars, that by the time they paid expenses the thousand fish had cost a dollar each. He and the men he worked with made $1.50 for a twelve-hour day.

There were fish aplenty in the Stony Creek in summer—catfish, sunfish, mullet. But bass; it made him smile to think of how good a bass would taste.

Nora would be there, he knew. He had so little time now, what with working, attendance at evening meetings, and his obsessive record keeping. Now he went to the lake only when he was sure to find her. Sure to leave and receive a note, although they were no longer really notes. They had become long, revealing missives, shot through with shy confessions. Tentative admissions.

"We should meet," he wrote that summer of 1886, to a seventeen-year-old girl he barely knew. The fact that he was quick to anger, quick to judge, that his passions were vibrant but disorderly detracted from what he had to offer, his many gifts. He was rash and bright, and was held in esteem by much older men, union figures. He was trying to organize a strike; he had sedition on his mind. He'd had sex with several women; with Marie, he had exchanged sex for information. But with this girl, he was someone else. With her he was neither confrontational nor careless. She made him feel hopeful. Even as he almost blinded himself reading, and became irritated easily by the issues and questions that consumed him—about disparities in wealth and power, the inequalities that made the world seem unjust and skewed and all but doomed—his connection to her softened him. They were not alike, and yet they had come to feel a sympathy for each other. He imagined, in a way he had not thought possible, that she understood him. He wanted to resist her, the idea of her, but every time he saw the swirl of her handwriting, every time he saw her kneeling with her magnifying lens, bent so earnestly to the task of seeing the smallest things, bent to the task of understanding, something stirred in him. They were not alike. He knew that all he felt for her was futile. And yet he had begun to think he loved her.

"We should meet," he wrote.

He would rest his fishing rod against a rock. Bend to tuck the note in the pages of her workbook. He knew he shouldn't, but he had to take a chance. He'd risk everything, then fish as he had planned to. Come home with a bass for dinner.

It was unusually warm in Cresson that summer. In July, Carnegie brought Matthew Arnold there, apologizing for the heat, as if he, who believed himself to be in control of everything, should have managed the weather better, and would have had he only been more focused on it. When the heat became oppressive, Carnegie had thought to postpone the visit, but he'd been promising he'd bring Arnold to the mountains since the night they'd met in London years earlier. "My Cresson," Carnegie had called it, when he spoke of it, describing the roll of the hogback hills, the pine-scented air, the simple beauty of the Mountain House Hotel. It was his hope that a trip to the redolent mountains would turn the poet back to poetry, a gift Arnold seemed to have all but abandoned for a life as school inspector, theorist, critic. Arnold was young enough to reclaim his art, just sixty-four. Carnegie believed so utterly in the revivifying properties of Cresson that he felt there was every chance that the Muse might visit Arnold there.

So he had brought Arnold to the mountains, arranged a room for him with a kneehole desk, placed paper and pen and ink in a small red-cedar box that had been especially made. He planned excursions into the countryside for early morning so that afternoons could be preserved for rest and writing. Solicitude shadowed every moment, every turn; it was what made it possible for one to like Carnegie. And Arnold did. He enjoyed spending the mornings with him, enjoyed observing the sweep of Carnegie's mind, his sheer expansiveness. So unlike him, this unlikely friend. Who had ever been quite so considerate of him? Once, while on a coaching trip through England, Carnegie had stopped at Pain Hill Cottage to retrieve Arnold, and then taken an unnecessary but touching detour to Hursley Churchyard, where Arnold's godfather, John Keble, was buried. Together they had walked in "the silent graveyard," and together touched the stone. Who before had so unabashedly admired him—minor poet (or so he feared), tired bureaucrat, he who had given up poetry for duty? Each morning in Cresson the trim light wagonette was waiting in front of the Mountain House Hotel, as were Carnegie and his driver. Two sure-footed horses drew them through deeply shaded forests, past gorges that sliced through the hillsides and gave passage to insistent streams. In the evenings Arnold wrote enthusiastically to his sister about exotic flowers that he found. "Veronica Virginiana, from three to five feet high, with great spikes of white flowers, and the pokeweed, a great herb yet taller." So taken was he with the wild extravagance of floral life that Carnegie had his carriage stop so that they could fill their arms with flowers. The poet and the philistine gathered Kalmia and rhododendrons which tumbled from the boggy edges of the streams. A week into his visit, the weather broke, frost tipped the grass, the cool invigorating mountain air Carnegie had promised made it necessary for them to wear light paletots on their morning rides, to add to their gear a plaid lap rug for extra warmth. Each day they ventured farther from Cresson in their explorations, and then on the morning of his leaving, Carnegie took Matthew Arnold to see the South Fork lake. A weft of mist hovered on the lake's calm surface, the sky was empty of clouds, arching, startlingly blue.

"There is something untouched, prelapsarian about it," Arnold said, or had Carnegie guiltily imagined it, this poetic envisioning of the earthly beauty that existed before men arrived to interfere and alter it? Real or imagined, the word stayed with him, a lingual gift from a poet friend.

After Arnold left, after the last of the summer visitors had decamped and all grew quiet, Carnegie and his mother had stayed on, well into the fall, at Cresson; she, because she always stayed with Andrew, always watched him, especially since he had involved himself with the Whitfield woman, whom he had actually brought there, to Cresson, just that summer, flaunting her; he, because he had grown fatigued and blunted and thought he needed rest. He was fifty-one years old, in the throes of an ardent, almost adolescent love, but unable to marry and commit to it because he was unable to defy his mother. He'd spent the spring and summer reorganizing his business to accommodate the acquisition of the Bessemer steel plant in Homestead, and he had been laboring incessantly at what he thought of as his "writing life," penning the last draft of *Triumphant Democracy*, his screed in praise of wealth and industry and all things American. By the time fall arrived, by the time the oak and ash trees blazed with color, Andrew Carnegie felt weary, lonely, middle-aged. He hoped an extended stay at Cresson would energize him, and it soon became apparent that it was essential to his mother. Dr. Dennis had insisted on a postponement of their return to New York because Margaret was seventy-six and had become a frail, uncertain version of herself, unfit for travel.

All three of the Carnegies—Andrew, mother Margaret, Tom—became ill that autumn. Each lay in a different room wondering feverishly about the others. In Homewood, Tom was stricken with a sudden, fulminating pneumonia. In Cresson, Andrew was afflicted with what began as an annoying, enervating rash and fever that, as it worsened, was diagnosed as typhoid. Margaret, bedridden in her room across the hall from his in Braemar Cottage, was simply fading from her life, relinquishing it, too weak to struggle against the fluid filling her lungs, threatening to drown her.

November snows that year were wet and heavy in the mountains. The hundred-room hotel and all the other summer cabins stood dark and empty, the sky the color of a dove, the branches of the pine trees snapping in the high wind, yielding to the weight of accumulating snow. The doctor, his sleeves rolled above his elbows, moved anxiously from room to room, watching the raised red rash of typhoid spread, checking Margaret's shallow breathing, hoping he could manage to save somebody, anyone at all. Tom, the baby, died in Pittsburgh only three days after he fell ill. Margaret lingered a short while longer, and when she did die, Dr. Dennis insisted that her coffin be lowered by ropes from her bedroom window, so as not to be seen by Andrew as it was carried past his door. Carnegie became better, relapsed; fear for him mounted and was finally assuaged as his recovery progressed and his strength began to slowly return.

It was late November when Louise Whitfield received a note scrawled feebly by her erratic, desultory lover. "Louise, I am now wholly yours—all gone but you." Louise had received bulletins from Carnegie's secretary throughout his illness, but this was the first word from Andrew. She was tall and self-possessed; during the weeks of fever and uncertainty she had confided her fears to no one, not even her mother. Now there was no one with whom to share her guilty triumph. Margaret's death had been a necessary prerequisite for Louise's marriage; she'd prayed for it. But when the letter from Carnegie came, she realized that she had all but given up hope of ever receiving the news it contained. Once she had it in her hand, she found that she could not grasp it. Five years' anguish, waiting, and in that moment, when the news came to her, her heart and her fingers failed her. The note fell from her hand and banked like a gliding white bird past her wrist, her waist, her gathered skirt, in its flutter toward the floor.

"Wholly yours."

Nora found it difficult to forget the overheard argument between her father and Colonel Unger about the widened road across the dam. Prior to that she had thought of the dam as a boundary, as the great wall that contained the South Fork lake. Archaeological, indestructible, something rooted to the earth that would remain there always. Now she, too, noticed how close the water level was to the top of the dam. She became aware of how often there were work crews laboring on it, how haphazard their efforts seemed to be when they heaved shovels full of dirt and manure and straw onto the dam's steep side. She wondered how it was that she had never noticed it before, why she had never paid the least attention. She began to ask herself why what her mother called her intrusive, unbecoming curiosity had not directed itself toward the dam. How foolish was she?

In late September, Nora and her father came for a long weekend to the South Fork Fishing and Hunting Club. Since that summer, the summer of the argument, James, who had always been on club committees, who had always been a part of the seasonal decision making—what trees to plant, when and if they should have indoor plumbing built—had become even more involved with the administration of the club, fretting over details that he feared were not being tended to by others. This sense of responsibility meant that he spent at least one weekend every month throughout the year at South Fork, and extra days during the summer as well. It pleased Nora when she was able to convince him that she should be permitted to go along. She wanted to be necessary to him, and she wanted to be at the lake. She had developed asthma in the city. South Fork had become essential to her health.

But while she was glad to be there, she grew more and more concerned about her father. He had lost weight. He had become quick to anger, accusatory and demanding.

When she stayed on beyond the summer with him, she had her routine and he had his. He had become consumed now by the minutiae of the club, even the things Crouse or Unger regularly attended to, such as the price paid for oats to Mr. Roland, the wages of the wait staff, the regularity with which the paths were maintained, the trees were trimmed. He routinely got out of the carriage bringing them from South Fork as the horses drew it onto the breast of the dam. Telling the driver to stop and wait while he stepped down, strode to the dam's edge, to the side that faced the valley, looking down at South Fork, then staring at the dam's face, as if focusing the whole of his attention on it, as if his gaze conferred strength and were keeping the thing intact, hardening the crumbling core. Nora watched him with a womanly concern.

She had other concerns as well. "We should meet," Daniel had written at summer's end. Now she found she had no way of answering. As the cold weather came and the earth began to harden, she had had to abandon her many woodland stations, to close her various "laboratories," to put her summer life away. Daniel's note asking to meet her had come too late for her to leave some final word, and by the time of her November weekend with her father, she was longing for some contact. He had chided her the previous summer with the note left on her pillow: "You forget yourself." Now she wanted to explain, wanted to say, But you see, I come here now alone, without the others, without the elaborations of the summer, without the costumes. Now I come as I did when you first saw me. She wanted to be found by him again.

But while she waited, hoped for his return, she spent more time with her father. Clearly he knew things about the dam that she did not, and with his knowledge came the dread of rain, some deeply felt fear of it. More and more, whether she went briefly into the woods for last efforts at collecting or was in her studio compiling notes and narratives, she came to dread the sound of thunder, too. She came to know that when it rained, whether night or day, he donned gum coat and boots, and trudged through mud beneath a sky crisscrossed with lightning, always, she knew, heading for the dam.

They were two days into their September visit when, in the middle of a moonless night, Nora was awakened by the dull roar of thunder in the distance, and she heard her father in the next room in the clubhouse rising from his bed. She heard the clicks and thumps of hurried dressing—drawers tugged open, pants pulled on. He moved quickly when he feared rain was coming. She heard his footsteps as he passed her room, heard rattling and the thud of gumboots being taken out of the mudroom closet, the groan of the front door opening and closing. She was fully awake by then, and what she thought might be a shower had become a full-fledged storm, moving on the clubhouse with a vengeance; tree-bending wind, rain bulleting the windows, sluicing through the gutters. No kind of night to be outside, and suddenly she had a premonition, a foreboding sense that she hadn't had before, that he was in particular danger on *that* night, in *that* harsh storm. She rose from bed, threw a shawl around her shoulders— ridiculous, she knew, to fear a chill when she was certain to be soaked with rain. But logic, reason, had been utterly replaced by fear, by a panicked sense that she must follow him. When she opened the door, the wind all but tore it from her hand. She had to use her full weight to press it closed and latch it. She tucked her chin then and set herself against the wind, marched into it. The sky was livid, white; she'd never seen lightning like that, washing the sky as well as ripping it.

She found the path he would have taken, pressed on with her nightgown trailing heavily beneath the slicker she had found. She cringed in spite of herself each time thunder struck (and "struck" was the word for it; it felt as if the entire planet would be cracked, the earth would open), fending off the mix of blinding lightning and impenetrable darkness with a kerosene lamp, following the distant dot of light made by the lamp her father had had the sense to bring, as it streaked and threaded through the rain-blurred distance. She wondered what possessed him. What drove him out into such a night? She tried to run when the path cleared enough to make running possible. Her nightgown grew heavy with accumulating mud; an edge of it snagged on a bush, making her pursuit that much more difficult.

The rain had slowed a little by the time she caught up to him on the road that crossed the dam.

She called to him, as if he might hear in spite of all that wind, and some sound, some sliver of her call, must have reached him. Because he turned toward her, raised his lantern toward the improbable, bent, slicker-bundled figure approaching him. "Oh, child," he said when he realized who it was. "What in God's name are you doing here?"

"Looking for you," she answered, breathless. "Trying to find you."

"But on such a night . . ." He was shouting to be heard above the water crashing over the rocks at the spillway.

"Why are you out here?" She made a visor of her hand, shielding her eyes from the sting and slash of rain. "It isn't safe. Suppose you were to fall, suppose you slipped? Who would find you?"

He shook his head, cupped his hand at his ear to indicate that he couldn't hear her. Then reached to take her arm, gestured to her to put down her lantern.

"Come, come," he shouted. "Leave the lantern here. We'll get it in the morning. Hold my hand, stay close to me. The rain and night . . . can't see a thing . . . The mud makes for tricky footing. Hold my hand," he said again, and she obeyed him. And they sloshed back through the woods that way. The wind, finally, whipped the lantern from James's hand, extinguishing it, sucking it up into the dark spinning mayhem of treetops and limbs, whirling leaves, bending, cracking branches. The only visible landmark was a tiny pearl of light in the far distance, the one kerosene lamp that he had left lit at the clubhouse.

Once they were inside, James sent her to her room to change into dry nightclothes, told her to bring her blanket, return to the main living room, where he would light a fire. She was still shivering when she returned to him, when she curled into the armchair he had drawn close to the fireplace for her, chilled through, surprised at how cold a mountain rain could be in autumn. With the hubris of the young she had believed that she knew these mountains, what to expect from them.

As soon as he had settled her, James left to change his own clothes, left her in the armchair, thinking. The giant fireplace was the mainstay of the room, its great carved corbels shadowing the hearth. Dried logs ignited quickly, and the fire crackled and blazed.

It was the first time she had ever been alone in this room; when she came to the club, it always seemed to be full of people. Once warmed enough to venture from the fireplace, she wrapped herself in the blanket and walked slowly around. She looked at it from a new vantage point, that of sole proprietor. There was a diorama on the wall close to the entryway, something "the children" (as everyone beneath the age of twenty called themselves, would always call themselves throughout the years, no matter how old they would become, no matter how far away they drifted from the innocence of childhood) found oddly fascinating. It had been there since the day of the grand opening, some sort of commemorative marker. *South Fork Fishing and Hunting Club* engraved on the brass rim that encircled a woodland scene ensconced in glass. A diorama; real twigs and branches, trifold leaves, a painted landscape for the backdrop that was supposed to be a reproduction of the lake from a distance: the lake, the mountains, the fringe of trees. Nothing in the scene was quite to scale, and Nora had always thought that there was something odd, even grotesque, about it. The grotesqueness amplified by the diorama's centerpiece, the object around which the scene was organized. It was a frog seated on a toadstool—a little green frog, killed, eviscerated, stuffed, a sacrifice of nature, a watchful, ever-present sentry. Its eyes were perpetually open, its slippery frog lips sealed.

"Has the fire helped? Are you warm now?" Her father had returned, boiled wool slippers on his feet, his dressing gown wrapped tightly around him. She wondered if he would be angry with her, if there would be a lecture or an explanation offered, or a threat of punishment for following him when she oughtn't to have. She returned to her chair, tucked her feet beneath her. She undid her thick braid, spread her hair into a dark sheet over her shoulder so the fire's heat might dry it.

James sat silently in a chair across from her.

"I was frightened for you," she finally said, hoping to preempt his criticism. "It was dark and I thought you might be in danger outside. And I was frightened. That's why I followed you."

"I understand," he said, surprising her. "I apologize, Nora, for causing you undue concern. When I heard the rain, I felt compelled to go out to the dam, to check on it."

"Check for what?" His openness had made it seem possible for her to question him.

Instead of answering, he questioned her. "Did you know there was a death the summer before last?"

"A death? Here?"

"Yes. Well no, not here. In Johnstown. The city farther down the valley."

"Was it someone we know?" she asked, presuming that here, in their world, they knew everyone.

"No. Not really. But he was a man who was a member of the club."

"Then we must have known him. I thought we knew all the members. By sight at least."

"Not this member," her father said. "His name was Daniel Morrell. He'd never actually taken part in a season here. He came to business meetings on occasion. I suppose you could say he was inactive. Especially in recent years. He had been ill."

The fire crackled and spit, and an ash flew from it over the protective screen, drifting in a languid flutter toward the high ceiling.

"Did *you* know him?" She hardly dared ask, but he had brought it up; she wished to believe that he wanted to have this brief, quiet time, this small effort at sharing a confidence with her.

"We'd met. But only briefly. Early on, right after the club was chartered, there was an exchange of letters. As attorney for the project I participated in the drafting of them."

"I don't understand. Letters about what?"

"He lived in Johnstown," James offered again, as if unaware that he was repeating himself. "About fifteen miles from here. It is one of several cities near here, but it's the largest. He was an important figure there. From what I've heard, he was beloved. He ran the Cambria Iron Company."

There was something about the dreamy abstracted way in which he spoke, the contrast of her father's voice and the hissing curl of the fire, with the press and pounding of the storm outside, that charged the air. Her unbound drying hair gathered static electricity and spread in disarray around her.

"He was a friend of Mr. Carnegie's, then?" An assumption on her part. In the same business. They'd surely been friends.

Her father leaned his head back against the antimacassar that protected

his wing chair. "No, I wouldn't say that. I wouldn't say that they were friends."

Silence then.

"You mentioned letters?"

But she realized at that moment that she had lost him, that he was no longer part of this exchange, that it had stopped being a conversation, a give-and-take, and had become, instead, a gathering of James's thoughts, a speaking aloud of his private musings.

"I read in the local paper that there were thousands of people at that funeral. And tonight, when I had trouble sleeping, I kept thinking of him. Then, when I heard the rain, I thought I should inspect the dam for him. Stand in his stead. That's why I went out there tonight." He rubbed his hand across his forehead.

She remained silent, waiting.

"I've always thought that he and I were bound somehow. That he and I, together, were keeping watch, each in our own way, over the dam. A foolish thing, I suppose, imagining this sort of bond with someone I'd never spoken to, never knew. Nonetheless, I have been thinking of him all day."

She thought he'd been unusually quiet during dinner, strikingly without appetite. He'd barely touched his wine.

"Watching for what?" she pressed. "Tell me, please, what are you watching for?"

Instead of answering her question, James continued with his soliloquy. "And as I thought of him today, I found myself wondering, Who will mourn for *me* when I die? Who will enumerate the things I've done?"

"Oh, don't say that. Don't talk about dying." The words came rushing. "Don't even think such things. You're a lawyer. Everyone respects you." Something, in fact, that she could not attest to. Even as she spoke she realized that she had no idea what his place in the world was. She had no way to evaluate such things. He never spoke about his work. She never saw him with colleagues or business associates except here, at South Fork, where congeniality, polite engagement, was the rule, where, on the surface, everyone was full of goodwill and affability.

"Papa," she ventured. A term from childhood. Long ago replaced by the more formal "Father."

He looked at her apologetically. "I'm sorry, Nora. Don't mind me. It's late. I'm tired. You must be, too." He rose as she did. Moved to gather her

blanket around her, to place the edges in her hand so she would not trip on it on the darkened staircase. "Hold tight to the blanket now so you don't stumble. Follow me." The second time that night he'd invited her to stay close, to go where he led her. He moved toward her, took her face between his hands, kissed her forehead.

"You have your grandmother's hair," he said. It took her breath away. This small suggestion that there was a past, that he'd had a life, that she was rooted in the world.

She did as she was bid, stayed close behind him. He was not a big man, and he had realized when he kissed her how tall she'd grown that summer, how likely it was that very soon she would be as tall as he. The thought came to him: *She* is the good thing. She will be the thing for which I'll be remembered. He would lose sight of that again and again in the years that followed, and then, at the crucial time, he'd forget it tragically. And he'd forget to ever say this aloud to her. But he'd given her some sense of it that night. Something she could carry like a talisman.

LOVE, BETRAYAL

"Small is this balance of life left to you. Live as on a height . . ."
—Marcus Aurelius, *Meditations*, Book X, Number 15

"Scones?"

"Which I baked myself."

"As busy as you are, you shouldn't have taken the time." Grace lifted the edge of the linen towels and bent her face toward the fresh scent.

"I found a recipe in a book which I checked out from these very shelves last week."

Grace smiled. "I loved scones once. It was my favorite treat at tea when I was a little girl."

"I cannot imagine growing up in a household where tea was served. What other things besides scones did you love?"

Grace hesitated. "What about you?" she said evasively. "What did you like as a child?"

"Oh, many things. The scents of smelling salts and alcohol. My father's office made the whole house smell medicinal and . . . safe in some way. It made me think that nothing could ever harm us."

"Even with all the sick people that came to see your father?"

"Even then. Of course, what do children know? It was foolish, obviously. I realized that as soon as my mother died. Once that happened, I realized that we were safe from nothing."

Grace reached up to the shelf for teacups, a small tin of sugar. She folded a tablecloth in half and laid it on one end of the long library table. It was the afternoon lull. February 1887. The sky beyond the library's tall windows was gray, end-of-day winter darkness beginning to encroach upon it. The day shift at Cambria Iron had not yet ended, school was still in session. When Julia came at this time of day they could be fairly certain to have the library to themselves.

"And what else?"

"What else did I love? I loved Chicago. I loved the wind from the lake. Or at least I thought I did. A few years ago that was all I could think of. How everything that had been happy in my life could be gotten back if I could return to Chicago."

"Really? You thought of leaving here?"

"Yes, really. Now I realize how ridiculous that was. A facile solution to an impossible problem." While the tea brewed, Julia walked the few steps to the table where the returned books were kept, waiting to be shelved. She picked one up, examining its spine. "I asked Daniel recently about the time when you taught him Greek." She looked up, met Grace's eye. "It's the first time I've ever asked him."

"So it's a good thing, having him home?"

"Well, Frank wanted him to stay in school, to finish. And I know he's right, that Daniel should do that. But yes." Julia nodded slowly. "It's a good thing. He said that you and he read Thucydides."

Grace laughed as she poured the steaming tea. "Bits and pieces. The whole thing would have been quite an undertaking."

Julia nodded. "My father told me that Pericles once gave a funeral oration for Athenians who had died in battle. In his speech Pericles said that the vanishing of young men from the country was as if the spring were taken out of the year. My father told me that when we were on the train coming here, right after the war. He's a very intelligent, very thoughtful man. A man not afraid of taking risks. I've not always admired him for that. But that's neither here nor there now. What I was going to say was that I remember how powerfully that idea—spring being taken from the year—remained with me."

"Yes. It's so apt somehow."

"It was like that for me when Claire and Louis died. Spring disappeared."

In the three years that the two women had known each other Julia had mentioned those children only once. All conversation had centered on Daniel and Caroline, more recently Caroline's new baby. It was from Daniel that Grace knew the story of the other children.

"I blamed Frank. Really, I blamed everyone. My father, Frank, even Daniel. I couldn't help myself. I wanted someone to be responsible."

"It must have been a great suffering for you. I can't imagine, Julia. Who would not understand the blaming?"

Julia broke a scone in half. "Who made scones for you when you were a girl?"

"Oh, my mother. Or maybe it was our cook. We had a very good cook."

"Do you cook? Now? That you're by yourself?"

"A little."

"You should let me cook for you. You should come to our house for dinner."

Grace shrugged and blushed in a way that surprised her. Frank came so often to the library now, so often asked for her advice on what to read, solicited her opinions, it seemed unwise, embarrassing to imagine trying to mingle those relationships, sitting at the dinner table with them. "It would complicate our friendship, don't you think? I rather like our teas, the dressmaking you do for me. Things that are just ours. I find myself wanting to be selfish."

Julia smiled. "Yes, I like that, too. I have not had such a thing before."

Grace bit into the scone.

"It's the cream that makes the difference. It tastes like nothing else but itself. It must be because there's cream in it," Julia said.

"What do you suppose it is about blaming?" Grace mused, a crumb dropping to the surface of her hand. She licked it away. "It feels like such a good idea. It feels so helpful when you do it, and then you discover that . . ."

". . . you're a disappointment to yourself. That it's something that ought to be beneath you. Does Daniel ever talk about me? I know he is fond of you, I know he still visits. Does he mention me?"

Grace was uncertain how to answer. "He says you seem changed since he's come home. Since Caroline married. He says you seem younger."

"Younger? What a sweet thing. He's been so solicitous of me. And all my activity seems to please him. He doesn't even mind the bolts of fabric, the boxes of trim and rickrack that have taken over the house." Julia smiled. "You've helped me become an admirable person, Grace. It is a gift from you." Julia handed Grace another piece of scone.

Grace looked away, thinking of how she had once wished to steal Daniel from his mother. How in some small way, she wished it to still.

"It's hard to explain to Frank about how changed I feel. When I detached myself from him, when I lost myself to bitterness, to mourning, he grew impatient with me. I can understand that now. I understand. But I'm not sure how to involve myself with him again. How to invite him back."

Grace thought about Frank, about his initial odd approach to her, their conversation about Dickens. "Maybe he's just waiting. Had you considered that? One move on your part might be all he needs."

"It's much easier to talk to you. I wonder why that is. Why it's so easy."

"Because I'm a stranger," Grace said simply. "Because I came from nowhere and might be gone tomorrow. That makes it easy to talk to me."

"I don't believe you'll be gone tomorrow. I think you'll remain here and we'll always be friends." Julia blew across the surface of her tea. "Why didn't you ever marry?"

The library door opened and Horace Rose walked in, hearty, bustling, brimming with greetings. Grace realized that it was four o'clock, that there would soon be others following close behind him, the afternoon crowd. She felt relieved that she wouldn't be further pressed for confidences.

"So," she said as she pushed her chair back, smiled at Mr. Rose approaching. She looked down at Julia, still sitting. "You'll come to fit my new dress tomorrow?"

"Saved," said Julia, as if reading Grace's mind. Julia stood, too, to take Rose's hand, to allow her cheek to be kissed by him. Even though a sweet formality prevailed between them, she felt that there was also an intimacy, a product of his help when the children died, his goodwill toward Daniel. They'd been through a lot together. He looked older to her, standing in the library's afternoon light. She supposed it could be said for all of them. Frank, Grace, her father, even Daniel. Time seemed to be rushing by. She watched Grace and Horace Rose in animated conversation. She thought of Frank. And it occurred to her that she ought to see to it that no more time was wasted.

"Marriage brings luck," Frick insisted that March during breakfast at the fishing and hunting club. When it was as empty as it tended to be in the off season, the clubhouse looked like the center of a feudal empire, the turreted cottages splayed off on either side like battlements, placed strategically for the protection of the liege. The off-season weather—hail fat and hard as marbles and snow that clung to the roofs—had washed the painted siding of the buildings with a soft patina; vivid greens turned mossy, the red trim at the windows faded to a cinnamon brown. Sun and snow had blistered the wooden porch posts. In the cottages that were not used at all, that remained closed all winter, the plaster grew damp, wallpaper peeled. Spiders, able to work without interruption in the stable, spun webs the size of sails. In the seven years of the club's existence the boardwalk had weathered to a shade of driftwood gray. And beyond the windows of the dining room weeds thrust themselves through the boardwalk's planks, forsythia twined through the handrails. Soon crews of men would descend to plant and trim and tend, to triumph over nature. But it was only March, and the overgrowth, the insistence of it, the way it seemed to claim what men had carefully constructed, made each building of the compound seem inexorably rooted to the land.

Marriage brings luck. Frick and his breakfast companion were the only two diners that morning, and their waitress, once she'd served them, stood at a discreet distance, watchful, as she had been trained to be, but out of earshot. Poached eggs quivered on beds of toast. Frick's empty water goblet cast a prism of sunlight onto a nearby wall. They had come alone, Clay Frick and Andrew Mellon, urged to this retreat by the wife of one. "This prolonged grieving is unseemly," Adelaide Frick had said to her husband. "She is dead four years. He should go out when he is invited to things. He needs to be in society more. He needs to marry."

It was not the kind of thing men talked about, but Adelaide had been uncharacteristically forceful in insisting. So much so that Frick finally felt he had no choice but to make a stab at it. "We'll walk the footpaths, breathe mountain air," he had said in an effort to stir enthusiasm in the unenthusiastic Mellon. When Frick first approached him, Mellon had looked at him in bewilderment, as if an Arctic expedition had been proposed, something life-endangering and outlandish, rather than the simple trip it was. "It's why we are club members, isn't it?" Frick had asked, sitting across from Mellon, at the desk in his large office. "For the quick getaway, an easy outing, a spur of the moment change of scene?"

Frick never knew what made the reclusive Mellon reluctantly agree to it. But he did. They had arrived the night before in Pitcairn's private train car, then settled into their rooms. Each of them noticed the obvious emptiness of the place, but neither commented upon it. Frick was thirty-eight in 1887, in his ascendancy. And his marriage *had* brought luck, that luck having begun on his wedding day. When he should have been attending to his boutonniere, to Adelaide's wedding ring tucked snugly into his breast pocket, when love and love's ceremony ought to have absorbed him utterly, he excused himself from his best man, in the anteroom beside the sanctuary of the church, risked delaying the start of the entire well-planned wedding in order to wire a response to an invitation from Carnegie, who'd suggested that the newlyweds come for lunch with him while on their honeymoon. "Dine with us while you're in New York," Carnegie had written, and Frick had left the church to dash to the telegraph office, to wire "Yes."

When he and Adelaide had arrived at the Windsor Hotel, Carnegie's manic volubility was like wind in the room, battering and blustery. Frick had sat in what had come to be his trademark pose—silent, judging—as the older Carnegie charmed, flirted, and laughed at Adelaide's coy willingness to be so flagrantly, shamelessly engaged. Margaret Carnegie at her son's right had matched Frick for humorlessness, and was dour in black silk. The two men had forged their partnership that day. There had been toasts, Carnegie had called him, embarrassingly, "pard." The uninvited familiarity made Frick flinch.

A toast on a honeymoon had been the beginning, a single moment that bloomed to wealth beyond even what he had imagined. Yes, marriage had brought him luck in business, luck in his life. Two children now, a boy, a girl, a wife who did not question. When he needed an estate in which to house his growing family, he'd built Clayton. Now he and his Adelaide were filling it with Chippendale and French Empire furniture. Theirs was an ideal life with little lacking. But industry, *his* industry, had made Pittsburgh a dirty place, a place from which one needed to escape. A mountain lodge, a sweet retreat, clean air for his clean, pretty children.

As Frick waited for a reply to his observations about marriage and good fortune, he slowly sipped his coffee. "I do not wish to interfere. But I would like to see you settled, happy. You seem . . ." Frick hesitated.

"Unhappy?"

A smear of egg yolk had gathered on Frick's lip, and he dabbed it with his napkin as he looked out the window at the boardwalk terracing the little hills and hummocks. "Yes. Unhappy."

Mellon was thirty-two years old and still barely capable of being touched. He found himself wanting to share some confidence, wanting Frick to understand his feelings. And that wish made him think about his mother.

He had been thirteen, and on the anniversary of his sister Annie's death, she had asked him if he would hitch the horses to the brougham to take her to the grave. He had said yes, but the request surprised him. It was early fall, a Saturday, a rare day without school for Andrew and his younger brothers. He had risen early to work in the kitchen garden, to turn the moist earth and strew hay over it. The last of the radishes, onions, and young carrots had been picked the week before. Working alone suited him, the isolation of his family in their large house on their large property, his lack of friends. His garden efforts were a kind of requiem for the last vegetative offerings of summer. There would be potatoes now, then turnips, pumpkins that he had planted. Winter food. It was in the garden that his mother found him, there that she asked if he would be her companion.

She made this cemetery trip three times a year, dressed in mourning black, in honor of her dead children, but as far as Andrew knew, she had always gone alone. He had watched her in the past, watched her summon one of the boys who worked for them to see to the horses, to help her up into the buggy, hand her the reins. Andrew might have wondered why his father never went, but he had not been raised to wonder. Nor had he been raised to deny his mother. She was the only woman in the Mellon house, the only woman in the world as far as the experience of her sons was concerned, and so she was acknowledged to be another kind of being. She was of them, but not *with* them. Her dresses were dark, their sleeves were long; light could not pierce her. She wore a simple brooch at her stiff little frilled collar, and no other adornment. Once, two or three summers earlier, he'd stumbled upon her underthings drying on a clothesline. White, lace-trimmed, delicate: surprising. The summer air brushing at the hems of the chemises made them seem possessed, inhabited. He could feel the presence of a woman in them. How, he had thought, had he never seen these things before? How had they been washed and worn and washed again, then hung to dry, in the hush of secrecy, out of the sight of his male household? He saw his mother differently from then on—as someone with a furtive, private, frilled white life.

It was rare for Andrew and his mother to be alone, rare for him to be in such close proximity to her as they were in the carriage. He looked at her in profile. Her mouth was thin. In the style of the day, she wore her dark hair parted precisely in the middle, pulled tightly over her ears and gathered at the nape of her neck into a bun. Her eyes were deeply set, large-lidded, the irises a pale and fragile blue. Eyes like his. But her face was without the emphatic planes and angles that his face and his father's shared. Looking at her as he urged the horses forward, he became aware of how much he looked like both of them, to what degree he was a product of their union.

The year had been 1869, the war blessedly over. In adherence to their father's wishes, Andrew's older brothers had avoided serving. The air on that Saturday had the decided weight of autumn air. The leaves had just begun their shift in coloration, and the morning light seemed crystalline, distilled.

"Thank you, Andrew, for doing this," she said. "I probably should not have taken you from your apple picking."

Each fall since his ninth birthday, he'd been selling apples from their orchard, saving the money, as his father had instructed him to do, hoarding it, without plans for any pleasure it might bring. He'd had a bushel basket with him when his mother found him in the garden, in anticipation of going directly to the apple picking, with no break between the gardening and the orchard labor. He wanted to be thought of as purposeful. Purposefulness pleased his father.

"I'll see to the apples later," he had said to Sarah.

She made observations, which she shared with him, about the way a cloud formation heaved its way across the sky, the muted nature of the late-September sun, and the sweet decaying scent of the detritus of summer. "The autumn always moves me," she announced. Andrew nodded as if he shared her capacity to be moved by a season. Her mood, her strange wish for his company, made him think it would be best to be agreeable and humor her.

At the cemetery, he drew the carriage up to a hitching post, tied the horses to it, and wedged a sprag between the spokes of the wheels to keep the brougham from rolling. It was a short walk to the gravesite from the road, and the tall grass was crushed and flattened by someone who must have recently preceded them. Sarah knew the way; Andrew followed. The hoop of her skirt (still so much the style then) swayed heavily from side to side, scything at the grass and widening the path. It was only as Andrew walked behind her, when a gust of leaf-strewn wind brushed past her toward him, that he realized she'd perfumed herself. She smelled of lavender, of Parma violet. He'd always believed that she shared her husband's distaste for finery and show. She, like the judge, had seemed little given to personal enhancements. Now her son discovered that his impression of her had been a false one, that she had bent to vanity. He wondered what had possessed her, what she had been thinking when she pressed the scented powder to her skin. Perhaps she thought the freshness of the day, the persistent breeze would dissipate the scent, so that by the time they returned home her husband wouldn't notice. Perhaps she thought that an embracing of the feminine was fitting for a visit to a daughter's grave. Then it came to him—maybe it was rebellion, maybe she felt shackled by his father's punishing, exacting standards. He almost asked her, Are you happy? Do you love him? The questions formed in his mouth, but he did not ask, because he feared she'd disappoint him with her answer. Because in that moment what he wanted from her was rebellion. There they were—thoughts of treason, a longing to escape from his father's scrutiny and judgment. And what came with his acknowledgement of that part of his character was a yearning for a partner in it. He wanted his mother to give some indication to him that she understood, and even shared his urge to kill the tyrant, to overthrow the monarchy.

The path they trod turned abruptly and wound up a small hill. In tight single file they threaded their way through the varied markers, some large and looming, some sites planted so heavily with mums and zinnias that they looked as if landscape architects had been employed for their design. The script on some had the look of runes, ancient, indecipherable, the stone worn by weather and time's passage. He was surprised when his mother approached a place where there was no obvious memorial, no cross, no attending angel. She stopped, then knelt to part the overgrowth of grass and touch each of three flat stones. He had imagined something less severe, less absolutely ordinary. He held to an adolescent logic in which the grandness of the monument was reflective of the love felt for the one who lay beneath it. The plainness of the site offended him.

Sarah Emma, Annie Rebecca, Samuel Selwyn. Names, birth and death dates—the simple facts engraved on simple markers. She knelt, he stood. He imagined she was praying. The sun reached its midday peak, its light rained through the orange and amber leaves of the tree that spread its shade over the graves. An American elm; Andrew knew from the vase-like shape of trunk and splaying limbs. As the air moved through the branches, he saw that the play of light and shadow brought an incandescence to the site. At least there was that, he thought. A natural beauty.

He hardly remembered his sister Annie; he'd been a toddler when she died. But as he watched his mother, images of her, and of that time, slid through his mind. The images came to him not as scenes, but in a barrage of indistinct and dreamlike fragments. Himself in a dark room, sent hurriedly to bed. And then the late-night waking, the sick and sudden fear he felt. Muted voices came from outside his room. "Sh . . . sh." A whispered warning. "Mustn't wake the children." It was his father's voice. "Sarah, Sarah." The only time Andrew had ever heard his father call his mother by her name. In the presence of the children he had always called her Mother. When she spoke that night, the young Andrew had begun to cry at the coldness of her tone, her hard authority. "She must have a place beneath a tree." He had never heard her insist on anything, but then, the night of Annie's death, she had insisted. The choice of where her daughter would be laid would be her choice. In that one thing, she'd have her way.

At the graveside Andrew reached to take Sarah's elbow as she rose. In another year his father would retire from the bench and turn all his prodigious energies to banking. Andrew knew that of the five surviving boys, he was the chosen child, that one day he would be his father's partner. He was, at thirteen, already thin and scrupulous, honed to his essential self: wary, focused, grave. His slenderness made him look ill and hungry, as he would throughout his life, as if something made it impossible for him to take nourishment and thrive.

His mother turned to face him, and reached to straighten his shirt collar, smooth a wrinkle from it. It was a gesture better suited to a younger child, someone eager and pliant, but he didn't shrink from it. "I would have preferred raised stones as markers," she said simply, and he understood that she was confiding a deeply private thing to him. "I imagined something upright, tall, with chiseled angels rising from it. I wanted a curved elaborate script to spell their names, a poem or a prayer carved into marble. I wanted a building built. A mausoleum." She sighed. "I wanted something as magnificent as grief."

At thirteen, Andrew Mellon had not heard grief described in such a way before. He had not understood. Once Laura died he did, and now he wished that he could bring Frick to that same understanding.

Instead, he said, "I fear I have been a burden to you and Adelaide. My moodiness, my unhappiness, as you describe it. I would never want to be burdensome."

"No, no. It isn't that," said Frick, although it was. Mellon had grown marmoreal, closed. Absent as a dinner partner, drifting and inept when engagement and conversation were required. But even as Frick tried to broach this, to maneuver toward frankness, truth, he knew that he could not go on all weekend in this way, that this thing that was needed, this speech of encouragement, must be gotten over with so that they could spend the rest of their time on more solid ground, with talk of price indexes and interest rates, and the problems with the Iron Clad Agreement Carnegie was attempting to impose on all his partners. And art. Frick went regularly to Europe, to New York. Wouldn't it be easier to talk about art? Rembrandt's self-portraits, Bellini's startling composition of St. Francis in the desert?

"I will try to be less bleak, if you and Adelaide wish it. But I cannot promise to be much good at it. I never have been, you know? I'm afraid I'm a little bleak by nature. You know that, don't you?"

"I know. I know. I don't mean to criticize, God knows, but . . ."

"Of course you don't. I take this to be what it is—an expression of concern. So let's say I'll try to get out more, become more accessible and social. And then we'll agree to talk no further about it." He managed a slight smile, one that failed to reassure. "I will do my best. Will that do?"

How was it, Frick wondered looking at him, that this one man, of all the men he knew, had provoked such affection in him? He didn't like most people. He had never understood exactly what had attracted him to Mellon. Even now, when he seemed so unavailable for friendship, so mired in his own dark inner life, Frick envied him. Poor bastard, he thought, but there was a split between thought and feeling, pity and jealousy. He could not conceive of a love for a woman so intricate and fathomless that the loss of it could do such damage. He couldn't conceive of it, but at the same time he could envy his friend for having had it.

Mellon pushed his eggs away, turned to the window, taking in the view. "I like the fact that the Allegheny Mountains have no real peaks, that the tops of them are rounded," he said, a merciful and gracious change of subject. "They look from a distance like the brownish backs of elephants, especially now, with the trees still bare, not quite blooming. On the train I kept thinking about that, I found myself imagining a safari, some African adventure."

Frick moved, with relief, to talk of travel. "We should go. To Africa, that is. We know we travel well together." The tension eased from Frick. They could reminisce, recall the European trip they'd taken years earlier.

Mellon nodded. "The Blarney Stone. Remember that? Our July Fourth visit there?"

"Yes, yes. We were so . . . so exuberant that day." Frick shook his head.

"What was so funny? Do you remember? I can't, but I remember that we laughed and laughed . . ."

"And we had those little American flags that I had bought . . ."

"And the beaver hats."

"Which your father told us to dispose of when we returned. He said we looked like dandies." Frick smiled.

"You let me lower you to kiss the Blarney Stone." Mellon leaned toward the table, his untouched eggs, his friend across from him. How unlikely it all seemed to him. Breakfast, talk. Hadn't they gotten too busy for this, hadn't they lost the knack? "It surprised me when you trusted me to hold on to you while you lowered yourself to kiss the stone." One had to lie on one's back, extend the body out over a ledge to reach the Blarney Stone. Thin air and a long drop waited for anyone who slipped. Mellon had held Frick's legs and ankles as Frick lowered himself, and he still remembered that day, the sense of having someone's life in his hands. "I was so inexperienced in every way. What was it that made you trust me to hold you?"

Frick's face clouded. Introspection did not interest him. "I don't know. I suppose that I thought, even then, that you were sound. That we were alike in some essential way." He remembered that he had thought it would be fun to lie on his back, extend himself, to be upside down. He had recklessly offered to be the first to do it, and then been unprepared for the sick sensation: blood rushing to his head, his back arched, throat extended in a posture of complete vulnerability, the shifting of his center of gravity as he inched toward the stone. And the panic at the moment when he realized that the upright universe could in an instant become so foreign and fractured. Sheer will had kept him from yielding to the panic. He had gasped for air, saying to himself, Do not yield to it, do not yield. Mellon's hands held his knees and ankles, Mellon's grasp kept him from crying out, from humiliating himself by screaming. His grip had felt remarkably strong, especially for someone as thin as he.

"Alike? Do you think so? How are we alike?" Mellon leaned back as the server poured each of them more coffee. It was out of character for him to press for the sharing of thoughts, but a need to know seemed to have gripped him.

Is this what Adelaide had had in mind? Frick wondered. This drift into intimate terrain? Something akin to the panic he'd felt at the Blarney Stone flooded him.

"The lake *is* beautiful," he said with a false and firm exuberance, gesturing to it. "A lovely spot." Movement, he thought, get moving. He pushed his chair away from the table, folded his napkin, pressed both hands emphatically on the tabletop, as if to press himself to his feet.

Eloquence is what is promised to those who kiss the Blarney Stone. Each of them had done it.

In the clubhouse dining room Mellon took Frick's cue, rose from the table as Frick did, and he found himself wondering what error they had made in the maneuver at the Blarney Stone that caused them to be denied the gift, and to be denied it so completely. Eloquence so far beyond their reach, they had barely managed to stumble through this breakfast. And yet Mellon remembered how much he had wanted it that day. He would have given anything for eloquence.

"Yes, beautiful," he said obligingly about the lake, standing at the window, shading his eyes against the sun glinting off it. "I've often thought that someone should do an oil painting of it."

"Someone should. But who?"

Each ventured opinions. Whose brushstrokes would best capture its vastness, who was daring enough with color and contour to evoke the insuperable variety and beauty of the trees?

"About the club; I've gotten a letter from a lawyer," Mellon ventured as they stepped out the door onto the veranda.

"We all have. Ignore it." Frick thrust his hands into his pockets.

"Is the dam a problem, as he insists it is? I'm no expert, but it looks fine to me. Massive. Substantial."

"Of course it's fine. Repairs were seen to long ago."

"And the crew here has been charged with its maintenance. Am I remembering that correctly?"

"Absolutely. That's why we have a staff. That's what people are paid for," Frick said with unexpected hostility. He hated complaints and contretemps. He loathed distractions.

Concern dismissed, the briefest fog of worry was cast aside, forgotten. "So," Mellon ventured. "Shall we walk a bit?" But even as he spoke, he was looking over his shoulder toward the clubhouse door, the shadowed entry, the stairs beyond it, which led to the second floor and his room, blessed solitariness. He knew that walking on the wooded paths would require energy and affect. Even if the subject of his heartsickness didn't come up again (and he felt sure it wouldn't), there were so many other things that would demand comment and attention.

"I think I won't," said Frick about the walking. "Actually, I brought a bit of work to do, so if you don't mind . . ."

Fine, of course. They shook hands, exchanged reassurances. Good, yes; lunch, then? Lunch at one? Then Frick floated an idea, Mellon grasped it. Not spend a second night? Well, that was true, why have a private train car at your disposal if you can't change your plans? Of course, absolutely, good idea. Of course Mellon could see the wisdom of returning to the city sooner.

Mellon entered his room, pressed the door closed behind him. Shouldn't they have talked? Should it be so difficult? He ought to go back into the hall, down to Frick's room. He felt seized by a wish to tell him what he hadn't over their perfectly cooked eggs; that sorrow such as his could not be willed away; that he, Mellon, who had not so much as a whit of talent, that *he* wanted to paint the portrait of the lake; and that in Ireland he had been naïve enough to trust a myth, to believe that eloquence could be had so easily.

He stood beside his window. How he wished that time would move backward. He wanted the beaver hat, Laura. He wanted naïveté and foolishness returned to him.

It flattered Frank when Mrs. Hirst and Grace began to think of him as a library regular, even though there were weeks, months, when he couldn't go at all. Too busy, he would say to himself at those times, and there was some truth to that, but an uneasy guilt played a part in it as well. Guilt at the way his eyes strayed so easily from anything that he was reading whenever Grace was near. Guilt about the boyish pleasure he took when he began to be identified as a favorite, when Grace began to offer him tea. And guilt became especially acute when Julia entered, when he saw the two women together. The attachment of each to the other was obvious, and Julia had become lovelier because of it. There were days when she seemed almost happy. Some old tenderness, some signs of connection to the world were evident in her again. She was a grandmother now to the baby girl of their only daughter. The bond linking mother, child, and baby vivified them all. It had made Julia more available, more interested in him as well. It was a thing that should have touched him, and on certain days it did. But he could not quite bring himself to soften toward her, trust her. He couldn't quite forgive the way she had left him to do her grieving separately. And his growing admiration for the lovely Grace made it difficult to exert much forgiving effort.

It was on a winter Sunday, early 1888, that Frank first volunteered to walk Grace home from the library. He had stopped to return a book for Daniel, just as Grace was closing for the day. It was dark and blustery and cold; Julia would have insisted Frank escort Grace had she been there. He knew she wouldn't have wanted Grace to walk in the dark alone.

A starless night. The bitter nip of a storm in the air, snow coming, that little tinge of electricity that barbs the nostrils just before the clouds collide and release their load of snow. Grace wore a camel's-hair ulster pulled snugly against the cold. Her cheeks were flushed before she could lock the library door. She talked eagerly of Julia, about what a friend she had been to her and how when she'd first come to town she'd felt despairing, desperate, and how . . .

"Desperate?" He took her elbow as she stepped from street to sidewalk. It had been a slip on her part, he could see. Her arm tensed.

She laughed at herself in that deliberate and easy way she had. "Perhaps that's too strong a word. Too melodramatic, certainly. I meant to say alone."

"And why is that? If you don't mind my asking. I've been wondering."

Perhaps there was just enough wind that night, enough of a covering murmur of wind through trees that she thought she could say it aloud, give words to her past and in that way be rid of it. As the wind rose, she might have told herself that, in such a wind, if she spoke softly, no one, not even Frank walking beside her, would really hear her story. The running away. The breaking of vows. The abandonment. The fact that she had never even bothered to divorce him, that it might have been possible, but she hadn't deemed it worth the time. That that was the kind of woman she was. The kind who ran away. She spoke so quietly that he had to bend toward her to hear her; her jet bead earrings hung daintily. Such unlikely closeness to a woman other than his wife, in a shadow on a street corner, just out of the glare of the white arc lights that bleached the streets with brilliance. He'd bent his head toward her. Was that how easily one veered off the course of an entire life? A course that had been charted by love, by an elaborately developed sense of honor?

They walked and walked that night. Down Walnut to Main Street, past the opera house, the Johnstown *Freie Presse*, the bank, the Odd Fellows' new building, called Alma House. It was solid, brick, four stories tall, its face studded with sash windows, a store and the gas office on the first floor, law offices and rooms for lodgers higher up. Daniel was thinking of moving out, taking rooms there.

Frank stayed close beside Grace and listened carefully. Then he spoke about things he had never even thought to articulate, about Julia, the children, the way diphtheria had stopped their lives. Things she must have already known, of course, from Julia or from Daniel, but it seemed important that she hear it all from him. By the end of an hour and a half of walking, by the time he tipped his hat to her on Clinton Street, leaving her to go to her upstairs rooms, she knew all his secrets.

Grace was unable to sleep that night. What had she done? She hardly knew Frank Fallon. She had no idea why she had decided to trust him, use him as confessor. She had, until the words poured from her, not even known she needed one. He had surprised her by seeming so accepting of what she said. It was as if, in his life, he had stepped beyond the need to judge. Prior to coming to this city she had been ruled by codes of conduct, biting disapproval, the certainty of ostracism for anyone who stumbled. Now here was someone, a man who might be thought of as a friend, who had listened and who had not reproached.

"I ran away," she had said, and he simply nodded.

LIKE LOVERS

Nora marked a large X through the date. May 29, 1888. This year's schedule would take them to South Fork in July. Only forty-seven days of waiting.

From downstairs she could hear the sounds of her parents arguing. There had been a time when they had tried to disguise what was going on between them, for her sake, she supposed. Now it seemed to her that each year the arguing escalated. They were like two generals who had honed their expertise, amassed new weapons, relished each new strategy for cruelty.

"Letters? Are you mad?" Evelyn's voice, lighter, carried more readily; her diction clipped the very air with fricative, deliberate sounds.

What would her mother do if she knew that Nora mailed the letters for him? He had finally confessed his concerns about the dam to her, the morning after the storm, after their late-night talk at South Fork—the history of poor repairs, the slipshod maintenance, the weight of water in a 450-acre lake. Twenty million tons.

Nora, a clever girl, one accustomed because of her scientific interest to measuring and weighing, could not quite comprehend the figure. She tried to think of it in terms of the everyday. How many locomotives, bricks, books would that be? Twenty million tons. How many people? A workbook on her desk had calculations scribbled in the margins. How many horses? How many hens? What were the physics of it?

Now she was the one about to go to a college outside Philadelphia. In the fall she would step out of the confines of constricted life. Half-finished needlework could be abandoned, piano music with her teacher's chiding annotations packed and stored. In Philadelphia there would be courses in zoology. Someone like J. Henri Fabre might become her mentor. She had formed a mental image of him, this professor who would at once recognize her talent, her precocity. He would speak German and several other languages. He would wear glasses because his vision had been sacrificed to the miniature world. The thumb and digit that had so diligently gripped and manipulated tweezers and other varied instruments would be permanently ridged.

She wished the bell would ring for dinner. Once she had been ashamed at the thought that Eliza overheard her parents battling, but all such delicacy had come to seem contrived and stupid. She had moved beyond it. Eliza tippling in the kitchen, neat little flask kept in her apron pocket, her eyes rheumy and overbright with drink, dinner served when serving suited her, all protocol abandoned, replaced by sullenness and daring. What could they do to her, after all? Dismiss her? Set her loose in the world with all she knew, all her stories?

"You have become a whore to appearances, to fortune. Does human life not mean anything to you?" James flung the word at Evelyn. His vocabulary of disgust had grown far-reaching, vile. Nora took the book that she'd left opened at the foot of her bed and sat in her rocker. "There is no outward difference between the two sexes of the *Scarabaei*," she read. The pages of *Souvenirs Entomologiques* were dark with marginalia, stained.

Downstairs, Evelyn might have been wearing a sack slung over her shoulder where she stored all manner of munitions. She dipped with relish into her vast arsenal, chose sarcasm, mockery. "Oh, the histrionics, the hubris of it. *You* know more than all the other clubmen. *You* speak for oppressed man, all the nameless little lives."

Nora's eyes leaped from her reading. She did not mean that, she said to herself. It was rage speaking, she was a foolish woman but not a cruel one; she didn't mean to speak of people so cruelly. The phrase reminded her of something else. Ah, Maeterlinck, she realized, writing about insects, their "almost nameless little lives."

"I did this, don't you see? I filed the papers. If the worst thing happens, it all comes back to me."

Nora winced, hating it when her father pleaded for her mother's understanding. Dinner, where was dinner? Should she try to slip downstairs without being noticed by them? Past the partially closed pocket doors, into the steaming, reeking kitchen? Move things along? Ring the bell herself? She could do those things, but instead she plunged back into her reading. Of the praying mantis Fabre wrote: "Apart from her lethal implement . . . she is not without a certain beauty . . . her slender figure, her elegant bust . . . her long gauze wings." She closed her book abruptly. How she longed for South Fork, for space, for the tempering effect of crowds, of good society. The wounds and weaponry left here, to be taken up again with renewed ferocity when their holiday ended, but nonetheless abandoned, briefly. The thought of a reprieve from this made Nora want to weep.

"You think this will be accepted? This letter writing, this hectoring? You think we'll be welcomed at the club?"

Nora had not let herself think of that. Suppose South Fork was taken from her? Suppose she was denied her Alexandria? Daniel would be waiting for her at the boathouse as they had finally agreed he would. This was the year, this the summer. Suppose she could not get there? He would believe she had misled him. That the things that had passed between them had been a mere divertissement for her. Would he think that? In her mind she planned for every possible eventuality. She had his address, she would go to Johnstown. It wouldn't be difficult to find him. In a few months she'd be going all the way to Philadelphia. Surely she'd have no trouble finding Johnstown. How often she'd tried to imagine it—the shaded streets, the mosquito hum of the new telephone wires, the stone swans Daniel had described to her, fixed sentinels, in the fountain in the park. She could go to the *Tribune* offices and ask directions. Fallon, she would say, and there would be smiles of recognition, directions offered, the suggestion that the new Hulbert House Hotel would be a comfortable place to stay. She was not a child, not without resources. She would resist whatever force might attempt to keep her from him. She was weak in a thousand other ways, but she was a skilled resister.

Finally, mercy in the form of sound, the dinner bell. Now she could descend the stairs, now they could sup together. The argument (was that the right word for these bloody campaigns?) suddenly set aside, the voices lowered, cold politeness reinstated. Her mother's foot would move to the buzzer imbedded in the hardwood floors to summon Eliza, who had summoned them. She would join in the pretense that Eliza had not been drinking.

Nora checked her image in the mirror. Tied a grosgrain ribbon at the bottom of her braid.

Just forty-seven days.

That year, their Pittsburgh house, the seat of her pride and vanity fallen into desuetude, began to feel burdensome to Evelyn. A dinner party was beyond her ken; the extra bedrooms, meant for guests, had become well-furnished reminders of the son not had, of the disappointing daughter on the verge of leaving. The words "laundry," "linens" sounded like a curse to her; the kitchen, so utterly given over to Eliza, felt like an empire from which she'd been denied all access. The paint on the shutters peeled and flaked, the plastered walls began to crack; the pocket doors worked their way out of alignment, became sluggish and stubborn, reluctant to move smoothly on their tracks. July arrived just in the nick of time for all of them, just when another day of waiting would have been more than any of them could bear. Just in time, the trunks were dragged down from the attic, the fishing rods, the tackle box, the flies were packed, even though James hadn't fished in years. Evelyn tried one more time to convince Nora that her braid had become ridiculous, an affectation, and even this—this futile battle—reminded them of earlier years, when excitement at the possibility of one more magic summer still infected them, still made them sleepless with anticipation the night before they left.

In that way, nothing had changed. The lake, the dam, the brilliant summers. Pretend the world's the same, Nora advised herself as they left the train at the South Fork station, as she watched their things loaded on the spring wagon, as she let the horses nuzzle at her back. Emma Ehrenfeld still sat in the telegraph tower, the horses would stop on the road across the dam's crest, so that the passengers could catch the first sight of the lake. This world, she told herself, was still the same. But she had changed. She'd grown more interior, more serious than she had ever been. She was nineteen.

———

Two nights after their arrival at the club, Nora waited at the boathouse, which was empty but for the sculls which were upended and held by the U-shaped racks that jutted from the boathouse walls. The sailboats were still in the water, tied to posts along the dock, their sails rolled tightly and covered, their hulls dipping, rocking in the light night current. Daniel had insisted that they meet and she'd resisted it. She had feared changing the way things were, feared that he would be disappointed in her. He had written to her that perhaps the opposite was true: that her fear was that he would fail to be what she imagined.

"Never," she wrote as her reply.

It was just that, in some way she could not quite articulate, the notes, the letters had seemed enough. Those and the fact of his awareness of her. Because of that her life had come into sharper focus. She had become larger, more significant, essential to the workings of the universe because she was essential to him. She was afraid to tamper with that. It seemed like a tempting of fate.

Once he'd left college, started working at Cambria Iron, he was often not able to come to the lake when she was there, at least not with any regularity. So they exchanged addresses. And once that correspondence had begun, the notes left on the South Fork property grew more and more infrequent but, at the same time, more precious—an indication to Nora that he had been nearby, an indication that he'd seen her.

She struggled to make a case for keeping things as they were. She told herself that his life, after all, was fraught and busy. Busy with his twelve-hour shifts, his union organizing.

"And girls?" she'd asked after he'd written a list of all the things that busied him. Her question mark was large.

"We should meet," he wrote. Just that. Evasive when it came to his romantic life. But quick with his answers, quick on his feet.

"Soon," she wrote, again and again during the months that followed; as she wrote to and received word from several universities, as she began sorting through things, choosing what she could take with her when she left her parents' home. "Soon" in her Christmas card, "soon" inscribed on the fly leaf of a book she inscribed to him. There were so many postponements that it began to seem impossible to keep putting him off; until it began to seem cruel.

"This summer," she had written in her Christmas letter, 1887. She'd surprised him, and it undermined his quickness, tested his nerve. He'd been all talk, all certainty. "Now I'm worried. What, I wonder, will you think of me?"

She had pictured him a thousand times. Now short, now tall, now too serious, now jug-eared and freckled.

She should have brought her challis shawl to the boathouse. It was cooler than she'd expected it to be.

Lakewater lapped against the wooden pylons. Crickets chirped, a dog howled at the silver disk of moon.

"Nora."

He was much taller, broader in the back, a bit more hesitant than she'd expected him to be. His voice was a deep baritone; moonlight sifted through the trees and lit his auburn hair. His legs were long, his hands were at his sides. He was partially hidden by the shadow of a tree.

She felt terribly uncertain, and suddenly afraid. A leap of faith would be required here. She took a step forward, reached her hand out to him. "Come," she said. "Into the light. I want to see you. Come here to me."

The hand he placed in hers was rough. As she looked at his face she thought, There is something raw there. She knew a thousand things about him from his letters. So she knew to reach up to him, to undo his top shirt button. She knew to stand on tiptoe, to kiss the scar there.

Nora surprised Daniel when she took his hand. He had expected to lead in this; he was older, more experienced in every way. But it was she who reached for his hand, pulled him into the light, then said, We ought to move farther into the woods. We might be seen here. So she pulled him along, her hand lost in his enormous one. She was the one who had memorized the landscape. She knew where she was going.

The pleasure of holding hands surprised him. The pleasure of fingers webbed through his. Flesh and bone, a beating heart, someone beside him. Nora had insisted that the letters were enough. Now he knew how wrong she'd been.

They took the path along the lake bank, the path on which she had pursued her father the night of the fall storm. "Step carefully," she cautioned. "There are woodchuck holes and knotted tree roots. It's easy to lose your footing."

Her small size surprised him. From a distance she had looked tall. He supposed the braid helped in creating that illusion, a thick black dart that drew attention to itself, so straight, so long, so perpendicular. Distance had skewed his vision, it would seem. He wondered in what other ways he was mistaken about her.

"Where are we going?" He had a long stride and was following easily.

"To a secret place," she offered.

They had dropped the half-whisper they'd used and spoke aloud, secure now in the distance put between them and the boathouse. The sounds of a banjo had long since faded; they could hear the water rushing over rock—the spillway. "I know all your secret places," he said.

It was daring to walk across the dam's breast, two lone figures silhouetted, visible even from afar, away from the protecting cover of the trees. But the whole enterprise was daring; they did not care. She stopped at the spillway.

"I once thought the dam was a wall of a lost city. I thought it had always been here."

"And in that scenario, which is the lost city?" he asked, gesturing with his head. "The club or the valley?"

"I didn't think about that. Until fairly recently, I never thought."

"So think now. What do you think?"

"Not tonight," she said. Was she so wrong to want the first time with him to be without controversy? Which is the lost city, how strong is the dam? "Not tonight," she repeated.

But he found he had to say it, at least once. She was this person, this girl, here with him, but he could not deny that at the same time she was also one of the summer people. A member of the club. "Everyone believes that the dam will fail one day." A sheer fog was rising from the lake. The lights of the clubhouse blurred behind them.

"It's poorly made. Carelessly managed. It could fail, Nora. A thing like that could happen."

"So my father says. He says something should be done."

"Something should, but something won't be."

So cynical, she thought. But of course, he had every right to be.

"I don't mean to sound resigned to it," he went on. He spoke this way to steelworkers when he wanted them to organize. No drama, no inflating of truth, no lies. "I just know that efforts have been made, and that your people won't see to it." *Your* people.

The expression stung, and she grew silent. He tried to be gentler. "In any case, I'm not sure what can be done. Empty the lake so that discharge pipes can be installed? Close the club for a summer to make repairs? I don't imagine that being decided, do you?"

She wondered if her father could see to that. A summer skipped, work crews installed in the clubhouse, an engineer hired to oversee.

She asked him if she could come one day to Johnstown, if a visit could be arranged. "It's your home, I'd like to see it. You've seen mine." And really, he had. Because this place was as close to a home as anything she knew. She had no other.

He wondered if she sensed how uncomfortable he was, how uncertain about being there. He had pressed for this, and now, as they walked together, he found he doubted her. He knew her heart because he'd read her letters, but this was different. Now *she* was really here. This young woman who lived this other life. A life among people he had no wish to know, could never admire. He observed her closely. She wasn't beautiful, she almost worked to see to it that she was not. And yet her smile was lovely; her lips on his scar had been benevolent and sweet. What could she be to him, ever? Why would she want to come to town? What did she think she'd find there?

"Do you ride?" he asked, something he had failed to learn about her.

She nodded yes.

"Then one day we'll do it. I'll get horses from Snavely's. We'll picnic along the way." But he said it as if it was something that would never occur. His tone suggested too great a distance, too little time.

"Tell me more about Johnstown. You've told me a little, but I want to know everything."

He laughed then. "Tell you about it? What would you like to know?"

"Why do you like living there? Why do people stay?"

"Why do people stay anywhere? There are ties that bind. Besides, the fishing's good," he said, and she laughed.

When they reached the spillway, he made a place in the grass where they could sit together. The spillway had been cut into the rock-hard hill into which the east side of the dam was anchored, and after the spring rains the overflow of water from the rising lake poured into it and made a waterfall, a small Niagara. The press of the water from the spring-fed lake, the sudden rocky drop into the valley, the water's seething force as it fell misted the fragrant, summer air and the grassy hummocks just beyond it on the hillside; it was a cool, enchanting place to picnic.

"What else besides the fishing?" she pressed. He could see that she would not be deflected from knowing.

"Ice-skating on Von Lunen Pond in winter. We have two opera houses, traveling theater companies come. There is music. A very good library, and a wonderful librarian. Grace. She's been very, very generous to me. And a literary society. Oh, and there are fortune-tellers." He reached for her hand, turned it palm up in his as if he could predict her future by examining the lines there. "And friends," he said, stroking her hand. "Good people. People who will give you credit when credit's needed, and who'll carry the caskets of your dead for you."

"So we'll go next summer?" He was here with her, and yet was not quite. She felt somehow that it was important to elicit a promise from him.

He curled her fingers into her hot little palm. Brought her hand to his lips and kissed it.

Who knows about the future? Promise, he said to himself, promise anything. "Fair enough, then, Nora. Next summer."

He should go. He'd accomplished what he'd come for; he'd heard her voice, he'd held her hand. It would be best to let it go at that. Best to be done with it.

He reached behind her, took her thick braid in his hand, so consistent, so substantial; it never changed. He wanted to feel the weight of it, such hair.

She pulled it over her shoulder to give him better access. The ribbon tied at the end of it was maroon velvet. The color of a bruise. One small pull on the ribbon's end and her hair would come tumbling down.

"May I?" he said.

And she said, "Yes. Untie it."

The hair came first. And then the tucked and layered muslin petticoats, the little Paris tournure bustle her mother insisted on, the corset cover, the cambric drawers, lace-trimmed chemise. Too many clothes.

She had heard, been told, that this was done in darkness. That clothes were pushed aside, fumbled with, buttons undone, but that none were removed. Summer picnics at the spillway with the other young people had given her a glimpse, an inkling. On those picnics during recent summers, the sound of the falling water at the spillway had smothered every other sound. The young men and women, in whom the summer heat had bred new and pressing passions, found hiding places, moist mossy beds, rock-and-forest-sealed. Where a curve of breast could be laid bare in leaf-filtered light, where wet white thighs became moss-smeared and musty, lust-laced to a pale viridian. When these furtive lovers had returned to the picnic site, a space was made for them on the rough blankets, the easy give-and-take of talk flowed forward, the surface life continued uninterrupted. How well inculcated were the rules, how easily they were broken. No one saw the grass-stained blouse, the beard-roughened neck, pine needles nestled in gathered hair. Summer lust brought summer blindness. This she knew. But she did not know that this thing could be done openly, that clothing could be shed, removed. That his hand could brush past her knee, her inner thigh, to find the top of her silk stocking. Piece by cumbersome piece, he took her clothing from her. She watched him as he watched her, as he savored each inch of flesh as he bared it, astonished at his tenderness. Her own body surprised her. The hardening and rising of her nipple in his hand, the flush and hum of her own arousal. When he kissed the inner aspect of her upper arm, she bit softly at him, his neck. She wanted to devour him. He turned her onto her stomach, and she let him move her, arrange her as he wished to. She was supple, her spine curved into him. That once-stiff spine. He kissed each sculpted vertebra.

The ground was wet with nighttime dampness. How wonderful the spongy darkness was. She was exposed, but covered wholly by him. She let him caress her, spread her legs, extend her arms above her head and hold them there. Understanding that he wanted the entire length of her, from fingertip to toe. She felt dreamily like the insects that she loved, collected. Their bodies spread, admired, pinned. Pinned easily and cleanly. She was a virgin, he knew certainly, but there was no sign of it, no resistance. She was utterly penetrable, and he knew no one would ever have her as he had tonight. Whatever happened to them, it would not change this. What he couldn't know was that all that watching, all that waiting had been a kind of sacrament. He was bound to her before he ever touched her.

Too many clothes. They made an enormous heap, like a prehistoric rock formation. An earthworm nestled in the soft white folds of Nora's petticoat. A black bass jumped. The sky was pierced with brilliant stars.

The Club's Final Year

"Time is a violent torrent."
— Marcus Aurelius, *Meditations*, Book IV, Number 43

Nora sat in the college library reading room, folded a letter, and tried to return to her work. But concentration eluded her, uneasiness would shadow the rest of her day. Her father's concern about the dam had shaped itself into obsession. He'd grown careless about all other things. She knew from her mother that his law practice was in disarray; his eating habits arbitrary, strange: fish, apples sliced thin as paper, an occasional root vegetable. His dishevelment in dress was such that neighbors, their minister, and, more ominously, his colleagues had begun commenting upon it. When he wrote to Nora, he wrote of little else besides the fishing and hunting club. It was as if nothing there could occur without him; the boats could not be launched, the flag raised. Nothing could go forward without his tense presence. "Won't you meet me there?" he wrote. She had been told that morning by the bursar that her school fees had not been paid. She knew she ought to be ashamed for thinking of herself, but she had hoped that there might be money in the letter. It was February 1889, and he had asked her if she wanted to go to South Fork for the Memorial Day weekend.

Since her night with Daniel, she had grown inward, contemplative, as she tried to make sense of, impose some order on her life. Childhood seemed suddenly, completely over—she had a lover, after all; surely that marks the end of childhood. Her parents and their marriage seemed to be unraveling, yielding to some shared bitter history. The word "mistress" came frequently into her mind, unbidden. She was someone's mistress. Although of course that was an exaggeration. It had been one night, one evening. She had returned to her room, slept in her high bed, as she had on so many other nights, then returned to Pittsburgh with James and Evelyn when she woke up in the morning. Sex with Daniel, the strange tumult of feeling it produced in her, had only since been spoken of in letters, and only indirectly. Absence had not diminished what she felt; her thoughts were crowded with him. She tried to find words for what was happening but was unable to. Something had changed and changed essentially for her. A boundary had been crossed, fate tempted. No avenging god had forced her to pay pleasure's toll with a pregnancy, no shame or regret tortured her sharp conscience. What would he become to her? She had no way of telling.

In the library she pushed her books aside, drew a sheet of paper from a folio. To her father she wrote reassuringly a confirmation of dates, promises to write again after train schedules were consulted. The letter's complimentary close was "dutifully yours."

Then immediately she'd reached for another sheet and wrote to Daniel. *We won't have to wait until summer. I will come to you in May*. She supposed she ought to ask—can work, your other occupations, be put aside for me?—but she felt calm, utterly sure of him. So that there would be no confusion, she underlined the date. Friday, May 31, late afternoon. The spillway. Now there would just be the waiting to endure.

So this was love, she thought as she attended Meeting at her Quaker college, as she read *The Guide to Quaker Practice* in her theology class. Love was the sheer impossibility of waiting. She memorized plant genuses and species, dissected small mammals in zoology. Because her material future seemed so uncertain—she knew she would not be permitted to remain at school if money from her father wasn't forthcoming—she made maximum use of the library and laboratories, all but living there. For thrift's sake she skipped meals, and sometimes she hid in the stacks at library closing time, emerging only after all was dark, to sleep sitting at one of the library tables, arms crossed on the smooth surface, head cradled there. Everything but work and Daniel seemed precarious to her. Her attendance at Meeting every week was required by the school. There, she tried to clear her mind, to let God enter it.

Impossible.

And impossible for Daniel, too, this love, this anarchy of feeling. Nora's letter had arrived and he didn't hesitate: of course he'd go. But even as he agreed to it in his mind, and then on paper in a letter to her, he wondered what the future was of this impossible thing. As he waited for L. D. Woodruff's printing press to roll out flyers, waited with the scent of ink and oiled gears, he tried to imagine himself entering her world, or her entering his. Letters were inadequate for all that had to be decided.

In the early months of 1889, questions of duty and love had kept Grace awake as well. After one particularly restless March night, she had opened windows, aired winter's oppressive staleness from her rooms. She had come to realize that Frank Fallon wanted her. She saw it in the way he watched her at the library, in the awkwardness of his approaches and retreats. Recently he'd asked for *Plutarch's Lives*. He said a friend from the war had recommended it. And for weeks he'd sat, an hour here, an hour there, poring over it, elbow on table, forehead in hand, his face dense with concentration. He renewed the book four times, finally prompting her to ask one night, "Why this book? What about it means so much to you?"

She had been locking the library doors, he standing beside her. He was often there, the last of a day's swarm of visitors, waiting while she wound the clock, as she did each evening, waiting while she extinguished the lights. Then holding her bag while she locked the door. Sometimes he walked part of the way with her, sometimes not, in that way making his attendance to her seem occasional and accidental, and avoiding any appearance of impropriety. The night she asked him about *Plutarch's Lives*, he had fallen into step beside her.

"I was wounded in the war, at Fredericksburg, and spent the night in a field. By the time the fighting was over, it was too late in the day to clear it, to differentiate between the dead, the wounded, so I was left there— many were—with the corpses. Or if not corpses, then boys who had been blasted, who were about to die. They came and got those of us who were alive the next morning. My knee was wrecked, the doctor said; the joint was shattered, there was lead lodged in it. They'd have to probe and lay it open, see what they could do. They had some chloroform, but the pain was fearsome. I didn't know if I could stand it. Captain Bill Jones stood at my head, right by my ear through the whole thing, reading to me. Later he told me that he thought words, a familiar voice, might help. I was drugged and sick, out of my mind with pain, he could have been reading anything to me. But this was the book he carried with him everywhere, so this is what he read. Ever since then I've meant to read all of it, but never made the time. And I've decided, I don't want to live that way. I'm going to do things, seize opportunities."

So eager was she *not* to be aware of what was developing between them that it took her months to understand what ought to have been obvious—that it was she who drew him to the library. He was there because of her. This good man. It would be so simple to encourage him, say yes, to take this chance, and in taking it, just once and briefly, to be loved elaborately. She imagined herself growing old, a caricature of a spinster librarian. Her skin becoming powdery and gray, her narrow life the subject of sympathetic whispers. She could imagine dying without being loved by any man—father, husband, son—and she could hardly bear it. She hadn't pursued him; she had stopped hoping for and had not asked for love. But there it was. Throughout that spring, when she slept she dreamed of Julia, so she hardly slept at all. Then he said he wished to see her the day after Memorial Day. He had proposed a walk by Von Lunen Pond. He said he had something to tell her.

Memorial Day, 1889, a rare holiday in Johnstown. Frank Fallon had worn his army uniform, had marched with his son in the parade. That morning he had stood at the washbasin in his skivvies. Soap, straight razor. He had poured water from the pitcher into the washbasin, taken a hard look at his reflection in the mirror. I am a stranger to myself, he thought. He tilted his head from side to side, regarded himself in profile, ran his hands through his hair, hardly any gray there, lucky; perhaps that was one of the things about him that she'd found attractive. He turned away from his reflection then. "Good God," he said aloud. "Get away now. You're too old, too old for vanity." And with a hand poised on either side of the washstand he leaned toward the basin, toward the quivering water, as if he might find some submerged truth there.

But he was only fifty-one and he didn't feel old, that was the thing. For the first time since Claire and Louis died, he did not feel old.

After the night he had walked Grace home, after she'd told him the truth about herself, there was embarrassment between them. So much had been confided so openly. One week later, they had exchanged notes. Hers to him: "Thank you for allowing me to unburden myself." His to her: "Your trust has touched me deeply." Each of them telling themselves that nothing had really changed, and certainly nothing had happened. This would be a friendship, one of depth and dimension. That was all. Unusual, because such friendships rarely formed across the boundary of the sexes, but its uniqueness certainly did not make it wrong. There would be no betrayal of Julia, they each said to themselves without the knowledge of the other, unaware that subtly, insidiously, without their assent or awareness, the notion of betrayal had entered into their thinking, crossed their minds. No, absolutely never, they each said silently. Julia would never be betrayed.

And she had not been. His library visits had continued; he walked Grace home on many occasions. They had become good friends, they had kept faith with Julia and with one another. Then Frank asked Grace to meet him, the day after the parade and picnic.

Each year when Julia fried the chicken, when the plaid blanket was aired, Frank imagined that this would be his father-in-law's last Memorial Day. No one lives forever, but sometimes Frank thought perhaps Dr. Strayer would. He had kept the same hotel rooms he had taken when he first arrived with Julia. He paid the same rate he had always paid. Chambermaids gave him special consideration. The thickest, newest of the hotel towels were commandeered for him. In the dining room his tastes were known, wishes anticipated—toast with a wash of jam and warm milk for breakfast every morning; one single glass of sherry before dinner. Every Tuesday Julia joined him for dinner there, and in that way, and with his almost daily visits to the Fallon house, he watched over her as if she were still the girl he'd uprooted and brought here. Frank sometimes thought, Dr. Strayer will outlive her in order to be with her at the end—unlikely, of course, he was eighty-one, but maybe the love of a parent could bring about that sort of miracle.

Frank stood on his front porch, waved to a passing neighbor. Frank and Julia had once more gone to the cemetery together that afternoon, once more come home exhausted. Julia's hands were blistered by the force with which she used her little spade to turn the top layer of earth (as she did each year) so she could plant summer flowers, could turn the children's place into a circumscribed, bright garden. Now Dr. Strayer and Caroline, Ezra, and the baby were with Julia in the kitchen, unpacking the picnic basket, planning a lunch at Caroline's house on Sunday. Later, after they were gone, Frank and Julia would sit together, eat the last of the crisp chicken. Then tomorrow, when his workday ended, he would meet Grace near Von Lunen pond. He would hold her hand as they sidestepped their way down the embankment to a safe secluded spot, and he would kiss her. There. He knew the exact spot, beyond the rough benches where children sat to lace their skates in winter. Frank had rehearsed what he would say to her: You are the one. Grace had not asked him to declare anything, but it had come to his mind that he ought to choose, and he chose Grace. And tomorrow he would tell her. She would resist, she would be loyal, object to his presumption, but he would make her understand. She deserved love, and he had a great, great unused store of it.

From inside, Frank again heard Julia at the piano.

"How lovely it still sounds," Dr. Strayer said.

Frank had had the piano tuned each year for her, even after the children died, after she stopped playing. No doubt it was wasteful, but he had feared that not tuning it would imply the giving up of hope—in her, in himself, in everything, and it was a giving up that he was not prepared to do. So each year he had stopped on Clinton Street and arranged for a place in John Schrader's busy schedule, and on the appointed day he stood with his hands in his pockets, watching the tuning tools appear from deep within the felt pouch, listening to the unmelodic pings that issued forth as the strings were tightened, loosened, brought to pitch, the sounds declared to be on key. For nine music-less years, he nodded agreement to the lie when John Schrader smiled as he finished and said, "Like new." Frank understood it would never be like new, this early eager token of his love, purchased with money he'd saved in a sock. He didn't really even need for it to be. The purpose of the tuning was to indicate to Julia that he had not given up, that there were things waiting for her. Music, two living children, him. That everything and everyone were waiting.

Frank didn't know when he'd grown tired of waiting. He thought it might have been the year that Daniel left for Philadelphia, or the winter after, when Caroline was married.

He hoped the weather would hold. Dark clouds were forming in the distant sky.

A parade, a picnic, a visit to the graves. By four that afternoon, all that had been accomplished, another Memorial Day attended to, fallen soldiers, dead children honored, remembered as they deserved to be. A light mist began to fall, just enough rain to cause the draped buntings along the Main Street parade route to droop, then tear. On the front porch of the Fallon house, Dr. Strayer said no to the umbrella and slicker Julia and Frank offered him. He had always believed in nature's invigorating power. He thought a few blocks' walk in the rain would clear his head. Caroline and Ezra had taken the baby home a little earlier. Daniel was not there when they said their goodbyes. He had skipped the cemetery visit, too, instead making a stop at Snavely's to confirm the arrangement he'd made for a horse for himself for morning. Few shops had been opened today, but by five even they were closed, their proprietors knowing there would be little business on the evening of a holiday. By six a sleepy silence had settled over the city, punctuated only by the toot and flare of train whistles, the insistent bell on the street railroad car that shuttled back and forth to Woodvale. At the corner of Franklin and Main Streets, the clack of typewriter keys echoed from the open window of the *Tribune*, where George Swank worked on the parade description that would appear in the next day's issue.

At the South Fork station, rain fell, too. As Nora stepped from the train, she saw a mass of storm clouds. Stray wisps of hair curled tightly at her temple, the air was filled with static. A spark jumped from her fingertip to the train car's brass handrail as she descended. Her father, coming from the opposite direction, would arrive in half an hour. A carriage waited, the lantern in it already lit against the encroaching darkness. She sat in the shelter of the depot roof's overhang, mist moistening her face. A strange peace came to her now that her weeks of waiting had finally ended. How tired she was. Rain drilling softly on the clubhouse roof would be just the thing to help her sleep.

When they arrived at the club, there were more people than she had expected, more than she wanted to see. The young chief engineer, a man named Parke, and the club's manager, Elias Unger, were both on hand

and much in evidence, there to manage Italian laborers, housed in tents, who had been brought in to modernize the plumbing. The kitchen quivered with activity; the meal saved for Nora and James, for their late arrival, was left over from the food served earlier to the Italians—large, lavish portions, two meats, five vegetables, biscuits, food for workingmen, ditchdiggers. Her father, fish eater, grown monkish in his sensibilities, pushed his plate away when it was placed before him.

"Now that your tastes are so particular, you ought to wire your food preferences ahead," Nora offered, thinking she would leave a note for Colonel Unger reminding him that a black bass ought to be caught tomorrow for her father's dinner. The sight of so much food sickened him, but courtesy required James to stay with her while she ate dinner. To sip wine, to speak of neutral things. Bulbs that had been planted last year at his insistence in the bed to the right of the clubhouse veranda had bloomed successfully, he said. Yellow irises and crimson tulips. He said he thought he would go to the boathouse in the morning and row to the dam instead of walking. She agreed that it would be good exercise. He commented upon her kindness in coming. "It is not kindness," she said, reaching out to touch his hand. "I am always glad to see you."

He had read the paper on the train trip. "The forecast is for rain," he said, worry clouding his already-clouded face.

"Please," she said, imagining him racing to the dam again. "Sleep tonight. There are others here to do the watching. Colonel Unger. Mr. Parke. Take advantage of their presence. Look at us, both tired from travel. Tomorrow you can see to things. Tonight we ought to rest." He looked to her like someone who had not been sleeping, his face seemed caved in by exhaustion.

Once in her high-ceilinged room she undressed quickly, slipped with a shiver into her nightdress, into her bed. It was cold for May; the rain intensified the chill. She would need the flannel drawers she'd brought, the woolen cape. The last thing that flitted through her mind before she slept was the hope that rain would not make the journey difficult for Daniel. She was not much given to extravagant and melodramatic thinking, but she felt that her very life depended on seeing him tomorrow.

A moonless night, a pitch-dark room. Her dreams were vivid, brilliant. Dreams of sun.

Outside, it was a night of upheaval, of branch-snapping wind, an unexplained and otherworldly midnight roar. Funnel clouds, water spouts, ten inches of downpour, thunder striking with force enough to shatter an upstairs window at the club. Lightning whitened the sky; rain battled lightning for predominance with its force and density, rendering the world opaque, invisible, sight useless as sense. Mountain creeks swelled, then grew devouring and monstrous with swift currents, brown with mud. The lake was bloated, grotesque in its rapacity, swamping pastures, taking fences, markers, uprooted trees with it. The gods ravishing the landscape showed pity only once that night, and only briefly. They let Nora sleep.

The Stony Creek and Little Conemaugh both choked, gagged, and spewed their watery overload into the streets of Johnstown the next morning, into the first floors of houses and businesses. By then, after the night's fierce downpour, the water bore detritus as well as mud. Small logs, shrubs, elder bushes that had been washed from the river banks tossed crazily in the water. Spring flooding, someone said, but it did not feel like that. Cows were moved to high ground; men who worked the morning shift in the Cambria mills were told to go back home, to see to their families. Horace Rose hitched horse to wagon, took his sons, Forest and Percy, to his office to move documents and books to high shelves, where rising water couldn't reach them. The Reverend Chapman sat in his study, working on Sunday's sermon, the lamplit windows of the parsonage glowing like lighthouse beacons. Word came that railroad tracks were washed out in the mountains, trains were held, travel interrupted, mail delayed. Travelers were required to wait in passenger cars, which grew stale and stuffy. The *Chicago Limited* sat idly at South Fork while the crewmen came to the telegraph tower to wait for messages relayed from down the line. Two sections of the *Day Express* were held at the spacious marshaling yard at East Conemaugh on the northern edge of Johnstown. The passengers in one of the cars were players of a theater company who had just closed their run of *Night Off* at the Washington Street Opera House. Tired from their long night of entertaining, faces smeared with the residue of stage makeup from their last performance, they leaned familiarly against one another, snug as children, dozing lightly. All was stayed, as if time itself had been eerily suspended.

Later, Nora would not remember who first let on how serious the trouble was. But the world she woke to at the South Fork Fishing and

Hunting Club, when she woke at six in the morning, was not the one that had existed the night before. Dressed, standing on the veranda, she saw that mud had taken over. The clubhouse lawn had disappeared in it, the boardwalk had been broken into bite-sized boards and swallowed. She was forced to hope that Daniel would not try to make his way in this. The sky was black as mourning crepe, black as coal, and only in the wash of lightning strikes could she see how rapidly the lake was rising. How unlike itself it had become. She had imagined sea monsters in the lake when she was young, and now it seemed as if they'd roused themselves, as if they'd churned to the surface and brought the muddy bottom with them. Debris whirled in the angry currents—rail ties, tree branches, rats, the corpse of a Persian cat that one of the gardeners kept as a pet. A piece of wood siding, a wagon wheel, a plow, wildflowers. The current and the force of it all pressing toward the dam. Where it would harry and weaken it, before it gathered to obstruct the fish screens, to make spillage from the spillway, the only remaining outlet for overflow, impossible.

Twenty million tons of water. Plus the weight of creek overflow, the weight of rain.

Imagination began to animate her understanding, but she felt rooted, paralyzed. Only when a girl who helped in the kitchen spoke the words "How will the dam withstand it?" did Nora realize fully, deeply, that the worst would happen. That the world would end that day. That's when she rushed to find boots and a slicker and raced out into the mud. That's when she found the path that led to the dam, and to her father.

At two in the afternoon, the rains continued and Daniel was almost at the lake. Rain pouring from the sky, sluicing from his hat rim, made it almost impossible to see. He knew by then that he should not have tried this, that he should have stayed to help his father and mother. All this rain; water would be high in the Johnstown streets by now, houses flooded; furniture would have to be moved upstairs. He'd come too far to turn back now, and yet was not near enough to be certain he could make it. Pearl was his mount that day, and the mud made it hellishly hard for her to keep her footing. Daniel kept urging her up, to higher ground, trying to find some semblance of a trail.

As Daniel struggled to make his way to the South Fork Club, Grace purposefully made hers down in Johnstown. Her clothes were packed, her ticket purchased, but now the street outside her door was knee-deep in dirty water. More water than there had been in past springs of her brief, and happy—yes, she would say happy—life there. Her mind was made up, and yet she hesitated, trying, hopelessly, to make some case for staying. Some way, any way, to justify it. If she did not move quickly and get to the train station, Frank might come to her rooms, might try to find her. She'd have to hurry if she was to catch the *Day Express*. She looked up at the relentless sky. An umbrella would do no good, and her suitcase would be cumbersome. She abandoned everything, gathering her skirt in her hands, leaving her suitcase and umbrella on the hall floor behind her. The water in the street had developed an angry current. But she could not let that deter her. She closed the door for the last time. She stepped lightly, waded in.

Frank waded in as well, waded all the way home. The iron works were closed, the men allowed to tend to their families and the flooding. Everything about the water rising in the streets looked serious. So much for his planned rendezvous. Grace would be needed at the library to move books endangered by the flooding. Julia would need his help at home. The rain dictated, and it declared all human wishes futile, all plans irrelevant.

When he got there, Julia was making her eighth trip up the stairs, carrying small things—the mantel clock, his mother's Bible, a vase of flowers, the painting that hung on Frank's wall the day he first took Julia to his little house. When Frank stepped through the door, Julia's arms were full of Charles Dickens. Tucked under her chin was a sock. She looked like a girl to him at that moment, flushed and breathless.

He reached to help her. The skirt of her dress was soaked and clinging to her, her forehead moist from effort. When he had taken half the books from her, he realized that the sock she'd rescued was the one in which he saved for the piano, and just then he became aware of how the water was rising up the legs of it, rising toward the keyboard. Julia saw what he did, then gestured with her elbow, indicating that they needed to get Dickens up the stairs. "We're strong, but we can't take that," she said, nodding at the piano, and she laughed in a way that lit her face, that made him momentarily, intensely love her. "Besides, I've got the sock, Frank. That matters more. It was all that saving, all that love that mattered."

He heard a roar then, not thunder, but something more strange, more ominous. He was too caught in the moment to wonder what it was. As he followed Julia up the stairs, he thought of their long life together, what they'd been through. They'd lose furniture and rugs this time, trinkets that they'd grown attached to. But they'd lost things before. They'd manage this somehow, he knew.

He was reminded of how much he still felt, how much he admired her. He admired her back as she went up the stairs before him. He admired her legs and the nape of her neck. He admired her hands and her heart. He shifted the books in his arms so that he could touch her there, just so, on her thin hip.

Nora could describe the sound later, but only to herself. Only to relive it privately throughout the years that followed, when she wished to be punished, to be made to suffer. Or when dreams of it woke her. Only at those times did she allow herself to recall it, the sound of the end of everything, of life on earth. The sound of the whole world crumbling. She had been watching from a hillside some fifty feet from the dam, while her father raced back and forth, his wet hair plastered to his head, his voice hoarse from shouting. "Clear those fish screens, get some height on that sagging center." The sky was roiling, dark, the rain unrelenting. James took a shovel, cursed the Italian laborers for not working faster, for not performing the miracle of holding back the tide. But each strike of their shovels yielded only mud, and mud slipped down the side again. Rain blinded all of them, poured from her father, from his high-priced coat and his high, proud brow and his boots that were filling with the mud he was slinging. With every minute, every second, it seemed, the lakewater was rising, until the would-be rescuers were forced to run for high ground. To save themselves.

The water breached the middle first, a momentary gush of it, like the arch of water at the spillway on an ordinary summer afternoon. It was possible to believe, for just an instant, that that was all it would be, until twenty million tons of lakewater concentrated on that cut, that breach, and then ripped through it, slicing the earth face, the whip and curl of the tons of water, the awful force of it. It cut like a knife, and the dam face opened, like the great doors of an ancient castle, giving way, yielding to the water's heaving deep necessity. Trees were ripped from the hillside with groans so penetrating, so disturbing, that Nora thought hell itself had opened, that damned souls would come rising from the flood. One-hundred-year-old trees, thick as a giant's thigh, screamed and hurled themselves into the air, their roots like clubs, striking at the heavens that had brought this rain, this chaos. She covered her ears with her hands. The earth beneath her trembled. She knew at once how hideous the destruction was going to be. How total and annihilating. Her own breath left her, as if she were underwater with the valley residents below.

Ten minutes past three. It was the last moment that the lake was only water, roaring with a force equivalent to that of the Niagara River as it reaches Niagara Falls. Then it combined with everything that lay in its path, hurling into the narrow valley, churning, flinging, and scouring a high wide path, now narrowing, now broadening, depending on the land-scape it encountered, growing black, huge, monstrous, and fetid with debris. A black mist, a "death mist," as it was later called, hovered over it as it collected barbed wire, locomotives, railroad tracks, pulverized frame houses, keys and hobbyhorses, window glass, factory boilers, fuel. At spots where the valley narrowed the water wall grew to seventy feet, and more than once it blocked itself. A debris dam formed, and the killing wave paused, briefly, as if to reconstitute itself, as if accumulating force for its movement forward.

It took almost an hour for the wave to reach Johnstown, and once there, it gained speed and spread itself in three directions. Washington and Clinton Streets were crushed, swept clean. The stone swans were plucked from the park. Main Street yielded its handsome, proud brick buildings. The library and opera house, the railroad station, much of the iron works. All destroyed. Some frame houses were caught up whole, ripped from foundations, while others broke apart like matchsticks, their contents added to the rubble. Here and there a building was left standing. A church was spared, as was the *Tribune*. Because no real alarm had sounded, the awful roar gave the first warning of what was about to bear down on them. A roar, and heads turned in its direction. There were mad attempts to get away. People scrambled up hillsides in an effort to outrun it, or ran to brick houses and buildings, seeing safety there, only to be crushed when the wave collapsed the walls and crushed them.

Death was random and greedy. It claimed one of every nine. Drowned. Grace McIntyre, the *aurore du Bengale* dress that Julia had made for her floating like a pink parachute around her; Frank and Julia, who clung to each other, even when the weighty bloated body of a dead horse struck them; Caroline and her young daughter and husband swept up in a tangle of barbed wire. John Fenn and all seven of his sweet, fun-loving children drowned, as did Julia's father, who was caught by surprise as he sipped his sherry, and was later found impaled on a piece of the hotel roof that he had tried frantically to cling to. George Heiser and his wife, Mathilda. Young Elizabeth Bryan and Jennie Paulson, on their way to New York after a wedding, drowned when the flood swept through the train yard at East Conemaugh, where it pulverized the enormous round-house and gathered nineteen train cars into itself.

Death was arbitrary, ravenous, irresistible.

Daniel struck Nora when he found her. He struck her, and she did not raise her hand to stop him.

It had taken half an hour for the lake to empty, and by the time he got to the club, to the spillway, it was over. When, on his journey, he had realized there would be no turning back, he went higher and higher into the hills, onto one of the many paths among the tall pines, above creek level, out of reach of the rising water. And then he started down as he neared the club, descending slowly, carefully, toward the dam and spillway, because it was where they had promised to meet. It was only when he and his horse emerged from the wooded hillside that he saw that the lake was gone, leaving a giant cavern where it had been, fish flopping, gills clogged by the muddy stew. Daniel came over the crest of a hill, wiped rain from his eyes, and knew what destruction there would be. That life as he knew it had been obliterated, all loved things washed away.

He left his horse, slid and struggled over the last hundred feet of mud-slick terrain. Somehow in the chaos and its aftermath, he found Nora in the small cluster of soaked, mute witnesses who remained there even after the lake had emptied, unable to move, to comprehend. Italian workers, a few club members, the young club engineer, James and Nora. No one had thought to move or to find cover. What shelter would there be after what they'd seen?

Daniel struggled through the little huddled group, pushing everyone aside until he found her; in that crazed instant, she became the receptacle of blame. She of the summer people, whose carelessness had caused this. He hated her; he wanted her to take him in her arms and comfort him, even as he wanted to kill her. He stumbled in the mud, but he pushed forward until he reached her, and roughly grabbed her shoulder, spun her toward him. She had no idea who it was but turned instinctively to the touch, and when she saw him, saw the ruin in his eyes, when she felt the crack of his hand against her face, she welcomed it. She wanted to die for his sake, for the sake of all of them. A sacrifice, a pitiful, small retribution.

He raised his hand to her again.

Then her father had come between them. And after that she remembered little. A spring wagon, the wordless journey home. Home. Since all train tracks were washed out, the route by wagon was circuitous and long. Once in Pittsburgh, she stayed in bed in her darkened room, the curtains drawn, that day and the next. Evelyn tried to keep the newspapers from her, but on the fourth day James delivered them, understanding that she needed to know.

Two thousand two hundred and nine people died, she read. Nora sat in her rocker, her face appalled and gaunt, her thin hands cold. How had she become so cold? Two thousand two hundred and nine. More or less. It was as accurate an account as could be made, since, when the waters finally receded, there were some sixty acres of mud and brick and twisted steel and animal and human corpses. Four square miles of debris, including one hundred tons of barbed wire, some thirty locomotives, fifty miles of railroad track, brick and stone and shattered window glass. The ineluctable pounding force of the seventy-foot wall of water and all the detritus it carried severed limbs, ripped scalps from skulls. Both the dead and the living were later found naked, all their clothing peeled from them, their pale flesh pinched and puckered as if they had just been swimming, as some indeed had been, for their lives. A photo of the aftermath showed the body of a baby caught by the roots of a willow tree, her arms flung over her head, as if, Nora thought, she'd been playing a game of So Big.

How big is baby?

This is how big. So big.

But the baby's eyes were closed, her captured body floated, the bodice of her handmade dress was streaked with mud and shredded.

Paper after paper. Nora could choose among them. For days, across the country it was headline news. A stunned nation was transfixed, brought to a halt by it. Pittsburgh, Boston. In *The New York Times* she ran her finger down column-long lists of the names of the dead and missing: Renan, Riley, Richards, Rose, Souther, Stopple, Strause. Some corpses or portions of them were carried downstream as much as fifteen miles, flung onto muddy hillsides, onto the storm-bent, rain-soaked branches of surviving trees, as if into the arms of weeping mothers.

And then there was the fire. When the tons of mangled wreckage slammed into the stone railroad bridge that crossed the river just below the city, it wrapped and webbed and coiled through the horseshoe arches to form a buttress, an awful monument, a mountain of wood and flesh and twisted debris. Because so much of it was drenched in oil from derailed tanker cars, it was quick to ignite when hot coals swept from dying kitchen fires reached it. It became a pyre, a biblical inferno, and many who survived the flood were hurled, screaming, into it. The boards and beams they had clung to, that had saved them when the wall of water came, propelled them to a fiery martyrdom. Eighty people? Or ninety? Who knew, really, after they were burned? What exactly would survivors have been counting? The end of a charred femur, the blackened button of a brass-knobbed shoe? A child's detached arm tangled in the handmade leather collar of a matted, staggering, grief-crazed family dog? There was so much wreckage at the stone bridge, so much human debris, that they had to dynamite it later.

Fifty undertakers were able to make their way to the site by rail, finally, on Sunday, June 2, 1889. On the same day a freight train labored slowly over damaged tracks from Pittsburgh carrying nothing but an engineer and a fireman and eleven freight cars filled hastily with plain pine coffins. Nora imagined the rhythmic tick of the wheels across the tracks, the shudder of the coffins' slatted sides against one another.

Morgues had to be quickly organized throughout the city. Morgue A, the Adams Street schoolhouse; Morgue B, the Presbyterian church; Morgue C, the Millvale schoolhouse . . . Droves of dead. Nora envisioned the undertakers stumbling off their train that chilly Sunday morning. The step down to the sodden ground, the stench, the fog, the desolation. One of them pressed his handkerchief against his face, to keep from gagging. Another turned and said, My God, this can't be it. There can't have been a city here.

What could they do while they waited for the barrels of embalming fluid to arrive but try to label, mark, make some poor attempt at identification?

> . . . Unknown.
> Foot of female. High-button shoe. Black merino stockings. W. K. Endsley's bank book.
> . . . Unknown.
> Male. Age fifty. Weight 170. Height 5 feet 6 inches. Leather boots. Red flannel drawers. Blue drill overalls. White woolen socks. Gum coat. One week's growth of sandy beard mixed with gray. Silver open faced watch, Elgin movement. Silver chain. Leather coin purse. Ten cents. Bunch of keys. Scapular around neck. Found in Stony Creek near Brethren Church.
> . . . Little girl.
> Very light hair. Short gray flannel dress trimmed with three rows narrow braid, one and one-half inches from bottom, also three rows down front. Black hose. Spring heel button shoes . . .

In the end there were six hundred sixty-three "unknowns." Ninety-nine entire families. Gone. Ninety-six children, babies not yet ten.

For two weeks she did not leave her room, but sat in a sea of papers. *The New York Times*, the New York *World*. The Pittsburgh papers carried nothing else. In Denver, San Francisco, Boston, headlines screamed the news.

The day after the flood, members of the South Fork Fishing and Hunting Club gathered privately at the home of Charles Clarke to develop what they thought of as a policy. Initial reports suggested the worst, but they had agreed that silence would be the best response until more information was obtained. A worldwide relief effort had spontaneously begun, all goods heading for Pittsburgh, and out of a sense of civic duty, Robert Pitcairn, H. C. Frick, and Henry Phipps volunteered to chair the Relief Committee. They would oversee the heartfelt generosity—train cars full of shoes, pennies collected from elementary schools in Wisconsin and Georgia, money raised by a concert given by a group of freed slave singers touring Europe. Volunteers were coming forward. Red Cross workers led by Clara Barton were only waiting until a train could get them through. As befitted them and their positions, the club members oversaw these out-pourings, even as they decided that their own contribution ought to be a modest one—one thousand blankets. Heads nodded in agreement with the plan, eyes were averted. A low profile would be kept, a policy of silence adhered to.

While that policy was being discussed at Charles Clarke's house, in other corners of the city records were being gathered from law firm offices. Evidence compromised or hidden, lists of the names of members carefully destroyed. It was understood that the club itself would be abandoned, its history erased. With a little time and without much difficulty, it would be possible to think that the cottages and clubhouse had never been occupied at all. The silver and the china and the linens would be left, the writing desks, billiard table, the bowl on the sideboard where fruit had been kept. The clocks would wind slowly down, then stop forever. The sailboats, anchored in the earth and rotting, would be otherworldly-looking in this mountain setting, in a place that had no water.

As weeks went by, coroners' inquests resulted in public indictments of the club. *The New York Times* pounced: "An Engineering Crime; A Dam of Inferior Construction." Reporters tried to interview the few men known to be club members, but access to them was denied. The club was vilified, legal action threatened. But distinctions were quickly drawn between the club and the club members, and the club itself, that chartered entity, had few assets. It became clear that efforts to exact financial com-pensation would be futile. Later, small sums were donated guiltily, qui-etly, to the victims by the most visible clubmen. H. C. Frick Coke Company, $5,000. T. Mellon and Sons, $1,000. The Carnegie Company, $10,000. Nothing proportional to what they might have done, but they could live with that. Couldn't they? Frick wired Carnegie in France. He telephoned Mellon in the middle of the night. Couldn't they?

In a show of solidarity, schoolchildren in Omaha sent toys to the sur-viving Johnstown children. A stunned Walt Whitman wrote a poem of commemoration.

VIRGINIA, 1917

"All is ephemeral, both what remembers and what is remembered."
—Marcus Aurelius, *Meditations*, Book IV, Number 35

1917, Virginia. A small house, far away from any city, on a small, small plot of land. Lush land, lush flower beds, a little garden. Insects flourish in the dark alluvial soil. Gnats pepper the air like tiny dust motes. The air thrums with their sound. Plant roots and leaves, and spiky green lariope make food and hiding places for beetles, grubs, praying mantises. For them the garden is home. Flowers bloom in vivid disarray, as if all attempts at planning have been abandoned, containment having no place here. Virginia creepers. Night-blooming cereus. Beside the house, star jasmine climb a snake-rail fence. White buds spray along the thick green vine. Bees nuzzle, prod the tiny star-shaped blossoms, releasing perfume, so that the damp air feels thick, overburdened with their scent. Spring, but hot already in Virginia. A good day for being out-of-doors, for digging in the dirt.

In an upstairs bedroom a woman dresses. Button boots with high heels. A dark brown linen suit. The jacket falls to well below her hips. The skirt beneath it is unadorned and straight—two simple tiers; the hem of the lower tier grazes the indentation at her ankle, the edge of bone, the inner malleolus. The waist is high, the collar round. The cloche hat, leather gloves, and slender book-sized handbag which will complete the outfit are laid carefully across the bed. She watches herself closely in the cheval mirror as her hands work at fastening the jacket buttons, and she sees in an unexpected slant of light that there is dirt beneath one of her nails. Inadvertently she moves her hand to hide it. Then smiles and shakes her head when she realizes what she's done. Forty-eight years old, she chides herself, and still hiding from her mother. When she was young her white dresses were voluminous and long, replete with fabric flowers, folds and flounces—easy hiding places where imperfect hands could disappear. She reaches up to touch her jacket collar. The war has brought with it a new simplicity. In this costume, in this time, there is no place for hiding.

She'd seen a picture of a suit like this in a magazine, had surprised Mae Goodman at the local store when she'd inquired, while slowly fingering the bolt of fabric, where she might have it made. In her life, on her land, which is not a farm, she has always dressed like a farmer. In loose-fitting muslin dresses, with sleeves rolled past the elbow, cassocklike aprons on which she can rub her dirt- or bloodstained hands. But on this day in April she dresses not for work but for a journey. There is a train to catch, a son to see, a boat to take that son away. For him, she wishes to be beautiful. It is for him that she is taking pains.

"I've changed my mind. Please come," he'd said the last time he'd written. "I think it might bring me luck if you were here to say goodbye to me."

The boy whom she employs as her assistant has borrowed his father's truck to take her to the train. An old farm vehicle, she can hear the spit and whir and clank of it as it lumbers up the road. The toot-tooting of the horn. It has been a long time since she's been away. She'd stayed up the night before, head bent over her diary, writing.

Nora, at her mirror in Virginia, takes the cloche hat from the bed. Tucks her still-dark hair into it. In shape, in silhouette, it is not unlike the photographs she's seen of the helmets that the British Expeditionary Forces wear. And when that thought passes through her mind, her hands begin to tremble. To steady them she focuses on the working of her fingers into the leather fingers of a glove.

Beneath her window, the truck horn sounds again. A summons. A light breeze stirs the not-quite-transparent window sheers, and they billow like fog into the room. The heat, the flower-scented breeze—it could be summer anywhere. The sound of the truck horn could be the whistle of the little steamboat that churned so pertly every summer at the lake. Her porch, the boardwalk; the sighing wind could be the voice of her dead mother.

"Hurry, Nora, or the boat will leave without you."

Nora remembers well the excursions of her childhood, the gradual upward movement as the train charged from the city toward the mountains. The sense of rising. Of coming out of herself, out of her life, things falling away behind her. Now, earthbound, in Joe's father's truck, the dirt road rutted by long-evaporated rivulets of rain, the chassis swaying heavily, her shoulders rocking with each pitch of the truck, each heave, she is surprised by how easily she can slip back through time, how mesmerizing memory can be. Her eyes slowly close, she recalls a different rhythm, train wheels clipping over tracks, the easy sway of it, the sense of speed, of regularity. What was there about it that had always made her feel so buoyant, so unencumbered? More than once on her way to South Fork she had held her hand up to the window on the train where the sun slanted through, and her hand suffused with light seemed luminous to her, transparent, light as a feathered wing.

"So you'll wire, then," says Joe. "About when you're coming back. When I should meet you at the station."

Her eyelids flit open when she hears Joe's voice. She sees her hands, gloved and in her lap. She hears her own voice, adult, politely modulated.

"It should only be a few days, but yes," she says. "I'll wire."

"I'll take good care of everything, so don't worry," he assures her with a hearty, touching earnestness. She feels his devotion to her so keenly, it is like another presence in the truck. She looks across the angled metal column, the burled wood knob that is the gearshift. A boy, she thinks, as she does each time she looks at him. He should be in school instead of helping me. If I were a better person I'd insist he go to school. Although what good an education will do if this war continues she does not know. They'll all be called, these "boys," regardless of how educated they become, how much their mothers wish to spare them. She curses circumstances, fate, the January day in 1889 when Crown Prince Rudolf of Austria shot himself and his teenaged lover, Mary Vetsera, at the hunting lodge, in the snows at Mayerling. When Nora had read about it in the newspaper that January afternoon, she'd thought briefly of the romance of it, illicit love, twenty years old herself, so caught up in a passion of her own. Had the Crown

Prince lived, *he* would have been heir to Franz Joseph's throne. The course of history might have been altered. Franz Joseph might not have asked his nephew Franz Ferdinand to make the trip to Sarajevo. Shots might not have been fired. War might not have come. What if, what if? Since Samuel enlisted, Nora has stopped reading the paper. The litany of battles, the names of French and Belgian towns, the tallying of casualties.

The truck's front tire plows over a fist-sized stone. There is a bump, a vibrating metallic shudder. She lurches forward, presses one flat palm against the roof of the truck, while the fingers of her other hand grip the frayed edge of the seat. She wonders if the ship that will carry Samuel will pitch and roll this much, if he'll grow ill in the plunge of heavy seas, and if he does, who will be there to stroke his back and wipe his forehead as he heaves. She feels suddenly weak with gratitude that he has found this friend he's mentioned in his letters, that, at least in the beginning, on the voyage over, there will be someone he knows beside him. She imagines herself taking the friend aside, telling him her grown son's secrets — that he's a little vain, although reluctant to admit it; that he never learned to swim; that he believes that luck is a profound and potent thing, more powerful than diligence or talent. She would tell his friend every detail of her intimate maternal knowledge so that he could take her place if necessary. Minister to him if ministering is needed.

"Rough ride," says Joe, master of understatement. Characteristically laconic.

"Yes. But we're almost there. The station can't be too far now." She smiles at him. He, so generous with time and truck, so eager to make things right for her, to please her.

At the station, Joe kisses Nora on the cheek goodbye. Assuring her again that everything will be fine in her brief absence. Leaving her to wait alone.

She is going to New York, but that is all she knows. The sea attacks by German U-boats have made secrecy as to the exact time and place of troop disembarkation crucial. Samuel has written that he'll make contact with her once she's in the city. She presses her hands together in her lap.

War fills her mind then, and she finds herself thinking of her father's generation, their conflict, their war. Only in recent years has she come to be aware of herself as someone whose life has been caught, suspended between periods of war, and all that war brings with it. A kind of hardening, a turning of the heart, a greediness for life, a willingness to declare men enemies, to regard those enemies as "other." She knows all too well what the Civil War had done to her father. It is yet to be seen what war will do to her son. He is just a college boy, and like so many of them, who are so fervor-filled, he has never even held a gun. How on earth will he be a soldier, she wonders, when he's never held a gun? What to make of it all, she wonders, and can make nothing.

Read; she should read, and she opens the satchel she has brought. *A Tale of Two Cities*, a small volume of poems by Tennyson. Turgenev's *First Love*, its binding worn, the leather cover so soft, so familiar to the touch. How foolish she is, the way she carries it everywhere with her, this gift from her youth, this problematic treasure.

It has been a long time since Nora has been on a train, and it seems to her that they have become more functional, less grand. As she settles herself in a window seat, she removes her gloves and splays one hand across the clean pellucid pane. Taking note of her hand, the slenderness of her fingers, she reminds herself that she must eat. She has let herself become too thin. More often than not, she forgets meals. Forgets the passage of time, lost in the world of her bees and bugs and butterflies, the keeping of the record of her deliberate, careful observations of them. She has become well settled in Virginia, content to stay and work on her self-fashioned experiments. Her science. The papers she is publishing, the lectures she's been asked to give. This life's work of hers that had begun as a youthful fascination with the natural world, the world that had hummed so insistently at South Fork. Or did it? So often now she wonders if all her memories of that time are faulty, wanting. She has come to doubt her own trustworthiness. She sees it all as through a scrim.

Her seat is not as plush, not as comfortable as the ones she remembers from her youth. The upholstery is stiffer. She remembers the time when men of importance had their own private train cars, moving offices, living quarters on wheels, which could be attached to the last car of a train on any railroad line, according to the whim, the influence of the man. The nature of his power. In those days, word was simply sent to the railway station. A wire was delivered, arrangements followed smoothly.

Nora's train lurches. Huffs. Then huffs again. There is the click and grind as the piston presses the drive wheels forward. Slowly at first, then gaining speed. Leaving, Nora knows without looking. The depot recedes behind them; and there, she is committed to it now, this trip; there will be no turning back. Soon enough they will be traveling full-tilt, "full chisel." An expression she'd learned from her father.

She tries to read; she has brought a paper with her which is to be published soon, with the editor's suggestions. But concentration eludes her somehow.

From the train window Nora watches the scenery and light change. Rolling hills and sun-shot greenery. In fields, dark cows stand grave as idols. Tatters of the black smoke from the locomotive streak the air.

Train travel might not be as grand as it once was, but it is faster; Nora arrives in New York sooner than expected. She had been there only once before, in 1889, the year of the flood. There had been some vague and ill-conceived plan on her father's part to find Andrew Carnegie, to demand that Carnegie take responsibility. It was James's notion that he'd "make him pay." When Evelyn refused to accompany him, it was Nora who went and waited in the lobby of the Windsor Hotel, where James had heard that Mr. Carnegie still kept a suite of rooms. It was Nora who watched as he insisted that Mr. Carnegie be told that he was waiting; Nora who tried to keep him on the banquette beside her, next to the potted palm, to keep him from going to the desk clerk again and again, angrier with each approach, growing increasingly certain that he was being lied to. It was Nora who assured the security guards who were eventually summoned that she would see to it that James did not return; yes, she was willing to swear; no, please, you have my word, there is no reason to detain him. Nora who held his arm as they stepped into the New York winter, burying her hand in the crook of his elbow, like any young woman with her father strolling on Fifth Avenue, except that they were not strolling, except that her hands clasped around his bent elbow were holding fast, white with the pressure she applied, the strength with which she held him and propelled him, kept him going forward. She was trying to keep him from bolting, turning back to enter the Windsor, which he did in fact do two days later, this time to take the desk clerk by his lapels, threaten him, and get arrested. When Nora held his arm, she was holding on to James for dear life—hers and his.

She transfers her valise to her left hand, leaving her right hand free to hold the banister as she begins her ascent of the marble stairs, her exit from the railroad station. One, two, three, four. Counting, inadvertently attentive to everything, an acquired predilection, the habit of someone used to measuring and marking, taking note of and classifying each and every experience that presents itself to her. Without even intending to, she will remember the number of stairs, the symmetry of the swirls in gray-white marble. The fact that the young woman who races past her at that instant, who almost knocks her down, is also named Nora. "Nora," the young soldier calls to her as she falls into his waiting arms. He takes her by the waist, sweeps her off her feet momentarily, and then she lets herself be kissed by him, publicly without embarrassment. How much times have changed. Love, she thinks, and then thinks of herself at that age.

She is looking off to the left at the other Nora and her soldier, when an angular, good-looking boy draws her attention with a full-armed, attention-getting wave.

Samuel. She drops her bag, lets it thud to the marble floor, opens her arms to him, as she did when he was small; half-expecting him to run into them and to allow himself to be scooped up by her. But it is he that does the scooping.

"Good God," he laughs, stepping back, looking her over. "A hat? You?"

"It is the very height of fashion," she says with a mock primness, turning to allow him to admire her ensemble. "Honestly. What do you think?"

"I think I'm glad to see you."

"And I too, dear one. I too." She touches her hand to his chin. His hair is dark like hers, but straight, combed back severely. He's lost weight while training for war; he looks alert and ready.

He will take her to her hotel, he says. That night they'll go somewhere quiet for dinner. Then tomorrow, she can see him off. "You can wave your handkerchief. Blow kisses to me," he says, trying to make light of it all. And as he describes the traditional scenario—kisses, waves, he and his compatriots with their heads thrust out of train car windows for one last look, one final falsely spirited adieu—she wonders how, exactly, she is going to get through this.

She wishes she had some advice to give him, tonight, tomorrow. But all she can think of are tired clichés. What does she know about fighting? Nothing. What wisdom can she share? She wishes his father were here. Or hers. She wishes for a man.

"I could have gotten to the hotel myself. I wouldn't have minded," she ventures. The kind of remark a mother would make: "Don't trouble your-

self, don't fuss, don't mind me." She's always tried every conceivable way
to avoid that sort of thing, to avoid the suggestions of martyrdom, self-
effacement, false feminine humility—now here she is. "I could have gotten
to the hotel myself, but I'm glad you came to meet me." A corrective. A
reassertion of the honesty she values. "I wanted to see your smiling face."

Nora's father had spoken against the club members' policy of silence. He
had condemned deception and written incoherent letters to newspapers
(which were never printed), and in November 1889 he began his sorties
against Carnegie in Manhattan. After five days of trying to see the Scots-
man, three nights spent in jail, months of trying to insist that someone feel
what he felt, that someone share his guilt with him, he hanged himself in
his hotel room when Nora went out to get a bite to eat for them. When
she returned to the room, she knew he was dead before she even touched
him. Whom should I call? she wondered. Who in the world is there to
help me? She pulled a straight-backed chair across the room, climbed up
on it, and struggled to bear the weight of him as she undid the belt buckle.
It seemed important to bring him down herself before she summoned the
hotel desk clerk or a doctor. Hard work, but she did not want anyone to
see him that way. Once she'd gotten him to the floor, she placed a pillow
underneath his head and carefully covered him with a blanket.

She had written to Daniel to tell him about her father. So accustomed
had she become to writing to him about everything that mattered. But she
had sent the letter to the only address she had for him, and it had been
returned. The address no longer existed; it had been washed away. There
was no way for her to know what had become of him. She might have
found that out. In a thousand instances she had proven herself to be a
most resourceful girl. But she kept hoping, believing that he would contact her, and when he didn't, when months passed and no word came from
him, she understood that he must not want to hear from her or see her.

James's small estate had made it possible for her to finish school, to find
a job as assistant to a well-known entomologist, an apprenticeship which led
to her own independent work and a career as a writer and researcher. Evelyn, abashed and humiliated by James's suicide, sold the Pittsburgh house
and moved back to Wilmington, and within six months had remarried.
Security was hers in the form of a banker husband. The settling of her

mother had been a great relief to Nora, at a time when she thought that she
would never feel relief, pleasure, happiness again. It had given her a sense of
freedom. That and the other part of her very small inheritance from James.
His will revealed that her grandfather's large Virginia farm had been broken
into smaller sections and confiscated after the war, but that he had managed
to retain a fraction of it, a birthright for his son, now passed on to her. A
small, small plot of land. She had thought of J. Henri Fabre, of what a paradise a plot of earth had been for him, and she hoped she'd be so lucky. Her
father had taught her how to love a place, lost to her now. At the reading of
his will she had hoped she could learn to love Virginia.

That night, at dinner, on the eve of his departure, Samuel reports that there
are to be no farewell rituals, that there will be no gathering on the platform
next to the departing trains. No waving handkerchiefs. No blown kisses.
The announcement had been made after he had dropped her at her hotel.
The families would all say goodbye in a large anteroom at the station, one
with a high domed ceiling. And then the inductees would be whisked away,
transported to secret disembarkation sites. "It will be better that way, don't
you think?" Samuel asks her. He reaches across the table for her hand.

"Perhaps," she says.

She has a gift for him. She'd been saving it for a moment such as this.
Something of his father's. "Here you are, then." She slides the carefully
wrapped box across the linen tablecloth. "For luck."

"What's this?"

"I've always meant for you to have it."

A pocket watch. He takes it from its cotton batting. Holds it to his ear.
"Father's?"

"Indeed. Open it."

Inside the lid a photograph has been trimmed into a perfect circle. Cut
to fit.

He looks closely at it. "You?"

"Your father and me."

"And a sailboat? I didn't know you'd sailed."

"Oh, I have many secrets," she says, smiling. "That's how your father
and I met. I lured him to me. I forced him to teach me how to sail." She
had married Edward, had his son. He had died before they'd had to admit
how ill suited they were to one another.

How clever Louis Clarke had been to keep a record. Samuel's smile makes her happy that she'd kept that photograph.

"I wish I'd known him," says Samuel, so unused to giving voice to his young longings. Now, on the eve of war, he wishes for his father.

"Ah, yes. I wish that, too. I'd imagined we'd grow old together. Who would have thought he would die before you were even two?"

"Were you good at sailing? Did you love it?"

"I did love it once. And your father and I did it well together. We made a very good team."

It pleases her to be able to say that.

They might have talked all night. That's how much she wants to keep him with her.

But of course she can't. So they part, and she does not sleep. And too quickly morning is upon her. Time for the real goodbye.

In her hotel room Nora dons her suit again, places her hat at a rakish angle. There you go, she says to her reflection in the mirror. You can do this.

The crowd that has gathered at the station is a large one. There are hundreds of young men leaving, their families clustered around these boys like moons around bright planets. She will miss Samuel every day. She will die if he dies. She is certain of it.

"Listen," he says. It is a desperate time. Anything, anything at all to postpone the agony of leaving. "That friend I mentioned in my letters. The friend I made in training. He's over there. He'd like us to meet his family."

"Oh, Samuel, I don't think so. Dear one, please. Let's not." But she will do it if he wishes it. She will do anything he wishes. She begins to follow him across the room, and halfway there she sees through the throng of people that the man standing beside the boy in question is Daniel Fallon. The mahogany hair shot now with silver, the particular, quizzical tilt of his head, the red scarf. Could it be the very one she gave to him so long ago? But then he turns toward her, and she quickly realizes that it isn't Daniel; that she is, once again, mistaken. So often she sees a familiar profile, a walk that is like his. She is hopeless in this, even after so many years. Everywhere she goes, she thinks she'll see him.

She can never know what became of him. How their connection to each other might have grown. But she believes that she is all that she is because of what once had been his love and regard. She has become the scientist she'd sworn she'd be; she has designed experiments and written books that are models of precision and clarity. She is quick to correct error when she sees it. Now, all these years later, every day, she wishes that she could talk with Daniel one last time, that she could know that he is well, that he survived his losses, that the universe went on with him in it. She wants to tell him that if she has become good at all, at anything, it is because of knowing him.

"Samuel." She fears the leaving now and takes his arm. "Let's not. I think it would be best if we were alone when we said goodbye."

"But we can talk with them awhile. It's not quite time yet." There is fear, a hint of desperation, in his voice. He takes hold of her hand.

"No. Listen now. You know me. I'll cry." Her other hand is on his cheek. "It would be so embarrassing. Me crying in the presence of your friend. I don't want that."

"But we're going together."

A bell sounds, the signal for departure. There is movement in the crowd.

"I'm glad you'll be together. I really am. And I want you to take care of one another. But I can't share this goodbye."

"No," he says. He looks steadily at her, with great care, as if to memorize her face. "You're right. I know."

"So." She makes herself smile at him. "Keep your head down."

Samuel shakes his head and laughs.

"Lead with your shoulder. Is that the kind of thing people say to young soldiers?"

He puts his arms around her, pulls her close. "Go, then."

"Yes." A kiss for his cheek.

"No looking back now. Don't look back," he cautions.

"I won't."

"No tears."

"None. Go to your friend now."

"Yes."

"Tell him to keep an eye on you for me."

"I will."

And then she turns from him. That awful turning. That almost impossible leaving of the room. She takes the first few steps, and then the next, and then she is at the large carved doors leading to the street. On her way back to the train. Back to Virginia.

The doors swing open, then close behind her.

And he is gone.

ACKNOWLEDGMENTS

A portion of this book was written during a residency at Yaddo. I am enormously grateful to the wonderful staff there. The time and freedom to write were remarkable gifts.

I was helped by many people, both materially and psychically, in the writing of this book. It is a story I have wished to tell for a long time, and without them I would have been unable to do it. Laura Furman, Richard Howard, Beverly Lowry, Willard Spiegelman, Aryeh Stollman, Susan Tifft, and Wallis Wilde-Menozzi have often lit the way for me through the muddle of the writer's life. James McLaughlin and Jorge de la Torre gave me the gift of understanding. My children and stepchildren have been loving and patient even when my work has taken me from them. And my husband, Glenn, has read every word of every draft of this novel. Nothing would have been possible without him.

My agent, Heather Schroder, is a constant source of encouragement and support to me. Her contributions to this effort are too many to be counted.

I am awed by and grateful for the help of my extraordinary editor, John Glusman. His commitment to this book, his willingness to talk and think aloud with me about it, as well as his skill in shaping it into the story it wished to be, have been invaluable. I am, as always, deeply in his debt.